ARAKSI

&

THE

GERMAN

CONSUL

Carlos José Saenz

HEDDON PUBLISHING

First edition published in 2017 by Heddon Publishing.

ISBN 978-0-9932101-9-8

Cover design by Pablo Barragán

The cover image is *A Harem Beauty Holding a Fan* by Gabriel Joseph
Marie Augustin Ferrier (1847–1914).

Book design and layout by Katharine Smith,
Heddon Publishing.

www.heddonpublishing.com
www.facebook.com/heddonpublishing
@PublishHeddon

About the Author

Carlos José Saenz, a native of Buenos Aires, Argentina, is a film director and scriptwriter. He completed his secondary schooling at Colegio Champagnat in 1969 and studied Law at the Universidad Católica Argentina.

From 1977 to 1980 he studied film-directing and scriptwriting at the Centro de Estudios Cinematográficos, and play-directing at the Payró theater. He wrote and produced several short movies, among them *Reflex*, widely shown in his early film-making career.

Mr. Saenz has written and directed important full-length documentaries, including *American Rendez-Vous*, on the history and restoration of the Palacio Bosch (the US ambassador's residence in Buenos Aires) between 1998 and 2001, shown in the United States. He authored *Cuatro Escultores Argentinos* in 2004 for Canal Arte, Cablevisión, and Multicanal, and *Teatro Colón de Buenos Aires, historia y restauración patrimonial* in 2009, sponsored by the city's municipal government.

He was executive producer, in co-production with Spain, of full-length fiction films such as *Nunca estuve en Viena*, and *Chukker* for the United States and Britain, and *In the Footsteps of Bruce Chatwin in Patagonia* in collaboration with the BBC.

Mr. Saenz has dealt with varied movie topics, such as sports, art, and culture, and was contracted to write scripts for several fiction films, still in process, as *Capital aventurero*, *Montoya*, and *Cazar un tigre* in collaboration with writer Jorge Torres Zavaleta, among others.

This diversity provided Mr. Saenz with ample full-length scriptwriting experience. It was thus that in 2003 he was one of the winners of the 'Raíces' joint prize of the Instituto Nacional de Artes Visuales and the Instituto de Cine of Spain, for the script of the full-length historical movie *El león de las sierras* at the Mar del Plata International Film Festival.

Araksi and the German Consul started out as a movie script written in collaboration with Jorge Vartparonián. This story is the basis for an epic-historical super-production presently at the financing stage. It is Carlos Saenz's first novel.

PART I

CHAPTER I

ARAKSI

Erzurum, March 1915

STORM CLOUDS ROLLED ACROSS THE STEELY BLADE OF THE MOUNTAINS, as though fleeing from the morning light, without delivering a spring shower. Coming apart and separating as they moved towards the horizon, the sky cleared up completely and a fresh breeze blew across the table-land. Over this fertile land, wheatfields shone under the sun like gently swaying patches of gold thread.

An open coach, a two-horse phaeton, crossed the inner farm tracks of a large rural estate in Erzurum, Anatolia, in the Ottoman Empire.

At a cautious distance somewhat behind, two farmhands on horseback followed the coach which was driven by their boss Zareh, a rich Armenian landowner. Owner of the large estate, Zareh had inherited it from his father and grandfather, and his great grandfather, and so on. Back into the mists of memory of the region, when Armenian knights were the lords of Anatolia and the Christian Armenian kingdom had not yet given way before the great Turkish invasion which, from the Bosphorus to Russia, and from the Black Sea to the sands of the desert, was to extend its imperial boundaries for centuries.

THE RUINS OF AN ANCIENT FORT dominated the high part of the land, a rocky area. The carriage was rounding the hillock when the voice of his daughter, Araksi, who sat with him on the driver's seat, brought Zareh back to the present. The figures of knights wielding swords and pennants vanished into the hillsides of his imagination. With the reins, Zareh urged on the draught animals and looked at Araksi, the youngest of his five children, on the eve of her 20th birthday. She was an extraordinarily beautiful dark-haired girl with large black eyes. A strand of black hair fell across her forehead.

1

"Papa... Papa..."

"Yes, my girl, tell me, my love," he answered absentmindedly.

"You aren't paying attention to me, Father."

"Forgive me, Araksi."

Zareh smiled at her, tidied her hair with tenderness and looking behind, signalled to a farmhand to look into the distance of the fields, where the other crops began.

"Yes, Baron," said the farmhand, bringing his mount alongside the carriage.

"Abdul, I want to have a look at that field before we go back to Erzurum."

"Very well, my Lord."

The Turk, around the same age as his boss - who was 65 - nodded and rode forward, heading for the great open space of the plain. The other rider remained behind, leading a magnificent, saddled white-faced chestnut mare. He was riding with caution so as not to overtake the phaeton.

"How extraordinary the harvest will be this year, Araksi, in spite of the war," Zareh commented to his daughter. "Not even the Russians have been able to stop our production. I suppose the Valee will demand a few bags of food for the troops but... that contribution is fair in the circumstances. We're very fortunate, my daughter, after all... it will all blow over... and these fields will never stop providing us their bounty. We must thank the Lord, Araksi. How happy I am to be with you, my love..! It brings me memories of when you were a little girl," Zareh sighed. "I feel these are the last of our outings, as very soon we'll be preparing for your engagement and you'll no longer have time left for me."

"Don't say such things, Father. You know that I'm happy to come with you. And besides, I'll always have time for you," said the girl, leaning her head on her father's shoulder. Zareh maneouvred the reins and left the road, leading the pair of dark horses towards the uncultivated plain.

"Do you remember, Papa, when we used to go at full gallop from this very spot up to the ruins? Do you remember that none of the boys could ever beat me? You would give the starting signal and Tavel always came in last. Only Krikor was able to win, just once. It was on the way back when they drove the horses down the hill and mine rolled over, getting caught up with Tavel's... I panicked and never did it again. My poor horse had to be put to sleep. Do you remember that, Papa? That was the only time the boys were able to beat their younger sister," she said, smiling.

"You could have died... your mother and I were so worried! But I must admit that of all my children, you're the best rider. I'm very proud of having taught you to ride, Araksi."

"Neither the boys nor Mavush should hear me say that," thought Zareh aloud. "But of course... each child is special in a parent's eyes. Look, Araksi, look at the wheat in that field, see how it gleams. Without doubt these are the best lands in Anatolia, as your grandfather always said. One day everything that is mine will be for all of you and your children."

Zareh sighed, exaggerating his sorrow. The years were beginning to take their toll on the old man's character, and he took advantage of this, especially with his daughters, although Araksi did not pay much attention.

"That's the way it'll be, when we're no longer around," dramaticized the patriarch.

"You'll always be with me, Papa. Please don't make me suffer, don't go on like that. Let's just enjoy this moment. Don't think of anything else. Don't make me sad!"

"Don't pay attention to me, girl. It's what happens to parents when their children are about to leave home... although I can hardly imagine anyone in Erzurum as a better husband for you... Diran loves you. Besides, your mother and I have always considered him as one of the family, from the moment he first appeared... He must have been around 14 years old then, perhaps?"

"Thirteen," Araksi corrected.

"Thirteen, you're right. It seems like yesterday that he arrived from Tiflis and remained under my tutorship."

"It's true, Papa. Everything happens too quickly! Ah,

Daddy, I don't want to miss anything. There's so much I haven't seen yet. I want to travel around the world, walk along the streets of Paris, buy dresses in fancy shops, go to gala performances at l'Opera, just like when you and Mamma met! Maybe study something... study... why not, Papa? Some girls are already doing it. Is all this an illusion; youthful dreaming before a lifetime of motherhood? I have no right to complain. I know it, but... haven't we been born to experience that marvellous freedom?"

"Don't rush, child. Everything in its own time. Besides, women have a duty and that is to follow their men. The rest will be given to you automatically. There are destinies that don't allow us to do what we fancy but rather what our position dictates to us."

"I know that, Papa. Yet I can't resign myself altogether... I know I love Diran but there's something in me, I don't know... Why should I live a life that depends on others? It frightens me that any attempt at happiness could just be blown away in a country at war, Papa... We're so close to the frontier that the Czar's army could get to Erzurum in only two days. Then what might happen to us? People say that if that happens, the government in Constantinople will take special precautions with the Armenians."

The Turkish farmhand galloped very close to the carriage but Zareh made a calming gesture to his daughter and continued the conversation in French.

"Araksi, my dear, look at our farmhands. They're very faithful to us. Look at Abdul. He's been with us since your older brothers were born. We've lived with the Turks in relative peace for centuries. Why should all this change now?"

Araksi gazed at the plain as her father spoke tenderly to her in the elegant accent he had learnt as a youth at his school in Paris.

"If things change in Turkey it'll only be for the better. Do you imagine that if I believed some danger could arise, I wouldn't have taken some precautions at the bank? Wouldn't I have thought of you all, who are the most important things in my life? In my position, one can anticipate events and I can see no cause for concern. This war will come to an end at some moment and we'll carry on in Erzurum because it's our home, always has been, and always will be. Remember this, my dear: we must always be equal to the level of our duties and our tradition. Don't forget it. The wealth the Lord has generously granted us, we can only be worthy of if we respect our deep roots, which we must never betray. They are the foundation of the beginning and ultimate end of the family and, for as long as this is so, our Armenian spirit will always be present and will never die."

Araksi looked at her father with love and admiration and, kissing him, said with a merry smile, "Yes, Papa. You remind me a lot of Grandfather when you speak like that, serious and old-fashioned. It makes you seem older, you know."

Zareh grumbled without being able to disguise his weakness for his daughter.

The second farmhand was riding and trying to control the spirited white-faced chestnut, which was prancing self-importantly, demanding freedom with every tug.

Araksi felt the same unrestrainable impulse as the chestnut passed by. She stretched out her hand, trying to fondle it. Zareh stopped the coach and the farmhand did likewise.

"May I? You won't be angry, will you, Papa?"

"Of course you may, Araksi. Go ahead, my dear... What I would give to ride on horseback at the moment, if it weren't for this hip of mine!"

Araksi got down from the coach and with expert skill mounted the horse, smoothing her skirt down. Then she was riding side-saddle away at a gallop, across the undulations of the land.

Zareh watched his daughter with pride as he drove the draught horses forward. The phaeton followed the track up to the gate where Abdul was waiting for his boss to go through. Without stopping the coach, Zareh looked at his property, which extended in all directions, and thought, *Oh God, I never want this moment to end.*

CHAPTER II

THE WESTERN FRONT

LORRAINE

MAX VON SWIRSDEN-RIGHE remained alert and still at the observation post not far from the artillery. His horse shifted nervously as, through his binoculars, Max studied the maneuvers of the French enemy in the trenches.

The lieutenant's posture was worthy of note — the balance and strength of his legs, body positioned in a straight line, broken at the waist and matching the horse's movements. It could be said that, in his own style, Max represented the classical image of a young German officer.

Stationed at Straubing in the 5th Cavalry Corps, Max was somewhat dark for the Baltic German stock he came from. He wore metal-rimmed glasses; a reminder that when he was called up and incorporated as a reserve volunteer, he had interrupted his studies for a doctorate in Chemistry. But now — war! The front in Lorraine and the tense calm that put the German soldiers' nerves on edge in the trenches as they waited for the next barrage from the French. That was their worry, and that of the entire regiment under Count von Preysing.

The violent artillery fire started again between the two fronts and the first shell landed close to Max. All at once the noise of the guns became deafening and a dusky smoke covered the sky; the mud in the trenches became mixed with pieces of twisted iron that killed and maimed the hapless German soldiers.

Controlling his frightened horse, Max sank his spurs in, endeavouring to find a safe shelter at a fast pace. Leaning low over his mount, he galloped downhill and, on reaching his own lines, he jumped down to the ground. A piece of shrapnel from a shell hit his face. It was hot but did no harm so he picked it up in his gloves and looked in all directions. It was enough to remind him that death hovered very close by that afternoon.

He measured the distance to the nearest shelter and ran to the trench, panting and sweating without cease. Around him, orders to regroup arose among the sergeants and soldiers; others stooped within the trenches, holding their rifles. Enemy blasts followed one after another with increasing intensity. One German officer, covered in blood, stopped Max and grabbed his sleeve. With the difficulty of a dying man, he stretched out his arm, trying to show Max the trench he had come from. Without doubt or hesitation, Max pulled the first man onto his shoulders. Then, crossing the trenches, he deposited him in the camp, safe from the shooting and into the hands of the stretcher-bearers of the rear-guard. The bombardment from the French batteries was becoming more intense and the place was turning into a veritable inferno.

Returning to the trench, Max repeated the feat, shouldering another casualty; he had to make haste in getting him out, taking pains to ensure he would not remain among the pile of corpses forever. With another burst of energy, Max was back in the safety of the rear-guard. He lay down, sweating and exhausted, his strength gone. He saw the ambulances making their way with the dying and mutilated. On the battlefield only smoking craters were left. Among them, the bodies of dozens of German and French soldiers sprawled in the mud.

CHAPTER III

FAREWELL TO MUNICH

THE IRON CROSS, the prestigious decoration, was passed around amongst the dinner guests. *'Honor for bravery in battle'* was inscribed on it; the distinction the army bestowed on its officers and subalterns who stood out in battle. Each guest congratulated Max as, in turn, they held and respectfully handled the cross, which hung from a blue ribbon, until it finally came full-circle and returned to its owner.

Max discreetly put the decoration away in his pocket, holding it firmly in his hand for a while without letting it go. Like all of his male guests, he wore a tail-coat. He sat at the head of the table, befitting his position as host.

Hildegard Countess von Swirsden, his wife; attractive and of undeniable poise at 40, in fact nine years her husband's senior, presided at the opposite end. Hildegard beckoned the butler to clear away the dishes and serve the coffee.

Some of the gentlemen lit cigars and everyone seemed comfortable and relaxed as they conversed at the after-dinner table. One old gentleman, with a great white moustache and typically Prussian features, lifted his glass and proposed a toast. "To you, Max, for your valor and service to the Fatherland... and to you, Hildegard, for your constant abnegation as the wife of a German soldier... Gentlemen, to the Kaiser. Long live Germany!"

Everyone repeated the toast and raised their glasses as they faced their hosts.

Talk continued, agreeing with the imperial policy, or discussing the disagreements between the Russian Czar and his cousin Kaiser Wilhelm II, and how blood-ties sometimes provoke the most extreme kinds of hatred in families.

"Just remember Cain and Abel, dear Professor," observed a distinguished baroness, referring to the Bible story.

At the other end of the table, reserved for the younger guests, two brothers were chatting with Lieutenant Thiele. The three youths, barely 20, made no secret of their admiration for the honor received by their host, who was a reserve officer and novice like themselves.

It was only three months earlier that Max had joined the 5th Cavalry regiment and he already had such an enviable distinction in battle. They felt profound pride. The memory of the great assembly in the regimental square on their return from Lorraine, and the commander's address about the recipient of the decoration - in front of everyone - remained fresh in their minds. It was an honor and achievement dreamt of by every soldier, whether raw recruit or veteran.

"To your health, comrade," said Rolf, lifting his glass.

Friedrich, being slightly tipsy, on seeing his brother breaking the ice of so much formality, came up with his own toast. "Colonel von Preysing is a legend. We'd all have liked to be in your place, Max... Gentlemen, I propose a toast to reserve Lieutenant Max von Swirsden-Righe and his Iron Cross."

Max thanked him and asked for everyone's attention. "Many thanks, my friends, comrades, Hildegard. It's a great honor for me but I did no more than duty called for... Please — please listen. I have certain news I should like to share with you.... In fact, this evening is not only one of thanks for this celebration you're all accompanying me in, but also one of surprises and farewells."

Hildegard looked at her husband with curiosity.

Max continued, "Soon after we returned from Lorraine, our commander, Colonel von Preysing, was summoned to Turkey by the High Command... You all know that already. It seems he has declared his intention to take some officers to the Eastern Front." Max paused. "My friends, we may not see each other for a long time. My orders are to leave immediately for Turkey and join the command in Constantinople."

There was a deep hush. Hildegard remained silent with surprise at the news.

One of the gentlemen was first to speak. The old

colonel, a veteran from the times of Bismarck, stated with a gruff voice in his old-fashioned military manner, "Well, if that isn't an opportunity, Max! Turkey. That's our real national objective! The old German dream, as you well know. As all we Germans know!" Very sure of himself, he added, "Gentlemen, whoever dominates the Hinterland will dominate the whole of Asia. I congratulate you, it's a wonderful destination, Max! The mission of our officers in Constantinople will be very useful to our Kaiser's purposes."

The old man's comment related to the standard subject matter at any meeting of Munich society and in each corner of the German Empire. Those not sent to the front due to their condition as exempted civilians, or because their age precluded them from active service, exalted the military virtues even more than the soldiers themselves. The latter were aware of the reality; the distance that existed between the reality of war, the actual danger they faced in front of the enemy, and the hawkish talk expressed in the comfortable salons of Munich. However, such talk helped gain a promotion, a good destination, or a desirable command.

Max was courageous. He had proved this on the battlefield. He was not beyond the ambition of making a name for himself by taking advantage of every opportunity that offered itself in these changeable times of war. The military nobility of Germany claimed for itself the very glory of the Empire, reserving the most prestigious posts for its members. In this sense, Hildegard was the ideal companion. In his ambitions, Max had no better partner than his own wife. Hildegard nurtured his drive and ambition, taking advantage of the elegant and influential society she frequented thanks to her position as a Prussian noblewoman.

ALL AT ONCE, A HUBBUB of various opinions arose. Everyone seemed to be talking about the war theater of the Eastern Front.

"Kaiser Wilhelm is convinced national progress will come from expansion in Mesopotamia. Besides, we have no other choice. Every German must realize that our natural borders are in the heart of Asia, the land the Aryan race derives from." The guest drank a small glass of liqueur he was then offered, enjoying the sound of his own voice as he went on. "The Sultan of Turkey — Muhammad, am I right? He has personally entrusted His Majesty with the construction of the Constantinople-Baghdad railway. I, gentlemen, definitely support that policy. We must populate that strip with Germans the whole length of the territory..."

Immediately, the table turned into a meeting of experts.

"The good dividends we'll collect from that alliance with the Turks. At this very moment the cruisers we sold them are bombarding Sebastopol — obviously with our admirals in command! In Turkey, arms and the leadership of the troops depend on us, ladies. German nature always imposes itself in war."

The young Bavarian baroness interrupted her husband, speaking up in her high-pitched voice. "I have read that three military men took power: the Young Turks; the Ittihad? It's said the Sultan is a powerless puppet, totally under their sway. Is that true, Max?"

Max nodded politely."That's correct, Franziska, you're well-informed. I'll try to make it simple," he took a knife and marked out by way of illustration a rough geography on the tablecloth. He smiled.

"What an odd alliance. I can't conceive any civilization more unlike our own than the Turks," opined another of the ladies.

"Don't you believe it, my dear," interposed someone at her side. "According to some theorists known to inspire the Kaiser, there is more than one similarity between their mentality and our own. Especially, I'd say, in the way the Turks have of considering themselves as a nation, very like ours, no matter how peculiar this comparison might seem."

"Interesting... I'll have the chance to learn about this," said Max. "In Turkey, as a secondary scene of the war, we must create multiple forces against the Russians: isolate the Czar completely from his British allies at the same time as building bases to attack the British in Egypt and the Suez Canal. At this moment, England is in control of the area. Remember, gentlemen, that between Germany and Turkey there lie neutral countries and our armies are prevented from getting to the Bosphorus. German officers who command Turkish troops are at the head of regiments and the German embassy in Constantinople is a veritable centre of diplomatic and military intelligence."

Hildegard was following the conversation with a certain uneasiness. Her guests were absorbed in the attraction produced by the strange alliance with such an alien culture. 'Germanizing', 'Turkifying'... these were the words beginning to be used.

"Lieutenant General Liman von Sanders has a detachment of 40 of our army officers in Constantinople, and Colonel Preysing is part of that elite group. A world unlike our own, unknown but similar, and useful in the circumstances." Max stressed the details as he glanced at his wife from time to time.

"Persia will open up the way to India, won't it, Max?" Friedrich asked.

"That is so," replied Max. The older Germans around the table nodded enthusiastically.

Friedrich, excited and still filled with the celebratory spirit, raised his glass once again. "Let's also drink to this magnificent dinner, madam."

Hildegard smoothed the necklace of precious stones which she had inherited from her mother and bowed her head slightly, thanking the young lieutenant. No one could have read in that calm face what her real feelings were. Hildegard would never have allowed herself to reveal them. The duties of her social position were beyond any show of character. However, she was unable to stop thinking that this might indeed be the last farewell from her husband. Turkey... Constantinople... these words sounded so foreign and distant. Together they had faced other dangers in the past, in their native Riga, but this separation would be different.

WHEN EVERYONE HAD LEFT and only a few candles were alight in the house, Max and Hildegard continued talking in the drawing room.

Hildegard felt deep melancholy. Approaching her husband and reclining against him, she sought his embrace. Her long dress spread out with a rustle. Max raised her skirt and caressed her, running his hands up her calves and thighs.

Countess von Swirsden was an extremely attractive woman, with deep blue, somewhat hard, eyes that only softened during intimacy with her husband, regarding him with fondness and sensuality. The difference in age did not matter yet and Max's youth provided an erotic element for the couple.

Hildegard's somber countenace expressed her sensitivity and, as Max caressed her and loosened her hair, she asked, "My love, why didn't you tell me sooner? Why did it have to be in front of our friends? This news has left me distressed."

Max did not reply, instead kissing her neck and ears, removing the earrings that matched her necklace.

"I'm very proud of you, but this separation..." she continued, "Suddenly I'm on tenterhooks again. We've only been together a few months this time. I was hoping you wouldn't be transferred from Straubing so soon."

"Munich isn't Riga, Hildegard."

"I know, Max. I suppose friends will keep me company while you're away, but... Turkey seems so remote. It's as though the distance increases the danger and that's how it'll really be: I'll never know if the news I get from you will give me real peace. It'll always be outdated. If anything were to happen to you, my love..."

"Forgive me, my dear, I thought there'd be no other chance to take my leave from our friends. Besides, it's good for you to grasp the reality of the true dimension of this transfer. Turkey is very important for the future of my career and so for the future of both of us. Constantinople is the place for initiatives. All decisions originate there at the embassy," Max explained.

"But they'll send you to the Russian Front, Max,"

answered Hildegard, stroking her husband's skin.

"Listen to me, Hildegard. In Constantinople, generals and colonels are in close contact with subaltern officers, which happens nowhere else in the German army. Do you realize what that means? Any lieutenant that stands out in a mission will be promoted. In the Turkish regiments, our officers command the troops. No reserve lieutenant like me could ever rise so quickly. It's likely that Preysing will offer me a command. Do you understand, Hildegard?"

A teardrop ran down Hildegard's cheek. "Don't pay attention to me, Max. I'm the wife of a German officer, and have accepted to support you at every chance and always wait for your return. I'll be strong while you're away. Don't mind me."

Hildegard embraced her husband. The embraces turned into passionate kisses. Max bared her shoulders from her dress. Hildegard stopped him. Taking his hand in hers, she stood up and led him up the stairs to the bedroom.

MAX LAY ON THE BED for a few minutes, his shirt open and his trousers still on. Meditatively, he gazed at the bedroom ceiling. Hildegard finished combing her hair, turned down the night-table lamps and walked over to the bed.

Naked and embracing each other, they made love. With their bodies entwined, Max felt a certain sadness. A feeling of far-off fondness for his wife took hold of him; a certain absence. He was unable to explain it — a kind of fraternal sensation as though, after the emotions he had experienced on the brink of death, of extreme danger, his body required a different carnality; something more brutal and impassioned. He ascribed this to the excitement of his mind at the uncertainty of what he would have to face. Soon fatigue overcame him and he fell asleep in Hildegard's arms.

TWO DAYS LATER, OUTSIDE Max's house, the military assistant sent by the regiment was helping to load Max's luggage into the back of the car. The morning was grey and along the street only a few cars could be seen.

Soldiers were being transported to the front in trucks, driving on ahead, silent as though absent, disappearing along the boulevard.

Max was in uniform. He and Hildegard held each other's hands, proudly defiant in not making a public display of their emotions.

Hildegard said in his ear, "Never forget how much love and pride I feel for you, Max. Now I'm the wife of an officer decorated with the Iron Cross... Write soon, my love."

"I'll write as soon as I arrive in Constantinople. It's the first thing I'll do, my love. You know I carry you in my heart. Neither distance nor the unknown will separate you from me."

"Be careful, be very careful, my heart," Hildegard said with contained emotion.

The car was moving away and she remained on the porch, standing on the entrance steps. That was the last image Max had of her as he waved through the window. Then the car disappeared along the boulevard on its way to the train station.

CHAPTER IV

CONSTANTINOPLE 1915

THE DOMES OF ST. SOPHIA were the first thing that would strike the gaze of any newly arrived visitor. They would go on to lose themselves in wonder at the roofs and minarets of the Turkish palaces.

That bright winter morning, a fine mist was rising from the sea and spreading through the air, giving the buildings the impression of magical suspension which only increased the exotic beauty of the scene.

Standing before the window of his office in the Imperial German embassy, the ambassador Baron von Wangenheim looked out on the view of the Bosphorus. This well-built man, venerable and energetic at 56 years of age, wore a thin moustache. As he restlessly toyed with his watch-chain, he spoke with two German gentlemen. Colonel Count von Preysing and the chief of the German military mission in Turkey, General Bronsart von Schellendorf, both wore the uniform of the Turkish army. The Imperial flag waved outside, providing a background for the ambassador's profile. Wangenheim paced back and forth, his hands clasped at his back, eyes fixed on his steps. In the background, a huge tapestry depicted scenes of ancient Teutonic legends, while a portrait of Kaiser Wilhelm II imposed itself on the room with imperial majesty.

Wangenheim was musing aloud. This diplomat was responsible for the whole of German policy in the territory of the Turkish allies. "To bring about the greatest damage to the Russians on the Baku oil-pipeline and then take possession of the oil ourselves is something no one questions any more.... As you will appreciate, it falls to me to deal with the diplomatic aspects. However, to carry out the military strategies which his Imperial Majesty orders is your territory, gentlemen." He spoke impatiently, "Really, it is with unusual incompetence that our Turkish allies lost an entire army in the mountains, led by no one less than the War Minister. An unfortunate adventure that must be a lesson to us. It is clear that the Turks can lead whole divisions to disaster without as much as going into battle. We must find a different strategy. How do you feel, von Schellendorf?"

The general made himself comfortable on the little padded seat facing the desk and, crossing his legs, made ready to answer as he accepted the cigarette Wangenheim offered him. "The Turks' methods have been mistaken, without doubt, your Excellency. Napoleon also suffered defeat by the cold but he, in contrast with Enver Pasha, would never have taken an absurd detour, burying the troops to the knees in the snows of Kars before attacking the enemy and going down in history for his incompetence. Enver Pasha's defeat at Sarikamish has set us back and hampered our chances in that region. Now, in general terms, we know the Czar must be cut off from the English, so we need to penetrate Persia despite the failures on the Kara-Kilisse-Koprikoy line, gentlemen. At the same time we should bear in mind that Liman von Sanders' victory in the Dardanelles gives us considerable time to come up with new plans against the enemy."

Colonel von Preysing agreed with a nod, blowing a puff of smoke upwards with an elegant gesture.

The Turkish military uniforms of both contrasted with their undeniably Teutonic figures. That was the norm in Turkey and it was commonplace to see a high-ranking general or officer wearing a fez.

Bronsart von Schellendorf went on, "We agree with you, Wangenheim. The Russians cannot control so many kilometres of the frontier. Infiltration would appear to be a suitable tactic. Furthermore, other units could be deployed to bring about an earlier end to work on the railway, in accordance with his Imperial Majesty's wishes."

"Preysing, I understand you have already ordered the transfer to Constantinople of persons who have stood out on the Western Front..."

Count von Preysing leant forward and, opening his portfolio, extracted a folder. "That's correct, General."

Wangenheim finally stopped pacing around the room and deposited himself behind the great desk. Behind him, an enormous window allowed in the morning light. He was fiddling with the silver cigar box, absorbed with an idea running through his mind and delaying the colonel's report.

"Infiltration... infiltration in Russia... A year ago, in this office... right there where you're now sitting, General, I received a visit from the so-called 'Agitator Parvus'. You will have heard of him, gentlemen. A thoroughly uncouth and disagreeable man... This Russian kept walking about without coming to the point of his visit. His beating around the bush was beginning to make me impatient, so much so that eventually I had to ask him directly. Parvus suggested destroying the Czar by sending Lenin to Russia. Yes, gentlemen, introducing the Bolshevik virus in their midst... Those were his exact words, I remember them well. So I asked him why we should back this individual... Lenin. The Russian very self-assuredly answered, 'Lenin will be in charge of organizing a massive revolution that will bring Nicholas II down.' I still wonder, gentlemen: if Lenin were to succeed in Russia, wouldn't the upheaval end up affecting Germany as well?"

The two officers listened attentively.

Wangenheim continued, "Anyway, gentlemen, your objective is the Caucasus... This Lieutenant Swirsden-Righe we are waiting for must be in the anteroom by now. If you please, Colonel, we should like to go over his dossier before my assistant shows him in."

"By all means, Your Excellency," answered Preysing.

MAX RESOLUTELY WALKED DOWN the embassy passages. As he passed through the neoclassic halls of the former Turkish palace, he glanced at the magnificent decorations on the walls and the enormous portraits. Carrying an attaché case, he broke the silence of the place with the click of his army boots. As he came to the end of the corridor, flanked with doric columns, the orderly guided him to the ambassador's office.

The impressive stairway opened upwards to the right

and left, its curved brass banisters flaunting eagles' and lions' heads at each end.

Max fastened the last button of his jacket and put his cap under his arm. His head was shaven and his metal-rimmed glasses gave him an intense and resolute look.

Meanwhile, beyond the doors, von Preysing was already reading Max's service record.

"Within a month of his recruitment at Straubing he had already stood out among the reserve lieutenants, receiving the Iron Cross for Bravery in Combat. I myself pinned on the decoration. It was my last line-up as regimental chief," explained the colonel without raising his eyes. "Excellent horseman. One of those individuals able to profit from any event that crops up." The colonel looked at his superiors' faces. "He has no lack of courage or ambition. Fought in Riga, his native town, in 1905, at the head of a Cossack regiment to defend Count von Swirsden's factory against anarchists that were threatening to sack it and set it on fire. After these events, Max Righe — that's his surname by birth — began his career in Chemistry."

Bronsart von Schellendorf and the ambassador were listening attentively.

"Very soon after, he married Hildegard von Swirsden, his boss's daughter, whose surname he took. Due to that family's lack of male heirs he ended up being adopted by his mother-in-law, in accordance with our prevailing inheritance laws."

Baron von Wangenheim smiled slightly, while Bronsart von Schellendorf nodded; a knowing, ironic gesture.

Count Preysing quickly read through the service record. "Speaks Russian as a native as well as perfect French. Your Excellency, General, I think reserve Lieutenant Swirsden-Righe is the right officer for this mission."

MAX WAS STILL SITTING outside the office doors, waiting to be ushered in.

The ambassador's secretary answered the phone, hung up, and walked over to the lieutenant. Max got up and the doors to the office opened. Max stood to attention before the imposing figure of the ambassador.

Wangenheim gestured with his hand to Max as he introduced the two high-ranking officers.

"Welcome to Constantinople, Lieutenant. This is General Bronsart von Schellendorf, military commander of our combined forces. And of course you already know Colonel von Preysing."

Max shook hands with Wangenheim. This was the first time he had been in the presence of such high-ranking chiefs and, in addition, the man that managed German diplomacy in Turkey. He had to remind himself to remain nonchalant, as if such an introduction was an everyday occurrence.

"Thank you, Your Excellency."

"Please be seated, gentlemen," said the ambassador. "Let's get down to business. Lieutenant, I am officially informing you that your new function in Turkey will be that of Vice-Consul in Erzurum, a city in the Interior of Anatolia."

Max's nose twitched: the post carried diplomatic responsibilities.

Wangenheim went on, "You are already aware that it is a war zone close to the Russian border. Erzurum is a key point of union between Russia and Mesopotamia."

The speed of his designation gave Max no chance to come up with a suitable answer, but he realized at once that he was the recipient of a great distinction. After all, he was in the presence of the highest political authority of the German Empire in Constantinople. He had not been mistaken in dreaming, prior to his departure, that his transfer to the Eastern Front would grant him the benefit of rubbing shoulders with the highest echelons, something inconceivable for any obscure lieutenant in the normal context of war.

The ambassador offered further details: "Erzurum is the only German legation in a 400-mile radius between Tabriz and Mosul. I think you might continue, General," said Wangenheim, inviting Schellendorf to speak.

"The vilayet is in the heart of Anatolia, a region inhabited by Armenians for over 3000 years. From there you are to organize an expedition to the Caucasus, with the object of de-stabilizing the Muslim nations on Russian territory: Persians, Kurds, Chechnyans and Daghestanis. You are to create light combat units able to withstand the climatic extremes of the territory: 20° below zero in winter and summer temperatures rising beyond 111°. The 9th and 20th Turkish armies — 80,000 men — have just succumbed in the mountains under Enver Pasha's command. Over-equipped at the start and then divested of their backpacks so as to be able to advance in the snow. A true catastrophe of the War Minister's, for which reason we will be facing the offensive with fewer troops attempting alliances with the tribal chiefs of the Caucasus."

Schellendorf signalled to von Preysing to provide greater details. The colonel took a pointer, approaching the great map on one side of the desk. "Your command, Lieutenant, is to penetrate Russian territory and reach the Baku oilfields. You are to blow up bridges and destroy railway lines that you come across on your way. Your orders are to inflict the greatest possible damage on the oil pipeline on the shores of the Caspian Sea. If you succeed we will then redirect the pipeline towards Turkish territory."

Max was listening attentively. He began to assess the real dimensions of the task he was being ordered to carry out.

Bronsart von Schellendorf, in a martial tone, expanded further, "Persia is hovering between the British and the Russians. The objective is to nudge Persia in our direction and, fundamentally, to prevent them from joining their battle fronts. Russians and British together would squeeze us as in a vice."

"Of course, Sir," Max agreed.

"Also, remember we are not to meddle in Turkey's internal affairs. What they do with their population is no business of ours. You are to report to the Turko-German military command and to Ambassador von Wangenheim himself on the opinions, movements and intentions of the Muslim peoples under Russian rule. Have you understood?"

"I have, General," was Max's reply before being warned about the perilous journey over sea and land to Erzurum. If the Russian submarines trapped the torpedo-boat or the convoy's cargo vessel in the Black Sea crossing, they would inevitably be sunk. Everyone knew the enemy dominated the sea.

Colonel von Preysing looked at Max and warmly wished him luck. Max stood to attention before the chiefs then left the ambassador's office as the new military Vice-consul in Erzurum. The excitement of the unknown gave wings to his feet.

CHAPTER V

A FAMILY

THE ARMENIAN CATHEDRAL was filled to capacity. The principal families of Erzurum were sitting in the first pews; a tradition everyone respected. The building, vaulted with stone arches, evoked, grotto-like, the great mystery of faith. The church, not only a place of religious worship but also a meeting place, had hosted the prayers of the faithful since time immemorial in Armenian history. The great majority of the congregation wore European clothes.

On observing the sector of the most important individuals, and to judge by the elegant air and delicacy of the girls and ladies, one would be forgiven for thinking they were at a Sunday service in some Paris church or at a church in any city of the eastern United States. However, the heavy habits and dark beards of the Armenian priests and the impressive choirs accompanying the lengthy service, punctuated by prayers sung in an Oriental liturgy, reminded one that this place was the heart of Anatolia. Eurasia by its geographical denomination; Turkey by conquest and territorial invasion over the preceding 700 years.

The religious community went back to the time of St. Gregory the Illuminator in the year 301 of the Christian era, when the kingdom of Armenia adopted Christianity as its state religion, becoming the oldest Christian nation in the world. Despite the uninterrupted domination of the Sultans, Christians lived under the tolerance of their Islamic compatriots. Turkish history records the bloody exception of the late 19th century massacres of Christians during the reign of Abdul Hamid II. Yet, though the indelible memory of 300,000 Armenians murdered in 1895 remained strong among the elders, the present time had brought a certain liberality and even participation in public affairs of state for Armenian citizens.

These conquests were auspicious and arrived under

the authority of the Young Turks' party, also known as the Ittihad, which, overthrowing the supreme authority of the Sultan, adopted certain European airs of modernity.

SITTING AT THE FRONT of the cathedral were Zareh and Mariam, his wife; the rest of the family were at their side. All were listening attentively to the Sunday sermon.

Mariam was a distinguished 60-year-old woman who was beginning to age gracefully. Dressed in the latest European fashion, she retained the broad-mindedness and sense of patriotism that came from a family connected to public posts and dignities. Her brother was a Member of Parliament in Constantinople, and an uncle, her mother's brother, was Bishop of Erzindjan.

Mariam's romantic spirit and her well-known good taste put cheer in Zareh's life and that of all the family. They were the result of a happy childhood and youth spent in Paris with her parents. Family friends often said Araksi was the spitting image of her mother and, except for Mariam's blue eyes and calmer disposition, Araksi was indeed a copy of her mother, her beauty much noted among the inhabitants of Erzurum.

Tavel, the eldest of the sons, was 34 and a banker. He worked with his father at the Ottoman Bank. As the first-born he was the one of choice to take charge of the business and the family fortune, which extended beyond Turkey to Europe and the United States. Both father and son had seats on the board of the Erzurum branch and maintained good relations with the Turkish authorities, being recognized as members of the local Armenian elite.

During the ceremony, Vartuhi, Tavel's wife, attempted to keep their three children still, although they persisted in trying to climb and slide along the church pews, ignoring the grave words pronounced by the Bishop of Erzurum.

Further along sat Krikor, a military engineer aged 30 and an officer in the Turkish army, wearing his uniform and ready to be called to barracks at short notice, in view of the imminent war situation.

Then came the elder sister, Mavush, 28, mother of two

well-behaved children, and her husband Levon, who occupied the end of the pew.

Araksi, sitting among them, kept looking back from time to time, as though looking for somebody.

Meanwhile, from the pulpit, the bishop was speaking to the congregation in Armenian. "Dear brethren, we have all seen with pain and sorrow the return of dead and wounded soldiers from the defeat at Sarikamish. We must remain faithful to the fatherland where we live together as brothers and citizens, albeit of different faiths, especially in these times of extreme uncertainty and ordeals. The Armenian people will once again know how to behave in solidarity and cooperation in the face of the threatening war situation. A terrible struggle in which we are involved as members of the Ottoman Empire and in which today our kinsmen are fighting at the enemy front, causing us sadness and confusion at seeing lives lost and families destroyed by so much horror."

At this point in the sermon a slim, lithe young man walked up the central aisle of the cathedral, his tardiness drawing the attention of those present. On seeing him appear, Araksi gave him a look of disapproval.

Diran looked his age, 25, and was of a pale complexion, with straight, dark hair and a hooked nose. His face was well proportioned and intelligent. He wore a dark suit and was looking for a seat. To get to Araksi, he was forced to walk the entire length of the pew, obliging the whole family to move along, and they took turns in letting him pass. But, far from feeling put-out by his late arrival, they greeted him affectionately. The cordial gesture and smile of his mother-in-law-to-be lessened the looks of impatience the bearded priests cast in his direction from the altar.

Araksi whispered, full of love, "Diran, you're almost 50 minutes late."

He answered in her ear, "Forgive me, my love, something unforeseen held me up," and sat down, somewhat agitated.

The bishop went on with his sermon. "I urge all my brothers and sisters to show resignation and Christian

25

forgiveness. Should the vicissitudes of the clash of nations come to rebound on our homes, we shall only find protection and fortitude by invoking the Lord, assured that Good will finally triumph over Evil. We must ever be prepared by trusting in the Highest. Let us keep this in mind today, Sunday, and in all the turns of fortune that may befall us along our journey through this vale of tears, but also of hope. Let us pray for Turkey, for her leaders, and for all of us, my brethren, that this war may soon come to an end."

Diran was listening sceptically to the Bishop's words as the choir of deep voices rose throughout the church, bringing about a moment of intense piety. The faithful bowed as a sign of worship.

Diran looked at Araksi kneeling at his side, her eyes half closed. Though held in place by a mantilla, wisps of her hair fell over her forehead. He felt he loved her with all his soul yet he was unable to avoid the inner thoughts that disquieted him to distraction. He observed the whole congregation; the women, children, elders, people of all social statuses together, fragile, hopeful, bowing towards the altar, and seeking protection from all the dangers looming, all with the hope of being heard by Him.

Diran found it hard to give himself up to Providence. His very life had been a trial of great suffering, all the way from childhood. He took Araksi's hand and, murmuring a prayer, following the rest. Araksi responded lovingly, her tenderness towards him and the closeness between them evident to any who cared to look.

When the ceremony finished, the families met in the entrance atrium and on the cathedral steps. The Armenian group was dressed in all its finery and the women wore dresses bought in Paris and London shops.

"How are you, Baron?" was often heard as members of the community came up to greet Zareh.

Some girls, wearing pink and blue ribbons in their hair, came up to Araksi.

"*Bonjour, mes petites élèves,*" she greeted them.

"*Bonjour, mademoiselle Araksi,*" the girls responded to

their teacher then ran back to their parents, somewhat shy and excited.

Diran smiled as he lit a cigarette and chatted with his future brothers-in-law. Discreetly, he put his arm around Araki's waist, drawing her close.

Cars and horse-drawn coaches pulled up in a line to pick up the families and drive them to their homes. The Turks regarded the scene with ease and familiarity. Many of them were clients or neighbors of the people coming out of the cathedral and many stopped to chat when they met after the service, wishing them well.

ZAREH'S AND MARIAM'S HOUSE was a luxurious one. Built in stone, it was located on high ground, thanks to the undulations of the land. The gardens reached to the end of the street, following a gentle gradient. Several similar properties separated by high stone walls made up the concentration of the most important residences in Erzurum. In the back gardens there was space for stables and the servants' quarters. Rich families usually owned some cows in a small dairy and even a stable for their carriage horses. Zareh's stables also housed the finest horses he and his children used for riding, like Araksi's favorite, Akyuz, the feisty chestnut.

The two-storey house boasted a spacious living-room. The furniture was European, interspersed with small Oriental tables and couches. There were crystal chandeliers and display cabinets full of silver. Armenian and Turkish tapestries and carpets stretched out in every room and a few French paintings interspersed with Oriental ones. In the dining room was a table which allowed 20 people to be comfortably seated. The whole family would get together in that room after the service.

The small children tirelessly ran about the ample living-room, playing hide-and-seek and stealing into grandfather Zareh's library, where they could slip away from their governess and the maids' watchful eyes.

Zareh, at the head of the table, helped himself to another plate of roast lamb then took a sip of the French wine he had brought up from the cellar. Mariam, at the opposite end, was conversing with her daughters. Diran, sitting next to Araksi, was arguing with Levon. The scene was typical of every Sunday.

"Look, Levon, I totally disagree with you. We've listened to the bishop more than once. Admit that the clerics themselves, in private of course, consider Germany is responsible for this war and has dragged the government into our having to face Russia. This is almost shouted from the rooftops, Levon. There's no more room for lukewarm attitudes."

"As far as I'm concerned," Diran lowered his voice, "I'm completely in favor of the Armenian volunteer movement in Russia. That's our only hope of liberation. Do you know how many men we could arm, Levon? General Antranig puts it at between two and three hundred thousand young Armenians, counting military and civilians. We would then be a powerful army and I doubt the Turks could prevent it. That way we'd shake off our burden in this country once and for all, Levon. It's a unique opportunity! But the people prefer to carry on not reacting. They believe that by remaining loyal to the Sultan they'll be rewarded afterwards. Naïve, all of them. Naïve!"

Diran was raising his voice, getting everyone's attention.

"You're wrong, Diran," Levon replied. "You can't overlook the participatory political measures we've obtained with this government. Our Uncle Vahan's in Parliament... you know."

This reference sounded like a familiar set phrase. Diran made a gesture of frustration.

"Whatever you like, Levon. Personally, I'm not taken in at all by the tolerance and integration nonsense of the Committee of Union and Progress," retorted Diran. "In the long run, as we are Christians the Turks will never stop squashing us, nor are we nor will we ever be free. No Member of Parliament can assure us that persecutions will never happen again in Turkey."

Diran's strong opinions were beginning to annoy the others at the table, prompting an interruption: "What, politics at the table again?"

Zareh, making a sign, intervened, requesting silence: "God forbid, Diran. Those are not convenient opinions to express in public. If you plan to build a family with Araksi you should watch for exposing yourself to suspicions of collaborationism or possible sedition. We're at war, Diran. A simple statement contrary to the policies of the Empire in unsuitable surroundings could cost you jail or death on charges of treason to the fatherland, don't forget it. Even," added the patriarch ruefully, "if your words are true."

Araksi remained attentive to her father. Krikor, who seldom intervened in political discussions, adored his younger sister Araksi, and felt a deep sympathy for Diran.

Using a conciliatory tone as he turned a silver napkin ring round and round, he stated, "If I may be allowed, I believe the work on the Baghdad railway through Mesopotamia is bound to have a significant commercial impact on everyone — and I mean all of us... not just the Turks and the Germans — and that is the crux of the matter, Diran. Once the war ends we'll enjoy the benefits, just wait and see! There'll be huge business opportunities all along the belt of new towns."

Disquieted, Diran answered, "Yes, especially for the Germans."

Mariam, hearing Krikor's words, was conciliatory as she spoke, "I think the same as you, son. Germany is European and Christian. Sooner or later it will influence the thinking patterns of the Young Turks, and those changes will end up being irreversible. I'm sure you have a far broader outlook than we have, and those works will be of use in civilizing such inhospitable regions. Incidentally, Vahan has written to me this week," continued Mariam with pride as she looked at all of them. "You ought to read the latest news your uncle sends from Parliament. The Sultan has congratulated the Armenian deputies for the loyalty with which our people are contributing to the war. My dear," she said to Krikor, "I agree with you entirely."

"Thank you, Mother," smiled Krikor.

Tavel, who remained quiet and pensive, added: "It's

simple. Look at it this way. Europeans need us to be able to invest in Turkey. They always look for partners of Ottoman nationality that have a fluid rapport with European culture. It's impossible for foreigners to manage alone with the Turks. They need Armenians for any business to function."

Mavush changed the subject. "Talking of Germans, I've heard the new German consul's arrived in Erzurum: Count Max von Swirsden-Righe. We ought to make his acquaintance soon, Father? You knew..?"

Zareh interrupted. "Of course, my dear, but we haven't met him yet. I got on very well with the former consul."

Vartuhi added, mischievously, as she scoffed meringues with honey and fruit, "Mavush surely knows every detail of the consul's life. There's nothing that gets past her in Erzurum."

Everyone laughed.

Araksi spoke up for the first time, "At the school they've called for volunteers for a blood hospital at the German Consulate and I didn't hesitate for a moment in offering myself as an assistant nurse... the doctors simply can't cope with the wounded arriving from the Russian Front," she added enthusiastically.

Mariam started. "I don't think that's at all suitable for you, Araksi. You should have asked your father and me."

"It's for a noble cause, Mamma."

"Yes, child, but it doesn't seem proper for a young girl to be in contact with the soldiery, besides seeing so much suffering. There are other ways of helping."

Mavush interrupted, "Araksi, what's going to happen with your French classes? Are you going to abandon your pupils?"

"I've been given permission, Mavush. They couldn't say no for a couple of weeks."

Zareh calmed his wife: "She can go for a couple of days. Then she'll get tired or feel horrified at the butchery... Just let her and she'll soon lose some of her altruistic ideas about going in for medicine."

Diran appeared surprised but said nothing, considering any attempt to oppose Araksi as useless.

From his very early youth, Araksi had been part of his life plans. They had always been attracted to each other and the secret Diran held was to accept her as she was: full of life, resolute, and having an enormous will to live, overriding all obstacles. He, in a certain way, also loved action and unsteadiness, but knew the value of waiting for the right moment and never yielding in his purposes. Getting married was a natural consequence of that mutual attraction, enhanced by the circumstance of their having almost grown up together. He hoped Araksi would make up her mind once and for all to marry him. After all, he had done his bit, he had just begun his professional life, and with Zareh's and Mariam's backing everything would be very easy.

The gramophone in the library was playing a tango. The men smoked, and Araksi was dancing with Krikor. They exaggerated and clowned their sensual turns and twists, creating excitement in the children, who imitated their seniors under their grandparents' benevolent eye.

Zareh put his cheek close to Mariam's. With 'cortes' and 'quebradas' they showed a talent apparently picked up in Paris salons that elicited applause and cheers. Diran took Araksi's hand. Following the elegant rhythm of the melody, he led her to the small side-room out of everyone's sight, where they might enjoy a little intimacy. Among the curtains, Diran kissed her passionately.

"I love you, I love you, I really love you, Araksi. Let's get married soon, my precious."

"Diran, you're mad, not here... in front of my parents? I also love you... be careful, someone could come in... I'd die of shame if they caught us..."

"I'm authorized... I can demand my rights, don't you think?"

"Oh, yes? How sure do you feel about me?" she asked coquettishly.

Diran asked, as though he had been waiting for the opportunity, "What's all that about you being a nurse at the hospital, Araksi?"

"Yes, Diran. I've already decided."

"You'll be surrounded by hacked-up Turks."

"I don't care. It's what I must do. That way I'll know all about the suffering of others and perhaps... become a doctor some day." She smiled seductively.

"You wouldn't have time left for me."

"We'll have it later, Diran... Aren't we together now, silly?" she countered, giving him a passionate kiss on the mouth.

CHAPTER VI

THE CONSULATE

THE IMPERIAL GERMAN flag stood out against the sky above the table-land. "Stand at ease!" commanded General Posselt, the highest ranking officer.

The ceremony was brief but full of martial spirit. It seemed as if the Germans had set out to show their Turkish allies and the tribal chiefs of the Caucasus region that they were in the presence of the Kaiser's greatness, as represented by each one of them.

Max was reminded that his new office came with a promotion: from now on he was to be Lieutenant Swirsden-Righe. He thought of Hildegard and smiled inwardly as he returned the military salute of out-going consul Colonel Schwartz.

"Congratulations, Lieutenant. Now the Erzurum Consulate is your personal responsibility," said Schwartz, accompanied by a corporal of the Turkish army. The Turk, Tahir, had a rather neutral look, though not completely exempt of features of loyalty and shrewdness.

"Tahir will be your personal assistant, Lieutenant. He speaks Russian, Turkish, Kurdish, Persian and Armenian to perfection, but neither reads nor writes," stressed the colonel, adding in a somewhat confidential tone, "He is totally trustworthy, and will be indispensable to you in this Babel of personalities you will have to deal with."

Impressed at such linguistic prowess, Max understood the interpreter would be his own voice in a territory so vast and peopled by different ethnicities.

He greeted Tahir in Russian. After all, it was his native tongue. The Turk smiled on hearing the German's perfect accent. Normally German officers and gentlemen, and some Turkish, spoke French besides their own language. A current of mutual sympathy was established between them at once.

The unmistakable sound of hooves on the paved central square caught everyone's attention. From the stables of the building an elegantly dressed soldier was approaching. He was leading by hand two magnificent thoroughbred Arab horses, duly saddled. The beasts pranced around nervously and reared, revealing their noble blood.

Max looked on with delight. Everyone present stood aside to make way for the groom. It was then that General Posselt smiled, "They're for you, Swirsden-Righe. These outstanding beasts will come in handy on your lengthy Caucasian campaign. How do you like them?"

Max remained speechless with wonder as the Turk handed him the reins.

The dappled horse moved restlessly. Its dark nostrils and fetlocks of the same color showed flowing, harmonious lines such as Max had never seen in any European regimental horse. He usually rode Hanoverians or Westphalians, the best national breeds to be found in Germany, and of an enormous size, suitable for jumping, horsemanship and war. He would ride them on outings with Hildegard in the Bavarian woods. These horses, however, were the stuff of dreams, worthy of sheikhs and princes.

He looked from one to the other, inspecting the animals' fineness. The chestnut pricked up his ears on seeing Max, fixing his dark, somewhat mad eyes on him, offering an invitation to live wild adventures at full gallop on his back. He pawed the ground with his hooves, alert to the slightest movement of those cavalry officers, who marvelled at such beauty. It was a smooth-skinned Arab horse with a black mane contrasting with the reddish brown of its body, with perfect lines inherited from the most faultless specimens the Sultan and the Military Junta offered the German commanders from their stables at Constantinople.

Tahir translated for Max the soldier groom's words: "That's Kismet," pointing at the dappled horse, "and this is Pasha," fondling the chestnut.

Max had already made his mind up and, stepping into the stirrup, mounted Pasha. The animal, spirited but docile and well broken in moved only a little and, responding to Max's hand, allowed itself to be led in the small circles the rider ordered to test the softness of its mouth. Everyone admired Max's equestrian skill.

After a short ride around he dismounted and, after thanking General Posselt for the gift, walked to the commander's office for the reception. The new consul was overwhelmed by all these excitements, one after another.

Later, in front of a huge map of the region, the general set out to explain to Max and the others the nature of the military mission in Erzurum. "You are aware the Turks conquered Tabriz — that is, under the orders of Lieutenant-Colonel Stange, the commander of the 10th division of the Turkish army... Right here, do you see?" He indicated with the pointer. "In Northern Persia. Now we're expecting the Russian counter-offensive. It can come from practically anywhere on the line from Tabriz in Azerbaijan, a territory of the Shah of Persia's, to Mosul, our great base." Posselt marked the line on the map.

Max absorbed with interest each detail about the exotic region that destiny had awarded him. The general went on, "In the meantime, this triumph gives us an opportunity of entering the East Caucasus."

"Lieutenant," he said, "your first task as Consul of Erzurum will consist of taking charge of the wounded. A hospital will have to be improvised in the Consulate. There are so many wounded that the city hospitals couldn't possibly cope. I've issued orders for the work of accommodation to be carried out and for nurses to be recruited among the local poulation."

General Posselt felt further explanations were called for. "I expect you've heard what's happened. Enver Pasha, the War Minister, led the 9th Infantry Corps to disaster in the mountains... They left their knapsacks in Erzurum so as to make passing through the high mountains easier. 80,000 Turkish men went down in the snow, frozen through lack of equipment... and because of hunger. The rest were made prisoners. Do you understand the sheer number of wounded that can be expected to arrive in Erzurum?"

"Yes, Sir. I've been informed of the defeat at

Sarikamish," Max replied.

Schwartz, the outgoing consul, was sitting in a large leather armchair. Noticing his successor being somewhat troubled, he suggested, "Lieutenant Swirsden-Righe, this consulate covers an enormous territory and the image of the Imperial German Consul inspires deep respect. You'll find the civilian population of Erzurum to be inclined to cooperate in any way you may ask them to."

The time had arrived to detail the military status between the German military mission and the Turkish command in the region. Before Max was able to raise any questions, General Posselt cleared up his doubts about fulfilling orders. "Commander Taksim Bey will be your military superior in the region, to whom you will report periodically. Taksim Bey is above any civil authority in the vilayet of Erzurum. Have you understood?"

While the general declared the meeting over and everyone in the room stood, he added one final recommendation, "Always remember, Lieutenant Swirsden-Righe, that we are never to meddle in the internal affairs of Turkey."

"I understand, General. I will try to live up to what's expected of me," Max answered, standing to attention before the chiefs.

While the officers left the building, Max appeared on the terrace and looked to the snow-capped mountains surrounding Erzurum. The streets, with their irregular levels, sloped down abruptly, lending the buildings a quaint arrangement. Some distance away, the occasional minaret overlooked the remaining roofs.

He allowed free rein to his thoughts and mulled over all he had experienced that day. He thought of Hildegard and finished his cigarette, sitting down at his desk for the first time, right outside the bedroom. In one drawer he found letterheaded notepaper and, dipping his pen into the inkwell, made ready to write his wife a letter to inform her of everything that had happened since his arrival in Turkey.

First, though, he selected a gramophone record from a collection of operas he found next to a bookcase and, laying it on the turntable, set the apparatus for the music to start playing. The notes wafted him away at once, very far from Eastern Turkey.

THE FOLLOWING DAYS WERE USED by Max for studying and planning the political functions of his post. He had little time to familiarize himself with the operation of the consulate before trucks rolled up and unloaded oxygen tents, operating tables, surgical instruments, lamps, and everything necessary to receive the wounded. Very soon the recruited military and civilian doctors quickly took up their positions in the building, turning it into a blood hospital.

Max supervised the work. He rapidly came into contact with the Turkish world and with chiefs of staff of the regional regiment. Normal communication between Germans and Turks was in French, a language Max knew perfectly. Some of the Turks had attended German schools but they were a minority, so his first language, Russian, would be very useful to him whilst on the campaign.

WEEKS LATER, THE GERMAN CONSULATE building was in veritable turmoil. Not even the outside courtyard had been exempted from the new tasks. Carts and ambulances arrived without cease, loaded with the seriously wounded from the Front. Most of the men, besides wounds and mutilations, showed horrible signs of frostbite and gangrenous limbs. The stretchers on which lay those needing attention were out-of-doors, below a long gallery, waiting for the death of a wounded comrade in order to free up a bed in the pavilions.

The soldiers' dirty, bloody faces and their screams of pain made the gravity of the situation more than clear. On all sides, people ran about asking for surgeons, drips, a free operating table, or nurses that would carry bandages and water to the thirsty. There were, in the Turkish army, Armenian, Kurdish and Caucasian soldiers, and even a few Germans, but in their pain they were indistinguishable. They all proffered similar screams of despair and anguish, whatever the language they expressed them in.

Max walked among the beds in the great main hall, observing everything around him. At the far end of the hall, which was normally the staff canteen, curtains had been set up to act as separators between the operating tables. Trying to overcome his apprehension, he walked over, keeping a prudent distance.

All at once a nurse went by, staggering. She was leaving the improvised operating theater on the point of fainting, either from fatigue or the effect of such a horrendous spectacle. The Turkish doctor, without removing his mask, and covered by a blood-stained apron, commented, "She was unable to stand it." He beckoned to another nurse to take her place. At a neighboring table, the group of doctors stopped struggling and gave up their useless efforts. The dead man was removed and they began cleaning the table, preparing it for the next casualty.

Max moved even closer. The opened curtain allowed the operation to be seen: a surgeon amputating a young soldier's leg. Faces were tense and sweat ran down the physician's forehead. The nurse, Araksi, handed him the instruments. They made desperate efforts to save the wounded man. The young girl's courage overcame the effect produced by the terrible carnage. In the presence of pain, her sense of compassion was endless. From time to time she wiped the poor unfortunate's forehead, caressing him with great care.

The consul looked on the scene, moved by the young woman's composure. The patient's blood was flowing copiously and the volunteer nurses went back and forth with bowls and bandages. The surgical mask covered the girl's face, but allowed her lovely eyes to be seen. The German felt a deep attraction to her — instantaneous, almost irreverent — and he realized that his presence there was disrupting the doctors' work.

He felt strange, since he was used to controlling his acts and emotions. He kept staring at the girl throughout the whole operation. Araksi did not once notice him, her concentration on her responsibility leaving no room for even the slightest distraction.

When her replacement arrived, the girl left the operating table and, removing her mask, revealed the full beauty of her face. A surgeon went by in a hurry. Max caught his arm and the doctor halted for an instant with considerable surprise.

"Doctor," Max began.

"Sir?" said the doctor, a middle-aged Armenian.

"That young nurse there, the one that helps the chief surgeon — who is she? Do you know her? She seems to resist the sight of suffering very stalwartly. Others have had to leave the scene horrified, on the verge of fainting."

"Yes, sir, she's a young Armenian. Her name's Araksi. She belongs to one of the most important families in our community, she's the daughter of Baron Zareh, head of the Erzurum bank."

"An Armenian?" repeated Max, almost curiously.

The doctor, realizing the German Consul's lack of information, said briefly, "She's been here for two days helping us... If you'll excuse me, Sir, I must get on with my work."

Max, dazzled by Araksi, observed her tied-back jet black hair and a figure he imagined as perfect, even beneath her nurse's apparel. He ran his eyes up and down, unable to check himself, the harmony of her arms and the perfection of her hips. He was lured by her color; a gentle matte complexion. Araksi wiped her forehead with her hand, showing exhaustion, then lost herself amid the dividing curtains.

Max came back to reality, disturbed from his rapt contemplation by an assistant's call to come between the wounded men's beds. A strange, unexpected emotion had taken hold of him at the most surprising moment and in the least suitable circumstances.

ALONG THE ALLEYS of Erzurum, people moved around the bazaars just as on any other day. The scene was undoubtedly that of an Oriental town. Outside the residential area of great houses and public buildings, the 500,000 people who lived there, barring the 60,000 Armenian residents, led their lives in small shops and industries. Even though Erzurum lay in a zone threatened with a possible invasion of Cossacks under the command of Nikolai Nikolaevich, the Czar's cousin, war had not yet touched the city.

The women's clothing, covering them from head to foot, demonstrated to European visitors the isolated and traditionalist spirit of the population, which seemed to have come to a standstill in time. The Turkish shopkeepers exhibited their wares in baskets outside their shops. Carpets and cloth hung from poles and beams everywhere. Max made a habit of looking over and discovering the various parts of Erzurum and its surroundings. The hospital had been dismantled and the sick transferred to numerous different places for their recovery, until such time as the expedition to the Caucasus was organized.

He jumped up onto Pasha, his magnificent chestnut mare. Soon he was able to see that, as he had been told in Constaninople, the figure of the German Consul, as representative of a great European power, inspired enormous respect.

Tahir, his assistant, mounted on the dappled Kismet, would ride ahead, opening up a pathway among the townspeople, preventing carts or some animal from interrupting their progress or getting disrespectfully in the way.

IT WAS JUST AFTER MIDDAY when the riders went by the French Institute on one of their usual excursions. It was the time the children came out of classes. The consul held Pasha to rein, the animal snorting at so much hustle and bustle.

Araksi and another young teacher, Armenuhi, descended the steps of the main entrance, making their way through the little children now out of their classes.

Without stopping his horse or showing special interest, Max observed the noisy pupils striving to reach the school gates. Yet his lack of interest soon turned into curiosity and the glance awoke a memory. But from where and when? He remembered a feminine presence that had struck him before in some way. There in front of him stood the image that he remembered with pleasure and he drew his horse closer to see the young woman better, as close as the mass of children and mothers in the broad street allowed.

His memory didn't deceive him and he saw the young teacher who was now wearing her dark hair loose and which the wind ruffled irresistibly.

She was laughing as she walked with her friend of the same age, another Armenian teacher, Max imagined. From time to time they scolded the noisier children. He was sure the young woman was Araksi, the same woman who had fascinated him a few weeks ago at the consulate hospital, only now he was able to see her full beauty. Both girls were dressed in the current European fashion.

People in the street whispered at seeing the foreigner and his assistant. Soon Araksi and Armenuhi noticed the looks the German was giving them and Araksi curiously and somewhat cautiously took in the consul's composure. Maybe it was the novelty, the German uniform, the authority of the person that she hadn't seen in the improvised hospital those few weeks earlier.

She held his look for a few instants and immediately a spark of mutual attraction became evident. She looked away, blushing a little, as she continued coming down the steps.

Armenuhi could not avoid commenting: "Araksi! That's the new German Consul. Did you see how he stared at you! He stopped in front of everybody. Do you think he's handsome?"

"I think he was looking at you, Armenuhi... I didn't even pay attention, what do you think?"

Max and Tahir rode on at a trot. Max looked at the young woman just once more and thought, *That's her, Araksi... Araksi, the doctor said... Armenian. Why should I have passed by this place at this very moment?*

"Tahir, is this school for Armenian children?" he asked.

"Yes, Lieutenant, it is the French Institute, but Turkish children also go to it," the assistant remarked.

Max remained pensive for a while. He was bothered

that a thought so alien and improper to his function in that place should occupy his mind.

The riders left the broad street and then followed the road that left the city towards the high plain. Several carts and goatherders driving their flocks crossed the road.

Once out on the plain, Max and Tahir gave free rein to their thoroughbreds and soon there was no room left for any other thoughts.

THE CONSUL OF ERZURUM'S FUNCTIONS were linked to reports that had to be presented periodically to the Turkish regiment of the region, based in Tartum, a two-hour ride away. These journeys enabled Max to get acquainted with the vilayet and the military commands of the Turkish army his own authority depended on. But as the weeks wore on, his own office began to be visited by certain regional personalities who brought him useful news about the campaign to Persia, which the Germans were about to launch through the high mountains. A complex web of alliances needed to be established with the local tribal chieftains, adding them to the offensive against the Baku oil pipeline at the Caspian Sea in Russian territory.

It was a normal afternoon at the Consulate when suddenly an orderly entered the office, interrupting Max's work.

"Excuse me, Sir. You have a visitor. Amir Aslan, Prince Khoisky is requesting a meeting. He says he's the representative of the Mahommedan organizations of the region. Will you receive him, Sir?"

Max looked up.

"Amir Aslan, the Daghestani chieftain?"

"Yes Sir, he's in the room outside."

"Show him in."

The soldier respectfully clicked his heels and left the room.

Minutes later both Max and the chieftain were seated opposite each other in the lounge armchairs. On the wall hung a large map of the region.

Amir Aslan was wearing a costume proper to a

character out of *A Thousand and One Nights*. From his waist hung a long sabre. He was fond of reminding those newly acquainted with him that in the past he had undergone military studies at the Saint Petersburg Military Academy and served as an officer of the Czar in Moscow. He belonged to one of the thousand families the Russian Empire recognized as princes in Daghestan.

The two men spoke in Russian.

"Committees of the revolutionary type are increasingly numerous, Consul. Elisavetpol is the principal base of the tribes." He indicated a spot on the map. "Rumors are circulating that Count Vorontzoff-Dachkoff, the Czar's civil and military governor, has retired, much weakened. There are no police there and discipline in the army is very bad. Muslims desert from Russian regiments and many Armenians, in turn, join Cossack units. This will surely bring about very severe measures against the Armenians of Turkey. Look, Consul, maybe you ought to be on the look-out and avoid possible uprisings right here in Erzurum."

Max looked at the prince in surprise, not entirely grasping what he meant. After all, the Armenians of Erzurum vilayet were peaceful people and he considered them foreign to this business.

Amir Aslan went on, "Count on the Daghestani tribes and the other organizations I represent in carrying out your campaign. We will be backed by the Baku oil barons... with sufficient arms, ammunition, and money to combat the Cossacks. If we agree to ally ourselves to the Turks we will cooperate in the general uprising in the Caucasus against the Russians. But then, Sir... Germany must guarantee our subsequent independence — our independence from Russians *and* Turks," he emphasized.

Max stood and walked before Amir Aslan. It seemed as if his attention had remained stuck at some previous point of the conversation. "It seems opportune.... The moment seems ripe. The Russians may reinforce that battlefront.... And what if we entered their territory by way of northern Persia...?" The Daghestani's warning went round and round in Max's mind. "But tell me, Amir Aslan, do you believe that those insurrections, the Armenian insurrections you spoke about, could spread to the whole of Anatolia? The Armenian population here in Erzurum is 30%, so that is a really troubling thought."

The prince nodded assent, and was categorical. "Blood is going to flow. You do not yet know the Turks, Swirsden-Righe!"

Max was dumbfounded by the reply. Later, when the prince left the office, he remained thoughtful, looking out of the large window.

CHAPTER VII

ARMENIAN BLOOD

THE SECRET MEETING had been convened in the crypt of the thousand-year-old Apostolic Church of Erzurum. The group of young conspirators were speaking in an undertone with a certain complicity and evident fear. The candle light cast eerie shadows on the stone walls and the vaulted ceilings of the aisles. They were in the very catacombs of the church.

Diran and eight young rebels of the Armenian resistance movement were challenging authority. The crypt was the safest and most hidden place in all Erzurum.

Although the meeting could cost them their lives if they were discovered by the zaptiehs (the Turkish police), the urgency of the circumstances justified every risk they were taking. By now the Armenian resistance youths knew the time to act had arrived. Stone sarcophagi eroded by time along the naves caused a certain shudder in the young men's spirits.

The voice sounded deep and determined, with an Armenian accent that seemed to come forth directly from ancestors lying in the vaults, below crosses and fleurons wasted away by centuries in that place of death and eternal reverence. "The resistance of our brothers in Van has been heroic. The Turks have tried to exterminate them and if we don't extend the rebellion to the whole of Anatolia as soon as we can, a sure death awaits us all. Comrades! We shall fight until the last drop of blood. There will be no alternative this time. Understand that we could lose our lives on this mission but it will be so the Armenian nation may rise once more!"

Diran raised the collar of his leather and fur coat and contemplated this in silence.

"The Czar is on our side," exclaimed another youth, "and when the Russians cross the border we'll be free. Already, thousands are joining the Cossacks."

The one that seemed to be the leader spoke again. "Yes, but there are many more that won't react. There's no time left for conversations: each of you knows the orders. The telegraph line must be put out of action. Diran, you will go with them, we'll gain time, and the Turks will be disorganized for a few hours. Then the second group will march on the guard posts along the mountain highway and transmit a message to our brave comrades in Van and the other cities. We must create chaos. Perhaps that way conformist Armenians will come out of their lethargy and, realizing the gravity of the situation, join us. The advance from Russia will do the rest. Now, comrades, let us all swear to fight for liberation or death... That the sacrifice of our brothers in Van shall not have been in vain."

All the men joined hands as an oath of loyalty to the cause. When the moment to disperse arrived they came out one by one, in silence, stealing along the tunnels. As they climbed the narrow steps, they proceeded to the little hidden trapdoor behind the altar dedicated to St. Gregory the Illuminator in one of the side naves. The choir of deep voices at the religious service being celebrated could be heard.

Passing through the sacristy, Diran looked up at the stained glass window which showed sacred motifs and, despite the religious scepticism he felt, in his own way he asked the Highest for protection in the risks they were about to face. It was his task to take charge of his first action in the combat group, a sort of baptism of fire.

THE TELEGRAPH LINE COVERED hundreds of kilometres and news travelled from town to town throughout Turkey. The Van rebellion had already broken out. Thousands of Armenians died and were killed in defending themselves from the violence let loose by the Turks in this city not very far from Erzurum. This was the message the wires carried.

The group of Armenian combatants had reached the nearby mountains surrounding Erzurum. They had to prevent gendarmerie detachments — the dreaded zaptiehs — from receiving the orders to repress which, coming from Constantinople, buzzed through all the telegraph lines of the empire.

Hanging from wires and divided into groups of two, the young men cut telegraph lines while others kept watch at a bend in the road to prevent the appearance of some patrol alerted against possible sabotage. The zaptiehs' response was not long in coming. At the police post, Turkish soldiers tried to telegraph in vain, proving that the lines were dead. The patrol left the guard-house at a full gallop and minutes later a dozen soldiers from the detachment boarded the truck that would take them to the mountains.

Meanwhile, Diran, high up on a pole, struggled with pliers to cut the wires which resisted his efforts. From the ground, Tigran, his companion, warned nervously: "The police are coming, Diran. Hurry, hurry, or we're dead men."

Diran, sweating despite the cold of the night, carried on until the flash of a short circuit announced his work was completed. The cut end fell to the ground with a lashing movement and went on throwing out occasional sparks. Some distance away, a group of eight Armenian companions took out their guns.

"Everyone to the bush!" yelled the leader. "Diran! Get out of the way, hurry or they'll kill you. There's no time left. Those at the rear, cover the retreat and start shooting as soon as you see headlights appear round the curve."

"Get down, get down from the pole once and for all. What the hell is happening to you, Diran? Shit! They're almost on top of us," yelled Tigran as, behind him, he saw headlights piercing the blackness of the moonless night.

Diran was trying to loosen his boots from the tangle of wire and, finally managing it, crossed, crouching, almost crawling, to the other side of the road. Tigran, having no time to escape, faced the gendarmes, firing his rifle at them. From the undergrowth, each on his own so as not to reveal their position, the Armenian combatants shot a rain of bullets against the military truck.

The young Armenian leader was able to make out Diran, illuminated by the flashes of gunfire, dodging the shots and throwing himself into the shrubbery at the side of the road. He also saw how a shot shattered Tigran's shoulder, who fell wounded while covering Diran's escape. An expression of intense sorrow fell across the group captain's face. An immediate decision was called for.

They looked at one another for an instant. There was little to be added. They had pledged themselves to advance to Russia. It was pointless to resist. At any moment, more trucks would arrive. Everything was lost for the stragglers by now. Tigran, lying on the road, pulled out his handgun from among his clothes and with a slow movement attempted to shoot himself in the temple. A Turkish corporal arrived just then and, stepping on his arm, prevented the suicide.

Diran, hiding in some bushes, managed to hear, "Leave this Armenian dog alive. He has a lot to tell us. Let the mounted group run no risks. At dawn we'll scour the mountains to the East. Take him away quickly so he'll spill the beans before he croaks."

Diran realized by now that it would be impossible to catch up with his comrades. The zaptiehs straddled the road. The only remaining option was to return to Erzurum. Sweating and panting as never before in his life, he ran downhill among the bushes. He would often fall over and pick himself up to carry on running until he no longer heard the sound of shots. He took the mountain path and an hour or so later he could make out shadows coming closer. He waited, hidden behind the rocks, as he heard the squeak of a wagon and a voice that, on becoming closer, became clear and familiar to him. It sounded like a chant in Armenian, surely a lonely shepherd coming down the mountain to get to the city market at dawn, urging his old mule on.

The young lawyer sighed with relief and came out onto the road. The old man, startled, gave a shout of fright but heard Diran's pleas and without asking questions allowed the young man to conceal himself beneath a load of hay. He had looked at the young man for an instant and seemed to understand without needing further explanations.

Two hours later, still before dawn, Diran exited the cart in the streets of Erzurum. He immediately headed for Zareh's house. Jumping over the stone wall, he let himself in at the back to avoid being seen by the servants.

Everyone was sleeping. Making one last effort, he climbed up to the overhangs of the house and, holding on to the balconies, managed to reach the first storey. He opened the large window and entered Araksi's bedroom. She opened her eyes and saw Diran - covered with dust, sweat on his clothes and his wild, haggard look - all the while asking her to keep quiet as he gently covered her mouth with his hand.

He sat down on the edge of the bed as Araksi sat up.

With an agitated, broken voice, he said, "We destroyed the telegraph line. The general revolt is spreading to every city. Don't ask me any more. All I ask from you is to let me rest here for a few hours. It's very likely they're searching for me. When day comes, I'll slip out and lose myself among the city crowds. One of us tried to kill himself but he was taken alive. They've begun eliminating us, like in 1895, Araksi. The Russians say this will inevitably happen in the whole of the empire."

Araksi embraced him, worried. "Since when have you been part of the armed resistance?"

"Forgive me, Araksi. I took an oath to fight in secret."

"Do you realize what you've exposed yourself to, my love? You're completely pale. Diran... Diran, have you killed anybody?"

"No. In the gunfight some died. The rest of my group escaped to the East. Give me water, Araksi!"

She got up and handed him the large bottle and a glass. Diran took great mouthfuls until he had emptied the container.

"I seriously believe that within a few weeks nobody's going to escape the Turks' fury. The most sensible thing to do is to flee to Russia as soon as possible, Araksi. That I didn't do it tonight was because I'd never have been able to leave without you."

Araksi walked over to the wide door to her bedroom and signalled to him to remain silent. She barely opened the door and, peering out at the passage, she confirmed that everyone was asleep. The house was huge and the other bedrooms were some distance away. She shut the door again and huddled on the fur carpet. She needed to think. Diran's appearance had startled and confused her. She had to organize her thoughts. What was happening would permanently affect her family and herself.

"My parents' position and the family's influence... Uncle Vahan will intercede for any of us in Parliament if anything so serious were to happen... We'll always be protected from any danger. Papa has told me so... The war's against Russia. The Sultan himself congratulated the Armenians for fighting against the Russians. Diran... Diran, are you listening to me?"

Diran moved his head, weighed by tiredness. "In 1895 many were killed, Araksi, among them my parents... You know that's impossible to forget."

Araksi caressed Diran with great tenderness. It was still dark outside the windows. She embraced him more closely as fatigue overtook him and she nestled him as a child in her lap.

HOURS LATER, A RAY OF SUNLIGHT entered the room. Araksi watched how her fiancé's face lit up. She remained immobile until he awoke. They embraced and kissed over and over again. For a while they said nothing. Then Diran decided it was time to leave the way he had come in.

He dropped down from the rear window of the room, this time making sure he was not seen by the stable-hand who was milking the cows. Araksi watched as though she expected the worst, following his every movement until he dropped down on the other side of the garden wall.

MAX VON SWIRSDEN-RIGHE read aloud a cable in his office, where he often received callers. Sitting in front of him, the Bishop of Erzurum was listening with a somber look to the news arriving from Van. Max read on: "The fierce armed resistance in the city of Van by Armenian guerrillas developed into a full battle, leaving thousands of Turkish citizens dead, with the resulting bloody repression of the

Armenian population ordered by Djevdet Bey, the military governor of Van."

Max looked up and, removing his steel-rimmed glasses, asked, "What consequences will this uprising bring, Bishop?"

The bishop half-closed his eyes with heavy-heartedness and, leaning forward, answered, "It has been in legitimate self-defense, Consul. Violence is absolutely to be condemned from our pastoral point of view. You must know that one third of the population in the vilayet of Erzurum is Armenian... Our people, Christians the same as you Germans are, have for centuries lived peacefully alongside Turks." The cleric spoke with great sadness. "At this very moment in Constantinople, while you and I talk, they are murdering the most prominent men of our community, even Members of Parliament. Do you not think that a provocation of such gravity has unleashed the Armenians' reaction? The Turks are taking revenge on us for the defeat at Sarikamish. And I ask you: what is Germany's role in all of this, Sir?"

Max felt the intense look of the bishop from under his dark, bushy eyebrows. He did not know what to answer.

"Did you know that in towns and villages a deportation to the Mesopotamian deserts had begun? It is rumored this is an idea of the German allies, who aid and abet the Young Turks. I answer for my flock in Erzurum, Sir, and assure you no one will betray the fatherland, but our first kingdom is Christ and I sense that the Turks want no other population than Muslims. What, then, will the Kaiser, who presides over a Christian nation, do, Mr. Consul?"

Max looked worriedly at him. This was a grave measure he knew nothing about. At that moment the secretary interrupted the dignitary, announcing that a group of 20 notable Armenians urgently wanted to participate in the interview. Max consulted the bishop, and immediately agreed to receive them.

They came in at once. Among them were Zareh and Tavel. Diran was also present. The bishop introduced all in turn, explaining to Max the position of each in the community. No doubt they were the most prominent men in the city. It was Zareh's turn to speak.

Max recognized the surname, immediately associating it with the dark-haired girl who had so impressed him weeks earlier. "I know who you are, Baron. Your daughter collaborated as a volunteer nurse in helping the wounded, and worked indefatigably alongside the surgeons. Her great work in this improvised hospital has not gone unnoticed."

"My daughter is a very worthy young woman, Mr. Consul. I thank you for your comment. I'm proud of all my children. Their mother and I have educated them to be equal to their duties, in whatever circumstances of life they may find themselves." Tavel and Diran came forward to be introduced. "This is my eldest son, Tavel. He is my best employee at the Ottoman Bank. And my future son-in-law, Diran, soon to marry Araksi."

Max von Swirsden-Righe experienced a certain distaste for Diran, but gave himself no time to admit these feelings as he shook hands with the young lawyer and held his gaze. Diran, in turn, took an instant dislike to Max. He was probably jealous, knowing Max had taken notice of Araksi. He saluted in Russian, not in French as the others present had done.

"Are you Russian?" inquired Max.

"I am Armenian, born in the Russian territory of Armenia, which one day will be a united Armenian state," Diran replied.

"And I am a German Balt, from the Russian side, which will be a part of Germany once more," replied the consul, bothered at the young Armenian's improper and challenging tone. He immediately turned the conversation towards other topics. "Gentlemen, this military consulate is informed about what is going on. The bishop has enlightened me on certain aspects I was unaware of based on our reports. I will try and guarantee the safety of Armenian families and individuals as far as my authority allows in the case the crisis should spread throughout Anatolia, but I have express orders from Constantinople not to intervene in the internal affairs of your country."

Diran openly answered him: "Sir, I know the zaptiehs are detaining all the notables of our people in Constantinople. If they are doing it there, where Enver, Talaat, and Djemal Pasha exercise their authority, and in front of all the foreign legations, what can we Armenians expect from the persecutions in the interior of Turkey? Could it be that the German generals in Constantinople just turn a blind eye to it?"

"I will do all I can to safeguard the life and goods of the Armenian population, particularly yours and that of your families," Max promised.

The bishop intervened. "Gentlemen, it is a terrible event of the last hours that violence has broken out in Constantinople. I can't understand how you know, Diran, but I cannot do anything other than confirm the news of persecutions and deaths."

A chorus of worried voices rose among those present. Some looked at each other in dismay, while others picked up their hats with the intention of leaving the place soon and joining their families. Those left behind at the meeting speculated about taking precautionary measures and travelling to Russia, leaving Turkey via some Black Sea port. The bishop requested them to calm down as Zareh and the rest took their leave, to put their faith in the German Consulate's protection.

"IT SEEMS THE APOCALYPSE has been let loose on our people once again, my dear Mariam."

Mariam read the letter over and over, shedding tears of great sadness. Her crying appeared to be in harmony with the dark stormclouds crossing the Erzurum sky that afternoon, which threatened to enshroud the entire region. Seated in the library, she was unable to stand the warbling soprano on the gramophone any further. With a gesture, she asked the maid to remove the record, which the girl did clumsily, scratching it and producing a distorted, horrifying squawk.

Mariam's disquiet heightened and she continued reading the tragic news from Constantinople.

Dear cousin, I can find no means to soften this terrible news. Vahan, your brother, has been murdered. He was hanged somewhere outside Constantinople by the police, together with hundreds of the best public men. Hide your goods, everything you can. You know... Zareh will know what to do with your savings at the bank. Escape as soon as you can... Understand that I cannot give any more details. May the Lord have mercy on us, dear Mariam, my beloved cousin.

Drenched in tears, Mariam fell heavily into the armchair.

FROM HIS OFFICE at the Ottoman Bank, Zareh, along with Tavel, observed through the glass that partitioned the offices how the employees, having heard the news, whispered with suspicion among themselves. They observed with little concealment the reactions of the managers and Armenian directors. Although they could not be heard, Zareh imagined some of their comments. Not in vain was it said that his financial shrewdness consisted of always being a step ahead of others' reactions.

Sitting down behind his ample desk with leather armchairs, as a director and financial manager, he told himself the time had come to take precautions to protect the family capital and that to delay the move for a day, even hours, could prove fatal and irreversible.

Coming close to Tavel, he confided to him deliberately casually: "Son, listen. I've been thinking. There's no other way out. We must clear out our strongboxes as soon as possible."

"What do you mean, Father? Are you serious?" asked Tavel.

"Very much so. We'll go down to the vault and take out all our deposits. We'll do this after hours, when the employees leave. This very afternoon."

"And what then, Father? Do we drag home the jewels and pounds along the streets?"

Zareh put his back to the glass division so that the group of Turkish employees and orderlies should not see him and realize his disquiet. The clock on the wall showed it was 5 p.m.

"Tavel, I want you to bring the car around to the back of the building. We'll load it all into the trunk, go to the farm, and bury everything somewhere on the property. Then, God knows what'll happen. I have the strong feeling that the bank will be sacked in a few days or even within hours. The London and New York accounts won't be accessible to them if we take away the numbers and records. The Turks will never find them. Quick, Tavel, open that drawer and hand me all the papers in it."

"Father, we are bankers! Do you intend to bury a fortune in the ground and leave it there, just like that?"

"It's the safest place. In an instant the bank could become exposed. This is the time for an immediate solution and nothing else," said Zareh without so much as a hint of doubt.

When they went down to the vault later, no employee remained in the building. They could work in peace in the deserted chamber. They kept silent. Tavel looked at his father, who had a grim expression unknown to him until then. He was sweating profusely and his shirt was becoming soaked below his tail-coat. Precious jewellery, gold coins and thousands of pounds were transferred from the seven strongboxes to two large sacks. The remainder went into the pockets of their suits and overcoats. It was a sizeable fortune in any country of the world.

"Is the car ready?" Zareh asked his son.

"It's at the back exit," said Tavel.

"Stuff these jewels under your overcoat, son. The guards won't realize," Zareh said, shutting the doors of the vault. Looking casual but laden with packages in their overcoats, they crossed the hall of the bank up to the rear door.

It was still twilight as the car drove through the countryside on the outskirts of Erzurum. Tavel was at the steering wheel, feeling very nervous. They reached the hilly road that ran through the first gate of the farm.

"Tavel, take the road futher away from the house. I

don't want the farmhands to know we're here at this time. They'd be suspicious."

"Where are we heading for, Papa?"

"The ruins," answered Zareh.

The black Daimler rolled along the inner earth roads which skirted the wheatfields. Arriving at the slopes of the first hills, they stopped. Father and son got out of the car and began climbing the slope, hauling bags up to the ruins of the fort further up the hillside, around 200 meters away. It was cold and night had already fallen.

Breathing heavily from the effort, Zareh said, "If we need to get away from the house for a while, this will come in handy to buy some transport and get to some port in Russia, or maybe Europe or America... wherever God leads us, where the whole family can live without problems until we are able to come back... safe and sound."

Tavel was a few feet further up the steep incline. He looked at his father behind him, somewhat lagging. Besides his youth, he knew every stone of the pathway, which he had climbed countless times with his brother Krikor and their friends. He felt a twinge of worry about his father making such an effort. "Give me your bag, Papa. Do you really think we'll have to leave Erzurum for good, Father? Our properties, the house, the farm?"

"Thank you, son." Zareh lay a while to get his breath back. "I hardly imagine things will get to such a pitch," he said, "but it might be wise to get away from Anatolia for a while, so it's best to prevent sackings and confiscations. The truth is that, though with distaste, I must acknowledge what Diran often says... the Russians are our protectors and they are nearby. And they may well be our solution... temporarily!"

Zareh's breath became progressively heavier. They carried on climbing, their suits covered with dust, and they were forced to take big strides to balance themselves and get a footing on the rock, until they reached a pathway, even steeper but easier to negotiate with the bags on their backs. From there they were able to see the ruins of the old stronghold in the moonlight.

Tavel asked breathlessly: "What about Germany?"

"Germany won't allow murder. This isn't 1895, nor is the sultan Abdul Hamid II. The Ittihad prides itself on a certain modernity. The savagery of the past can't be repeated. Well, we're here. My heart's about to pop out of my mouth."

"Are you alright, Papa? Have a rest, sit down a bit. What do we do now?"

"I'm fine. Let's not waste time."

Zareh looked around and pointed to a spot. They dragged the sacks. On removing the rocks from an old derelict wall, the shape of a stone arc was revealed. They dug a small vault. The chosen wall retained a lintel showing fragments of carved Armenian characters, archaeological remains from the ancient fort of the knights, the scene of defensive actions against invaders.

"Remember the exact point," said Zareh.

Tavel nodded with concern: though there was no time for arguments, it was impossible not to remember they were interring a great fortune, part of the family wealth, from which would possibly hinge all the luck they might have in the following days. It would be left to the elements and buried underground. Everything had begun to turn crazy.

They came down from the ruins to the road, the descent much easier for Zareh, and they got into the car and sped away from the place.

Driving in silence, reviewing what had just taken place, they realized that they had taken the track closer to the house, which passed by the farmhands' post. In the distance, lights shone in the house.

NOT FAR FROM THE ROAD, Abdul, the old Turkish caretaker, was riding back to the post across the fields. He saw the car lights straight away. They did not call his attention, as he was familiar with the vehicle. But it puzzled him that his boss's car should drive by without stopping and, even more, that Baron Zareh should have driven round the property in the middle of the week without letting him know.

It's odd, mused the Turk.

CHAPTER VIII

THE NEW POLICY

AT THE BACK OF THE ERZURUM HOUSE were the stables. Nothing could be seen from the street and the wooden gates were almost always closed. The old shepherd knocked several times. Finally, a maid opened the small wooden door, which was used for greater practicality. It was unusual to get callers at night time. She opened it a crack and saw the old Armenian shepherd who, without much explanation, handed her a letter addressed to Miss Araksi. His task accomplished, the old man departed wordlessly. Further back, in the garage, a car could be seen which had just arrived from the fields covered in dust from the roads.

AS ZAREH AND TAVEL came into the library, tired and filled with disquiet, they found Mariam in tears. She was still holding the letter. Zareh crossed the room and embraced his wife. Tavel joined his parents. He felt all the frailty of the world descending on his family. He poured himself a liqueur and shut the library doors.

The first to speak was Mariam. "Vahan's been murdered in Constantinople. It's here in the letter... My heart's breaking with grief... dear Vahan... my beloved brother, the pride of our family. I'm frightened of what may happen to us, Zareh! Read it yourself."

Despite the sorrow possessing her, Mariam noticed the look of father and son. She found the untidiness of both very unusual.

"Tavel, your shoes are all dusty and you, Zareh, have your suit all soiled and torn. What's wrong, my husband? I've never seen you looking this way. Where have you come from? Tavel, answer me!"

Zareh took his wife by the shoulders. "Mariam, do be quiet, please," he said. "I'm deeply sorry to hear about Vahan. It hurts me as much as you... Listen carefully now. We've taken out all our deposits from the bank; the gold, jewels, two sackfuls of pounds, everything that was in the vault. Everything's been hidden on the farm, do you understand? Two sackfuls. They're buried just below the lintel of the ruins, where there's a sign in the stone. You must dig there if something happens to us. Nobody else knows about it. Tavel, quick, give me the books with our accounts in the States and Switzerland. Where have you put them? We have to hide every reference to the deposits." The young man handed his father the leatherbound book. "Do you see? These documents are really important: shares, insurance policies, etcetera."

"But have you just left a whole fortune buried in the ground? Are you mad, Zareh?" Mariam reacted in frustration. "And you, Tavel, you're just like your father. Haven't you had the sense to stop him? What'll happen if we have to leave in a rush, with no time to go to the farm? We may never even have the chance to recover the sacks. Someone will find them. Oh, God! You've gone completely crazy. You should have brought everything home."

"No, Mother, Father's done the right thing. It'll be safer there than in any bank vault. The zaptiehs will come looking for gold and jewels if things get worse. Papa's idea is good. If the worst comes to the worst and we have to escape to Russia we'll have a chance later on to come back to the farm, without making anyone suspicious, and dig up all that fortune."

While Zareh ruffled through the papers in all his desk drawers he said, "It'll be convenient to keep a few pounds on hand. You know, son, the police could get difficult. I've set aside a few thousand."

The library doors burst open just then and Araksi ran in to hug her mother.

"Father, Mother!"

"Araksi," they chorused on seeing her run in.

"Mamma..." she wept, frightened, "the zaptiehs are patrolling the streets, and I've had no news from Diran for two days. I'm so worried about him."

Zareh approached the great window and peered out. He immediately ordered them to shut all the blinds in the house. "It's better that Mavush and Levon stay here with

59

the children. Call them. You too, Tavel, for tonight. It's better... I think Krikor will be arriving any moment. He had time off from the barracks this afternoon, didn't he?"

"Normally he should, yes," agreed Tavel, "but maybe he's been confined to barracks. They'll let us know. Listen, Father, I was thinking we might go down to the coast, by car to Ordu, and there get ourselves passage. Better still, buy a vessel and travel by sea to Batum, and then go on to Tiflis or Erevan."

"Let's not get alarmed just yet," counselled Zareh. He was relying on sanity to prevail. He was a cautious man but no alarmist.

THE HOURS WENT BY AND WHEN, not long before daybreak, he was alone and the rest of the family slept, Zareh pensively, holding a glass of liqueur, contemplated the great portrait of his ancestor, a noble medieval knight. He felt a whole chain of ancestors were with him that night of great worry, helping him to make grave decisions — for, deep within, he vividly felt that the flood of time never held up, and that what was today could tomorrow be the complete opposite.

No longer being sure of anything, he felt the weight of his responsibilities to his wife, children, and grandchildren, who had always trustingly relied on him for their security. He was their guide, the protector of them all, but now he felt that events might overwhelm him and the fortitude he always showed became sterile in the face of the authorities' insanity. After years of peace and quiet his people were threatened once again.

On the gramophone a singer could be heard intoning a timeless melody. The library doors squeaked open and Araksi appeared in her dressing gown. In the semi-darkness of the room, her father was barely visible, illuminated only by a candle.

"Papa, are you there?"

"Yes, Araksi."

"I can't sleep either," she said, pouring herself a glass of liqueur and sitting in an armchair.

After a few moments she asked again, troubled, "Will

we have to leave our home, Papa? Will we have to give up everything?"

"I NEVER GET TIRED of this piece of music, my dear. Do you know that your mother and I were at the gala performance at L'Opéra? The audience gave the diva a standing ovation for half an hour, till one's palms hurt, but admiration overcame the pain, Araksi. The theater became a heaven and your mother, radiantly beautiful, was admired by everyone... *le tout-Paris* were at the theater that evening."

Araksi realized her father was taking refuge in his memories, which made her even more apprehensive. In her pocket she had Diran's message. Just a smatter of lines from her fiancé confirmed the danger of the moment.

"Each time I hear this aria it's as though we were in Paris once more," reminisced Zareh. "Once again, every evening, as that time at the opera..." With a paternal gesture he invited his daughter to sit next to him. Araksi huddled in his arms.

"Come, little one... We'll be alright. The German Consul gave us hope. He seems a decent man... born in Riga, you know? He's a Russian German. There have already been irreparable deaths, your poor uncle Vahan... You know, Araksi, it's almost 3000 years that we've been in these lands. Never forget your heritage, girl. Never, ever forget you carry in your veins the blood of the knights that defended the fort against Tamerlane: the Knights of the Banner of the Rose."

Zareh stroked Araksi as though she were a very young child and enfolded her in a great paternal embrace. The young woman looked at him more worriedly than before, perceiving a certain weakness in him. She felt Zareh to be aging, fleeing from the present.

"Go to bed, Araksi. I'll stay up a little longer. Good night, my darling."

"Good night, Papa."

As Araksi left the library the gramophone was still playing the singer's romantic voice. She glanced at her father; immobile, almost in the dark. A sensation of disquiet and uncertainty ran down her whole body.

THE CARRIAGE, ESCORTED BY two mounted Turkish soldiers, pulled up outside the German Consulate. Commander Taksim Bey alighted from the vehicle, showing an air of regal dignity among his subalterns. Max Swirsden-Righe waited for him at the door. The Imperial flag waved outside the building. The members of the legation's guard of German soldiers stood to attention, presenting arms to the military chief of Erzurum vilayet. A bugle sounded a salute. Max and Taksim Bey entered the building.

Taksim Bey was slim, middle-aged, around 40, with a thin moustache and distrustful look. He wore a general's uniform and his tone of voice was controlled, but as the two men talked in French, Max found it difficult to identify the Turk's real intentions from his tone.

"After the Van rebellion and the defeat of our army at Sarikamish we know that Armenian conspiracies will multiply. Be warned, Lieutenant, for a general uprising in Anatolia is possible. Many Armenians flee to Russia and join the Czar's army. That is treason to the fatherland."

Max replied, "Commander, we have found neither bombs nor conspirators in Erzurum, and the Armenian Bishop has explained to me that they feel a sentiment of patriotism and belonging right here in the Ottoman Empire, much more than under the Czar's authority."

The general responded at once, "We have had telegraph lines cut, and there are clear signs of sabotage planned by organized groups."

Taksim looked arrogantly at Max, as though to say, *Why the hell is this newcomer meddling in the country's internal affairs!*

The consul carried on voicing his opinions: "In Russia, Armenians are just a community of economic and religious interests. Obviously the Czar is a natural protector towards them. Sir, I believe these people are reacting in self-defense. However, in my meetings I have purposely informed them of the true war situation so that they will not entertain any pro-Russian hopes. They know the Russians are being defeated in Europe, Sir."

"Look, Swirsden-Righe," said the Turk huffily, "your

explanation is unnecessary. Don't justify them. As regional commander I will not accept the least hint of Armenian disturbances and insurrections. This will in no way be another Van, have you understood?"

"Yes, Sir," replied the other.

The commander cast a quick glance round the room and left the office without ceremony. During the whole time the meeting had lasted, the Turk - lord and master of the region, and on whom depended the entire population's fortunes - had told Max in few words who gave the orders there, and that any initiative in the military matters of that nation was not to be questioned by any German ally. Confused and irritated, Max saluted as his superior departed in his carriage.

THE VILLAGE WAS ONE of many in the region, a humble settlement of Armenian herdsmen on the plain. Flocks of goats could be seen grazing, watched over by old people and children. The animals' bleats accentuated the quietness.

A group of children were playing among the sheep when, over the near horizon, from behind a tall hill, the figures of horsemen appeared. First, their white fur caps. The little shepherds and the old men were paralyzed for an instant, and all turned to look at the figures, armed with knives and short swords, in a formation extending across the horizon. The Kurdish horsemen carried swords they unsheathed from belts crossing their chests. In the rearguard were Turkish officers who, smiling, anticipated what was about to happen.

Everyone ran, shouting in panic. The elders rounded up the children in a vain effort to protect them from the mad rush of the Kurds. The herds of animals dispersed in terror at the galloping horses that pushed into them from all directions.

The band of riders killed the first men they came upon in their swoop. Then they rushed into the houses in the village, sacking them and striking the women, some of whom were dragged by the hair with savage violence.

The hovels were set on fire, smoke covering the village.

The Kurds raped the women, while others captured the children, who were desperately screaming as they were lifted onto the riders' saddles.

In just minutes, the Turkish and Kurdish soldiers were gone, driving away the livestock, leaving destruction and desolation in their wake.

The groans of the dying could be heard everywhere. Those victims; women, children, elders, who had until that morning led a peaceful, modest, simple existence, now lay strewn upon the plain, turned into mutilated corpses.

CHAPTER IX

KRIKOR

THE TURKISH AND ARMENIAN battalions were lined up, awaiting the presence of commander Mahmud Kamil Pasha in the great square of the Erzurum regiment. The sun shone straight down in mid-morning Tartum and the troops had already been in the barracks for two weeks. At the head of the men in his unit, Krikor, a lieutenant engineer, straightened a button on his jacket while in the ranks orders were given to line up. The call to attention resounded throughout the barracks. The squadrons turned their sight to the regimental chief. A rumor was going around that, since the rebellion in the city of Van, certain precautions would be taken. Nothing concrete, everything rather uncertain and contradictory, yet, all the same, a reason for worry among the Armenians.

The second-in-command, a colonel, ordered the troops to stand at ease after the salute and then Mahmud Kamil Pasha placed himself at a certain height, dominating the military line-up. Some distance away, in the middle of the formation, battalions of Armenian soldiers and officers were organized, surrounded by Turkish ones.

Mahmud Kamil Pasha said in a blunt, martial tone, "Soldiers... the way of serving the army and the fatherland will be modified as from now. All units of Armenian men will be deployed in the service of road-building and construction of war routes. Other divisions will replace you. Artillery and engineer officers will continue at the head of their men in this new assignment. The orders will be carried out as of this very instant."

From the corner of his eye, Krikor looked at the other Armenian officers. Four machine gun batteries became visible, pointed straight at his men, among whom alarm made itself felt. In the Turkish lines some soldiers grinned; others looked with hatred at those that, moments earlier, had been their comrades-in-arms.

Everyone knew what was going on, but no one dared

say it openly, not even the commander, who carried on giving orders.

"The battalions will hand in their weapons, and will be provided with new tools suitable for the patriotic task imposed by the High Command. Unit leaders, proceed to disarm the troops," shouted the second-in-command.

Krikor, alarmed yet obedient from his military training, eyed his companions once more. No one reacted. A sense of enormous dismay ran through them. If anything had characterized the army it was recognition of the equal standing of Turks and Armenians; more so as he was a lieutenant of engineers, respected in the unit and possessing an enviable service record. For the first time in his life he felt a mixture of surprise, disappointment, and, above all, humiliation. As he unbuckled his holster and pistol and handed them over to a Turkish superior he thought, *All this time I've been mistaken. How many of my men are going to die?*

Hundreds of Armenian soldiers lowered their rifles off their shoulders and unhitched the straps. Then a slow parade began, watched over by Turkish soldiers and officers, until the pile of weapons, one on top of another, seemed like a mountain.

The columns of Armenians, disarmed and demoted to forced labor, marched on foot towards the plain surrounding Tartum. They were guarded by armed mounted officers. Krikor walked at the head of one division. He thought of all the ideals he had held as a member of his country's army. He thought of his parents' pride the day of his military graduation. He thought about his life being linked to his vocation of serving his country, and would gladly have offered it in the battles being waged against the enemy. He thought of all those that had never trusted the policies of tolerance installed by the Young Turks, and remembered the discussion in his parents' home. How much time had gone by since Diran had upset the whole family with his gloomy prophecies regarding the advisability of joining the forces of General Antranig, champion of the Armenian resistance? Just a few weeks, during his last leave.

He thought of Zareh and Mariam, his parents' happiness, presiding over the lunch table as on any Sunday, and his brothers and sisters, noisy and argumentative. Then he stopped thinking. The heat was stifling and his boots were enormously heavy with each step. Some of his men showed signs of heatstroke.

The sun shone directly above and the column of soldiers cast hardly any shadows. The whole countryside seemed bathed in a strange luminosity. The battalion of disarmed men was advancing towards the railway embankment. The business the Sultan had personally entrusted to Wilhelm II, the German Kaiser, had already found workers for the project. An army of Armenian youths, wielding spades, would be in charge of digging the ditches and laying the rails of the Constantinople-Baghdad railway. Krikor laughed inwardly. All the lunch table discussions struck him as absurd now, facing the embankments and the long line of lads and men appearing before his eyes, exhausted and sweaty from the effort and bearing the threat of lashes from the Turkish watchmen.

IN THE MEANTIME in Erzurum, a group of prominent Armenians, among whom were Zareh and Tavel, were having a meeting with the Valee, Taksim Bey — bankers, businessmen, lawyers, the notables of Erzurum, all of them standing to lose a lot, and therefore with good reason to be worried. The military governor remained seated behind his Commandancy desk, while the men had to remain standing to listen to him. A secretary took notes at a side table.

"The uprisings in Van have alerted military governors and commanders in the whole of Turkey."

Zareh and the others looked fixedly at the Valee so as not to miss a single word. The commander continued reading the communiqué without batting an eyelid: "On orders issued from Constantinople, any insurgency or sabotage by Armenians shall be punished with maximum severity, especially in regions considered war zones." The Turk paused, looking at all of them, then went on, "The goods of Armenian subjects in banks shall be protected and left in custody of the Armenian church."

There was a hubbub amongst those present. Zareh was the first to speak, "Excellency... we have heard that the Armenian battalions are being disarmed and their soldiers transferred to other destinations." Avoiding any show of weakness in front of the Valee, Zareh sought his understanding. "I have a son, Excellency, a lieutenant of engineers, in the Erzurum battalion. His mother and I are very worried."

The Turk emotionlessly raised his sight. Looking straight at Zareh, without changing his flat tone, he answered, "This is a precautionary measure taken in consequence of those Armenians that fight against Turkey, but this need not worry anyone, particularly if your son is a disciplined officer."

Greatly troubled, the Armenians understood it was time to depart from the governor's Commandancy. There was nothing to add to what they had just heard from Taksim Bey. Rather, they departed thinking that their properties and fortunes were in danger. All those present had their valuables deposited at the Ottoman Bank in Erzurum and, save their foreign accounts, had made no provision in the face of a possible confiscation of their values. The Valee's comment was unmistakable: the Turkish government would take over all the deposits.

FROM OUTSIDE, THE MUEZZIN'S call to prayer could be heard. It was nightfall and through his window Max saw the town lights turning on one by one. He lit the gas lamps and carried on studying the possible routes for the campaign on a large map spread across the table. From the gramophone came the voice of the French singer he was so fond of. Interrupting his task and laying aside calculations and plans that forded river courses and traversed mountain passes, his thoughts changed direction. The music made him nostalgic, and a great loneliness came over him. His pen sped across the letterheaded paper.

German Consulate, Erzurum, May 1915

Dear Hildegard,

Never did I imagine, on taking over my functions, the unforeseen responsibilities that, to my mind, are about to present themselves. Turkey is another world. I will explain what I mean. I fear I am about to witness a great internal tragedy in this country. The solitude of wielding authority in these remote regions, so exotic and distant from Munich, from the motherland, from your love... and your friendship, which I so grievously yearn for, lead me to write to you after another day in Erzurum and to share my thoughts. From my office window I see the far-off blueish mountains that do not at all resemble the peaks and forests we used to frequent for outings, you and I, my dearest Hildegard, and which I carry in my soul, but... the satisfaction of fulfilling my military duty... makes me forget all nostalgia and all...

The muezzin's prayer invaded the air once more, sounding like a lament. It seemed as if those prayers from the minarets in the reddish sundown in the city were announcing the great tumult hovering over Erzurum. The deportation of Armenians from cities and villages was already an order proclaimed in every city throughout the Ottoman Empire.

Max wrote on as though nothing else existed. He experienced a kind of release in so doing. And the pages directed to Hildegard multiplied with details and turbulent passages whose contents in European eyes might seem incomprehensible. Max's confidences and descriptions were recorded in that correspondence as an irremediable foretaste of the tragedy about to unfold.

CONFUSION PREVAILED, and on the last evenings in every Armenian home it was difficult to sleep and keep calm. Those that remembered the slaughters of 1895, during Abdul Hamid II's sultanate, were given to relating tales of horrible deaths in streets and homes at the Turks' hands. And, even in the face of this, it was hard for such firmly rooted people to react and flee to Russia or Greece, or simply find a safe place within Turkey. Zareh worriedly and pensively walked up and down his library.

Mariam was unable to conceal her sadness. "Deportation... what are we to understand by that, Zareh? — because I find it offensive and terrifying. As though we weren't entitled to choose where to live. Where will we go, Zareh, where, my husband?"

Zareh remained quiet. He had no answer.

Mariam went on in despair, "What'll happen to the house if we leave it? Our furniture, the memories of our parents and grandparents? We can't just leave everything behind like that! Zareh, answer me please!"

"I don't know, Mariam, I don't know."

Araksi watched her parents. In her head a cloud of sensations was moving, finding no explanation for anything, and the fragility she saw in them was heart-rending. She had never seen either of them broken, even in the saddest and most difficult situations. Actually, nothing threatening had ever happened to the family, to the milieu into which she had been born. Her last 20 years, her whole life, had been of total harmony, love, happiness, and protection.

Mariam said, "It's as though they were wrenching my arm off, Zareh. What will we find when we return if we leave the house? Could we leave somebody in charge? How much will we be able to take with us? Is no one going to put a stop to this madness? Oh my God, you're not answering and I feel I'm going crazy."

"Nothing will happen to us, woman. Deportation is for the villages... the poor people, the ones with no money, Mariam," murmured Zareh.

Mariam looked away, towards the great painting of Christ's Nativity, the work of a renowned Spanish painter, given to them by a grandmother for the birth of their eldest, Tavel. She was seeking answers to senselessness. At that moment Mavush and Vartuhi entered, having heard the news. In silence they held hands.

"Let us all pray together. Only Jesus can help us. There's nothing we can do. We're all in His hands," said

Mariam, comforting the girls. "Call the children, but let's put on a brave face in front of them. They mustn't know... Zareh, you begin. Let everyone come. Mavush and Vartuhi, bring the children."

Once they were all there, a psalm was recited. Zareh led the prayer. "God, Thou hope of the persecuted innocents: I invoke Thee because Thou answerest me. My God, incline Thy ear and hearken to my words. Show me the wonders of Thy mercy. Thou that savest those that take refuge on Thy right, guard me as the children of Thine eyes. In the shadow of Thy wings hide me from the unrighteous that assail me, from the mortal foe that encompasseth me."

HUNDREDS OF SOLDIERS of the disarmed battalion sent to do forced labor were digging the soil and raising mounds. The length of embankment was taking shape.

The mounted officers watched over the troop. The sun's burning rays fell on the men. The groups worked in short shifts. Away from the work site, resting with his crew, was Krikor.

Every so often the Turks would take a group of men — 20, 30 perhaps — away from the main work area and lead them to a place beyond a great hill on the road. The men disappeared and did not return. Krikor was staring curiously at this movement — until he finally understood. The next group was his. He said nothing, half-closed his eyes an instant and came to an immediate decision — it was life or death in a matter of minutes. That was it. Actually, all of them were in line, sooner or later, for the Turks' butchery.

In the time it took for the guard to march up and down the area where the men were resting, he had to decide his fate. Just a few minutes. He decided he would run to the first hill, then there was the plain, without any chance of hiding, and then the forest. *Maybe on the other side, who knows... maybe there'll be a saddled horse somewhere,* he thought.

His instinct for survival was strong and suddenly Krikor was running. Other prisoners got up and, encouraged by his daring, did likewise, all of them running in different directions to increase their chances of escaping. Krikor ran towards the hill. As soon as he got over it, he hardly had time to observe the Turkish soldiers cutting the throats of the last group of Armenians they had taken away. The scene was ghostly, vertigo-like, soundless save the throbbing of his temples and his own breathing.

Krikor did not look back. He ran at full speed, being a strong, athletic young man. Bullets whizzed past him. All at once two mounted officers appeared at full gallop from the opposite hill. They were wielding yataghans which were pointed forward. Krikor suddenly changed direction and the horsemen bet each other who would overtake him first. The young man desperately ran to the next hill. The terrain was utterly bare, without trees.

Soon one of the officers managed to catch up with him. The Turk swung his sword but missed. The horse passed at full tilt next to Krikor, who rolled over and evaded the swing. The second rider was waiting at the opposite line. He took the necessary time and, giving his mount free rein, bore down directly on his quarry. This time Krikor did not run. He stopped. On the plain, the figure of the Turk advancing on him was clearly visible. Krikor knew that he had no chance against his pursuer. The forest was still quite far off. He thought: *You aren't going to catch me. I'm not your prey. I won't retreat.* He then began advancing towards the other, at a brisk run, disarmed as he was and at a total disadvantage, yet offering himself in an attitude of defiance, as if to attack. The Turk covered the distance at a gallop. He found the Armenian's reaction inexplicable. *What is this maniac doing?*

Krikor ran on, panting, as he saw the horse approaching at full speed, pounding the ground with its hooves.

The rider was accurate. As he passed next to Krikor, with a quick, clean swing of the yataghan, he sent the young man's head sailing through the air. The officers brought their mounts to a sudden halt and trotted back to the dead man's body. The killer dismounted and lifted

Krikor's head by the hair, while the other congratulated him, resigned to the bet he had just lost.

CHAPTER X

TERROR IN THE CITY

ARAKSI AND HER FRIEND Armenuhi left the school gates behind. Classes were adjourned at mid-day and the younger children went home for lunch. They walked through a small park and turned in the direction of home. Armenuhi lived in the same quarter as Diran, a well-built neighbourhood of houses surrounded by gardens, much like Araksi's. Therefore after classes the two French teachers walked home together. The bazaar was teeming with salespeople and shopkeepers. Nothing seemed different that day except that a police patrol was present amid all the multi-colored throng. The young women approached with curiosity. Some of the shopkeepers suddenly went silent, on recognizing what side they belonged to. A zaptieh was shouting out the official proclamation, announcing to the Armenian population the news of their deportation. Others pasted posters on the walls giving details of the Valee of Erzurum's orders, to whose authority all were subject in those war days.

By order of the General Command, Armenians are given 15 days to abandon their homes, shops, and other possessions in the city, and are forbidden to take away any merchandise.

The two girls looked at each other in alarm.

"Oh God, Araksi. Did you hear? Then it's true what my father says, that they're killing the Armenians in the army... that they take them to the work sites and there they murder them."

"Armenuhi! Have you gone crazy?" exclaimed Araksi, shaking her by the shoulders. "My brother Krikor's been transferred from barracks and we haven't had news from him for days."

Armenuhi wept as the two ran along the street.

"Oh, I'm sorry, Araksi, forgive me if you hadn't already

heard. The Turks are going to turn us out of our houses and then take over all our things... My God, where can we run? Araksi, my parents won't be able to move at their age. They'd rather die here. I can't abandon them, Araksi... we're lost... Araksi... Araksi, where are you going?"

Araksi hurriedly separated from her friend as they came to the town cathedral. "I must go into the cathedral, Armenuhi... I'll see you tomorrow, maybe. I can't explain now... Be careful, Armenuhi."

"You too, Araksi. God bless you. Pray for us. I'll do the same for you and your family."

They embraced before leaving one another and Araksi ran across the street to the cathedral. As she entered the church, she looked around her, as though wanting to find someone. There were few people there at that time. Deeply disturbed, she directed her gaze towards the great cross above the altar and prayed, kneeling in a dark corner of the temple. A few minutes later a sexton came along and asked her what her name was. A few signs sufficed for them to understand each other.

Araksi followed him obediently. Before entering the sacristy they went in through the little door hidden behind a large cupboard the clerics had used to store tablecloths and habits in the past. The sexton walked ahead in silence, making sure no one caught them there by surprise. Then, in a very small, closed-in space, Araksi noticed a stone cover on the floor. She looked at the sexton, awaiting instructions from him. He made signs that everything was alright, lifted the cover and invited her to accompany him to the cellars.

Together they went down steep stone staircases until they reached a tunnel below the cathedral building. The candle held by the sexton illuminated the stone passageways which were tall enough for them to walk upright but narrow and dank.

"Mind your step, Miss. At the end of the tunnel we'll come to where Diran and his companions meet. The cathedral is a construction of several buildings, one on top of the other, built over centuries. In fact the foundations of the temple are riddled with tunnels from diverse eras," said the sexton. "For centuries it was a refuge for Christians persecuted by invading armies. Since 300 A.D. our ancestors have taken refuge from numerous pursuers."

"I know our history very well," answered Araksi as she observed the ghostly shadows projected by the figures sculpted in the stone of the catafalques, illuminated by candlelight.

"Today the lads of the resistance have to take refuge here. The Bishop himself doesn't know about it. Duck down, mind that piece sticking out," cautioned the sexton. At each step they went by tombs of notable knights and Christian martyrs with Armenian inscriptions worn down by the centuries. At the end of the dark passage, candlelight shone. Araksi started at seeing it go out. The sexton signalled for silence, and then advanced a few steps further. Then his voice could be heard. The echo resounded down the passages: "It's me, Diran... There's no danger. I've brought Miss Araksi."

Araksi saw Diran in the darkness, illuminated by the light of a new candle being lit.

"Araksi?" said Diran, coming towards her. The two embraced emotionally. "My love, I was desperate at not being able to see you. To have shown myself on the streets would've been suicidal."

"The pastor gave me your message, and from then on all I could think of was to come and see you, Diran. The news is alarming and at home all I feel is sadness and fear. I've just heard we're to be evacuated from Erzurum. What's going to happen to you, Diran? What can we do?"

"Listen, Araksi, just listen. We foresaw everything that's going to happen. We know what'll happen. At least I tried to warn your father, your brothers and sister..." Taking her by the shoulders and stroking her dark hair, he looked straight into her eyes. "Tonight I'll be joining the group that'll cross the border. It's the last chance we'll have to get away. There's no other way left. It's either that or death. Come with me now, Araksi. We can still get to Russia before they catch up with us."

"I can't, my love... How could I leave my parents like that, and never see them again, disappear without their knowing anything about me? They'd die of despair. They're already in pieces because Krikor hasn't come home. Imagine — they'd die of sorrow... I can't. I haven't the strength, Diran. Understand it."

Diran became serious, but did not want to alarm her any more than she already was from the dire news about the fate of the Armenian battalions. "Many are going to die, Araksi. The Turks will go out on the streets to kill our people as in 1895. Our world is falling apart around us, and we'll only have this opportunity. If you don't come with me now we may never, ever be together again, my love. I have that feeling."

Araksi, crying, held tight to his shoulders, and shook her head.

"I have no choice, then. I'm a marked man. Araksi, the wounded combatant talked before he died. They tortured him and he gave our names. I'm a dead man if they catch me. Then how could I serve my cause, my free Armenia? I no longer exist in Erzurum... or anywhere else in Turkey."

Araksi wordlessly extracted a little bag from her overcoat, depositing it in Diran's hand. Diran could feel that it contained a few coins, hopefully enough to buy over any will on the risky way that lay ahead to the Russian frontier. They embraced, kissing passionately.

Tearfully, Diran managed to say, "Many times I thought I could never separate from you if I were confronted with this problem. I adore you more than anyone in the world, Araksi, but if I didn't pledge myself to fight for my principles I'd deeply despise myself for the rest of my existence, knowing what my duty was and running away instead. Maybe it'll cost me my life, and then you'll remember me as fighting for a free fatherland and not as defeated by my conscience. I prefer that, a thousand times." Weeping, Diran embraced his fiancée. "Goodbye, my love. Goodbye, Araksi..."

The sexton, who had kept vigilantly at a distance, approached the youths and, urging them to hurry, started off, torch in hand, to the first turn in the passageway.

Araksi looked at Diran one last time in the gloom of the crypt. Standing serious and resolute by the stone tombs of ancient knights, his lively, intelligent eyes shone in the candlelight. *What a contrast!* thought Araksi. In the gloom of that place of death and darkness, Diran's eyes cried to heaven for an existence of hope and love, far from the nightmare that had broken out in the country in the space of a few weeks, destroying all those born Armenian.

She kissed him one last time without a word, then gently let go of his hand and, not wishing to look back, followed the sexton out of that eerie underworld.

Once more they climbed to the central nave. Women and old people were waiting for the service to begin. Araksi looked towards the enormous stained glass window high in the walls: the figures depicted were of Jesus' baptism by John the Baptist in the River Jordan. A deep sadness in her bosom made her cry, and her pleas rose together with the prayers of the faithful present.

The chorus of deep voices, singing chords of the Oriental ritual, contributed to the dramatic atmosphere for those Erzurum Christians who were about to enter a time of great uncertainty, the greatest that would befall the Christian nation in the whole of its history.

RUNNING, CROUCHING against the cathedral walls, Diran moved several feet away from the building. Almost out of breath, he came to a stop at a corner. Further on, a police patrol with truncheons and whips were arresting two men on the street. Diran thought for a few seconds. The night was moonless, and that was an advantage.

With difficulty he climbed up to the projecting beam of a house and saw that on the other side of the low buildings, a block away, his combatant companions' truck was waiting for him, as arranged. They nervously and expectantly looked in all directions. Between his position and theirs was the zaptieh patrol, armed with pistols. Diran heard the harsh laughter of the Turks a short distance away. The night air carried their voices. They were laughing and horseplaying, as yet unaware of the truck's presence, which only he could see from the rooftops. He looked at his watch and saw it was 11:58 p.m. He was sweating buckets. Only two minutes remained to join the others, otherwise they would have to leave without him.

He climbed across the roofs and, letting himself down further along the alley, he ran as fast as he could under cover of darkness. He ran another hundred feet and came face to face with a new patrol of gendarmes, asking for identification and knocking at house doors. Terror reigned and yells for help reached him, begging for mercy.

Diran stopped dead. It was already too late. A gendarme pursued him, pulling out his gun. He ran and ran in the opposite direction. His comrades, still waiting for him with the engine running, were immediately alerted. One of them, up on a roof, kept track of each of the zaptiehs' movements but, looking at his watch, he saw it was past midnight. There was no option: they had to leave without Diran.

The group of young men quickly boarded the truck and, gliding down the alley, soon reached the open countryside.

In the meantime, Diran ran in exhaustion along the alleys back to the city in the opposite direction. The zaptiehs were almost upon him. Without any strength left in him, Diran rolled, tripping on the cobblestones. He felt the sting of a lash across his back and several kicks in his sides.

"Why were you running away, Armenian? Have you got a dirty conscience?" he heard next to his ear.

"Frisk him, make sure he's not armed. I don't want any surprises on the truck," ordered the highest-ranking officer.

While several Turks kept their guns pointed at him, others went over his clothes and discovered the bag of coins Araksi had given him. "Look at this. He doesn't seem to have needed anything, eh? Where were you off to with so much gold? You haven't got very far, you dog, have you..?"

The police dragged all the detainees to the truck. Using his whip, a sergeant yelled, "Say goodbye to this life,

Armenian dogs, you'll see what's good when you get to prison!"

Diran, sweaty and sore, sank his head into his shoulders as he was made to board the truck with another four individuals caught like himself in the roundup.

ARAKSI WAS UNABLE to get to sleep. A few gunshots could be heard resounding in the nearby streets. She thought of Diran and hugged her pillow more tightly. Two nights and almost three days had gone by since their parting. Surely he would be onboard a ship and sailing off to some Russian port. His words still resounded in her ears. Everything had become absurd and she was scared. Even if things were inexplicable to her on account of the amazing speed at which they happened, of one thing she was certain: she could not have stood escaping with him to Russia, causing her parents unimaginable pain. She knew they must all remain together, come what may. God willing, they would meet up again somehow.

The pain of separation and the uncertainty of ever seeing Diran again, her first and only boyfriend, the man she intended marrying, took hold of her once again. Strange buffets of destiny turning their lives about from one moment to the next like a hurricane... frightened of her own premonitions, she recalled having had similar thoughts about her father on their last outing together covering the wheatfields of the estate.

Suddenly, yells and crying startled her. They sounded as though they were near her bedroom. Araksi got out of bed to have a look. She discovered the crying and violent yells were coming from the neighboring house, which was separated from them by a high wall and several trees, at the back where the cattle pens and stables met with those of her own garden.

She knew that in the dark they would not discover her. Between the branches, she observed the police entering the house next door. With lashes and at bayonet point, they threatened the owner, a good friend of her father's. The police kept their rifles levelled at the whole family. The wife and her children begged for mercy but the Turks, impassive to any plea, continued the requisition and took away two fine draught-horses, which whinnied nervously, and the carriage. Further on, others cranked up a car and opened the gates, laughing and shouting. They came out of the stable with jewels in their hands, shouting like gleeful children at the fruits of their hoarding, "Look, look what I have found!"

Araksi felt her father's hand on her shoulder. Then Mariam came in and Tavel after her. In awestruck silence they watched the way in which the police drove away a whole family through the back gates. Araksi embraced her mother in terror. Mariam, breaking into tears, was only able to say, "Where can Krikor be now? I want to see my beloved son. I want to hold him in my arms right now. I want him to come back and all of us to be together. This just can't be true. When will Krikor come back and defend us? I can't stand any more of this! Zareh, you must know where your son is." Tavel and Araksi were holding her.

"Please, dear... don't let them hear us... Where are these barbarians taking them? What vandalism, what criminality! Tomorrow it could be us," babbled Zareh.

"Will someone have reported some misdemeanour against them, perhaps?" put in Tavel.

"No, son... in the whole neighborhood there are none as loyal and law-abiding as them. I know no better people. We all know why: it's because they're Armenians, so any excuse is good enough," Zareh answered. Drawing the curtains, he sat on the edge of the bed in great sorrow. "I'll try and see the German Consul. Maybe he'll listen to us and help us. I found him a reasonable and good man. In the middle of all this madness I can think of no other possibility. The Turks have gone crazy again, Mariam!"

ONCE MORE, MAX found himself facing Zareh and his son Tavel in the Consulate office.

"The purpose is to eliminate us, Consul. I was doubtful at first. I wanted to believe that a policy of massacres as we Armenians suffered in 1895 was impossible, that they were a thing of the past, of cruel governors that could not come back to life in Turkey... but I was mistaken."

Zareh was no longer the solid man Max had met on

arriving in the city. In just a few weeks he seemed more like a defeated father, thought Max, without interrupting.

"We were congratulated for our services to the country. My own son is an army officer, and now they want to evacuate us from the cities. This means death for many. Please, Swirsden-Righe... we need your intercession. Someone in his right senses will listen to the Kaiser's representative. We are unable to believe the German ambassador can agree to this arbitrary persecution, Consul."

Max took a deep breath to hide his powerlessness.

"If we're to be deported let them give us some opportunity of putting our affairs in order. What will happen with our properties, with our homes? What will we take with us? Where will we be resettled? I'm not a young man. My ancestral roots are here, and I have always been faithful and contributed to my country, which is the Ottoman Empire. I studied in France and have seen the world. I have businesses in the States, but nothing seems to matter now. If we have more than they have it's because we've been a hard-working and productive people..."

Swirsden-Righe looked down, feeling hand-tied. Looking at those men, he tried to imagine himself and Hildegard in a similar situation, but it was hard to do.

Zareh went on talking, his voice breaking. "My brother-in-law, a Member of Parliament, was murdered, and as for my son Krikor, confined to barracks in Tartum, I've lost all contact with him. We know nothing about him. His mother's desperate. What will our fate be, Lieutenant Swirsden-Righe?"

Max preferred not to comment. Finally, he chose his answer with care. "Sir, you know I have the highest regard for you and your family. I will do everything possible within my reach to help in this situation, despite my government's preventing me from intervening in the internal affairs of this country... I'll do everything I can for you," he repeated.

Zareh and Tavel looked at each other, somewhat discouraged. Still, they took their leave gratefully. As they got into their car, Max felt a certain impotence. Taking stock of the serious situation, he realized he had few resources on hand with which to protect those people.

CHAPTER XI

PRISON

IN JUST A MATTER of weeks the Armenians of Erzurum and all other cities of the Ottoman Empire were subjected to the same treatment, while dozens of criminals were released from the jails and sent out on the streets. As soon as the cells were opened, the guards lined the men up in the delegation courtyards and handed out clubs and knives. These bands made their way immediately, breathing vengeance, towards the neighborhoods inhabited by Armenians, and terror became the norm.

It was in those days that a Turkish police patrol burst into the Ottoman Bank building. Zareh and Tavel were holding a meeting in the directors' office with some of the staff. Then total shock was everywhere as a loud explosion was heard coming from the door. At first they wondered if a bomb had gone off in the building, but soon realized the noise was produced by sticks and clubs breaking down the doors. The zaptiehs yelled orders obliging the Turkish employees to leave the building while all the Armenians were to stay where they were. Everyone was terrified at hearing this. Zareh and Tavel soon found themselves surrounded by Turkish police who, armed with rifles and truncheons, violently burst into the room. The one in command of the operation yelled insultingly in their faces while he shook his whip, cracking it against the desks.

"All persons of Armenian origin shall accompany us to the police station. You will be interrogated on suspicion of financing the purchase of weapons for the Armenian activists. Move along now. You, Sergeant, get those men out from behind their desks and line them up. I said move!" bellowed the Turk.

THE CHILDREN, worried and alarmed, interrupted the lesson underway in the classroom. The shouts coming from the street below came progressively closer. Araksi stopped writing on the blackboard. Pupils and teachers ran to the windows to see arrested Armenians paraded down the street. A group of 20 men were being forced to advance at bayonet point by the Turkish police, who cracked their whips over the prisoners' heads.

Araksi did not take long to identify Levon among the captives. His hair was messed up and his face bruised. His coat was in tatters as he was pushed from the rear, raising dust as he shuffled along, bumping into the others. All of them seemed to have been dragged away from their desks and shops only moments earlier.

"Levon, my sister's husband," Araksi managed to say to her companions, covering her mouth in incredulity at what she was seeing. Some Armenian mothers broke away from the crowd and ran to the entrance door of the school, seeking shelter. The tiniest children covered their ears or their faces, not understanding why adults in the street were shouting with such hatred. Araksi controlled her own despair and attempted to comfort the children. She was hard put to keep her own terror in check, but as usual managed to take charge of herself in a situation requiring her whole presence of mind.

Next to her, behind the windows, an American couple of volunteer teachers looked on in horror. Araksi overheard their comments.

"I can't believe my eyes," said the husband. "Our ambassador in Constantinople, Mr Morgenthau, has got to be told about this persecution of innocents. This is inadmissible! We've got to inform the press in the States and the world about what's going on!"

"Let's do it right away, before the Turks requisition the cables," replied his wife.

The group of detainees marched away and no one else continued looking. Children and adults emerged from the building as fast as they could. Most of them were Armenian. Araksi ran the whole way back home.

ZAPTIEH PATROLS were arriving at the central police station with hundreds of prisoners. The trucks rolled up crammed full of men, most of them young, of weapon-bearing age, though middle-aged merchants and professionals were also captured in the roundups. The entrance to the building was pure chaos.

There the families of the detainees milled about, jostling to get in and find out the fate of the unfortunates. Some were freed, and made their way out through the multitude, showing signs of having been punched and tortured. They could consider themselves lucky.

Zareh and Tavel were shut up in one of the large cells. Dozens of citizens were crowded together, waiting to be interrogated under torture. Suddenly, amid all that confusion, Zareh saw Diran being led to the isolation sector of the prison. They looked at each other for an instant. Diran's face showed bruises caused by punches. He made a barely perceptible sign to the older man, warning him that the Turks might find a link between them. All three knew Diran would be tortured until he disclosed all the necessary information.

The two groups were separated by whiplashes and shoves. Diran looked with resignation at Zareh, the father of his beloved, and at Tavel, whom he loved as a big brother. His eyes disclosed a lot more than words could have said. The die was cast. Shackled at the ankles, he hobbled away under the lashes of his captors.

Screams of pain could be heard along the passageways. Within those walls, unimaginable horrors of suffering were taking place.

ARAKSI RAN NON-STOP. Breathless and exhausted, she covered the last blocks, the steepest, until she arrived home. As she approached, she feared the worst. On entering, she saw Mavush and her sister-in-law Vartuhi consoling Mariam, who was lying on an armchair and shedding copious tears.

"Mamma, what's the matter? Where's Papa? Isn't he back yet? Mavush, you know what's going on, don't you?"

Araksi hesitated to tell her sister the news, but there was no going back. "I saw them taking Levon away."

Mavush gave a cry of despair. "You've seen him? I knew it, I felt it in my bones right away... How was he? Was he hurt, beaten?"

"No, Mavush, I don't think so," Araksi soothed her. "They were taking him in a big group of captives. He was walking normally," she lied.

Worriedly, she looked all around. The study and the rest of the house seemed enshrouded in a sepulchral silence. "Where are Papa and Tavel, Vartuhi? Is there any news of Krikor?"

Vartuhi shook her head in hopelessness. Mariam kept looking at the windows as though expecting her husband and sons to appear any moment. Vartuhi and Araksi moved a little away to speak in undertones.

"She hasn't stopped crying. She's at the end of her tether, Araksi. The Turks have taken away all the men in the family. We've heard they might be at the police station. We've been told the zaptiehs are cruelly torturing the detainees. Sometimes they release some of them... after a few hours."

Araksi, standing in front of her sister-in-law, remained silent. She was thinking all the time. Yet what could a group of defenseless women do, who had depended on their men all of their lives? Araksi was not about to give up, though.

Knocks were heard on the front door. A chill ran down their spines and they kept quiet on seeing the maid come straight into the study. She went to Mariam.

"Ma'm, there are two gentlemen at the door. They wish to see you. They introduced themselves as friends of the Baron. They say they're family friends, and not to be afraid of them. What shall I do, Madam?"

She handed their visiting cards to Mariam who, looking at them, said, "Show them into the library. I'll be there in a moment."

Two well-dressed Turkish gentlemen stood waiting for her in the library. Mariam knew them. They were actually Zareh's friends, prominent Erzurum citizens and former neighbors with whom her husband and she had shared many a pleasant evening. On seeing them there Mariam had a few frightened moments of doubt, but the elder of them came forward, treating her with friendliness.

"Mariam, your husband and sons have been arrested

and taken to the police commander's office under the serious accusation of financing the Armenian guerrillas."

"But that's not true," Mariam answered. "You know that. He'd be incapable of doing anything like that."

The younger Turk interrupted, easing her dismay as they sat down on the armchairs.

Araksi felt her blood freezing, though she hid it as best she could. It was evident that if the Turks discovered Diran's participation in the resistance, matters would be much more difficult for her father and brothers. Maybe it was already too late.

"We're aware of your family's uprightness and are offering you our solidarity," the Turk assured her.

"We totally disagree with the persecution of Armenian citizens ordered by the Ittihad, Mariam. We'll do everything possible to intercede for Zareh and your sons before the Valee. Maybe we'll obtain some clemency in all this barbarous injustice. We've always considered you to be friends and distinguished neighbors of our city."

"Violence against the innocent is contrary to the Koran, and no good Muslim behaves this way... Count on us, Mariam," the other added, with a sincere, open tone of voice.

Mariam was unable to control her emotions. Moved by her neighbors' gesture, she burst into tears. The two gentlemen stood and, taking their leave from the younger women, deemed it opportune to go. Araksi hugged her mother, pressing her hard. She was hoping to find a point of support and be of use amid such vulnerability. She looked at the portrait of the medieval knight, that glorious ancestor in front of them, and felt a surge of inspiration, as she recalled her last conversations with her father in that very room. Her character would not allow her to give up to adversity without a fight but Mavush and Vartuhi were too weak and passive for her to rely on them in a crisis.

"Mother... let's ask the German Consul for help. Papa and Tavel trust him. Surely he'll be able to help from his privileged position. The Turks won't listen to anyone unless they consider them important; that means only their European allies and nobody else."

Mavush and Vartuhi were in agreement.

CHAPTER XII

KAMIL PASHA

THE CONSUL HUGELY ENJOYED the rides separating Erzurum from Tartum, headquarters of the Turkish regiment. Every time he had to report to Kamil Pasha, the regional commander, he rode across the plain and passed through some small villages of Armenian herdsmen.

Max rode Pasha, the magnificent Arab thoroughbred, accompanied by Tahir who was mounted on Kismet, the dappled horse that snorted its request for free rein while elegantly lifting its tail.

They rode at walking pace, talking enthusiastically, for the German and his Turkish assistant got on very well together. In fact, Tahir was a sort of alter-ego of the consul's — eyes and ears that translated every moment of any situation that cropped up in that complex Eastern world.

The animals snorted testily several times. They had caught the acrid whiff of smoke long before their riders. Presently, a column of smoke made by bonfires became visible. Tahir looked uneasily in every direction. They were approaching an Armenian village. The column of smoke grew as they came nearer and they began to see the unburied bodies of men and women strewn over the terrain. The horses pranced about, sensing the danger. Max, still disbelieving, took in with stupor the countryside dotted with death, as he rode into the desolation of that rural village.

They dismounted and Max went up to the smouldering ruins of a small church. The roof had totally vanished and the walls had collapsed. Among the remains of what had been the main space, he stepped against the carbonized mass of a body. Startled at first, he covered his mouth and nose. The stench was unbearable. He bent down and saw what seemed to be a surplice. Removing the ashes, he came upon a hand sticking out. With the tip of his boot, he cleared away the burnt remains to get a clearer view.

An object stood out from the blackened mass. The priest's hand was still clutching a scorched crucifix.

Overcoming the stench and his reaction, Max took the crucifix, prying open the fingers which still held it, and buried it alongside the body. He came out quickly, perturbed. Looking around him, everything was death and desolation. Tahir was walking among the rubble of the houses.

Gen. Kamil Mehmet Pasha, Commander, 3rd Turkish Army Corps

SO READ THE DOORPLATE of the reception to the great office of the Turkish regional commander.

Kamil Pasha was a man of aplomb. He took his place behind his enormous desk and invited Max to sit down. The general had adopted the diplomatic tone expected of him towards the consul of an allied power, but it was clear he was in no way comfortable about giving a simple lieutenant explanations.

"These are measures of a military nature. The inhabitants of the plains shall be resettled along the Euphrates... away from Anatolia," the general began.

"And the Armenians of the cities — will they be allowed to remain in their homes?"

Kamil Pasha was definite. "No," he answered unwaveringly.

"But a deportation of that size amounts to a massacre... Perhaps not even half of the Armenian population will make it alive across the desert, General," Max noted.

The conversation between the two was unfolding with cold politeness. Behind Kamil Pasha hung the portraits of the junta ministers that ruled Turkey, the so-called Young Turks, the Ittihad, who had raised themselves to power in the wake of the military coup that had deposed the last Sultan, representing the party called Union and Progress. There lined up, among the national flags, were the photographs of Talaat Pasha, the Interior Minister, Enver

Pasha, Minister of War, and Djemal Pasha, Navy Minister.

Kamil Pasha displayed great self-control at Max's brazen questions, answering without batting an eyelid. "They will be resettled in the interior of the country, among the Muslim population. Those that adopt Islam will not be deported. You need not worry, Lieutenant. The Armenians are our affair."

"General, so far only women and children and old people have been deported, and no attempt at sedition is to be expected from the Armenians in the region. From a practical point of view, particularly in times of war, don't you consider it would be inconvenient to deprive whole districts of a hard-working, productive population?"

Kamil Pasha's tone became impatient. "Under my command there are six provinces besides Erzurum. They all respond to my orders: Van, Bitlis, Harput, Dyarbekir, Sivas and Trebizond. The region is a war zone. The Russians have already penetrated my territory in the last months, shortly before you arrived in Erzurum. All the governors come under my authority and report to me so I, better than anyone, know what happens in each vilayet. The Armenians are a dangerous population, saboteurs and insurgents. Do not forget it, Consul." Kamil Pasha's continued drily, "If you have come all this way to report your personal impressions, kindly bear in mind that you are under my civilian and military authority while you are posted in the region. Good day, Lieutenant."

Max rose and stood to attention before his superior, about-faced, and left powerful General Kamil Pasha's office. He imagined he would find an understanding response to his worry amongst his German countrymen and, walking down the regiment passages, headed for the German advisors' section. The building was an old, almost palatial 18th century construction, housing cavalry sections and maneuver yards. Soldiers, officers and vehicles circulated everywhere.

Max had not resigned himself to Kamil Pasha's cold, harsh words regarding the measures that would affect the lives of thousands of human beings. He thought of the Armenians he had met — Zareh, the bishop, and the others... He immediately remembered Araksi, that Oriental beauty such as he had never seen before, who every so often would disquietingly return to his memory.

By then he was almost in the next pavilion, and the German spoken by officers walking down the galleries brought him back to the present, reminding him that he was now at the *'German Military Advisors'* section, as a bronze plaque inscribed in German and Turkish announced. Minutes later, Max was in the presence of Lieutenant-Colonel Felix Guse.

The office was conventional and very spacious. The flags of both empires hung at either side and the familiar portrait of Kaiser Wilhelm II held a place of honor. The German commander wore a Turkish army uniform.

With a tone of superiority, the lieutenant-colonel huffily rebuked Max: "I know you have just had an interview with Kamil Pasha and I'm reminding you that we are not, as German officers, to interfere in the internal affairs of our Turkish ally. You have been most imprudent, Lieutenant."

Max clenched his teeth as he toyed with the helmet in his hand.

"That aspect of the Turks' internal policy was pointed out to you by Ambassador von Wangenheim and General Bronsart von Schellendorf in Constantinople. They were very clear with you on giving you your orders. The Turks are taking revenge on the Armenians for what they did to them at Van. And d'you know what? They deserve every reprisal. The conditions in which the Turkish soldiers that put down the Armenian rebellion were left is terribly serious."

Max looked at his superior. Guse was nervously looking for papers in his desk. He was particularly irked by Kamil Pasha's call a few minutes earlier, informing him about Swirsden-Righe's impertinence.

"Sir," Max answered, "the Armenians defended themselves against arrests and provocations, and now deportations and deaths. I consider it a natural survival reaction to aggression. According to my own investigations and testimonies, they have never had the intention of fighting. We know of only a few isolated cases of sabotage they have produced, but I believe reports are being unduly exaggerated. I believe there's another, higher purpose behind it."

Lieutenant-Colonel Guse clasped his hands on the desk, leaning forward. "All important business related to our government's policies in this region passes through my hands. If I tell you the events in Van were a planned, anticipated revolt by an Armenian movement, it's because that's what it was. Have I made myself clear? What you consider is irrelevant, Swirsden-Righe. What matters for this command are the motives and strategies the Armenians hide... people of low morals and condition... dangerous, I would call them. Just keep to your duties at the consulate, concentrate on your own military mission, and don't get involved in other matters. Take my advice, Swirsden-Righe, you can do well on this campaign, and the results will not go unnoticed by your superiors."

The lieutenant-colonel looked straight at Max. There was nothing further to add. Kamil Pasha and Guse had been quite definite.

THE MUEZZIN WAS calling to prayer. The roofs of the city and its minarets stood out in the sunset, and the domes of Erzurum created an unmistakably Asiatic impression against the landscape.

This time of day put Max into a melancholy, nostalgic mood, yearning for his far-off Germany. Munich. Hildegard. It was not simple to understand this world with European eyes and culture. The ride and the events he had experienced that day had not spared him any tension. On the way back from Tartum, Max and Tahir had to make a lengthy detour to avoid passing through the burnt-out village.

They had just dismounted in the inner courtyard of the consulate, when an assistant came up to the consul, informing him that two Armenian women had been waiting for him for hours. Max, tired from the ride, tried to postpone the meeting, but the assistant insisted, handing him a note that explained the women's quest. Max read it attentively.

"I'll see them. Show them into the private room."

Max had bathed and put on a fresh uniform. He reacted warmly and was inwardly surprised at seeing Araksi and her mother, whom he had not met before.

Mariam got straight to the point: "We've come to see you, relying on your kindness and humanity, Consul. We can't bear this injustice any longer. I beg you to help us. My husband has been arrested, together with my eldest son, and they're being held at the Commandancy. My son-in-law, Levon, was seen by Araksi as he was being driven by blows along the street together with many others..." Mariam stood. "And my son Krikor... I've been told... but it's always obscure, vague... that he's been transferred together with his regiment to work on the railway embankments... Others have told me they kill the Armenian officers..." Mariam was unable to continue and her voice broke, disconsolately, in tears.

Max breathed deeply. He could not confirm or deny any news. "I promise I will speak to Taksim Bey to bring about the release of your husband, madam, whom I regard as a dignified, honorable man, the same as your son Tavel."

Araksi intervened: "And my brother Krikor, a captain of engineers."

Max looked at Araksi, marvelling at her beauty. She, conscious of the effect she had on him, made capital of it.

It was the first chance Max had had of speaking to her. "I remember having seen you attending to the wounded when this consulate requested volunteers. If for no other reason, I would be in debt to you and to your family for your act of abnegation, Miss..."

Araksi lowered her gaze.

"I'd recommend that you all remain together at your family home until all this is cleared up, or you know what will happen regarding the deportations."

The look that passed between Araksi and Max became intense. Araksi felt intimidated by the German. It was an odd feeling, somewhat out of place. Some inevitable attraction, she thought, but she never lost sight of the principal aim of their visit and she had to say what her mother had left out. Never would an Armenian or Turkish girl have said it to a man so directly, to a stranger, outside her family, or an authority such as Max von Swirsden-Righe.

"What will happen to our property in the outlying lands of Erzurum, Sir? What will happen to my parents' house, that previously belonged to my grandparents, and to their grandparents before them? Why have we got to leave when we have always lived on this land? Do they expect us to go away from one day to the next? Where?"

Max was dazzled as he looked at her. The young woman spoke perfect French. Her tone of voice sounded as though he had always heard it in his mind. It was strange. Araksi was the way he had always imagined her. She showed resolve and femininity which, combined with beauty, left an indelible impression on any man able to appreciate them, he thought. A maturity in accord with the behavior she had shown as a nurse dealing with others' pain. Effortless intelligence and natural sensuality, and a plea that did not lose dignity even in extremity.

She carried on looking into his eyes: "If this is the elimination and despoilment of our people, I ask you, Consul, on my parents' and my own behalf, that they might give us a chance to make ourselves ready, because it will mean death for many of us. They won't be able to resist it, especially the old people and children that live under the same care as any of you in Europe and with the same fears of losing everything that's dear to them. The German Government in Constantinople must know that the Turks are destroying the lives of thousands of innocents, and that these people have the same right to live as any other human being in the world."

Max seemed moved when Araksi had finished speaking. Once more he undertook to do the impossible, to intercede with the Turkish authorities. Mariam thanked Max for doing all he could for her family. Meanwhile, Araksi swiftly glanced around, her eye falling on Hildegard's portrait, then caught sight of a photograph in which the consul and his wife were smiling next to their horses somewhere in the Munich woods.

Mother and daughter left the consulate before darkness should catch them in the streets.

Max did not forget that meeting. Araksi's words went round and round in his mind. He flopped down on the sofa, heavily burdened and pensive.

CHAPTER XIII

TAKSIM BEY

A SMALL ORCHESTRA was entertaining the guests. It sounded sensual and discrete, almost like background music. Most of the gentlemen, in elegant European wear or Turkish uniforms, reclined on cushions. The women wore silk dresses and chatted in a side-room off from the great salon which was decorated with Oriental tapestries and canopies. A few of the men were smoking after the banquet.

Among the Valee of Erzurum's guests were the two prominent Turks who had presented themselves to Mariam with an offer of help. As they made themselves comfortable to eat fruit, they conversed with their host, Taksim Bey, and the group of military men around him.

"These massacres should be a thing of the past. The persecutions of Armenians were due to armed conflicts and by soldiers in fair fights. But I cannot agree with the present policy. Kill women, children, and old people, deport them to the desert? Why, Taksim? Since when have we resorted to such methods in Turkey? All this will only bring us great problems," said one of Zareh's friends.

Taksim said nothing.

Another guest joined in. "How many Armenians do you imagine will survive such a relocation? The truth is that such mass practices have never happened in this country. I cannot remember any Sultan having ordered them, not even Abdul Hamid II in 1895," said an elegant city merchant with displeasure.

A prominent elder added, as he chose a date from the dish, "This is a German idea, gentlemen. They are the ones that secretly influence the ministers, that's obvious. It's serious... very serious... I would say it's entirely contrary to the Koran and the behaviour of a good Muslim."

The gentleman that had remained silent next to Taksim Bey never stopped thinning his bushy brows. He blew out a puff of smoke and it seemed as if that gave him strength to express his opinions. Though he was among friends he was cautious in his words.

"They say the Kaiser is being advised by German ideologists. They also say the deported Armenians are 'useful elements' to be relocated along the strip where the Baghdad railway is to be laid."

Music from the orchestra sounded in the salon and cigar smoke floated around those present.

The first guest wished to add a further comment for Taksim Bey, who held the fate of the Armenians of Erzurum in his hands, to hear. "Honestly speaking, Taksim, you know we've never had trouble with the Armenians, as they're trying to make us believe now. Much to the contrary, we have always lived in peace with them in Erzurum, and some of us have very good friends among them. I am frankly alarmed at what may happen to them."

Taksim Bey listened in silence while he calmly smoked. His direct orders precluded any decisions. He was to obey orders and was not keen on going against Commander General Mahmud Kamil Pasha, on whom depended his military district and the whole organization being secretly set up to deal with the Armenian question. He clapped his hands for the large dish to be removed. Then the negro servants began serving coffee. The conversation drifted off to other matters and the subject was not brought up again.

CHAPTER XIV

MENACING SIGNS

THE HOUSE WAS IN DARKNESS. The front door opened slowly and a man's figure projected a shadow onto the marble floor of the lobby. Tottering with exhaustion, he closed the door with difficulty, making a noise that resounded in every room.

On the first floor, Araksi and her sister Mavush, frightened and in their nightgowns, carefully peered over the banister. Vartuhi joined them immediately. They had another look, warily going a few steps further down, until they recognized Zareh, lit by a ray of light from outside.

The three ran down the stairs and embraced their father. They turned on the lights and Mariam, hearing their voices, joined her husband and daughters with tears of happiness. Ashen-faced, his suit dirty and torn in several places, with evident signs of having been ill-treated, one cheekbone still bleeding, Zareh looked for something to hold onto for support. They led him to sit in an armchair.

With a thin, stammering voice as he spoke, Zareh pressed his wife's hand. "Mariam... my loved ones... I thought I'd never see you again. Tavel and Levon remain at the Commander's office... The Turks execute the majority straightaway. Others are tortured in the most dreadful way by these savage demons. I can't tell you all the horrors I saw there..."

Zareh sobbed as he spoke. Horrified, Araksi and Mavush looked at their father. Zareh continued, "They've got Diran, girl."

"What are you saying, Father? Are you sure? At the Erzurum prison? Then he never managed to escape to the frontier," Araksi was desperate and felt a rush of blood through her body.

"He was chained, darling. Araksi, you must be strong now... He may already be dead... We were only able to see each other from a distance... They had him in the cells where they take anyone that has murdered Turks... or are known to be combatants and saboteurs."

Araksi wept, and so did Vartuhi and Mavush.

"Oh my God," blurted out Mariam. "Poor Diran. May God and the Virgin protect him."

"Did you know anything about his plans, Araksi? The family will have been marked thanks to him," protested Mavush.

"Don't say that, Mavush. We're all condemned by hatred," chided Vartuhi, "What harm has Tavel done: being an honest businessman, a good family man, and a loving husband? Is that his crime, Father? The children and I need him." Vartuhi walked round and round in circles, desperate.

"Lie back, Zareh. Try not to worry. Ah, they've beaten you. My God. Girls, help me move your father," commanded Mariam, taking her husband by the arms, and trying to heave him into a more comfortable position.

Zareh said tearfully, "Listen, all of you: they're going to deport us. It's inevitable. Someone, I don't know who, interceded for me this evening. They said, 'Go home, Granddad. Thank your friends and commander Taksim Bey, but your son and son-in-law are staying here.'"

"It must've been the German consul," said Araksi.

"No," corrected Mariam. "It was our Turkish neighbors, Zareh. They did it. But where is Krikor? No one answers when we ask about our son. They should have some consideration and inform officers' families where their sons have been transferred to," she grieved disconsolately.

"I don't know, Mariam. We're in God's hands now," he sighed. All at once he broke down, babbling. "They must know something... something more. I wasn't able, I wasn't able... to resist." Zareh hid his face in his hands, pressing it in despair and impotence.

"They took us to the torture chamber... I asked them to take me in place of Tavel. I begged them not to harm him and the zaptiehs agreed. Beside me was a lad... he had a horseshoe nailed onto his foot... Yes, a horseshoe, as I'm telling you, soulless beasts, undeserving of Jesus' forgiveness. They nailed horseshoes on his feet so that he would talk. I've never heard such blood-curdling screams. I was next in line... I couldn't, I couldn't have stood it... I immediately confessed where we'd buried our jewels. That was their condition to let me go. The zaptiehs knew about the vault. All the safes at the bank had already been cleared out, and they immediately suspected."

Horrified at his narration, Mavush said, "But you saved your life, and maybe Tavel's and Levon's, Papa."

Zareh rubbed his temples. "I don't know how we'll pay for our trip. Don't you understand, Mavush? We're lost. The Turks only save those that mean more gold and pounds to them."

"We've still got something. You put away some gold coins, Zareh. They were here in the safe."

"No, Mariam, I had them on me when we were arrested. The zaptiehs kept everything."

Araksi felt at that moment that it was up to her to take the initiative. "Papa, tell me exactly where you hid the jewels on the farm, and I'll go and fetch them."

"It's no use, Araksi. The police will be there first thing in the morning to dig them up, or they may even be on the way there now. It isn't a job for a girl. We haven't got a hope. If only Krikor would come..."

"I'll leave right now. I can find anything there, day or night. There's no place in the world I know better. Please, Papa! Tell me where you buried them and I'll be back by dawn. Please! You've always said there's never been a better rider in the family than me. Please, Father, it's our last chance!"

"Let her, Zareh," Mariam ventured, hopelessly.

WITHOUT LOSS OF TIME, Araksi and the other young women ran to the backyard. Araksi opened the gate of the stable. Her feisty chestnut snorted nervously. Araksi patted him hopefully and, placing a bridle on him, led him out of the box.

The noise woke Nubar. Half asleep, the old Armenian odd-job-man asked no questions. Araksi ordered: "Nubar, bring me riding clothes, quickly — the ones you use.

Quick, Nubar!"

Mavush and Vartuhi looked on worriedly.

Vartuhi asked fearfully, "Araksi, what are you planning? You're crazy."

"Are you going to mount that horse in the middle of the night and ride out of Erzurum with all the police roaming around? Please, Araksi, don't go... Don't," Mavush pleaded in vain.

Araksi took the horse to the saddlery. She looked at the sky. The moon seemed to be clouded over. She was almost as frightened as the other two, but had no doubt as to what she must do.

"If I leave now no one'll see me. In an hour's time I'll be on the farm and I'll look for the jewels. I'll be back sooner than the zaptiehs even start out. They'll surely put it off until daybreak," said Araksi as she waited for Nubar to come back from his room. Staggering along, Nubar, around 60 years of age, brought back the apparel normally worn by men for rural work. Araksi took the garments and ran into the house.

"Vartuhi, come and help me. It's no time for crying."

Nubar finished saddling the spirited horse. He asked no questions.

Araksi reappeared, dressed like a Turkish horseman. A turban round her head hid her hair and she wore wide, loose riding jodhpurs. She was unrecognizable. She perfectly resembled a man.

Mavush and Vartuhi looked at her speechlessly. Worry turned into admiration at her courage.

As Araksi placed her foot in the stirrup, Mavush said, "It's total madness, Araksi."

"You're right, Mavush. Everything's total madness but now the men in the family aren't here and our lives depend on us." Araksi led her horse to the gate and Nubar, looking in every direction, signalled for her to go out. As she passed him, urging the spirited beast on, a tear ran down the old retainer's cheek.

MINUTES LATER, ARAKSI WAS RACING away from the houses. Crossing fields at a brisk pace and dressed like a Turkish rider, she arrived at the estate. She made her way through the wheatfields, always crouching over her mount. Further on, coming out of the fields, she headed towards the hillside.

She climbed a narrow pathway. The silhouette of the ruins could be seen higher up, at the end of the track. The horse was hard put to find a foothold among the loose shale. As they climbed among the rocks, Araksi urged the animal on, asking it for more effort. It responded untiringly, doing honor to its noble blood.

Getting a precarious foothold and on the point of tumbling down the slope at each instant, they continued the ascent. Araksi, huddled over the saddle, held on to the horse's mane. Finally, tense and overwrought by the effort, rider and horse reached the platform.

Covered in nervous perspiration, the young woman jumped down off the horse. The night was mild and the moon appeared, glowing brightly. Araksi told herself, *Keep calm. Control yourself. What did Papa say? Yes, lintels. Below them, the inscriptions.*

She began inspecting the tumbled-down walls, going one way and then the other. The moonlight helped her. Believing she had hit on the right spot, she began removing stones, digging and digging with her hands.

Bandolier-like, she carried across her chest a bag, which she soon deposited on the rocks. She also had an iron bar. She went back and forth among the ruins, then sat down to get her breath back. She was exhausted. Her eyes searched for the reference among the stones, and she struggled not to despair. A moonbeam illuminated a sector of the shadowy terrace at the edge of which there was a sheer drop of several feet. It was then that Araksi saw the stone arc of the millenary fortress. Above the lintel she was able to make out part of the sculpted rosette. She jumped up. She got close to look at the ancient carving and the inscriptions became evident. *That's them,* she told herself.

She cleared away and dug with her hands. Then she helped herself with the bar. As she pawed away the soil, the stones appeared that her father and Tavel had placed below to hide the sacks. She could hardly carry on for excitement, and from the soreness of her hands. Soon she had struck the metal of one of the boxes. She wept but, without stopping, hurried on, using the iron bar. All at once the silence of the mountain was broken by a sound at her back, as though someone had dislodged stones with a false step. The chestnut neighed an alert and Araksi turned in fright. The body of a large man was approaching her threateningly. Immediately, she recognized the old Turkish caretaker, Abdul, who had appeared from behind the ruins and was advancing towards her.

Abdul silently looked at her with malice. He laid his shotgun on the rocks and smirked with satisfaction, realizing his hunch had been right: the three boxes Araksi had just unearthed glittered with jewels and coins. Araksi instinctively moved back, seeking the protection of an outcrop.

The Turk lunged at her, trying to tear her clothing and undress her. Both rolled on the ground. Araksi resisted with all her might. In her desperation, she kicked one of the boxes to the edge of the flat ground. The metal burst open and the jewels were scattered, falling down the precipice. The Turk, a prey to his own greed, on seeing his booty disappearing, loosened his grip, giving Araksi a chance to breathe. He yelled with violent lust as he kept hold of her, dragging both of them to the edge of the terrace while trying to prevent the fall of the second box.

Araksi, almost out of breath, wrestled with Abdul, pushing part of his body to the edge of the precipice. Finally, the Turk, wearied by such extreme effort, lost his balance. Araksi still had one of her arms free. With a burst of effort beyond her strength, she managed to reach the iron bar. Holding it firmly with her left hand and allowing herself to be embraced by her aggressor, she dealt the man a brutal blow to the head. Abdul fell backwards into the chasm. A cry was heard, and then a little avalanche of stones accompanied the falling body.

Araksi stood up, trembling with fear. Looking down, she saw Abdul the caretaker's body stretched out below at the base of the hollow. One of the boxes had been lost along with the whole of its contents. She managed to take hold of herself, reminding herself that she had to think clearly. She began filling the sack, scooping out everything she could. The jewels and gold were very heavy. She worked non-stop.

The first blueness of dawn appeared behind the mountains. From the hilltop she had a view of the whole countryside. Below, on the plain, an army truck, surely full of zaptiehs, slowly advanced through the main gate of the estate. Araksi saw from her privileged position how the truck drew up at the foot of the rocks. A group of several gendarmes got down from the vehicle. The Turks discussed which path to take to reach the platform. Finally, with difficulty, they began climbing towards the ruins.

Araksi looked back and thought for an instant. She only had a few minutes left. She must go down the other side, unseen by the police. She walked to the edge of the cliff and threw the shotgun down into it. She grabbed the bag of jewels and gold and, placing it across her breast, again looked down into the cleft, trying to vanquish her panic. She realized there was only a rocky hillside to go down by. The slope, practically impossible for any horse to negotiate, was at a 45° angle, more appropriate for a mountain goat than her Akyuz. She recalled that as a child, neither she nor Krikor had ventured to ride down that way, where the probability of breaking one's neck was almost certain. Now there was no choice: it was either that or fall into the hands of the police, which could only mean a horrible death after being raped.

She secured the sack round her neck and hid the two boxes in a small opening in one of the projections of the platform. She knew that within minutes the caretaker's body would be discovered and perhaps the metal box with the pounds strewn around amongst the stones, but there was no more time to think. A fortune lay buried there, maybe in safety, or at the mercy of anyone.

THE ZAPTIEHS WERE STEADILY climbing the hill. Araksi mounted her horse and, digging her heels into his ribs, advanced to the edge of the opposite slope. The horse shied away, becoming restless. Araksi tried again, cropping him severely. The horse finally sprang towards the decline. It galloped downhill, on the point of rolling over in its mad race. Araksi, leaning back, bounced once again against the saddle, holding onto the reins and the mane, trusting that the beast would find its own sure footing. The descent lasted an eternity. She prayed that the horse would not break a leg in the fierce career. But heaven was on her side that morning and, holding fast to the saddle, she managed to reach the plain without losing control for a moment and without the slightest injury to the animal.

Frothy with sweat, Akyuz opened his eyes madly. Snorting for air with his blood-swollen nostrils, he lifted his legs with spirit, sure of himself once more now they had left the hill behind.

Araksi breathed deeply once again and looked back. The toboggan of rocks and stones had been overcome. She bent down without dismounting, to make sure her horse had suffered no injury, and patted him thankfully as she hugged his neck, at the limit of her nerves.

Knowing the chestnut's resilience, without loss of time she sped among the high wheatfields. She wept with emotion and fear. The tall plants covered her movement from the sight of anyone that might try to follow her along the paths that only she knew.

Araksi did not slow down once out of the property and on the open plain. The chestnut snorted, shaking his mane and obeying the rider. His resistance was exceptional. At a full gallop, they crossed the countryside. Dawn was breaking on Erzurum.

IN THE HEIGHTS bordering the great plain, the detachment of German soldiers had finished breakfast in the bivouac the Turks had set up for war maneuvers. They were patiently preparing the tackle, forming groups in front of the tents. The climbing exercises and practices for attacking enemy trenches had only just begun the day before. Joint operations by Turkish and German officers always demanded lengthy preparations in order to assure reciprocal understanding. It was the contingent's practice to camp out in the mountains, outside town, aiming to ready the expedition to the Caucasus.

Max von Swirsden-Righe emerged from his tent, feeling a little numb from the night-dew. The first rays of the sun filtered between the peaks of the neighbouring mountains. As he conversed with the sergeants, the consul turned his attention to the column of dust rising below, in the distance, travelling through the valley; a sort of minute, solitary whirlwind racing along. A horse full out. *Outstanding,* thought Max. Whoever the rider was, he was a real master, on an extremely fast horse. He had a look through his field-glasses and could hardly distinguish the figure. At that moment a gust of wind loosened the turban and released a cascade of hair. Max looked again with care. The jet-black hair floated in the wind... He was not sure... No, it could hardly be... but there was something familiar about that figure that seemed to be flying on its mount. He became convinced that it was a woman, an amazing Amazon anyway.

The Turkish lieutenant next to him commented in French, "It's surely some kaimakam's thoroughbred being trained for the races by its rider."

Max assented without comment.

ARAKSI RODE into the city. The horse moved at a walking pace. She was on the alert so as not to bump into any soldiers along the entrance road to the town. A few carts and several herdsmen driving their flocks crossed her path from time to time. The muezzin was calling to morning prayer from the minaret.

The chestnut was bathed in sweat. Araksi decided to dismount. She would be less identifiable on foot, mixed in among the townsfolk, than riding such a fine horse. She chose a solitary group of cottages in the suburbs and led the chestnut behind a shed, where no one was likely to appear at such an early hour. She quickly removed saddle and bridle and threw them among a pile of hides where they would draw no special attention.

The horse did not leave her side. Araksi stroked him

fondly for the last time and then waved her arms, shooing him away to a nearby field. Akyuz trotted a few feet away and remained grazing there.

Araksi continued her homeward journey on foot, in the guise of a Turkish laborer, mixed in among the people that walked along the streets. The sack with the pounds and jewels hung at her back. Thick tears rolled down her cheeks.

CHAPTER XV

HAMMAM – THE TURKISH BATH

STEAM WREATHED the room, giving the whole place a misty effect. Moisture rose from the hot water pools, covering the marble path to the bath-house, the main space of the building, like a gauze. As usual, prominent men were there, recumbent and half naked, being given massages or getting in and out of the heated bathing-pool. The hammam was an unusual luxury, used almost as a private club by the city's top functionaries.

Kamil Pasha, supreme commander of the 3rd Army, was talking in subdued tones with other high-ranking officers. Being of a well-built physique, he sweated profusely while he seemed to be issuing orders until, limbs akimbo, he stretched out, covered only by a small towel, allowing a negro slave to lather his back. The other officers, military governors of surrounding regions, and municipalities known as vilayets in Turkey, stopped their activities so as to listen to the general's orders. Kamil Pasha recited by heart and in a monotone the entire plan for the extermination of the Armenians that the Sublime Porte in Constantinople had commanded the main authorities in Turkey to apply without delay.

"Any Muslim that should feed an Armenian shall be hanged outside his house. For disobeying, his dwelling shall also be burnt," he proclaimed as he submissively offered his back to the pleasurable rinsing. Kamil continued reciting articles: "In the case of an army officer, he shall be degraded and court-martialled. If the individuals infringing these orders are sergeants or corporals, they will lose their status as such, and shall also face a court-martial. The Islamic precept of not committing forbidden acts, even under intimidation or duress, shall be borne in mind. Is that understood, gentlemen?" Kamil Pasha looked fiercely around. "These rules are to come into force as from this very day in Erzurum and the other six districts of the military region.

It is necessary to magnify the gravity and diffusion of any act committed by Armenians, as well as any report of sabotage or insurgency or violent reaction carried out by those subjects. Is that understood?"

Taksim Bey, the Valee of Erzurum, wrapped in towels, turned his head, the same as his colleagues, when a colonel dared comment on the given orders.

"Sir, Armenian women and children are innocent of any sabotage or insurgency. Besides, I think they are absolutely necessary to carry out productive work and provide food for our troops. We will have problems before long if they are no longer around to carry out these tasks."

Tensing his facial muscles, Kamil Pasha was not long in answering. "Colonel Nusuhi, what I have just stated are strict orders from Constantinople, without exception. Alright? Everyone will in his commander's office comply and make others comply with the plan of the Special Organization of the East, as it has come to be called. Of course, with the greatest reserve."

The officers looked at each other in silence, only to be disturbed by the sound of voices - deep, dramatic tones which reverberated in the dark, feeding the thoughts and worries of the officers' imaginations. The voices, filled with pathos, descended like light-rays from the skylights above, suspended in the mist of the pools.

With slow, relaxed movements, and making no comment, the military chiefs continued with the ancient ritual of the Turkish bath.

ONCE AGAIN, MAX VON SWIRSDEN-RIGHE was face-to-face with the military governor of Erzurum, Taksim Pasha, in the spacious office of the Turkish commandancy. He carried the telegram from Constantinople, received that very morning at the consulate. Max proceeded to read it with no further ado, skipping headings and formalities: "In view of such heinous deeds of blood, the prestige of Turkey has fallen considerably among her allies and neutral countries."

Taksim looked at Max with unmitigated hatred. The

Turk slipped his hand to his holster and slowly took out his pistol, leaving it so, always hidden below the desk, ready to fire if needed or if he were unable to control his rage. Max read on, unaware of the threat.

"We must energetically exhort, even allowing for the present war situation we are going through, that massacres and murders of an innocent civilian population be prevented. Signed, von Wangenheim, Ambassador."

Max looked up and met the commander's hard gaze.

"The telegram was sent to me this morning, Taksim Pasha."

"Yes, yes, these deeds are shameful," said the general, by way of a standard response.

"It is the local authorities' responsibility to prevent them with all possible means at their disposal. Surely you will not want to carry in the future such a tremendous responsibility on your shoulders?" Max pressured.

"I will do what I can to prevent such happenings," replied the commander, all the while keeping his hand on the gun and repressing his choleric nature, exacerbated by Max's insistence.

"Sir, it depends on what you consider possible to prevent them. Russians and Armenians will without doubt respond to violence with terrible acts of vengeance. Your own capacity for leadership, Taksim Pasha, will be judged by your superiors in the Turkish government before future peace negotiations, when these deeds are revised by the international community. Turkey will find itself in difficulties and will make foreign powers aware of the Armenian massacres... For myself, Sir, I warn you I will inform the Army High Command as soon as possible of any knowledge I come by..."

An uncomfortable silence ensued between them. The governor-commander was unable to control himself and, turning his apparent calm into an unequivocal grimace of displeasure, stood up, banging his chair. Max, expecting the worst, casually unfastened his holster, releasing the safety catch of his gun under the table.

Taksim now held his pistol in his right hand as he leant on his desk, the gun hidden behind some folders. With fierceness that sounded like a threat, he spat back: "Are you trying to save your own responsibility, Consul? Is that why you are acting this way? If you do not modify your posture *vis-à-vis* the Armenians, I will not be able to guarantee your personal security here."

"I have not asked you to guarantee my security, Commander, but there are certain Armenians I should like to put in a request for." So saying, Max handed over a list that included Zareh, Tavel and Krikor, as well as Levon, Mavush's husband, and finally Diran.

The Turk looked at the list with displeasure. "I have already ordered the release of several of these Armenians. Various Turkish citizens also interceded for them, but there are traitors there among them who will never get out alive."

The tension between them eased up. Taksim Pasha exhibited a certain magnanimity, perhaps reflecting on his own fortunes if Turkey's plans did not turn out satisfactorily at the end of the war. He thought for a few instants. "Alright... I will have a hundred gendarmes accompany the second contingent of deported Armenians... those travelling with women and children. Families without male support will be accompanied by certain men I shall release from the forced labor groups. Finally, I will have all values deposited in Armenian banks transferred to the Armenian Church, for their safekeeping. Are you satisfied now? Don't ask for any more, Consul. You know that more... is impossible."

Max knew he would obtain nothing further than that, and assented. Meanwhile, he casually pushed the safety catch back on his gun and eased it back into his holster.

CHAPTER XVI

GENERAL DEPORTATION DECREE

THE STREETS OF ERZURUM had been crowded with carts since the night before. They formed a long caravan with their pairs of oxen, carters in the drivers' seats, and ready to move off, lined up outside the houses of the fanciest neighbourhood. The whole of the city's Armenian population were being obliged to abandon their homes and be led through the deserts of Turkey to Deir-ez-Zor in the north of Syria. Travelling across rugged mountains and rough roads, and threatened by hostile populations, even imagining the route made it frightening. People from the smaller towns and villages, feeble old people, women and children, fearful and disconcerted by the sentence of eviction they had been condemned to in a matter of weeks, now faced the beginning of the general deportation.

Whole neighborhoods of Armenians, thousands of human beings, awaited orders to move. While some of the Turkish drivers chatted beside their carts, families loaded enormous packages containing the objects they wished to save, and continued to do so up to the very last moment.

Amid the dramatic scenes that arose, policemen, zaptiehs and mounted officers kept watch over the convoy, minding that orders were carried out. Mules, donkeys and oxen were made available to the children, old people and women, though only among those rich families able to pay the fare. The clothing of the better-off was generally also humble, playing down any show of possible wealth.

The remainder; that is, the vast majority, would journey on foot, carrying whatever they could in backpacks. The worst conditions awaited them during the march: miles through the mountains and then the desert. That was the uncertain prospect the Armenians would have to face until they arrived in their new home in one of the grimmest corners of the Ottoman Empire. The elders, torn with grief, wept disconsolately at the scene.

ZAREH GATHERED HIS CHILDREN TOGETHER. They all went into the house for the last time. They visited each of the rooms. No one spoke but they were heartbroken. They had spent the last weeks picking out the best things and selling the rest, although practically all the furniture would remain behind in the great house. They thought that perhaps, on their return, they might find it all in the same place. They held on to the hope that this terrible uprooting would pass, and that they would soon return to their ancestral home, Krikor among them.

Mavush, Araksi and Vartuhi quickly put on makeup in front of the great mirror in the library, making themselves ugly to disguise their attractiveness and youth. The time had come.

Zareh and Mariam gathered them all and, before the picture of the Sacred Heart of Jesus, they joined hands and prayed. Then they all burst into tears, and wished to have a last look around the house before boarding the cart. Araksi went to her room and, broken-hearted, went up and down the stairs as she had always done. Every happy and important scene she had experienced under that roof flashed through her mind in an instant. She would record them in her soul for the rest of her life.

One of the children, Mavush's son, locked the door and hid the key under the stone pathway. In his innocence, he said, "So that Papa and Uncle Krikor will come and be able to get in, and take care of it till we come back." They all wept bitterly but tried to hide their tears from the little ones.

In the street, Araksi viewed the three carts hired by her family. The caravan stretched to the end of the block. All the women were wearing long garments like her own, her mother's and sister's, their bodies fully covered despite the summer heat.

The convoy was composed of a group of 300 wealthy, prominent Erzurum families. They were leaving behind their great stone houses and the neighborhood that had seen the birth of each generation.

Finally, they got underway. The mounted police rode ahead and at the sides. Policemen on foot, armed with rifles, guarded the column that slowly advanced along the streets.

On the pavements and rooftops, the Turkish population of Erzurum crowded to watch the Armenians going by. Many shouted and insulted them, calling them Christian traitors to the empire and blaming them for war defeats. But it was not all of them who did this. A great multitude looked on in silence, struck by the forced exodus of those families suffering vilification by the Young Turk government.

Frowning, worried Moslems voiced criticisms under their breath, in total disagreement with the brutal deportation of Armenian citizens they had lived alongside for centuries in peace and prosperity and who now, wrenched from their homes from one week to the next, were marching towards the unknown and in the worst conditions any citizen of the Ottoman Empire had ever been subjected to.

Araksi, sitting on the seat next to the Turkish driver, looked all about her. She felt the target of hundreds of onlookers' gazes and a horrible humiliation, wishing it would turn out be a ghastly nightmare soon to be over.

MAX VON SWIRSDEN-RIGHE, leaning on the window sill of his office, first heard far-off shouts. As dozens of carts came nearer along the streets, their squeaking wheels and the voices of carters guiding their oxen grew louder. To this was added the clacks of saucepans and crocks banging against each other, till it became a noisy, dramatic symphony of the human condition on the way to degradation.

Max was unable to draw away from the window for a single instant. The tragedy of a people paraded along the street below. Nor was he able to make out the passage of the three carts in which Zareh, Mariam and what was left of that family were travelling, but he could not stop thinking of them.

As the long convoy of carts finally left the city, Max was heavy of heart, feeling great loneliness. The tragedy of that people was not like seeing soldiers dying in trenches.

This rather produced a strange, aching impotence. He sat down at his desk and began writing immediately. He imagined Hildegard reading his letter in the pathways of the park near Munich. He envisioned the trees of those woods he was so fond of, which evoked in the depths of his soul the homesickness of his Germanic spirit, sensing too that from those lines, Hildegard would realize they were confidences, as though they were conversing with each other.

In this way, for a few hours he managed to conjure up the weeping, prayers, and shouts of the deportees, whose echoes still rose from the street through the consulate windows. Well into the evening, by gaslight, Max carried on reporting to his wife the events in Anatolia, to the accompaniment of *Parsifal* playing on the gramophone.

Erzurum, German Consulate, May 1915

My dearest Hildegard,
It seems that, as Germans, we have no right to defend the innocent Armenians that are being deported, who lack all protection. So far I have only been able to speak out for the defense of their properties, protest about the deaths, and request that the expulsion from the war-zone they are suffering should be as humane as possible.

The governor, here known as the 'Valee', agrees with me, but insists he has no power to modify the orders he is given by the supreme command.

Incidentally, I have asked the general commander for his authorization to request the transfer from Straubing to Erzurum of our good friends Friedrich and Rolf Hüchtinger. Have you heard from them? If so, mention my letter to them. I would like them to join the Caucasus campaign I am preparing, which is my great project. They will bring me news from you and our beloved fatherland...

HILDEGARD, IN MUNICH, sitting on a bench in the shade of some trees, once and again went over the neat, compressed handwriting on the pages, and was able to sense that Max was there with her, at least in spirit.

117

CHAPTER XVII

THE CARAVAN OF DEPORTEES

WEEKS HAD GONE BY since they had left the city and crossed immense wildernesses. No one knew for sure where they were heading. The women in the family — Mariam, Mavush, Araksi, and Vartuhi — were travelling on the two carts, together with Zareh. In the third, loaded to capacity, went all their clothes, overcoats, kitchenware, beds, quilts, and the few things they had been able to include when choosing what to take with them and what to leave behind.

The children rode on the donkeys, amusing themselves and mindless of the journey, often unaware of the comings and goings of the Turkish gendarmes riding to and fro on horseback, keeping an eye on the people.

Sometimes the noise of the carts mixed up with the wind was so intense that it was impossible to hear the others' voices and shouts, even of those travelling in the next vehicle. The women's appearance had become unrecognizable by then. The dust and dryness of those regions formed crusts on their faces. Araksi's lips were beginning to blister from the intense sunlight. But it was the lack of water and the crowded conditions of the night encampments that were gradually undermining the strength of old people, women, and children, testing them severely while subjecting them to brutal rigors.

Behind those beggar-like countenances and discolored clothes travelled families accustomed to the best of everything, comparable to any polite, well-off family in Europe or the United States.

That was the transport assigned to Zareh and his family. Mostly, they travelled in silence, in a sort of dozing weakness. No one mentioned the worst forecasts in front of the children, but they realized the likelihood that all males of an age to offer resistance to the regime had been eliminated was almost a certainty by now.

Finally, they caught sight of the stream of a river.

Araksi, seated beside her father, was staring fixedly at the edge of the water. The reflection of the sun made her blink and she was suddenly startled. She was not sure but, as they came nearer to the edge, she thought she could make out the naked, dead body of an Armenian woman next to her little child, who was also dead. Araksi was dumbstruck and neither did her father, nor the Turkish driver, nor anyone else, say a word, but Mavush and Vartuhi covered the children's eyes and drew their attention away until the corpses had been left behind.

When the police leading the column decided to make a stop, it was a chance to distribute around the water canisters. The people moved around in the large circles formed by the carts, trying to quench their thirst and pleading with those that still had reserves in their drums. The police would not allow anyone to leave the circle. Hundreds of elders and women wandered among the carts and animals, begging, bartering, or buying water, which was becoming scarcer by the minute. Mothers desperately attempted to keep their children from getting lost as they played amongst themselves, oblivious to the dramatic situation.

The sadness of the deportation was reflected in the faces and spirits of all, and none attempted to inquire as to their destination. One thing was sure: by keeping to that route, they would come to the great mountain passes. Araksi wondered how much longer her parents would be able to hold out. Their appearance was deteriorating and they seemed to have aged several years in just a few weeks.

Mavush was horrified by the filth and degradation they were part of. She, remembered Araksi, who used to take pains each morning to tie her daughters' hair with pretty colored bows and who constantly scolded them if they did not come to the table looking their best. Yet at the same time their downtrodden appearance protected them from the zaptiehs' ogling stares, as they rode up and down examining and seeking out the prettiest girls.

Araksi left the mirror among the bundles of clothes and remained engrossed and troubled by dark thoughts.

Mavush and Vartuhi continued struggling with the children who, in turns, insisted on tugging the donkeys' reins, in peril of wandering away from the carts.

"We will all meet again with Papa after the journey. Don't stop praying. Jesus will help us. I've told you not to go far. Bring that donkey next to the cart. Do as I tell you right now!" Mavush desperately scolded.

Vartuhi tried to pacify her: "Calm down, Mavush, calm down. We should set the example. Let them hide away in their world. I myself want to believe none of this is happening. Pretend we're on a country outing... and we'll all go back home... It's just an uncomfortable ride... Let's copy the children, like this... All together now!"

Vartuhi started singing and dancing, showing signs of emotional imbalance. Mavush and Araksi looked at each other, alarmed at Vartuhi's state. Her face had taken on a strange expression of humorless laughter. She jumped and sang in a round with the children, using exaggerated gestures. After going round and round, she fell, caught up in her clothing. The children climbed onto her back as if they were at their kindergarten in Erzurum, playing their make-believe games, very far from everything around them.

Araksi and Mavush had to help their parents in all their needs. Little by little they went, limiting their movements to the most elemental, a prey to great sorrow. They often asked themselves, with monotone frequency, what would have happened if they had left Erzurum in time, following the example of a small number of friends.

At night the carts formed a closed circle and hundreds of tents were pitched as temporary shelters. There the people made do as best they could, always outdoors. The multitude of crowded Armenians squatted by the campfires among the filth, taking pains not to draw the attention of the Turks and sleeping by shifts, both to remain alert to the gendarmes' provocations and whiplashes and to prevent the constant thefts of what little food and water they had. The Turks grew increasingly crude as they moved away from populated centers, and lashes cracked overhead, often landing on the backs of stragglers. On one of those hot nights in the campsite and away from the guards' ever-present vigilance, Zareh and Mariam had taken the precaution of setting up the tents far from the general tumult. Zareh asked the family for their attention.

Without much explanation, almost in silence, he began handing out the gold and jewels that Araksi had been able to rescue. He ordered each of his daughters to take her share and blessed them all so that nothing might separate them until they were safe and sound. Zareh thought that was the safest way to leave the possibility of salvation open when they should arrive at some known destination.

The women hid the pieces among the folds and hems of their garments, even in their intimate undergarments. It was a small fortune in gold coins, pounds and jewels, enough to get to Europe and even possibly buy favors and passes at some frontier, perhaps at a Black Sea port, or even the Russian border. The largest pieces were hidden inside utensils and in the false bottoms of cans and flasks. They knew the police interrogated people, in search of details or hints during the day, until they detected jewels or money they would later snatch away during the night.

Shortly, rifle shots were heard, followed by shouts and yells breaking the silence of night. Everyone remained motionless and no one else in the camp was able to get back to sleep. The shadows of the attackers who moved among the tents, attacking and killing, filled the families with terror. The following morning, the bodies of the murdered just remained where they had fallen. If there were children in the group, others took charge of taking them with them, making room on their carts. The convoy was so big that only those who had been close by heard of the tragedies that had taken place during the night.

The morning light heralded a new day for the wandering population. The drivers hitched up the oxen and the carts were pulled back into line, while the Turkish guards tried to mobilize hundreds of people, organizing the caravan.

The enormous line of ragged, dirty, and badly-fed Armenians got underway, hastened on by the guards' yells and lashes. They took down their tents and once again stacked their belongings, portioned out in packs and bundles of clothes, as well as they could upon the carts. Forced nomads who, as days rolled on, went falling into increasing degradation until they sank into the most abject misery.

Araksi tried to have some tea and give herself the strength to face yet another day of this nightmare.

It was that morning, at some distance from the tent, where the camping space of the multitude ended, that she thought she saw an escort of mounted soldiers riding along the campsite borders. Her parents' carts and tents had remained at the centre of the concentration of humans, far from the periphery, according to what most recommended as safest against possible nocturnal raids by armed bands. Araksi looked again and this time made out German uniforms. She shielded her eyes from the early morning glare and unmistakably saw Max von Swirsden-Righe, accompanied by Commander Taksim Bey and an escort of Turkish soldiers.

She ran to let her parents know. Zareh, excited and still harboring some hope, got onto the cart to try and distinguish the contingent of riders better. There was little chance of being seen among that ocean of people. Father and daughter impotently watched the tiny figures that passed afar, with no intention of dismounting or entering the tangle of tents, oxen, and wagons.

Zareh saw the German Consul quickly riding away. He sighed in discouragement and carried on packing the crockery wordlessly. Then, "Go to your mother, Araksi, and you too, my girl. I'm very worried about Vartuhi. Sometimes she speaks to me as if she has confused me with Krikor." It was all he dared say.

Then the wagons got underway.

CHAPTER XVIII

HENRY MORGENTHAU, UNITED STATES AMBASSADOR

LIGHT SHONE OFF THE SMALL, ROUND GLASSES worn by Henry Morgenthau, United States Ambassador to Turkey. All the same, they allowed one to see how his stern eyes met those of his colleague, Ambassador von Wangenheim.

It was an intelligent, profoundly humane look. Morgenthau was the same age as his German host and had a pointed goatee beard.

The Baron paced the room from one side of the large window to the other, looking down. This allowed him to concentrate better. He looked up, evidently bothered, and let his counterpart have a good piece of his mind: "It seems that the only country that takes any interest in the Armenians is the United States, Ambassador. I know American missionaries are installed in Armenian villages of the Interior and that they send you periodic reports. Don't think I'm uninformed about it... and that in your country's newspapers the Armenian business appears as a matter the American public has adopted as its own." He spoke sardonically, continuing, "How can you expect me to intercede on behalf of the Armenians when you are selling weapons to these enemies of Germany? With what authority do you request it, Mr. Morgenthau? The Armenians — every one of them — act to destroy Turkish power." He stopped and looked at Morgenthau. "There is no other solution to their deportation."

Morgenthau reacted. "Nobody's going to swallow that version of the facts, Baron. The whole world will recriminate Germany for these crimes and the guilt, the responsibility, will pursue you forever. You are a Christian nation, von Wangenheim, and the time will come when the German people will call you to account for having allowed Turkey, a Moslem country, to destroy Armenia, a Christian one. Why are you trying to cover up the horrendous atrocities the Turks are committing?"

Wangenheim counterstruck. "The Armenians wish to destabilize and dismember the Ottoman Empire. Therefore they have forfeited all claim to live in its territory any longer. I'm sorry, Ambassador, but it's evident these two peoples can't live together."

He opened the box of cigars on his desk and offered his colleague one. Morgenthau thanked him but refused.

Wangenheim went on as he lit his, "You Americans should take a few Armenians to the States, and we could send a few others to Poland, and in their place we could send some Polish Jews to Anatolia, provided they left their Zionist tendencies aside. What do you think of that idea?" He smiled and continued: "Turkey wants to fix up its internal affairs... They have a right to. And we Germans have no responsibility or intervention in their affairs. I am not authorized to meddle in the internal policies of our ally. Our only purpose is to win the war."

Morgenthau was looking straight at the German. Making a show of perfect self-control, he answered, "Don't think, Ambassador, that the world will forget these crimes just because you look the other way and pretend it has nothing to do with you. Don't hide your head, ostrich-like. I am reminding you once more that I shall fulfil my duty and inform the State Department. I hope you will reconsider the matter. Good day, Mr. Ambassador."

Henry Morgenthau left the office feeling very upset.

The German, without batting an eyelid, blew out a jet of smoke and shrugged his shoulders, the other's displeasure a matter of little importance.

CHAPTER XIX

BODIES IN THE TIGRIS

THE BANKS OF THE RIVER TIGRIS looked fairly close to each other at this point of the river-course and thawing ice floes floated in the waters.

From time to time, Diran looked at the river indifferently, observing the sandbanks that interrupted the dark, driftwood-laden current. Anyhow, his thoughts were unconnected with the churning waters. Rather, they came and went among fragmented memories of the last weeks in the Erzurum prison and the reality he was now faced with. He was walking in a line of 500 men, all Armenian; prisoners from Erzurum and neighbouring towns, making up a long caravan of wanderers along the banks of the Tigris. Guarded by mounted police, the men, thirsty and exhausted, marched as though dragging themselves along.

He had been lucky. He could think of it in those terms, for he was still alive. He asked himself thousands of times why, after being interrogated with blows at the commander's office, instead of dying as the victim of horrendous methods of torture, or hanged in the prison yard like so many others, he had been forgotten in his cell so as to become a part of that caravan of condemned deportees that the Turks were taking who knew where.

It was not really luck, but he was alive. He attributed it to the confusion among the executioners, weary of killing, with their improvised lists of men condemned to summary execution, and thus to the immediate deportation of all of them outside the cities. Someone had probably died in place of him, thought Diran.

Tavel and Levon were also among the group of deportees, lined up with men of every condition, some very young, others older, but no one over 45, all destined to be the workforce of the Turkish army. They had been assigned to road-building and the transport of provisions like beasts of burden.

Tavel and Levon, unable to come closer and keeping absolutely silent, crossed glances with Diran, the code of the condemned. All suffering the same pain, they understood what could not be put in words.

As the road neared the riverbank, the officers re-organized the men into smaller groups. Diran saw that Tavel and Levon were at a small distance from his position. They were in a bad way, their aspect being evidence of the rigors of the forced march. Deep furrows had appeared on their faces. *They look like old men,* thought Diran — *our lives are no longer our own.* He struggled with his mind to avoid succumbing to the avalanche of horrors that constantly assailed him.

The caravan moved ever closer to the river, and the noise of thirsty men began to grow, turning into an enormous roar coming from all the lines. For days, fatigue, the merciless sun, and the Turkish guards' rationing kept them subjected to the worst of tortures in the death-like caravans: thirst.

There were shouts and desperate attempts to get closer and drink, but the Turks, setting bayonets, pushed the Armenians back into formation. They had made them walk on the plain for days with minimal water rations and now, just a few feet from the river, prevented access with whiplashes.

Sundown covered the formation with shadows and faces became unrecognizable. The long, snake-like line of captives looked like a group of animals rather than humans, jostling among themselves to dive into the river and quench their thirst.

They were at a rocky strip. At its edges, the Tigris formed into small beaches, and the sandbanks in the middle of the stream significantly reduced the distance to the opposite bank. Beyond, rocks covered by ice floes held up the passage of some tree trunks dragged by the current.

In Diran's section, three 30-ish Armenians were alert to every movement of the mounted gendarmes. Not so much as a whisper passed between them. They were waiting for nightfall. They seemed to be estimating with the naked eye the distance to the opposite bank. Diran watched them, intrigued.

All at once, the center of the formation overflowed. Unable to contain the milling horde, the Turks allowed a few of them to get to the water and drink. In vain, they tried to hold back the avalanche of the others who, struggling to get to the riverbank, fell over the first lot. The three youths next to Diran kept pushing, their faces furrowed and tense, looking at the river. Just then the one closest, the heaviest built, spoke to Diran for the first time. "It's now or never. This is the narrowest point."

Diran understood immediately and nodded. He looked at the sandbank and the rocky path to the further bank, and understood his compatriots' intent. He stood stock-still by them. The rest fell on the bank, swallowing as much water as they could while being stepped on by those behind them. With rifle butts and bayonets, the gendarmes tried to turn them back.

Diran saw Tavel and Levon running, out of control, towards the river. The Turkish guards sank their bayonet blades into them. Diran gave a cry of pain on seeing the avalanche let loose falling on his dear brothers; though not blood-related, members of a family dying out before his eyes. They who had fostered and nurtured him as another child during his happiest years in Erzurum. The beloved memory of Araksi was added to the horror. Was she still alive? He could not accept that any danger might have happened to her, the thought horrified him. Zareh and the women; had they managed to escape, or were they also innocent victims of this great madness? It all went through Diran's mind in a flash as he threw himself down on the sand.

Tavel's and Levon's blood mingled with that of a hundred others in the waters, creating a reddish tinge. A Turkish officer gave the order to hurl the horses upon the men, trampling all that fell under their hooves. In another sector, the police dismounted, shooting point-blank, non-stop, killing dozens of deported Armenians in no time.

The darkness increased the confusion. Yells were heard everywhere, and silenced with pistol shots. Fallen bodies piled up at the river's edge. Such was the number of bodies that they formed a barrier which diverted the flow of the river.

Diran and the three youths, moved by instinct and reacting in unison, began running along the beach to immediately hide beneath the dead. For camouflage, they smeared themselves with the blood of the fallen. Overcoming his horror, Diran soaked his hand in the warm blood issuing from a body, imitating the others. He vomited with repulsion and horror, but if he wished to survive he had to hide from the police, who moved along the beach, finishing off the dying. Darkness enshrouded the place. Dozens of bodies floated in the river.

Diran and his now two companions — the third had been felled by bullets — remained immobile under the corpses. The guards were still finishing off those still alive. The thickest-set Armenian peered out from among the bodies, looked in every direction, and understood this was the moment to make a break for it, taking advantage of the zaptiehs' distance. He and the other alerted Diran and without delay the three emerged from under the cadavers and ran madly towards the river.

As soon as he plunged in, Diran came up against floating bodies. As they swam the first few feet, all three felt the limbs of the dead entwining with their own. They had to swim a few strokes before reaching the sandbank, overcoming their horror.

The waters of the Tigris were freezing cold and the noise of the current was loud. The three jumped onto the first rocks. Some of these were covered with ice floes and accumulated branches. On the other side of the sandbank they saw that the strip of water separating them from the far side was narrower and shallower. They ran with the water up to their knees, avoiding driftwood and rocks.

Soon they gained the opposite bank and right away entered the immense dark, thick forest that stood in front of them.

They trekked on through the night, never stopping in spite of their tiredness, never looking back. The impulse to get away from that hell gave them renewed strength.

They advanced in silence. They only interrupted their journey to listen for some sound in the wood, wary of possible Turkish patrols or Kurdish bands that assaulted the caravans of deportees. They came across none of them in their flight. The immensity of the forest gradually erased the images of the butchery they had left behind.

CHAPTER XX

THIRST AND DESERT

THE CARAVAN SLOWLY ADVANCED across the arid plain. The wind was lifting dust clouds that reduced visibility to just beyond the oxen. Fatigue was general. Old people and women travelling on foot, following the carts, stumbled along with thirst. Their expressions showed terror and desolation.

Faces covered with rags to avoid the dust contributed to the drama of the Armenian wanderers' ruinous appearance, resigned to the brutality of the police officers who cracked their whips every so often, forcing them on. Those that had lost their wagons, for no longer being able to pay the Turkish drivers' services, were left on foot to continue the journey, carrying their bundles and children on their backs.

Araksi travelled on the wagon in the seat next to the Turkish driver. She protected her face with a veil, as did the others. She was deep in thought, looking ahead, almost falling asleep from the noise of the storm savaging the plain.

Amid the swirling dust, not far in front of the cart, a woman was advancing with difficulty, pulling the reins of a donkey on which her little boy sat. The mother's robe flapped in the wind and dust enveloped the scene. The backs of the oxen were barely visible. Araksi stared ahead without blinking, paying no attention to the monotony of the road. The woman on foot was tugging at the animal but going off course due to the raging wind. As if in slow motion, at the same time Araksi was jolted out of her reverie with fright. A figure appeared from nowhere, or rather from the dust cloud which was making everything yet more ghostly. But the vision became suddenly very real. A Turkish peasant sprang upon the woman and pulled away the reins with the aim of robbing her of the beast and, consequently, the child riding on it.

No one went to her aid, despite the woman's frantic

screams. No one but Araksi seemed to have even noticed the terrible event. Unable to take her donkey just by pulling, the Turk, determined not to lose his booty, unsheathed a yataghan at his side and unhesitatingly cut off the young mother's arm. He then fled into the desert dust with the donkey and the little boy, who was screeching on the animal's back.

Araksi covered her mouth with horror. No one stopped. At her side the driver carried on impassively directing the oxen. Araksi tried to jump off the cart to help the poor woman. The driver's hand stopped her and with a wordless gesture he made her understand the futility of her purpose.

The dust cloud enveloped everything once more. Soon the woman remained behind, stretched out on the ground while the caravan moved on. Araksi looked back into the wagon, searching desperately for Mavush. They were all asleep. She cried with impotence, bending over herself.

Some guards galloped by, repelling the attacking bands of Turkish peasants that sacked and killed Armenian stragglers. Then shots were heard, and screams of horror. The wind, blowing with increasing force, muted the sounds.

Every so often, they would go through little Turkish settlements spread out over the plain. The zaptiehs stopped at water wells to get new supplies. Long queues of women with their children and elders, by now a mass of dirty, ragged people, crowded around, carrying canisters and belongings to trade for water and food. The villagers offered yogurt, honey and water in exchange for gold coins. Situated all along the road, whole populations awaited these merchants of despair, and on their arrival the unfair trade began.

The guards were the first to approach and drink from the wells. With their whips they settled any tumult or argument that might arise among the thirsty throng who were desperate to fill their buckets; almost fainting, more dead than alive.

Zareh and his daughters finally found a good position to load their pitchers. Araksi covered her face to prevent the men from discovering her age and appearance. Both she and Vartuhi wore mud as a way of camouflaging their natural attractiveness, although this had been greatly reduced by the rigors of the journey.

After waiting in a long queue they had to haggle over the price with the Turks who administered the wells. Mariam was in charge of getting food. She went to the stalls that the village women had ready for the deportees. These improvised markets, set up for hundreds of thousands of Armenian wanderers, enriched the villagers along the route.

Around the wells, the Turks pushed away women and elders lunging forward to quench their thirst.

Zareh took out a coin of great value from among his rags to pay for the water and waited for the change. It was a mere six pails of water. The Turks looked at the coin and then laughed, shaking their heads. The former banker was soon involved in a heated argument with the villagers. Zareh demanded his change for the exorbitant price he had paid. The shouts and shoves quickly drew the gendarmes' attention. A group of Turks began to gather. Alarmed, Mavush and Araksi persuaded their furious father to leave rather than carry on arguing. Exhausted and at the end of his tether, he walked back to the wagons, helped by Araksi. His strength was failing. Close by, Mavush obsessively kept watch over the children to make sure that they did not get lost or kidnapped amidst the huge crowds. Survival demanded not shutting one's eyes by day or by night, especially when the convoy stopped somewhere.

Mariam and Vartuhi offered the village women high quality carpets and lamps, ready to exchange them for food. The women looked with wonder at the luxurious tapestries that only weeks earlier had decorated the floors of the house in Erzurum. An old village woman that seemed to dominate the others snatched the tapestry from Mariam but, not considering it payment enough for her wares, she wrenched away from Vartuhi the magnificent English lamp that had been in the study, adding it to her profit.

Then, as a token of exchange, she pushed a few containers of yogurt forward and separated away the pots of honey. Mariam did not argue and, bending down, even in her fragility, began carrying the foodstuffs away. Other village women gathered with curiosity to observe the misery of the Armenians fallen into misfortune.

Laughing amid the general mockery, one said to Mariam, "You don't need the lamp now."

Another Turkish girl joined in with relish on seeing Mariam's and Vartuhi's despair. "Where ye going not need that."

"Where then are we going? What do you know about that, woman?"

Vartuhi added after her mother-in-law, "Where are they taking us? Have you no children as we have? Are we going to the mountains or the desert? Where have they taken the Armenians from the other towns?"

The women burst out in mocking laughter. Without answering, they walked away towards the huts of the village, carrying their trophies. Mariam looked at Vartuhi in despair. They embraced, weeping.

Soon the gendarmes' yells announced that all were to return to their line and whips cracked overhead once more. Many had not managed to get to the wells. They begged the soldiers for water, dragging themselves with exhaustion, and receiving blows and insults. They knew a dreadful death from dehydration awaited them in the next few hours.

CHAPTER XXI

REINFORCEMENTS ARRIVE

THROUGH THE WINDSHIELD OF THE ARMY TRUCK the profile of the city standing out against the sky, at the top of the plateau, came into view. In the distance, the snowy mountain peaks rose majestically. Rolf was captivated as he contemplated the road leading to Erzurum.

The convoy of trucks, loaded with soldiers and carrying German banners, slowly climbed the slope. Shortly before the turn-off connecting with the main incline, they stopped. A gust of cool wind whistled when the doors opened.

Three officers in German uniforms got out to view the landscape: Rolf and Friedrich Hüchtinger, and the colonel, Count von der Schulenburg, the incoming Consul of Erzurum. The Europeans gazed with wonder at the end of their journey.

More soldiers got off the other trucks. They needed to stretch their legs after weeks of very bad roads and several combinations of sea and rail. From Europe to Constantinople, then the journey by sea and land to Erzurum. Lieutenant Thiele and a corporal jumped off the truck to help the doctor of the expedition, a portly man of Prussian aspect, who was stumbling giddily on alighting from the vehicle.

They enthusiastically observed the rolling road, climbing up to the plateau where the houses began. Rolf and Friedrich were anxious to meet Swirsden-Righe, their comrade from the Straubing regiment. It was several months since they had bid their farewells at the dinner at the Swirsden-Righes' house in Munich.

Max, on the point of ending his consular post, had asked the High Command for the brothers' transfer as reinforcements for his Caucasus campaign.

"This is certainly very different from Straubing," said Friedrich, taking in the impressive mountain view.

Suddenly, Rolf gave a shout, pointing at the curving

road. Riders appeared, one of them wearing a German uniform, riding easily upon their magnificent horses. Two Turkish soldiers followed, as an escort.

Max rode Pasha, accompanied by his assistant Tahir, on Kismet. The figure of both horsemen riding their Arab thoroughbreds, which snorted nervously at the brisk morning air, was a truly marvellous apparition in the eyes of those European soldiers just arrived in the heart of Anatolia.

"Look, look there, it's Max... Lieutenant von Swirsden-Righe," cried Rolf with childlike joy at meeting his friend in such a distant place.

"Is it Max?" wondered Friedrich. "Yes, Colonel... Look, up there at the curve. What horses — pure Arabs!"

The colonel smiled in agreement.

On arriving at the meeting point, Max dismounted and, after standing to attention before Count von der Schulenburg, his diplomatic replacement, he was unable to contain his emotion.

"Rolf! Friedrich! Attention!" Max embraced his old comrades warmly.

A few bottles of good German wine were produced from the truck while they all celebrated their reunion. The spirit of camaraderie reigned supreme on the mountain.

"Sir, Colonel, welcome to Erzurum. I am ready to transfer the command to you."

Schulenburg, military-looking but affable and youthful, patted Max as he held the glass of wine. "It has been a most incredible journey. Surely there will be a great deal to get me up to date with in this place. So we're at the gates of old Erzurum?"

"That is so, Sir, old Erzurum. This has been used as a stepping-stone by Alexander the Great, down to us Germans now... though as yet we're a small group. Prepare yourself to see medieval images right in the streets. I assure you they're here."

Max diverted his gaze to the trucks, which were loaded with young, Russian-looking soldiers.

"I see you've brought a troop of Russian prisoners along, Sir."

"They're Volga-Germans. You know, Russian prisoners of German descent can volunteer for heavy duty. They're sturdy — we'll use them for the Caucasus campaign."

Max had a good look at the soldiers and then the conversation became more general. Rolf spoke rapidly, with a certain agitation typical of his enthusiastic nature. He and Friedrich were little over 20 years old.

"Erzurum... It all reminds me of my reading *Tales from a Thousand and One Nights.*"

Friedrich asked directly, as he uncorked another bottle of wine, "I say, Max, on the last lap of the journey we were warned we might be ambushed by Armenian guerrillas in the mountains. How serious is it?"

Max did not answer. He sought to avoid personal comments in front of his replacement. Soon, the wine and the joy of the reunion created a relaxed atmosphere.

Max spontaneously but directly addressed Count von der Schulenburg. "Sir, why don't I hand you over the consulate here and now? We have a lot of planning to do and very little time before going off to the Caucasus."

The lieutenant-colonel replied forthwith, "The time and place couldn't be better. Thank you very much, Swirsden-Righe. Gentlemen, here at the city gates, I am taking charge of the Erzurum Consulate. Let us drink to a German victory at the siege of Warsaw and to the coming triumphs on the Eastern front. Long live the Kaiser!"

The officers raised their glasses. "To the Kaiser!"

HORSES AND CARRIAGES WERE LINED UP AT the doors of the Turkish Commander's Office in Erzurum. The band played solemn military marches, while the Guard of Honor of Turkish soldiers took up position on both sides of the entrance.

At the end of the long passage, Kamil Pasha, supreme commander of the Third Army, was waiting for the German officers and invited them into the main hall.

Lieutenant-Colonel Guse and Kamil Pasha were surrounded by Caucasian dignitaries and politicians, who moved around the salon dressed in their typical costumes. The newly arrived were awe-struck at such an exotic display, observing the Oriental chieftains' apparel.

Guse signalled to Max to come and in front of the Turkish commander of the region, declared, "Kamil Pasha, Lieutenant Swirsden-Righe is leaving the consulate. He will soon take charge of liaising between Germans and Turks and, needless to say, the Caucasian tribes that join the campaign."

Kamil made a gesture of approval, coldly shaking Max's hand and deliberately turning his back on him to carry on conversing with the new consul. Colonel Guse immediately sensed the uncomfortable situation and, taking Max by the arm, led him towards a group where a slim, refined and doubtlessly Asiatic man stood out. He wore a Chechen military uniform.

Guse quietly advised Max, as they made their way across the saloon full of Turkish officers, "Come with me. I'll introduce you to Omer Nadji Bey, the most influential politician in Turkey... educated in Paris and extremely shrewd. If he takes to you, half of the resources for the expedition to Persia will be yours. Omer Nadji will be general commander on that mission, together with you."

Max paid attention. Guse, just like all generals and superior officers commanding troops in large military units of the Ottoman Empire, were to wear their pertinent uniforms: Max was wearing the dress uniform of a reserve lieutenant of the German Empire.

As they got nearer to the group, the lieutenant-colonel elaborated further about Omer Nadji: "He isn't Turkish — he's Chechen. He's said to have more influence on the ministers of the ruling Junta than all the Turkish generals. Win him over to the cause, Swirsden-Righe."

The Chechen smiled affably on seeing them approach.

"Omer Nadji Bey, meet Lieutenant Max von Swirsden-Righe. He will be sharing the expedition to Sautchbulak with you," said Guse by way of introduction.

The men shook hands, studying each other. Max immediately perceived authority and intelligence in the man's look. There was a spontaneous current of empathy.

Guse continued: "Lieutenant Swirsden-Righe's giving up the comfort of the Erzurum Consulate to accompany you to fight the Cossacks, Omer Nadji."

Addressing Max, he added with a certain complicity with the Chechen, "I warn you, Lieutenant, that you are in front of the General Inspector of the Committee for Union and Progress - in other words, the highest political authority in the Empire. You definitely would do well to be on his side...."

They all laughed.

"It'll be a pleasure to share a mission of such importance for both our countries," answered Max.

The exchange was cut short. Commander Kamil Pasha, host and maximum authority, asked for attention. The Turks spoke French so that they and the Germans understood each other in an enemy language. Kamil Pasha addressed everyone present. His voice alone was heard in the salon.

"Gentlemen, please... Our objective is now the North of Persia. The new strategy for attacking the enemy will consist of mobile regiments of cavalry and infantry, few troops. Our combined armies will be able to withstand the rigors of the climate and penetrate the Russian frontier, breaking the line of the Czar's armies up to the Baku oil pipeline. Gentlemen, let us pledge ourselves to our nations and to the success of the conquest of the Caucasus. Prudence and courage for what awaits us."

CHAPTER XXII

THE SUBLIME DOOR

TURKISH FLAGS WAVED outside the building in Constantinople. Guards kept watch at the entrance and groups of Turkish military and politicians went in and out. The place was the seat of highest authority in the country.

The military Junta that ruled Turkey, the Ittihad, better known in the West as The Young Turks, and composed of three ministers, had replaced Sultan Abdul Hamid on deposing him and set up his brother, Murat V, as a kind of puppet governor in his place.

The three leaders of the party, Union and Progress — Talaat Pasha, Enver Pasha and Djemal Pasha — managed the destinies of the Ottoman Empire from the Sublime Porte. The inside of the palace was extremely luxurious. The passageways were decorated with magnificent chandeliers hanging from very high ceilings, and the walls of the salons were covered by beautiful ceramics and mosaics inlaid with gold. Huge portraits of the Empire's sultans looked down upon the carpeted passages, connecting enormous halls with marble columns abutting in whorls of bronze and gold.

The great double door at the end of the long passage remained shut, the reception space to Talaat Pasha, the Interior Minister's office.

United States Ambassador Henry Morgenthau did not easily take no for an answer. He patiently waited for over an hour on the reception room armchairs.

Talaat's secretary raised his eyes and met the irritated look of the ambassador, which said everything. He then stood and, gently knocking on the door of the minister's office, timidly went in, excusing himself. Talaat was talking non-stop on the telephone. The assistant approached the desk, reminding him of his meeting with Morgenthau.

Talaat was a heavily-built man in his late 30s. He wore

a small moustache and a tail-coat. He showed irritation at being interrupted. All the same, he signalled for the diplomat to be shown in while giving severe orders in Turkish to whoever was on the other end of the telephone before hanging up.

When Henry Morgenthau was seated in front of him, the two greeted each other as if they had met before.

"This is not a timely morning, Mr. Ambassador. I beg you to excuse me for having made you wait. Do you know that the British refuse to liberate my good friends Ayub Sabri and Zinnoun, imprisoned in Malta? We've been negotiating their release for months, and the British always backtrack, so I hope they don't come asking me for the release of any Canadian, and less still for any Englishman employed by yourselves... Ayub Sabri is my brother! Tell the English that on my behalf and let them set them loose right away!" the minister yelled in a rage.

"I'm here to ask you for the lives of other persons... who are neither Canadian nor British. I've come to ask you for the lives of the Armenians, Mr. Minister," replied Morgenthau.

Talaat studied him. "Why are you so interested in the Armenians? Are you not a Jew, after all? Those people are Christians, Morgenthau. We Mahommedans have always got on well with the Jews. Why are you insisting on behalf of the Christian Armenians? Here, Jews are well treated. Let us deal with the Christians in Turkey as we see fit, Morgenthau."

The ambassador took a deep breath. "That's not the question, Talaat. I'm not making my request for any race or religion. I'm doing this just as a human being. I'm not here as a Jew but as the United States Ambassador. In my country there are 97 million Christians and fewer than three million Jews, so as an ambassador I'm 97% Christian. This treatment of the Armenians is not placing Turkey in the progressive world, as you claim. Quite the contrary, it places your country among the retrograde and reactionary peoples." Morgenthau responded firmly to Talaat's platitudes.

The Turk remained motionless in a corner of the salon.

Morgenthau was determined to insist for as long as necessary. The news reaching him daily from each vilayet was too alarming. American teachers and missionaries were reporting abhorrent massacres and deportations. The ambassador continued: "Look, Minister, we Americans are disgusted at the persecution the Armenians are suffering. You must base your actions on non-discriminatory humanitarian principles. The people of the United States will never forget these killings... They will be considered premeditated murders. Exactly that. You yourself will not be able to evade such a huge responsibility. Your private status as Interior Minister will not protect you. For us United States citizens, this whole question flies in the face of any idea of justice."

Talaat, very upset, did not sit down again. He raised his head haughtily, aware of his power.

"This, Morgenthau, is definitely not the right morning. Those... people... helped the Russians. Then they rose up in Van. To defend ourselves in the future there is a single solution, the deportation of all the Armenians."

Morgenthau countered, "But, Minister, supposing there *are* traitors among the Armenians, is there any need to kill women, children, and old people?"

"Those are inevitable actions, Mr. Morgenthau... Today's innocents may be the guilty of tomorrow. Listen now, I will list the reasons. The Armenians have got rich at our expense, and are resolved to dominate us and form an independent state in Turkey."

Morgenthau tried to interrupt him, but Talaat went on. "They helped our enemies, the Russians, in the Caucasus. Therefore we will keep them harmless until the end of the war." With irritation, he seated himself behind his desk. "In fact, it is not worthwhile discussing the matter any further. We have already eliminated three quarters of the Armenian population. Not one Armenian will remain in Anatolia... Let them live in the desert... but nowhere else in my country."

The ambassador was horrified at Talaat's confirmation of the deeds.

"Ah, yes, Ambassador..? I was almost forgetting to ask

you for something important... There's something the banks in the States could provide us with."

"Provide you with?"

"We need a list of Armenians with policies in the insurance companies of your country. Since most Armenians will probably be dead and are heirless, the heir and sole beneficiary is the Turkish state. Would you be so kind as to transmit this request, please?"

Henry Morgenthau remained sitting, motionless, hardly believing what he had just heard. Alarmed at the Interior Minister's confessions, he took a few moments before finally standing. He coldly saluted Talaat and worriedly left the office.

CHAPTER XXIII

IN THE FORESTS OF KURDISTAN

HIDING AMONG THE TREES, Diran and the other two escapees studied the movements of a small Kurdish village. Their clothes were in tatters and they wore beards several weeks old.

The settlement was a group of 30 shanties on a thickly wooded slope, a clearing in the middle of the immensity of the forest extending over steep hills as far as the eye could see.

Wooden sheds penned in herds of goats. The light of the waxing moon allowed them to see the movements in the village clearly. Actually, nothing moved. Only the sound of cicadas broke the nocturnal silence. It seemed all the inhabitants were inside their huts, in spite of the heat.

They peered at the perimeter of the settlement. An old woman was collecting basketfuls of mulberries which she lined up outside the porch of her hut. She managed to drag into the dwelling the few her feeble strength allowed, leaving a small number for her next journey. Diran and his fellow fugitives were starving. They had eaten hardly anything for three days.

The eldest of the survivors, Manuc, the heavily-built Armenian who had urged Diran to escape across the river, said, "Maybe they're peaceful Kurds."

While it took Diran all his effort not to pass out, the third of them, Giorgi, crouching among the trees, added, "If the Turks are near, or have come by here, we're dead men. They'll raise the alarm at the nearest patrol."

Diran noticed that, further away, on a pathway separating the huts, an old man was holding a kid goat in his arms. He was carrying it to the shed with the rest of the herd.

"Shhh, there's someone there," Diran warned.

"He won't see me," answered Giorgi. "He's an old man."

Determined not to waste another second, Manuc

crawled in the grass as quietly as he could and came into the clearing. He had covered the whole way without being seen. On reaching the porch, he seized the basket. The door of the ramshackle hovel was open and there was nobody in sight. Gathering courage and egged on by hunger, he decided to enter the shack. He gingerly took a couple of paces and was able to see a pantry well stocked with cheeses, some fruits, and several pots of honey. A candle shone in the gloom.

From their concealment amongst the trees, Diran and Giorgi were startled by a noise among the leaves and a man came into view, carrying a crook in his hand.

Manuc emerged from the hut as fast as his legs could bear him, filling his mouth with some fruit and carrying as much food as he could. On finding himself discovered by the old goatherd, he made ready to run, but thought better of it. It was not a good idea. From some cubby-hole in the shack, the old woman came out in pursuit of the thief. The three lads realized that at the slightest cry of alarm the whole of the Kurdish village of goatherds would be upon them. They were too tired to flee.

The old couple said nothing. Standing still, they seemed to understand the situation. The old man began talking in a calm undertone. He spoke in Kurdish, using gestures and phrases that, though they were incomprehensible, were peaceable... They were inviting Manuc to stay and have some food.

From their hiding place, Diran and Giorgi watched every movement, getting ready to run for it. Manuc, caught at his thievery, was still undecided about the old couple's offer. He pointed at himself: "Armenian!" he repeated insistently.

The old couple looked at each other and then timidly said a few words in Turkish, accepting him. Manuc stood motionless on the porch, as though paralyzed. Looking all around him, he indicated the forest. "Friends over there... Armenians."

The old Kurd once again nodded agreement, urging them to make haste. Diran and Giorgi came out of hiding.

Inside the hut, the Kurds brought the lads plates of

food and drink. The fugitives hungrily fell upon the lamb and stew they were served. The old couple looked on with kindness.

Later, when they had eaten and felt their bodies alive once more, the herdsman led Diran and his comrades to a sort of woodshed next to the cabin, an underground storehouse made of logs and walls of stone and mud, where poultry were housed.

On going down into the shelter, they were surprised to find that someone else was there in the darkness. The shadowy figure started as Diran and his mates came down the steps, but relaxed on hearing them speaking Armenian. Coming forward, he asked in the same language, "Armenians?"

"You too?" they answered in surprise.

Manuc took the initiative. "We escaped three days ago. We're from Erzindjan, he's from Erzurum," he indicated Diran.

"We've been lucky to land up here. These old Kurds have been kind to us," said the shadow.

All at once they fell silent, hearing voices nearby. Through a crack between the logs they saw the herdsman greeting a neighbor on his way home. Very soon, tiredness overcame them and all four fell into a deep sleep.

CHAPTER XXIV

THE KEMAKH PASS

IT WAS NIGHT. The caravan stopped on the slope of the high mountains.

The deportees' encampment had been established in a forest clearing, just before the ascent of the steep Kemakh mountain passes. The tiny tents were spread out over a broad area. There was nothing new, just the usual survival routine, except for those that had gone falling behind, unable to carry on in those sub-human conditions and dying on the way. Then a new suffering arrived to terrorize the Armenians. As though at that stage of the journey the zaptiehs had decided to increase the people's woes, the guards began patrolling the tents in search of the money still hidden by those who had been marked in advance, or previously exempted from the requisitions.

Araksi and her sisters held the children tightly in an attempt to make themselves as inconspicuous as possible. All at once, Zareh unexpectedly entered the tent. He asked for silence and, using sign language, distributed the little remaining gold among his daughters. A group of officers was on the way, striking women and old people and snatching away everything of value they might still be hiding.

The zaptiehs' violence had increased since they had left the populated areas and entered the mountain passes. The money was essential to carry on paying the Turkish drivers, who every so often threatened to desert the caravan together with their carts and oxen if their pay was not raised. Not to be able to afford such extortion amounted to a sure death for any family left on the way, with no means of transport, carrying loads and children till they died of exhaustion or as victims of another menace more terrifying than the first: the bands of marauders that fell upon the caravans.

They had just arrived in the region terrorized by

Kurdish tribes, an Indo-European people just like the Armenians, but who were mostly Sunni Moslems, that the Turks had also subjected and now incited to attack the deportees. Zareh, Araksi and Mavush were able to see from their tent how the members of a family a few feet away were swallowing gold coins in case the police officers might discover them. The women almost vomited and the children overcame their fear of gagging as the coins went down their throats.

Somewhere beyond, by the light of a campfire, with yells and whiplashes, the Turks were obliging the people to hand over their last remaining valuables. When money was found, coins and jewels were set out on a rug and shared amongst the Turks. Zareh, Mariam and their daughters waited, shivering with fear, for the moment when they were to be inspected. Araksi felt panic overwhelming her. She tightly held Vartuhi's hand. Suddenly, the Turks began shouting and laughing with satisfaction. They were celebrating the find of a good quantity of jewels among some old people's clothes. Incredulous, they realized the great value of the gold coins and jewels they had discovered. Snatching away the booty, they struggled amongst themselves for a while and forgot everything else.

Araksi, Mavush and Vartuhi remained motionless next to their parents. The glow of the torches allowed them to see the silhouettes of the officers beating and stripping the unfortunates, until they moved away, satisfied with their haul.

Zareh breathed with relief. The women broke into tears of real panic, feeling the enormous powerlessness of their position and not being able to understand it. Mavush was terrified. Mariam vainly tried to comfort her. She could hardly say a word.

"I can't stand this hell any longer, Mamma... I can't go on... My strength's going and I can't find any reason to go on living. It's better to die soon," said the young woman, full of nerves.

"No, my sweet, no. Now is the time to show your faith in front of your children. This is a trial God is asking of us

147

and He will not abandon us. Let's pray together. Children, come! Let's turn this suffering into a prayer. This horror will pass by and we'll all go back home. You'll soon see, my dears."

Araksi tenderly caressed the little ones on Mavush's and Vartuhi's laps. They held hands and Zareh, with half-closed eyes, began praying aloud. "My God, hearken unto my cry, attend my supplication. I invoke Thee from the ends of the earth with a heavy heart. Take me to an inaccessible rock, for Thou art my refuge and fortress against the enemy..."

The train of carts was advancing along a narrow mountain trail, so narrow that the oxen could barely get by. The way soon narrowed down to a path that only allowed them to go in single file. Being unable to advance further, the Turkish drivers let go of the reins and began arguing with Araksi and her sisters. Zareh, much enfeebled, had entrusted his care to his daughters. The heated discussion continued until the drivers stopped their beasts and placed the carts across the pathway, demanding more money to continue providing transport.

Several zaptiehs came up, attracted by the carters' outrageous protests. Without the slightest remorse for their abandonment, the Turks unloaded the family's wagons, transferring only a few of the pieces of luggage onto the already heavily-laden donkeys. Immediately, they shook Zareh, frisking him and demanding more payment. Weakened and defenseless, he handed over without protest the last handful of gold coins, vital to purchase water and food.

Stark desolation lay ahead.

The Turkish drivers that had carried their belongings from Erzurum were leaving them to their fate. He and his daughters were incapable of carrying anything themselves. The carters about-faced, making the oxen go backwards, maneuvering in the narrow space between the abyss and the multitude, ignoring all claims or entreaties. Fearsome chasms opened out from that point on.

The officers hurried the winding human column

forward, obliging the people to climb, oblivious to the sorry state of those wretches that dragged themselves forward like automata.

Elders, women and children all carried on forward, indifferent to others that had fallen on the way. They even remained immutable to the animals loaded beyond all tolerable limits, which were falling down the precipices. Several mules lay on the floor of the chasm, still laden with all their load.

The ascent was continued on foot. The children and Mariam rode on two donkeys. Zareh, who could hardly negotiate the incline, had seemingly aged fifteen years in the last few days, and fatigue was about to defeat him. Every so often he fell back, leant on the rocks, agitated, breathless from the height and the tragedy, until he finally lay at the roadside. The multitude passed him by, slowly climbing. Araksi and Mavush walked ahead, dragging themselves, their garments in tatters, faces covered in dust and sweat, faint from the height and fatigue. The guards, ever behind them, would not allow the least delay. The caravan was an endless column of people that extended several miles over the mountain.

Mariam looked back and saw her husband left behind, lying to one side. She told Vartuhi several times to stop the donkey until the young woman helped her mother-in-law dismount and was unable to restrain her from going back to where Zareh lay in total exhaustion. When Mariam reached him, she knelt and embraced him lovingly.

A short distance away, the Turkish guards were shaking their whips and clubbing the stragglers in the ascent. On the wind, Araksi heard Vartuhi's desperate cries, asking her sisters-in-law for help with the older couple.

No one made room for them to pass back. Zareh and Mariam, hand in hand, knelt against the rock. Even in the dust cloud and pushed on by the caravan, they were able to see their family fading ever further away. In vain were the women's shouts and pleas to get back to where their parents were.

The two parents, invoking heaven in the same prayer,

watched their daughters and grandchildren disappearing amid the multitude round the next bend in the mountain.

"Farewell, dear children. May Jesus keep you... I shall forever inhabit in Thy dwelling, sheltered under Thy wings, for Thou, O God, shalt hearken unto my desires and shalt give me the heritance of them that worship Thy name..."

Araksi and Mavush, terrified, had time to notice how the guards, armed with sticks and rifles, were hurrying stragglers on. The wind muted their yells, rendering vain any entreaty. Their parents prayed in an embrace. When the guards came abreast of them they did not hesitate. They attacked with violence, giving them a number of blows. Then they plunged their bayonets into their bodies and immediately rifled through their clothing for anything of value. The deportees marched past the couple, who had been murdered before their eyes, with the indifference of exhaustion.

Araksi and Mavush cried in despair, hugging the children tightly, in pieces at what they had witnessed. The pain of seeing their parents die was heartbreaking, only made worse by their powerlessness in trying to go back against the crowds of people. In vain they tried to make way, but the turn in the road and the quantity of people pushing them prevented them forever from returning to Zareh's and Mariam's outstretched bodies.

CHAPTER XXV

OMER NADJI BEY AND

GETTING READY FOR THE CAMPAIGN

MAX ARRIVED AT HIS OFFICE. Omer Nadji Bey waited for him there, wearing a closed, tight-fitting suit as befitted the Chechen custom. His sword hung from a belt hitched up on his right shoulder. He wore a black lambskin cap on his head, which he kept on until Max entered the office and, taking it off, he stood up. They shook hands. Both spoke French with ease.

"Good day to you, Lieutenant. How are you?" Omer Nadji asked with a smile.

"Your accent is impeccable, Omer Nadji. Is that a throwback from your Parisian exile?"

The Chechen smiled and, accepting the seat Max indicated, sat down with elegance.

"I am a Caucasian from Chechnya... a Frenchified one," added Omer Nadji with refined humor.

"And responsible for initiating Enver and Talaat Pashas in the Union and Progress party... No mean feat," said Max, adding, "And your influence in the highest of Turkish affairs is undeniable. At least that is what is rumored in the uppermost spheres. I trust I am committing no indiscretion by mentioning it?"

Omer Nadji smiled modestly by way of all reply.

"The truth is we will need all the support of your government for our Daghestan campaign... Can I count on you for resources, Omer Nadji?"

The Chechen was looking straight at him. "I'm convinced that Turkish-German cooperation is indispensable for any military operation in the Caucasus, Swirsden-Righe. Don't worry," he assured Max. "We will ask the Supreme Command for everything necessary."

Max nodded in approbation as he offered the other a glass of brandy. The Chechen, after taking a sip, continued. "What have you in mind, an infantry battalion... a cavalry regiment? We could add a corps of Kurdish horsemen... Would that be enough?"

Max was watching him with enthusiasm. The offer surpassed all his expectations. There was no doubt he and Omer Nadji were going to get on well.

"Excellent! More than enough. It's going to be a hard campaign, but with well-equipped cavalry we will win over the Caucasian tribes as we go deeper into the territory." All at once Max changed his tone. "There is, however, one more thing I'd like to ask of you, Omer Nadji."

"What else do you require?"

"I should like to share the command with you, while at the same time not lose my condition as an officer of the German army. Is that possible?"

Omer Nadji looked at the other: this man no doubt made good of his opportunities, confirming what the German military reports included in this Swirsden-Righe's service record. They were certainly not off-track in granting him shrewdness. Omer Nadji swilled round the cognac glass for a few seconds. He was accustomed to giving orders and conquering wills. Despite having been born Chechen and not Turkish, he had risen to the highest pinnacles of power in Turkey's ruling party. Was it convenient to make a place for Swirsden-Righe in the command? Every structure in Turkey yielded to his political sway, but the German officer could be helpful to him during the campaign. Experience had taught him that incorporating people's enthusiasm into difficult missions paid good dividends.

Finally Omer Nadji gave his answer. "Are you aware that whatever officers pass over to our Turkish army lines do so enjoying a higher rank than in the German army?"

"I am... but to me that's a matter of indifference, Sir. I should like to retain my uniform."

"So be it, then. Though it is not usual, you shall be the exception. No one else commands troops in any other uniform than that of the Turkish army."

The two raised their glasses to the agreement. "*À votre santé*," toasted Max, glad at his achievement.

SEATED FACING MAX in the spacious consulate lounge, Rolf, Friedrich and Lieutenant Thiele went over reports and consulted one another about the meaning of certain Turkish words they had recently learnt. Max laughed at his compatriots' lack of linguistic prowess. Hung on a wall was a large map of the Caucasian frontier region, the limit with the Persian border and the extensive Russian one. Names of rivers, mountain passes and villages lost to Caucasian tribes dominated the conversation.

"Don't try it again, please," Max entreated the brothers. "Give my ears a rest. I've never known such little gift for languages, Rolf... And don't you laugh, Friedrich, because you're even worse. God deliver us from having to resort to this hideous gibberish in an emergency... Well, let's get down to business." Max stood and pointed to the map. "This is the line held by Prince Nikolai Nikolaevich, an uncle to the Czar, the new viceroy, and supreme commander of the Caucasus Army in Tiflis. Can you see?"

The officers paid close attention. Max went on. "The Cossacks and Russian officers must surely get their supplies from local resources. Evidently, they have no need of transporting equipment as we do. They have it stocked in each little town along the border. Unburdened in this way, it will be easy for them to advance against our expedition. Gentlemen, that means we must carry clothing for every climate of the most extreme kind: high temperatures in the deserts and snow in the mountains. Tents, mess-ware, rations... down to the last element needed to survive among rivers, plains, mountain passes, do you understand?"

The young officers were listening to Max closely. No one was smiling now.

Lieutenant Thiele interposed enthusiastically, "So the enemy must be destabilized on the inner front?"

"Exactly, Thiele," replied Max. "Our mission, gentlemen, is to penetrate Persia and take a few towns... On the way we will create uprisings against the Russians amongst the Muslim tribes — Daghestanis, the Kurdish leaders, and, of course, the Persians themselves. We will divide our forces. One branch of the expedition will be

153

under the command of Lieutenant-Colonel von der Schulenburg, and will march on Georgia, in the North. The Lieutenant-Colonel will be the overall commander of the campaign. You," he looked at each of them, "will be under my orders and those of Omer Nadji Bey, the political chief of the Turkish Government. On parts of the way we will be using the same route taken by Alexander the Great 23 centuries ago, following the course of the River Tigris as far as Mosul." Max marked the point on the map then added, "Mosul, the general base of the German Empire, on the frontier. From there, we will advance onward with all the participating forces."

The young men looked at the route without hiding their fascination at travelling through territories the great conquerors of the Ancient World had used as the stage for their exploits, campaigns written in the annals of the military history of mankind. They were to share the campaign with Caucasian warriors. The majority, as far as they had been able to ascertain, were more like soldiers of the Middle Ages than the 20th century.

Max continued. "Beyond the desert the mountains of Persia, the Cossacks, and winters 30° below zero, with snows up to the horses' necks, await us. Afterwards, provided we manage to overcome these minor obstacles," he said with a certain sarcasm, "if we can deal with the climate, only then will the battle begin in earnest for the occupation of Sautchbulak — here, you see, in this little valley, stuck amidst the mountains, is the village."

The three got closer to see the dot on the map. Among mountain peaks could be read 'Sautchbulak'.

Max observed his companions' reaction to what seemed a small, lost object - one might even doubt that taking it merited such a huge effort.

"Don't be deceived, gentlemen. This little village between the high mountains and the Russian frontier is the center-piece of the Turko-Russo-Persian front, and it will define the advance of our army. If we succeed we'll be able to get into Russia, reach the Baku oilfields, and take possession of the pipelines of the Caspian Sea. If the Cossacks defeat us, the Russians will find the way open through Persia to link up with the British against us. If it came to that, we should have no more chances open to us on the Eastern front. His Imperial Majesty's designs will then have been set at nought. Our country requires this mission, gentlemen. If we fail, Germany fails."

The young officers looked at one another, understanding the gravity of the struggle they were about to embark on.

CHAPTER XXVI

THE KURDISH VILLAGE IN KURDISTAN

A RAY OF SUNSHINE FILTERED into the woodshed where the fugitives were sleeping. Exhausted, they lay on sacks and damp straw. Diran was the first to awake. The place smelt of dung and dampness. What he saw further on, first of all, in a corner, was the other fugitive. The light that squeezed though the boards allowed him to assess his bearded, lean, scruffy-looking compatriot.

Who knows what he's had to go through, thought Diran — *well, the same as us... no more, no less.* He cautiously approached and the 25-year-old woke up with a start.

"Don't be afraid... I'm Diran, I'm from Erzurum... Actually, I was born in Russia but on my parents' death I was left to some relatives' care... my real family. They brought me up."

"My name's Agop, from Erzindjan. I escaped from a caravan. I got down under corpses and waited there."

Diran smiled bitterly: they shared the same fortune. Agop understood without needing further explanation. The other two companions, just awake, were listening with caution.

"Agop," repeated the stranger, pointing at himself. They spoke almost in whispers. "It looks like you all survived the same caravan as I did."

"It was as God willed it. The dead protected us. What did you do previously, and where are you going now?" Manuc asked drily and with mistrust.

"I'd just got back to Erzindjan from France, to visit my parents. I was studying economics in Paris. Now I want to get to Russia — where else? There's no one left alive in my town."

The other three eyed him with unease. Diran carried on in French so as to verify the truth of his tale. "We'll be joining the Armenian combatants. We're also going to the frontier."

"We must study the movement of this village. Let's not

waste any time," answered Agop in fluent French, and Manuc and Diran were persuaded that they should all remain together and leave the village as soon as possible, before they were discovered.

Giorgi, who was keeping watch, asked, "Where the hell are we?"

"Wherever we are, we're in danger. The Vali have all decreed that whoever shelters a Christian is to be hanged outside his own house. That discourages any gesture of kindness towards fugitives," answered Manuc.

Agop cut in. "Don't worry. The Kurds of this village are peaceful, and are proud of offering the hospitality of a good Muslim — or we'd all be dead by now. Not only the herdsman and his wife saw me arrive. Still, there are other kinds of more ferocious Kurdish bands all over the countryside, and they could appear here any moment. We've got to be careful."

The storeroom also housed some chickens. The men helped themselves to some eggs, eating them raw. No one spoke.

Diran, wiping his hands on the hay, broke the silence, "In jail I heard that the Kurds, encouraged by the Turks, fall on the caravans as soon as they enter the forests. They murder, and kidnap women and children with indescribable savagery. I wonder what'll have happened to my people."

Manuc comforted him with a pat and all kept silent, overwhelmed by a great melancholy. The sun was beginning to rise. They carefully left their hiding place. Mountains and forests extended into the distance. The village, in a forest clearing, a tiny speck amid that sea of plants.

Further along, the herdsmen led their goats with the help of their dogs. The old Kurd appeared with loaves of bread and milk, his wife behind him. They gave the lads woollen jackets and baggy, rustic trousers, a rig-out that would disguise them a little. The wife made signs for them to take off their dirty, bloodstained clothes. The bonfire quickly dealt with those traces of Armenian blood tragically shed on the banks of the Tigris.

After thanking the villagers for the change of garments, Diran walked a few paces away. He remained alone for a good while. He walked a bit closer to the slope, stopped there and, awe-struck at the immensity surrounding him, looked with misgiving at the enormous wooded extension of Kurdistan.

The herdsman came up behind and touched his shoulder. Diran turned. The old man had a clear, honest look, it seemed the only one Diran had seen in months. The goatherd was inarticulate in his rudimentary Turkish, but expressed a wish universally understood among people.

"Allah will protect you."

Diran's eyes moistened. Then the old man, leaning on his crook, drove the herd downhill as he was used to doing every day, along the path. The dogs pranced around; frisky and watchful, making sure none of the goats strayed away.

CHAPTER XXVII

THE HORDE

ARAKSI PLODDED ON, pierced with grief, but boredom and exhaustion lulled her mind. All those that had survived up to that point of the trek made up an immense file of ragged, starving wraiths. Some fell down dead along the way. Mavush and Vartuhi led the donkeys on which the children rode. Araksi's face, like those of her sisters, was blanketed with dust, agreeable features unrecognizable beneath the crust.

The guards continued cracking their whips overhead to emphasize their orders. At a certain point on the road, they held up the caravan. A Turkish officer rode up and from some distance had a good look at the women. Then he rode away. Everyone took the opportunity to rest. Araksi was too weary to perceive any reason for alarm: she was hard put to keep her instincts alert, what with minding the children and keeping her sisters close by. A copse of trees could be seen not far from the road. The mountain made way in particular areas for woods that descended several meters, alternating with huge boulders and steep precipices.

Araksi, delirious with thirst, bent down to drink water from the canister. Her feet were a mass of sores and her jet-black hair a tousled mass covered by a kerchief that gave little protection from the sun. She sat on a rock, and as she shared water with Mavush and Vartuhi, the reflection of the light blinded her.

All of a sudden, a noise from the copse thundered upon the land. A band of a hundred Kurdish riders, at full tilt and brandishing long knives, fell among them. The first to break into the caravan dragged away the women, who vainly tried to resist. The Kurds ripped their shreds off, revealing the age and appearance of each of them. Cries of despair were heard everywhere. Naked, panic-stricken girls fell to the ground, while others dragged themselves away only to be decapitated a few feet further on. Some men began raping the youngest of them, separating them from the main group and violating them on rocks or on the ground. The elders, men and women, who vainly tried to defend their daughters and granddaughters, were mercilessly knifed down at the roadside. Mavush and Vartuhi soon found themselves surrounded by a group of fierce Kurds wearing tall, white fur hats. As they were raped, their children, hiding behind a rock, covered their eyes in a state of utter anguish.

Araksi remained hidden next to her nephews and nieces. The Kurds had not noticed her. She hugged the children and folded them in the pleats of her skirt.

The succession of fierce outrages that in minutes had shattered the lives of dozens of young women, as if the very demons of hell had fallen upon the totally defenseless innocents, suddenly ceased.

A chieftain on horseback, accompanied by several officers, arrived at full gallop up to the mob. He yelled orders, preventing the rapes from continuing.

Then the looks of all the Kurds fell upon Araksi. Going straight to her and pinioning her arms, they roughly separated her from the children, and did the same with some other girls hiding among the rocks. The Kurdish chieftain looked meaningfully at Araksi. The captors kept a terrifying silence. Then, giving instructions in his dialect, he took up position in front of her, observing her from every angle.

One of the men came up to her and, dashing a bucketful of water in her face, immediately dislodged the dust and mud covering it, revealing her true beauty.

Amazed at the discovery, the chiefs separated Araksi from the rest, preventing the other men from touching her: it seemed they wanted to keep her in reserve, together with a group of other pretty girls. Araksi remained silent. She was sick with fear, but offered no resistance. Her mind was busy thinking of the children and her sisters, lying by the wayside, perhaps dead or dying.

All at once, Araksi was led to the copse, where the Kurdish horsemen kept their horses tethered, ready to ride off as soon as the price was agreed with the Turkish officers for the batch of virgins.

There, under the trees, the sale of the young women began. The Kurdish chief, after haggling over each of them — 20 all together — handed over the value in gold of all of them to the Turkish officers.

Araksi was roughly pawed over, as they came upon a few gold coins hidden in the most intimate parts of her clothing. The chief yelled in Kurdish, forbidding anyone to touch her face or mark her with lashes. Then, the same as the other 19, she had her wrists tied and was placed on a saddle, behind one of the kidnapping horsemen.

Vartuhi had died. Araksi managed to discern her stretched out on a rock in the distance. Next to her, her children were crying disconsolately. Then she looked a few feet further on along the road and saw Mavush, injured and bleeding. She had survived the rapes. Her beloved elder sister was regaining consciousness. The children surrounded her, impotent and torn apart with grief and unprotectedness.

Araksi murmured, drenched in tears, "Oh, my God, my God, take me as well, but I beseech you, protect the children, Mother of Jesus. What'll become of them?" She wept bitterly.

One of the children pointed at the copse, at the captive girls. The band of Kurds was preparing to leave. The white fur hats waggled with the horses' prancing. The men shouted, sated with violence, while the Turkish officers counted the gold pieces, satisfied at the treasure they had discovered.

Araksi, with her hands tied behind her, had time to look at the caravan for the last time. The figures of Mavush and the children receded into the distance. The images accelerated as the horse galloped faster, until they became a blur. The horses headed into the woods and she soon bowed her head, faint with the motion.

The Kurdish band galloped full out with the captives on their saddles. Then they passed through another wood and yet another, without stopping. Finally, it grew dark.

After several hours' ride, the horde stopped in a forest

clearing. They pulled the Armenian girls off the saddles. The girls could hardly stand after such an infernal shaking. Araksi and the others kept totally silent.

The chieftain gave orders and cracked his whip over the girls' heads. The place was a meadow in the middle of a forest. They tied the girls' feet to the horses' necks, so that they faced each other in double file and face-down.

Araksi wept silently. The Kurds huddled round a campfire to eat and drink. Night fell fully, and sleep overcame her.

When morning came and the Kurds approached the captives, Araksi, with her face looking at the ground and unable to raise her head, could only see the men's boots as they moved back and forth among the horses. No one touched the women. It was clear that they were meant to be delivered to more important people. The prospect terrified her. She refused to accept such a tragedy. The memory of her parents being murdered in front of her, the rape of her sisters by some of those men that walked around her, wrenched her soul to the point of wishing to die at every moment.

She saw the desperate faces of her companions in distress. Some showed resignation, but most of them could hardly stand the horrible nightmare which fate had brought upon them: they were slaves.

Mid-day came. The Kurds came to the young women and untied them, allowing them to stand for a few minutes. Araksi, numbed, could hardly move. The girls were given plenty of water and bread to eat.

Araksi drank with desperation, feeling her body revive, but almost at once the Kurds made ready to leave and all the captives once more had their wrists tied behind them and were sat on the horses. This time, the horse on which she was taken had a smoother stride, or maybe she had been able to get better used to the rider. The Kurd wordlessly led his mount along hidden pathways amid the thickets.

The cavalcade crossed the forests and then entered the plain. Araksi felt as though every step her captors covered was forever taking her away from everything she had known. Fate was swallowing her up for being who she was in a place and moment of history in which the innocent were guilty for being Armenian, to the point of no longer being entitled to their own lives.

CHAPTER XXVIII

THE DEPARTURE

THE MOMENT HAD ARRIVED to leave for the Caucasus. The war preparations for the campaign commanded by Omer Nadji Bey and Max von Swirsden-Righe had been carried out and it was now time to march against the enemy. The regimental band played military marches as the squadrons went, taking up position in front of the Commandancy building.

Turkish and German flags, held by the troops' standards, waved in the wind. The regiment of 500 infantry troops and 30 Kurdish horsemen were lined up at the front. Behind them could be seen the ox-wagon corps. The men carried ammunition boxes, hitched up cannon, and dismantled machine guns, all of them last minute adjustments for which the Volga prisoners were responsible; those Germans from Russia brought to Turkey by Lieutenant-Colonel von der Schulenburg to render service.

Max, about to mount Pasha, was bidding his superiors farewell: Taksim Bey, next to him, shook hands with the Turkish chiefs and the German Commander, Lieutenant-Colonel Guse.

Rolf and Friedrich, at the head of their respective cavalry squadrons, did not hide the fascination they felt at leading those Oriental troops. They gave orders using rudimentary Turkish vocabulary they barely managed. The Germans' excitement was plainly visible at the sight offered by the multi-coloured uniforms of the Kurdish and Daghestani divisions. They were aware of the privilege of being the first Europeans to visit regions almost never previously travelled by Westerners.

The Kurdish cavalry men rode spectacular Arab horses. Dappled and dusky chestnuts impatiently champed at their bits. All the infantry units awaited the order to march. Lieutenant Thiele took his place at the head of one of the units, and the Turkish interpreter, Memdukh, never left Max's side, as though he were an extension of his boss. He translated orders from German and French into Turkish and Kurdish and even struck up conversations in Russian and Daghestani dialects with awe-inspiring fluency.

When Omer Nadji and Max presented arms for the national anthems, Max felt he had achieved his purpose: he was commanding troops. He had arrived in Turkey a few months earlier as a simple reserve lieutenant of the Kaiser's imperial army and, in comparing his low rank with that of any other similar officer on the Western Front, he would never have headed an expedition escorted by the warriors of millenary tribes. What more could he wish for than a triumphal return and Germany's recognition of glory as a reward?

Finally, the column moved forward. Max observed Omer Nadji Bey, who rode next to him in his Chechen warrior garb with its tall, black goatskin hat and sword hanging from a bandolier: he rode blithely forth, deep in thought of high politics and the innumerable matters to be sorted out before getting to the battleground at Sautchbulak, the tiny village inserted amid the mountains, probably occupied by the Czar of Russia's Cossack cavalry.

CHAPTER XXIX

MAVUSH

Mavush trudged on very slowly, or rather dragged herself along, carrying her youngest child in her arms. She moved in obedience to the guards and at the limits of her strength, together with a handful of survivors. These women were the remnants of the 300 families that had left Erzurum and who, surviving the trek through the mountains and the attacks of Kurdish bandits, resisted death, fighting against the abuses of the officers, the scorching sun, and total lack of water, for the Turkish guards provided them nothing to drink.

Little by little they went falling by the roadside as they crossed deserts on the way to Deir-ez-Zor. The children were dressed in rags: her children, two boys and a girl, and Vartuhi's two surviving boys, kept apace of Mavush like sleepwalkers, thirsty and faint, hanging on to her tattered skirts so as not to be left behind. The skin of their faces was covered with sores from sunburn and they were almost barefoot.

They were nearing a Turkish village in the desert. Daylight reverberated intensely, so that the population some distance away seemed like a mirage to Mavush.

The inhabitants of the settlement, on seeing the Armenians arrive, lined up on each side of the column of survivors, in yet another macabre reception such as had become customary, ready to offer a few sips of water in exchange for all the money they could get out of the dying, as always with the complicity of the officers.

On seeing the well, the deportees lunged forward with shouts of desperation. The first of the women and elders to reach the watering place struggled and pushed each other to get something to drink. With their numb tongues and mouths they tried to sip the drops the Turkish guards ruthlessly spilt as they quenched their thirst from the buckets.

The women knelt, fighting each other. They desperately

166

sucked the Turks' wet clothing. Such was their thirst. The soldiers dipped the pail into the well time and again to pull up more water and drink more, warding off the women with shoves and lashes.

Mavush, unable to break through the crowd of Armenians, moved away from the well on the point of fainting, and then saw some village women, beyond the tumult round the well, who came out of their houses carrying pails full of water. She ran to them and, with the last gold coin she possessed, bought one from them. She immediately gave the children water. The little ones fell on the pail, trying to quench their thirst.

Mavush, in a near faint, looked at the desert around them, the Turkish village, and the sorry human remnants the best-educated Armenians in the vilayet had been reduced to in weeks of forced marching. From the settlement, a group of men and women approached them in an attitude of curiosity amid the swirling dust that enveloped everything. Mavush felt a pang of terror. The Turkish women fixed their gaze on her children and nephews, murmuring among themselves. They were five children. Though in rags and covered with grime, below their forlorn aspect the delicacy of their faces was still evident.

Mavush made them hold tight to her skirts. Her eldest son was five years old, the same as one of his cousins. The girl began to cry in despair at finding herself surrounded by villagers. The women came forward and examined the children's mouths and bodies for wounds or diseases. Then they caught them by the shoulders to draw them away. Mavush struggled against the women, until an old woman shouted, "Woman, let thy children live. Leave them here. They will work with the families, and will be fed and brought up by us. That is a better fate than dying in the desert. Woman... have none of you understood that none of you will get to Deir-ez-Zor alive?"

Mavush fought desperately. With her scant remaining strength she struggled against the ever-increasing tugs of the women that were trying to take the children away, balancing herself as she held the youngest child, barely a year old, who showed evidence of dehydration, while attempting to keep the women at bay with her free arm. The officers came up to the tumult and, overpowering Mavush, dragged the children away to hand them over to the villagers.

Mavush wept in her distraction. She still held the youngest. Overcome by her impotence, she was forced to return to the line at bayonet-point. With the remaining survivors, mute at the horror of having had the children taken from her, she carried on marching, hopelessly leaving two of her children and her two nephews behind.

The children were forbidden to look back at where Mavush had remained. The old Turkish women quickly ran off towards the houses, carrying the youngest children.

The children cried for their mother. They vainly tried, in their childish weakness, to escape from their captors. The Armenian women walking together with Mavush looked on helplessly, suffering, torn apart, in silence, as though what had happened to Mavush had been their own experience.

CHAPTER XXX

CAPTIVE

THE KURDS HAD NOT REDUCED the speed of their cavalcade. They stopped only to sleep and feed the 20 Armenian girls. When the rider carrying Araksi finally pulled up, she saw that they were approaching a tiny village on the plain, and that further on there was a town among the mountains. It was not long before they reached the suburbs of white houses built in a mixture of Turkish and Arab styles. The populace, on seeing their arrival, ran to the entrance of the town. The Turkish and Arab villagers mocked the women captured by the Kurds.

The band of captors stopped in a large stable for dromedaries and camels, where the Kurds took their captives off the horses and pushed them inside under the steady scrutiny of the Turkish merchants, who avidly examined them, ready to bid for those they found most worthwhile.

One of the merchants set his sights on Araksi more than any of the others. Without delay, he asked the Kurdish chief to set her and another two girls apart from the main group. Araksi, still dizzy, and with her wrists yet tied, in pain and with sores from the straps after several days' hard riding, kept her eyes lowered. With difficulty they advanced to a sector of the enormous stable. The gates were shut behind them. Daylight filtered in through the roof, where an open space allowed ventilation and a certain clarity into the place. The floor was covered with camel dung.

"They're going to sell us for prostitution, but if we're lucky we'll end up in a harem. That's why they've separated us from the others," said one of the girls, the first time in weeks that they had exchanged words amongst themselves.

"A harem?" Araksi was shocked.

They quickly broke off the dialogue. One of the Kurds entered the shed, and with rough movements untied the three girls' hands. He pointed at the food and water he was leaving them. Then he exited, shutting the great door behind him.

The girls fell upon the meal, consisting of lamb stew, potatoes and water. Then tiredness and sleep overcame them.

ARAKSI WOKE UP WITH A START. A hand was on her shoulder, shaking her. A few hours had gone by and the place was in semi-darkness. One of her fellow captives was warning her of the approach of men to the stable.

The noise of soldiers and the voices outside increased the girls' anxiety. Araksi and her companions embraced in terror when the gate opened. The group of Turks seemed to be led by a high-ranking individual, a hadji dressed in the traditional fashion of the Ottoman Empire. The hadji placed himself in front of the girls and, after some minutes of protracted observation, ordered the girls' dresses to be lifted in order to reveal their bodies. The men parted the girls' clothes and three of them stripped Araksi. The hadji judged her proportions perfect, his lecherous look intimidating her. Araksi trembled, her eyes on the ground. After a few seconds they covered the girls again and took them out of the stable.

Everything happened as in a succession of unreal, inexplicable scenes which Araksi refused to accept as reality. Her giddily experienced, adverse fate seemed nightmarish, a bad dream that was only too real, but at some moment must come to an end. She would wake up at home, in Erzurum, embracing her parents, her beloved brothers and sisters... Diran.

Where were they all? Was she not actually dead and being led down to who knew what hell? Indeed, what difference was there between the underworld and the horrors she had to live through at every turn? Cast to the will of malignant beings, reduced to the lowest degradation a human could descend to, thought Araksi in her hopelessness, as the three were made to get onto an open cart driven by the Turkish soldiers guarding the chosen captives' journey into the city.

The transactions between merchants and Turks went on in the stable crowded with buyers, while Araksi and the others shed silent tears on separating from the other kidnapped girls, subservient to new masters at an unknown destination.

CHAPTER XXXI

THE MOUNTAINS OF THE CAUCASUS

THEY CHATTED AS THEY LAY ON THE PASTURELAND, looking at the forests that extended as far as the eye could see. The morning was bright. Agop was listening to Diran's narrative as he chewed wild grass while trying to count how many goats there were in the scattered herd - little black specks moving peacefully as they grazed among the hills.

"All my people have left me, Agop. They've all gone to the other world... I've had to get used to this, ever since I was a child. My parents and siblings died in 1895, in Abdul Hamid's massacres. And now... the worst blow of all... Araksi was her name, of such loveliness as I'll never find again in my whole life in any woman. We were going to get married as soon as I landed a post at the tribunals in Constantinople, maybe in the Parliament... We didn't want to stay in Erzurum. Araksi wanted to see the world..." Moved, Diran interrupted his own story with a bitter laugh then went on. "It's useless to carry on reminiscing... We can't unwind time."

"It's roughly the same story for several of us," interposed Agop, making signs to carry on.

Diran calmed down. "No Armenian will ever again be able to live in Erzurum... We'll probably never meet again. Who knows what's happened to her... The only thing that keeps me going is the struggle for the fatherland. It's all that keeps me alive. My dignity as an Armenian is pledged to this. I swear it by what's most sacred to me, by the memory of my parents and my siblings." He began to weep. "One day the laws of the world will enforce the review and punishment of the crimes committed by governments against the citizens of their own countries, and the judges will represent mankind, not one flag or another, but just individuals, just human beings."

Agop cast the handful of grass in the air, watching the wind scatter it as he prepared to answer his companion.

"That's a useless way of speaking. No one'll listen to you... You're an idealist, Diran. Fight to defend ourselves; kill the enemy — that's all we downtrodden people need to think about. Don't expect any recognition of rights from the Turks or any other empire or country at all. We've lost too much time, and too many men of combat age who were unable to understand the call to arms at the right moment. That's the only question. Now they're all corpses, heaped up like dead rats on the banks of the Tigris and along the streets of the vilayets."

Manuc and Giorgi came up to the edge of the slope, looking worried and interrupting the conversation.

"The Russians are advancing and the Kurds are raising the alarm in the villages. Let's not put the old herdsman and his wife in danger any longer. We must leave as soon as possible," said Manuc animatedly.

"Let's see if the old man has any weapons. We could well do with one," ventured Giorgi.

THEY ATE IN SILENCE, next to the old couple. Giorgi kept looking at the knife on top of the cupboard, his gaze relentlessly returning to it. The old Kurd finished his last spoonful of stew and, laying the spoon on the table, looked fixedly at the lads. Then he handed the empty mug to his wife, who was clearing the table. Diran stood and gave her a hand with the washing up. She was a little surprised by his gesture, but accepted. Through the mild expressiveness of her sunburnt eyes and her wrinkled complexion she seemed flattered.

The lads came out of the cabin and, on looking up, saw that the clouds were blowing away across the night sky. The bright full moon was beckoning them to depart the village forthwith.

The old couple offered them food for the journey. They wrapped up some cheese and eggs, and a canteen of water. All this went on wordlessly. They were moved by the old people's generosity.

The couple blessed each of the men and shook their hands a little shyly. The old man went back into the cabin and immediately returned with the knife. Looking at them fondly, he handed it to Giorgi and said a few words in Kurdish.

There was deep feeling in everyone's eyes, which sufficed for a farewell. Turning tail, the four fugitives took the path leading down from the hill. The moon shone brightly upon the way, which made their descent easier. Not long after, Diran and his companions were once more on the long road to the frontier, rapidly vanishing into the thick, Caucasian woods.

THE VANGUARD OF RIDERS were far in front of the remaining troops so they could get to know the land. Somewhat behind, Max and Omer Nadji moved forward at a gallop through the rift in the deep valley. There was still enough daylight to make out the horizon. Below, shadows covered the hollows.

Occasional Kurdish wagons and herds of black sheep crossed the roadway. The riders in the vanguard held up to await the rest of the army. They were about to cross a stone bridge over the Murad Su.

Luggage and military implements swayed on the pack-horses and mules. The animals were laden with victuals, tents, collapsible cookers, and everything necessary for the provision of the expedition which was now entering the depths of Kurdistan.

Friedrich and Rolf brought up the rear, keeping an eye on maneuvers across the stone bridge. Max came and went up and down the whole formation. He brought Pasha to a halt on seeing Memdukh approach at a gallop, looking for him from the advance detail.

"Sir?"

"Yes, Memdukh. What news?"

"The Kurds say there could be Armenian guerrillas in the area," the Turk warned, pulling in the horse's reins. The animal's mouth was frothing.

Max looked up. They were at the bottom of the deepest part of the hollow. Thick woods climbed at each side of the road.

"If anyone attacks us now, this is the ideal spot to catch us with our pants down," observed Max. He moved his horse aside, alerting the various mounted scouts by pointing upwards. Then he gave the order for them to go forward. The Kurdish officers obeyed at once. Aware of the new formation, they opened up the way at walking pace.

On the hillsides along the pass, the afternoon sunshine shone weirdly golden and the men went forward in silence. All that was heard was the tinkle of harnesses and straps, then the neigh of their own horses. They were entering the depths, wary of the shadows that could render invisible any guerrilla lurking among the woods. They covered the initial stretches. Further on, the canyon narrowed and became covered with vegetation. Max looked at Omer Nadji. The Chechen looked serious, his head held high and pistol in hand, ready to deter any attack.

The young German lieutenants disregarded the tension of that moment, but to go through that canyon called for nerves of steel. It might be their baptism of fire in that unknown and dangerous Asiatic land. As they went, getting closer to the Russian enemy and the frontier line, the possibility of meeting some advance detail of sharp-shooters increased.

Max thought of the quandary this war meant: he had stood up for the Armenians of Erzurum, but that personal position towards the civilian population naturally contradicted the mission of combatting the Russians or any ally that embarked on hostilities against his expedition.

The crossing went off without incident. There were no shots or ambushes or indeed any trace of the Armenian guerrillas operating in the forests. It had been a false alarm. The military column continued marching until sundown. Fires had been placed along the whole length of the camp. Hundreds of white tents rose next to each other, covering a wide area.

The night was hot and officers and soldiers were in shirt sleeves. The men had eaten and kept themselves cheerful around the campfires, chatting and laughing loudly at the typical jests of soldiery. From time to time the strains of a Turkish mandolin were heard, and a chorus of voices joining in, singing songs of the land.

Max felt content. At last he had been able to give up his office work in Erzurum. He enjoyed walking up and down the camp, observing the men that made up his little army. He came up to Rolf's tent. Candles shone cheerfully and projected on the canvas the silhouette of his companion, engaged in writing upon a small table next to his campbed.

On seeing him appear, Rolf stopped writing and crossed his legs. He offered Max a chair he had beside him. Out of the corner of his eye, Max looked at the notebook, intrigued by his comrade's annotations, but he did not inquire into it.

Rolf took the lead: "It's a campaign diary, Max. I've decided to take notes on this adventure. Someone has to be the chronicler, don't you think? Who knows, maybe this expedition will go down in military history, just like the battles of Alexander the Great, Caesar, Hannibal, Scipio."

Max smiled.

"Our compatriots will remember us every time they read these chronicles. Maybe in a hundred years' time there will still be people interested in our adventures among the Turks and Kurds. Sautchbulak. The battle of Sautchbulak. Maybe they'll study it at military academies. Eh, Max, what do you think? You'll be engraved in bronze."

Max picked up the brandy bottle and helped himself. He seemed focused on far-off thoughts. Rolf stopped jesting and, getting serious, asked with certain misgiving, "Do you think I'll see my parents again, Max? Do you think we'll ever get back home?"

The lieutenant took a gulp of brandy, chose a record among those Rolf had brought along, and set the gramophone going. The strains of a Wagner opera were heard in the tent. The music merged with the buzz of the cicadas.

"Those that write history always return, Rolf. It's a natural protection destiny grants chroniclers. As for Alexander and Caesar, I'll be happy with a little less. Let's say, with the post of Commander when we advance on St. Petersburg."

"Next to nothing," answered Rolf, laughing as he accepted a glass. Then he went on with his diary.

The two of them listened to the opera with nostalgia. A few feet away from the tent, a group of German soldiers sang songs from the Volga. Max diverted his attention to that scene. The lights and shadows of the flames shone upon the youths' faces. A balalaika melancholically accompanied the deep voices of their spontaneous choir.

A Turkish lieutenant approached the tent, recalling Max to the present. "Sir, reports have just arrived from the vanguard in the villages. The Russians are near Lake Van."

Max thought this over for a few seconds. Obviously, Prince Nikolai Nikolaevich's troops would be concentrating at the Persian mountain range.

He turned his gaze towards the mountains. They looked close-by from a visual perspective, but were actually so far away and challenging; unknown and huge would the efforts be in attaining their objective.

CHAPTER XXXII

THE KAIMAKAM'S SLAVE-GIRLS

ARAKSI AND THE THREE OTHER CAPTIVE GIRLS had been sold to the kaimakam of the region. The Hadji's residence sat atop a hill on the outskirts of the town. The Turk was the most important local person in the district. He was rich and well connected with the military governors of the region.

Araksi and her companions were allowed to see nothing on the way to their destination. They were blindfolded and taken off the cart under the permanent guard of their new proprietor's helpers. Then they were taken indoors.

When the blindfold was removed, Araksi was able to see that they were walking through a long passage with a high ceiling; a damp, gloomy place. The whole building was ancient and looked like a fortress turned into a great residence. Three Turkish women and a black slave led the girls into courtyards surrounded by high walls. The corridor opened out into a huge, dark area, on the sides of which could be seen cells secured by solid wooden doors. Old stables and stalls that had once housed thoroughbreds now served the purpose of lodging the captives of the harem. As they advanced along the corridor they could hear the complaints and lamentations of a number of captive girls.

Araksi was horrified. If she had so far not fully understood that she had been bought for a future of prostitution, its reality was now undeniable, to the point of her soul bursting with such anguish that it took away all desire of carrying on living. She would never get out of there. She had heard stories of women in captivity, some of them Circassian girls destined for the harems, but those misfortunes of subjection always happened on other social levels. It was an unthinkable fate for a well-to-do girl from her community.

She was not unaware, like all women in Turkey, of the fortunes of those sexual slaves that lived behind bars, dedicated to satisfying their Turkish masters. From the palaces of Constantinople to the great residences of some kaimakams in the interior of the country, harems were kept. Araksi had been born a Christian, baptized and brought up in a family that was proud of its modern outlook in the world, without neglecting the age-old traditions of its lineage. She had lost her freedom and would be a plaything for those that, from now on, would be the owners of her existence.

As she walked down the passageway, she heard voices speaking in Armenian coming from behind the doors of each cell, and occasional laughter.

The first cries gave her goose pimples.

"Hello... hello... Please! I want to get out. For the love of God... Is anyone there that can hear me? I'm Armenuhi from Erzindjan."

"I'm Yugaper from Diarbekir," joined in another.

"And I'm Yevginé from Kharput," said a third as they advanced further.

The negro banged the doors with the end of his whip, for them to keep quiet, but the voices carried on.

"I'm Satenig from Sivas."

"Please, if someone can hear me... have mercy. I'm Noemzar from Erzurum."

Some voices sounded plaintive, others friendly, nearly all of them hopeful to explain that they were people with an identity. People coming from existing places and with real hope that whoever heard them might inform their families that they were there, lost to the world, forgotten by divine compassion. This world of wickedness and abduction that she could never have even imagined had no connection with any hope, thought Araksi in horror.

Tears came to her eyes and she was paralyzed on hearing the name of her city. She attempted to guess the faces according to the voices. All of them were her own voice, the entreaties of girls she might have known, with whom she might have shared friendship or gone to the same school, who perhaps had lived in a neighbourhood next to her own. On hearing the last girl, Noemzar, an impulse arose in her, and the emotion in her breast made her shout, "And I'm Araksi from Erzurum."

The negro cracked his whip above her as a warning. The report sounded right next to her, and the Turkish women, shaking her, thrust her into the next room.

The three women in charge of getting the girls ready stripped Araksi, as she chastely resisted the clumsy, insensitive handling of her body. As she was divested of her garments at the side of a steaming pool, the Turks commented admiringly on her perfect proportions.

Rarely had such a beauty been seen in that harem. They were amazed she had suffered no injuries or blows of consequence. All she had were a few bruises on her body and sores between her legs from the horse-ride, but these would soon heal with ointments and oils. The other captives were also undressed and subjected to the same cleansing: on the side of each pool the procedure was repeated. The Turkish women vigorously rubbed the bodies of those young Armenians intended to give pleasure. Soap suds fell everywhere, sliding away along the marble gutters. The place was a veritable turmoil. When any girl put up resistance, the oldest of the Turkish women, who went back and forth in the room, soon came to the bothersome or tearful captive and, with a few loud yells, put things back in order. Sunlight came in through a large skylight in the roof and descended as a misty beam that produced different tones of light above the water. At each entrance door the eunuch negro slaves wielding whips silently watched over the girls' bath.

When Araksi's turn came up, the women carefully rubbed her body and then soaped it, water and foam coursing down her curves. She remained tense, despite the women's attempts to make the captives relax, employing caresses and pleasant words but with coarse sensuality.

Throughout the whole of the bathing time, Araksi remained silent: her inner pride would not allow her to show submissiveness, just a few tears. Then she had her body oiled. She tried to overcome the apprehension she felt at strange female hands touching her intimately. Little by little, the oils loosened her tensed muscles.

Once more, she was rinsed. One of the women came up with bath towels and then indicated that Araksi was to dress in a light, clean tunic. Finally, she was given a pair of babouches to put on her feet. She sat on a marble bench and observed the remainder of the 20 girls in the swirling vapor around the pool. One of the slave girls came up to her and began combing her straight, jet-black hair. It had been Araksi's first bath in the months since leaving Erzurum. On remembering this, a stab of sadness and discouragement depressed her altogether.

The group of captives was led to another large room, decorated with cloth on the walls and small windows of wooden lattice shapes, far removed from the outside world. The negro slave indicated the cushions and carpets laid out on the floor and then shut the doors. Araksi was unable to keep calm any longer, and wept bitterly.

"Shut up!" snarled a blonde Armenian of around her own age. "We're in the same fix as you. We've been prepared to be raped, but we'll survive. The rest depends on you. Thousands of others haven't even had this chance."

"You shut your mouth. Let her cry. In the end, what difference does it make? We'll never get out of here. We'll live without ever seeing the light of day, having the Turks' children, or we'll end up somewhere a lot worse when no one is interested in us any longer," Noemzar defended Araksi, who hid her face in the cushions.

Another of the girls came to her, sat, and gently stroked her head as Araksi said aloud, "I'd wish to die killing those Turks. I don't care what happens to me. I'll kill whoever touches me. I swear it by the memory of all my dead ones."

From without was heard the Muslims' call to prayer. Araksi pressed her face into the cushion. She wanted to faint, to be free. There was intimacy only in her mind. She needed to resist the present nightmare and replace it with images of past times. The horror that had overwhelmed the Armenians made it impossible to even evoke that happy past. She filled her mind with the tender memories hidden in the depths of her thoughts, until she fell into a half-sleeping state; then the images appeared. She saw herself in Erzurum cathedral, praying next to her parents and Diran. The images of the Virgin and Christ, of the enormous, sunlit stained glass windows, appeared like dream-state transparencies, fused with the family's horseback rides among the damp grasses of the plain. Her ears heard the church choirs — vibrant voices sounding real in the depths of her soul, entwined in the laughter of her little nephews who smiled at her — or was it the innocent, childlike voices of her schoolchildren in the classroom?

Everything was falling back into place. Her mother's caresses returned peace to her spirit, rescuing her from any shadow.

So she remained, for who knew how long, until the door to the captives' room suddenly opened and the black slaves' yells brought her back to reality.

Araksi awoke with a start, still lying on the cushions. Soon she had to join the other girls. The negro eunuchs hurried them along, brandishing the whips above their heads.

"Come on, move. Don't keep the kaimakam and the hadjis waiting, you Christian bitches!"

Driven along the galleries, she was able to appreciate the importance of the place. There was wealth and a decidedly Oriental decor. She understood they were in the kaimakam's private rooms. She understood that the master of the place was a notable of the region, and that they were heading towards another sort of presentation, or perhaps to a new sale. As they advanced, the sensual strains of an orchestra could be heard.

Araksi and the 20 girls were brought to a large, plush room; seemingly the principal quarters of the residence. The place was brightly illuminated by ornate chandeliers hanging from the ceiling and carpets covered the floor.

Her sight immediately fell upon the stout individual reclining on a large divan. He was middle-aged, overweight, and wearing a Turkish-style moustache along with the typical garments of his country, comfortable and suitable for a social occasion.

This person was consulted by a secretary and by others

that approached him and laughed in reply to his comments. The smoke being exhaled bothered her, in addition to the fear that assailed her, provoking dizziness and a cold sweat.

He was the local kaimakam — a kind of mayor — and surely a rich man. Otherwise he would not have been able to maintain a harem and such a residence. Around him were other middle-aged Turkish dignitaries. Divans and cushions were spread out everywhere. At the girls' entrance, an expression of admiration and general enthusiasm was heard.

Amid smiles and comments as they pointed out the girls, Araksi, despite her panic, kept a haughty demeanour. Next to her, the other young girls seemed paralyzed, intimidated by the presence of the hadjis.

Some of the men ate fruits, while others reclined on the cushions, smoking from the narguile. They immediately paid attention to what was about to happen.

The assistant welcomed the girls in a loud voice, walking to and fro in the room. Approaching the group of Armenians, he ordered, "On your knees! The hadji has given you asylum in his home, and wishes all of you to pay for his kindness in saving you from the perils menacing your race. Show your gratitude for such generosity."

Deep silence prevailed, the musicians interrupting their playing.

The girls, still wrapped in their tunics, bowed to the kaimakam. The host and all his important guests continued to drink while they examined the girls, their stares overflowing with lechery. It seemed they were experienced in the art of assessing the beauty of young virgins; Armenians or Circassians assigned to give pleasure, some of them perhaps even becoming mothers of their children after being converted to Islam. That was the benefit of the best trophies from the caravans of deportees and the raids on Armenian villages.

Araksi remained standing haughtily. The other girls knelt as a sign of submission and gratitude towards the Turk that had bought them. The kaimakam set his gaze on Araksi, looking her body up and down, and then on her beautiful countenance. She was a twenty-year-old girl totally at the mercy of his authority, risking her life with her attitude – a combination of rebelliousness and great dignity. The assistant tried to force her to bow, but with a gesture the kaimakam ordered that she be allowed to remain standing. The Turk admired character and, even more so, reducing females to a state of complete humiliation. Quite surely that savagely sensual, refined Armenian girl was guaranteed to possess a passionate nature, promising unforgettable, lust-filled nights once she had been broken in and totally bent to his will.

After the girls had been examined with a first casual look, the slaves removed them from the great room.

Araksi and two other girls were taken back to the rooms to receive a suitable preparation. They were rapidly divested of the tunics covering their figures and piles of transparent silken and gauzy garments were placed on their cushions. The girls were pushed before mirrors, to be made up.

The eldest woman; a former beauty who, at the age of 45, devoted her efforts to organizing the kaimakam's intimate world of pleasure, gave orders to all the rest. Standing next to Araksi, she seized her by the chin and, looking at her as though seeing her own self some years earlier, said, "The kaimakam has chosen you for himself. You are very lucky, Araksi. Give him pleasure and your life will be transformed. You," addressing the others, "you are for the other hadjis that this evening are the master's honored guests."

The girls trembled with fear as they were made to don the silken veils that allowed their bodies to be seen. Then the babouches of different colours were put on. Finally, their ankles and feet were ornamented with bells.

They all looked at each other. The exterior transformation of those new captives had already been accomplished.

CHAPTER XXXIII

IN THE FORESTS

DIRAN AND HIS COMRADES were rapidly making their way through the darkness of the forest. Suddenly, Manuc, who walked ahead, made signs to disperse and keep quiet. They crouched without moving, looking out for any movement among the foliage. There was nothing within sight, but the sounds of engines could be heard approaching through the dense cover.

They promptly left the road and climbed an embankment, hiding among the bushes. Several army trucks carrying troops and machine guns were driving through the forest. The young Armenians watched the convoy go past, counting seven trucks. When the noise of the trucks finally receded into the distance, they once more took to the road and continued on their journey.

FURTHER ON, THEY CAME TO A RIVER running through the thickest part of the forest. Agop was the one in charge of replenishing their supplies at the river bank. Diran and the others threw themselves down under the trees, tired from their hike. Giorgi looked anxiously in every direction, desperately looking for something to eat. He plucked a few small fruits off a nearby tree, put them in his mouth, and immediately spat them out. They were sour. Foraging on the ground, he found some grasses and started chewing them. The others did likewise.

At the river bank, out of the others' sight, Agop was just finishing refreshing himself. He threw water on his face, concentrating on memories impossible to accept, the same as those in the minds of his companions. To his side, the sacks full of water hung from a bough, ready to carry back. A rifle came out from among the thicket, aimed at his neck. Agop felt the cold barrel of the gun and moved forward, paralyzed by the surprise.

"Don't move, you dog," ordered the voice. The Turkish officer, aiming at him, made him walk through the bush.

Diran and the other two began to worry about Agop's taking so long. Manuc looked towards the river. The darkness prevented him from seeing more than a few feet ahead, and the buzz of the cicadas only increased the lads' disquiet. Rising, he said, "He's taking too long."

Diran answered, "I'll go and see what's up."

"Take the knife with you," offered Giorgi.

Diran walked towards the river, guided by the sound of the current. When he got to the bank and there was no sign of Agop, he carried on walking a few steps and then suddenly came to a halt. He remained immobile on seeing his companion with the Turk's rifle trained on him. He hid behind a tree.

The two were coming in his direction. Diran nervously held the knife in his hands. He found his legs unresponsive, feeling immobilized. A sudden terror paralyzed him altogether.

His heart was pounding with increasing force and he found his body trembling. The knife slipped out of his grasp and fell to the ground. Diran was still stunned by fear. He could scarcely hold his breath. The two men were disappearing into the undergrowth. He was sweating buckets. He took a deep breath, bringing his tremor under control and, groping around on the ground, recovered the knife. Without knowing how, motivated by an inner impulse, he began running towards them.

The Turk, hearing the footsteps, turned his head round. Agop, not losing an instant, took advantage of this momentary inattention and delivered a kick to the soldier's arms. The blow made the Turk lower the gun-barrel. Without waiting another second, Agop fell upon him, rolling over on the ground and grappling for control of the weapon.

The soldier, obviously in better shape than the weakened Agop, soon recovered his bayonet and tried to plunge it into the Armenian's body. Diran had now reached them.

Agop yelled, "Kill him, kill him!" without letting up his struggle.

Diran fell on the Turk, stabbing him in the stomach

time and again until the soldier collapsed, bleeding profusely. Agop got up. He and Diran looked at each other without saying a word, picked up the rifle and got hold of the knife the soldier carried on his belt.

"Wait," said Agop, removing the soldier's boots. Diran was still perturbed at having killed a man for the first time in his life, and could hardly take his eyes off the body. Agop hurried him, taking him by the arm. "There's no time. Let's go."

They returned to Manuc and Giorgi as quickly as they could. There was no need for explanations. Almost breathless, they left the spot in pitch darkness. The response was not long in coming. Machine gun fire riddled leaves and branches near them. They moved without stopping, never looking back and at a run entered the forest thickets.

Almost at once, shouts and orders coming from the zaptieh patrol were heard in the wood. They had discovered their dead companion's body.

As they increased the distance from their pursuers, the shots diminished, and the pursuers' voices grew ever fainter for the four fugitives.

CHAPTER XXXIV

THE HAREM

ARAKSI, DRESSED UP AS AN ODALISQUE – a Turkish concubine - displayed all her astounding beauty and sensuality. Her face had been made up and a veil hid it up to the level of her eyes. Her hips and legs in full view through her transparent, baggy trousers produced admiration in the Turkish women. Her black hair cascaded down her bare back. They crossed a room where women were dancing with sensual movements, accompanying themselves with tambourines. Excited by the spectacle, the guests showed appreciation of the belly dance while lolling on cushions and smoking. A perfumed scent intermingled with the pipe smoke and once again Araksi felt dizzy.

The eunuchs forced her into a side room, half in darkness, with only a few candles by way of illumination. Golden cushions and a large divan served as an anteroom to the bedchamber with its enormous bed and canopy.

The doors shut. The sensual music drifted in from the neighbouring rooms. Araksi felt a male hand caressing her back and running down her shoulders and arms before finally encircling her waist. She became tense and tried to move away but the kaimakam pressed her hard, keeping her there.

"What is your name?" he asked.

"I'm Araksi... from Erzurum."

"Araksi... from Erzurum. Well, that's no great matter now," he answered.

The kaimakam took his dressing gown off, revealing a thick neck, breadth of shoulders, and paunch that filled out his shirt. He smiled, confident of his authority, and looked at Araksi lecherously, convinced of his possession.

He took an embossed crystal decanter from among several bottles and poured himself some vodka. Then he forced Araksi to do the same whilst he leaned on the cushions, observing her. The music seemed to be getting louder, as though the musicians were behind the curtains of the same room; so it seemed to Araksi in her state of confusion, mixed with the panic she was experiencing. She had never before been with a man.

She felt the alcohol going to her head and a stabbing oppression in her stomach. The man took her by the waist and drew her to him. The strength of his arms rendered any resistance useless. She began to protest but the kaimakam's thick hand immediately covered her mouth. Stretching out on top of her, he immobilized her. His breath grew more agitated. Determined not to waste a single minute with any form of nicety, he ripped her clothes off and began kissing and licking her entire body roughly, with irrepressible desire. He parted her legs. Neither spoke. All that was heard was the oriental melody of the instruments and the kaimakam's panting against the girl's mouth.

Araksi resisted in vain. When her strength no longer responded, her instincts followed the Turk's desperate passion. Tears of deep sadness and impotence welled up within her as she was forced to yield time and again throughout the whole night.

At dawn, daylight came into the room through the trellis windows. Birds could be heard flitting among the jasmines. Araksi's face, pained, with her sight fixed and distant, bore witness to the affront she had endured.

Her body felt exhausted. She remained stretched out, immobile, naked among the cushions. Under the body of the Turk, who was asleep on top of her.

CHAPTER XXXV

TWISTS OF DESTINY?

THE DESERT EXTENDED as far as the eye could see. The heat caused mirages on the surface, blurring the horizon. The last ragged survivors of the caravan dragged themselves along in the trackless sand, stumbling with fatigue: these were the Armenian women carrying their children through the entry to the Syrian desert. Reduced to skin and bones, and almost naked, with sores from sunburn, they were approaching their destination: the desert of Deir-ez-Zor.

Some lay dead next to their children, a short distance from the group.

Mavush shuffled along as though each step were her last, her eyes half-closed, her tongue sticking out from dehydration. She still held her youngest child in her arms, not realizing he was dead. All at once, unable to carry on any further, she collapsed, and remained stretched out on the sand.

The others passed by her without noticing her or turning a hair. Guarded by the mounted officers, these women were the last group of people or, rather, the remains of humans on the verge of death, who had left Erzurum — without water or nourishment, wandering deeper into the desert, the only place in Turkey suitable for Armenians.

DESPITE THE SHEET-LIGHTNING illuminating the sky and heralding a great storm for several hours past, rain had still not fallen in Bitlis.

Max, riding Pasha, headed the Turkish and Kurdish horsemen. They were approaching a town in the mountains. It was almost evening and the first rolls of thunder sounded like cannon rumbling above them. The men raised standards with the Turkish and German emblems and made their way at a gallop. On entering Bitlis, a torrential rain-shower burst.

Bitlis was a small town of large stone houses. What Max first saw on their arrival were the traces of the deportation of Armenians. Several children were taking refuge from the rain in the streets. Abandoned waifs, or perhaps escapees from Turkish captivity, separated from their parents and left to their own devices.

Max rode in silence. Pasha's hooves resounded against the cobblestones, as the horse snorted and exhaled vapor from its nostrils. Max patted his horse, calming it down. He felt an inordinate pleasure riding such a beast — tireless, of majestic movements, awaking the admiration of everybody as it passed. Never before had he had such a specimen as Pasha, thought Max. Not even in Riga, in his father-in-law's stables, had he come upon such an outstanding animal that made him feel like a conqueror. After all, along with the memory of a great warrior, it was his horse that was always remembered. He was proud of Pasha.

He turned his sight to his officers. Rolf, Memdukh the interpreter, and Stoeffels the physician were pointing at something at the end of the street. A group of military, protected in their black capes, were riding towards them: the Turks of the local garrison were coming out to receive them under the torrential rain. Guided along the winding streets, they headed for a great stone house and there dismounted.

On seeing the style of building, Max thought that it must have belonged to an Armenian family. The house rested on a hill, as did its neighbors, all lined up along streets that rose and fell.

The group of officers, sodden from the downpour, quickly entered the place. The house had been sacked and was empty of furniture. The Turkish military had set up beds, tables and chairs. A great hearth overlooked the main reception room. They immediately divested themselves of their wet clothing and, as they looked the premises over, Max commented to his men, "This house is typically Armenian. I've no doubt it belonged to a deported family And it is very likely that it was them that had it built." He remained pensive for a moment and then

191

continued, "The General Commander's office has set out a route for us, so that we shouldn't see the massacres and abandoned Armenian villages, but this neighborhood is clear enough evidence. After all, didn't you see all those ragged children in the street? They're abandoned Armenian children, orphans...."

The two brothers, Rolf and Friedrich, nodded, unable to believe it. They looked all around the spacious rooms as they unpacked their equipment. It was the first time Max had made any reference to the Armenians and none of them had heard about this chain of events since arriving in Turkey.

A FEW HOURS LATER, SITTING in front of the fireplace after dinner, Max, leaning back in his chair and crossing his legs, was finishing a story that his German companions followed with amazement. They listened to their commander with awe.

"That's the way it is, gentlemen. I did all I could to intercede for these people. When you arrived there were no more Armenians in the district... All of them murdered or deported to the deserts. Seventy thousand souls, who had lived there since time immemorial, a third of the population of Erzurum. God knows how few will have reached their new destination."

A pause ensued. Rolf wanted to know more. "Max, it's hard to believe that all those Turkish officers, who've been so kind to us, have taken part in such operations."

Friedrich commented, "We've heard about the city of Van, and the reprisals against the Armenians that resisted, but I can't remember the name of the Turkish commander. All those names sound like tongue-twisters." He smiled.

"Djevdet Pasha, the military and civil governor of Van," Max explained, and went on, "Djevdet, a great exterminator of Armenians, who happens to be right here, in Bitlis; he is married to War Minister Enver Pasha's sister. We'll have the opportunity of meeting Djevdet tomorrow at the celebratory dinner at the Commander's Office. There are those that say the most terrible tortures of Armenians have been carried out in his very presence."

Max stood up and stretched. The others watched the fire in the hearth, still disturbed at the stories they had heard.

"That's enough for one night. Take the opportunity to get some rest."

THE NEXT DAY, LIEUTENANTS Thiele and Hüchtinger walked through the Bitlis market. Many stalls were closed even though it was a morning like any other in town. They caught people's attention with their German uniforms and European features. The Kurdish shopkeepers offered them grapes and tomatoes as they passed. Everything and everywhere seemed full of poverty and abandonment.

All of a sudden, two children ran among the fruit stalls. They had just stolen something to eat. Escaping from their pursuers, they joined a group of 50 street children between six and twelve years old. Several dogs followed after the gang of hungry children, begging whatever they could get.

"Again, the Armenian children," observed Rolf.

No sooner had he mentioned them than a couple of middle-aged European-looking women approached them shyly and warily. They whispered in English to each other, and it was obvious they were Protestant missionaries, probably assigned to teaching in the interior towns of Turkey. One of them, a slim, bony blonde with deep blue eyes, addressed Max. She seemed to recognize him as the highest-ranking officer.

The whole group came to a halt. Max paid close attention to the woman's pleading tone.

"Lieutenant. I am Miss Shane. My colleague and I... are missionaries from the United States," she began. "We dearly entreat you to take charge of the Armenian orphans of Bitlis, Commander. For the love of God, don't allow this tragedy to continue, with us Christians turning a blind eye to the abandonment and massacre of innnocents."

Max seemed worried. Miss Shane carried on, "Look at these children, Sir. They'll never be reunited with their families, because their families no longer exist. It is reported that only a very few survive the deportation to the deserts. I beg you to use your influence among the Turkish military to get them out of here. I beseech you, Sir."

The two missionaries worriedly looked towards the bazaar in case they were noticed by the Turkish police. The other woman, Miss Randall, added her pleas in the same tone, deeply disturbed. "Miss Shane has spoken the truth. Humanitarian aid is urgent. We entreat you to intercede for us with the Turkish generals."

Max caught her arm to calm her.

The officers remained in silence at the missionaries' request. Their trust in the German army officers was plain to see. The Germans, European and Christian, were the last hope for those children left at the mercy of the worst fate.

"I promise you I will forward your request. Please be calm. I'll do what I can for them," Max von Swirsden-Righe assured them, and immediately ordered, "Rolf, make a note of where we can contact these ladies."

The women thanked Max and left. It was clear those two missionaries were the only people concerned about the Armenian children consigned to total destitution.

Misses Shane and Randall crossed the street and walked to the group of waifs that had congregated around a rubbish heap. Some of the tinier children were eating what scraps they could find. On seeing the missionaries they all surrounded them, tugging at the women's skirts and desperately asking them for food. The officers remained overwhelmed at the miserable picture they had witnessed. They continued their walk until night fell.

MAX SAT NEXT to Djevdet Bey, the military governor of Van. Djevdet laughed and jested in French, although from time to time he frowned and visually scanned the salon of the Commander's Office, decorated for the occasion.

Further on, at the table, the military commander of Bitlis and Omer Nadji Bey chatted with the thick-set kaimakam of the region, one of the important local people invited to the celebration in honor of the German allies.

The kaimakam was well-known among the highest military chiefs. Every time they came to Bitlis they were invariably invited by him to acquaint themselves with the novelties of his harem. He boasted of having lately renewed his team with a group of Armenian girls, as he enthusiastically confided to the guest beside him.

Waiters went to and fro, carrying platters of roast lamb and delicious side dishes. Great chandeliers illuminated the room from the ceiling.

Rolf, Friedrich and the other German lieutenants sat, alternating with Turkish dignitaries and several local tribal chieftains. They watched in wonder as the vodka flowed without limit into everyone's glasses. The atmosphere was festive and it was evident that the Turks had gone to a great deal of trouble to impress the Germans.

The general hubbub died down for a few moments when the regional Turkish commander stood up. He wore a uniform spangled with decorations, and a sash crossing his chest. He took a glass and, raising it, said in French to the assembled company, "Gentlemen... gentlemen, please. We have great reason to celebrate. The passage for the transport of arms, ammunition, and armies from Berlin to Turkey has been opened, and there will be no one to stop us now. Let us drink to Germany, gentlemen, and to the fall of Bulgaria."

All those present, Turks and Germans, stood and, raising their glasses, responded to the toast.

The expedition's Turkish physician, Dr. Fuad, clumsily trying out words in German and certainly encouraged by the vodka, stuttered, "I was forgetting... that... is... I would like to express a wish, a very important one and surely shared by all of us... Gentlemen, I drink to the rapid disappearance of all Armenians from our country!"

Max, who was eagerly awaiting the right opportunity to intervene, stood up. All the officers and Turkish commanders turned their eyes on him. They were expecting words of gratitude from their German allies.

Images boiled in Max's mind. Any request made in public could not be turned down by the military governors who, until a few moments earlier, had been unable to do other than celebrate the military alliance with Kaiser Wilhelm's army: that was the ideal moment in such a friendship.

"Gentlemen," he said, "I am grateful for the toast to our nations, and raise my glass in sharing the wish that both empires may defeat our enemies. I express my hopes that our expedition will succeed in its objectives." He took a deep breath before continuing, "Since we arrived in Bitlis I have been able to observe that we are in a city formerly inhabited by Armenians..."

The Turkish military representatives looked at him, puzzled at his having mentioned this topic. All those present looked on expectantly.

"I would like to make a request to the distinguished authorities in celebration of the alliance of our armies. Gentlemen — honorable governors and commanders: my request refers to the Armenian children wandering among the streets of Bitlis in a state of total bereavement. We have ourselves seen in this war zone the existence of children left to the elements with no protection whatsoever."

The Muslims showed discomfort at Max's discourse. Although whispers could be heard along the tables, in honor to Ottoman courtesy no one interrupted him. Djevdet Bey kept his eyes riveted on Max, showing no emotion.

When Max finished, the general took himself to be the butt of his comments and calmly answered, "In my district of Van many soldiers have died thanks to the Armenians and if these children are orphans the blame belongs to their parents, Lieutenant."

The Turkish officers were all looking at the Germans with frowns of evident displeasure. Max took the floor once more and continued, "Children have always been perfectly innocent in any armed conflict, the same as women, Djevdet Bey. What is the object of neglecting them this way? This very day, Commander, an American missionary, Miss Shane, begged me to appeal to the great gentlemanliness of the Turkish authorities, and moreover, that I should intercede for her to be given an interview with your good selves regarding the Armenian orphans. Sir, it is Miss Shane herself that wishes to present this problem to Your Excellency."

The silence in the room was deafening. The commanders looked to Omer Nadji Bey for him to give the last word. Smiling suavely, the politician took his cue and, for the sake of generally defusing the matter, made a joke of it. "Ah, what a sentimental consul. *Un consul avec des sentiments.*"

Everyone laughed, and the tension that had been growing amongst the authorities was dispelled by the politician's comment.

Max, from his place, was the only one that made any sign of displeasure. Determined not to be deflected from his purpose, he charged in once again. "When sentiments don't clash with the orders from our superiors, I see no reason to censure them, Omer Nadji."

Omer Nadji laughed and lifted his glass, as though to say *Touché!* The military commander considered it wise not to offend his German allies, of whom so much was expected, particularly in front of such a large gathering, attentive to each word that might keep them on edge.

Djevdet Bey, with a gesture of magnanimous concession, decided to present himself as tolerant before the public. When, moments later, Miss Shane entered the room, accompanied by Rolf Hüchtinger, everyone looked at the ungainly, fragile woman in long skirts, her hair in a bun. She came forward, intimidated by so many uniforms and the presence of such high-ranking Turkish commanders. Max stood and escorted her to the place where Djevdet Bey was seated. The governor made ready to listen to her. Silence returned to the room at Miss Shane's words. She spoke in English, with an interpreter translating into French.

"Excellencies — I thank you. I am a missionary from the United States. What I am requesting as a member of a neutral nation is permission to transfer 100 Armenian children at the Bitlis orphanage to Dyarbekir, where they will be safe... I appeal to your great Muslim magnanimity to make this transfer possible."

Max was listening with anxiety, just as the rest of the Germans present were.

Djevdet Bey was pure vanity. Making much of his authority which gave him power of life or death over the population under his command, he looked at the woman in a gentlemanly manner and said, "Let the missionary's request be honored... Translate for her that the children will be transferred immediately in safety in Turkish army trucks. They will travel with a military escort to guarantee the safety of the whole group."

Djevdet Bey took a deep breath, full of his own magnanimity: not only the woman would hear it, but the Germans would also take due account of the moment they were witnessing. "This is the spirit in which Turkey will not ignore the requests of our allies' friends," he declared.

Miss Shane's face lit up and, thanking Djevdet Bey, she turned about. She walked away amid the tables, delighted and also somewhat disturbed. When they left the banqueting hall, Miss Shane took Max by the arm. "I have no words to thank you, Sir... May Heaven guide you..! But I must ask you for yet something else. If I did not do it, my conscience would never forgive me."

Max looked askance at the woman.

"This I must ask of you, Lieutenant. There, do you see that man, the fat one sitting in front of the military?" Miss Shane discretely indicated the kaimakam. "It's a matter of captives, of girls kidnapped from the caravans. That man is the kaimakam of the region. He has several captive Armenian girls in his harem. Everyone here knows, but to them it's perfectly acceptable. The girls are Christian slaves. I beg you also to take action to rescue or intercede for those women."

"I'll see what I can do, Miss Shane. It may be that destiny has called on you to alert me about those poor wretches."

"No, Lieutenant, it isn't destiny. It's the Lord that is using us. We are just the instruments of His will."

Max did not answer. He summoned Rolf in a low voice, indicating the place where the kaimakam was drinking merrily. With the wine and vodka served at the tables, the general atmosphere was one of light-hearted camaraderie, and jokes were heard everywhere.

Max raised his glass and approached the kaimakam, inviting him to drink once more. The kaimakam smiled and returned the courtesy.

"Excellency — I've been informed that your taste for the most beautiful women is proverbial in the region... This evening has been a most pleasant one, and will always be remembered by my officers and myself. We will not always be so lavishly entertained before we cross the high mountains and go into battle. I've heard that your residence is much talked about with regard to women... It would be perfect if my men and I had the opportunity of meeting some..."

The kaimakam smiled and, placing his hand on Max's shoulder, interrupted him. "Say no more, Lieutenant... It will be my pleasure to offer you real hospitality at my residence in honor of our camaraderie... You have simply beaten me to it. There you will judge with your own eyes whether what is reputed of my house's tradition is true, or praise is lacking. You and your officers will have access to beauties worthy of the Sultan. Do me the honor of accompanying me right now, if you wish. Lieutenant, gentlemen, you shall presently know what a proper Oriental night is."

The kaimakam smiled and stood up, ready to depart with the Germans.

OUTSIDE, MAX MOUNTED PASHA. Rolf, Friedrich and Thiele accompanied him to the residence on their own mounts. The kaimakam rode ahead in his carriage with friends of his. Max looked at the new moon. It was a mild night. They travelled at a trot for around 20 minutes. His officers had not been given much instruction as to what was expected of them. Max preferred it that way, given the nature of the outing. On catching sight of the lights of the great residence as they came closer, Max made a comment to Rolf, his mind ablaze with expectations. "Write this down in your diary, Rolf. On this night of

October 1915 we are on our way to the kaimakam's residence to buy women — slave girls. Who said civilization had arrived everywhere, even in the 20th century? Makes you wonder how Germany can be partners with such people."

The officers looked at him without saying anything. They exchanged looks and smiles amongst themselves.

On arriving, they dismounted, full of curiosity and excitement. They left their horses in a large cobbled courtyard and went indoors, escorted by the house watchmen. The kaimakam was smiling as he led them in. With flamboyant gestures, he ushered them into the rooms. A penetrating smell of perfume mingled with candle smoke and incense in every corner. Rhythmical, erotic music reached the young officers' ears. The sensuality of the setting gradually took hold of them, and they commented to each other in an undertone.

On entering the main room, the kaimakam turned to Max and confided, "The girls that live here under my protection are trained to give pleasure. Nowhere else in the empire will you find such women as these in my harem. I'll confess this: some of them I've had to deliver over to Constantinople... As you'll gather, the exquisite services of some of them end up in the most important palaces. These women are the most beautiful in the whole of Turkey."

Everywhere there were cushions and divans upholstered in silk. The music intensified and the black slaves appeared from behind the curtains. Everything looked golden in the candlelight. The girls appeared in the room, swaying their hips. They wore veils and offered their bodies, at first a little intimidated by the German officers. In fascination, the young men watched the parade of the fifteen *godzes*, the harem slave-girls, who danced looking at them, mysterious and alluring.

Max observed that several were blonde and light-skinned. "Are they Armenians or Circassians?" he inquired out of curiosity.

"Most are Christian Armenians, some of them still virgins. Have whichever you fancy, Lieutenant. Then you'll find out if I was right or not," said the Turk. "You have a long campaign ahead of you... If you wish to have some for your officers, this can be arranged for a fair price. I'm ready to talk over the terms..."

Max interrupted, "I'm not about to haggle over the price of human beings. Whatever you say is right."

His host laughed heartily. "You very certainly are a sentimentalist, Sir."

Taking Max by the arm, the kaimakam led him to a more intimate room. They went through doors of finely carved wood. Negro slaves guarded the passages. The Turk, in a suggestive tone, urged the German to pass into his private chambers. "Come... come. I'll show you something very special for this unique night."

They went through curtains into the next room. The kaimakam invited Max to relax on some cushions. On a great brass tray there were liqueurs and incense sticks. Max felt slightly uneasy, but he still had his pistol at his side. The Turk stretched out on some other cushions and began smoking. Rhythmic music became audible from behind the curtains. At once a blonde Circassian with a perfect figure appeared, swaying her hips. She looked sensually at Max, offering herself as she danced. The kaimakam decided Max was about to be won over by the delights of the harem.

Max smiled at the young woman, admiring her. Then another dancer, light-stepped and with her back to them, came into the half-darkened room from among the curtains. She immediately caught all of Max's attention. She moved with extraordinary sensuality in the candlelight, moving her waist this way and that to the sound of the music. Her hips seemed to float above her naked, shapely thighs and calves with their perfect, slightly matt-colored skin. Her back reflected a golden hue and her shoulders were bare.

Max was captivated and subdued by the black-haired girl with enormous eyes that were visible above the veil concealing her face. He was utterly taken up with Araksi, although he had not yet recognized her. The Circassian danced close to him and did not let him see the dark-

201

haired girl's figure to the full but from what he had made out, it was a perfect figure, the best he had ever seen. The veils covering Araksi fell off, one after another, next to the two men. Immediately, he felt a flare of desire for the girl, but the sensation was a strange one. The memory of his senses took him back to other eyes, another time, but the strength of his immediate attraction prevented him from recalling the truth. He struggled with his will not to overlook the mission he had set himself. The young woman was dancing for the Turk, but it seemed she was turning towards Max while the kaimakam smiled lustfully at her.

When she dropped the veil that covered her features and, swivelling round, ended up facing Max, Araksi lost control for an instant, fixing her stare on the man in the German uniform. Her heart missed a beat then throbbed wildly in her breast. She could not think. Surprise and embarrassment interrupted her dance. Araksi stared at Max, a silent plea for help as he finally realised who she was.

The transformation she had undergone, unavoidable in view of the place she was in, revealed her sensuality but Max could understand the suffering it caused her. He remembered her as self-confident, self-possessed, and surrounded by an aura of pride in her race.

As for herself, Araksi felt too many conflicting emotions. She could not believe she was in front of that man in that place of captivity and degradation.

Her first impulse was to feel saved: someone she had trusted had appeared to rescue her, but straightaway, a different idea crossed her mind. Would the German not simply be another visitor seeking the favors of the young women in the harem? After all, he was an ally of her captor. Inhibition paralyzed her and the blood rushed to her face. On seeing Araksi interrupting her dance, the kaimakam lost his calm, as though awakened from his enchanted trance.

Max stood and put the matter to him directly. "I want that girl. She's Armenian, right?"

"Yes, but she's not for sale, she's *Gedikei Kadin*. Do you

understand, Lieutenant? She's for my pleasure."

The music played on, even though the two girls were no longer dancing. From a corner, they nervously looked at the two men arguing. The Turk clapped his hands impatiently and the musicians, somewhere behind the curtains, stopped playing.

Max, eyeing Araksi in a protective manner, went on, "I'm offering you four times what I'll pay for each of the remaining Armenians in gold, just for this woman."

The Turk shook his head, turning down the offer, but the large sum planted a seed of doubt in his mind. He was considering the deal.

Araksi was trembling. She realized her future depended on this haggling. Max increased the offer. "I'll take all the Armenians we've seen at the price you determine."

"Have them all if you like, but this one's not for sale, Lieutenant."

Max hesitated an instant and then increased the offer once more. At that moment, Rolf and Friedrich burst into the room. They had heard the kaimakam's raised voice and were there to assist their leader. Max made a sign that they were not to intervene. "I'm ready to pay as much for her as for all the rest together... in gold."

There was silence. The Turk shook his head from one side to the other, looked at Araksi and refused the bid. Araksi was clenching her fists, on the verge of despair. The Germans looked on, open-mouthed. Max had offered a fortune for that girl and it was clear he was interested in getting her away from the harem. No strategy was possible. That had to be the limit, that amount in gold was a substantial proportion of what had been allocated to purchase supplies.

When the silence became unbearable and he was about to withdraw from the room, Max gave the girl a last look.

The Turk stopped him, smiling. It seemed the German had suggested a price to his satisfaction. "It seems your interest in Armenians is not limited to orphan children, Sir. It would seem to be an unrestrainable passion in the case of women."

Max said nothing.

The kaimakam pressed on. "The price to take this woman must equal the sum offered for all the rest, and something more... Since you are so interested in her, I want something more..."

Max was listening.

"I want your horse. Yes, Lieutenant, I also want that beast, right away, just as you've left it tethered in my stable. It remains there, and you can have this and all the remaining Armenians. How about it?"

Araksi, guarded by armed eunuchs, trembled even more as the haggling advanced.

Max blinked. The amount was exorbitant and would affect the provisions and supplies meant for the army. He looked at Araksi again, whose luck depended on that instant. As for Pasha, he could never be replaced. The kaimakam knew the kind of animal the horse was, worthy of the sultan's stables, but there were Araksi and the other girls. Max hesitated no longer and accepted the terms.

"Take her away with you. No infidel is worth that much. You really are a sentimentalist, as Omer Nadji said. Have I your word as a German officer that you will pay me the gold tomorrow?"

"You have. Tomorrow you will receive the full amount, but this girl and the others leave with us tonight."

"I'll prepare a cart, and a carriage for yourself. By the way, she's from Erzurum, so maybe she was written in your destiny."

Araksi trembled with fear and emotion. Wordlessly, she looked at her companion's eyes as a farewell. An infinite sadness filled the remaining captive girl's face. Somehow she understood Araksi was regaining her freedom. Araksi gave herself over to Max's arm and they all went out to the courtyard, followed by the kaimakam and the house-guard.

Rolf, Friedrich and Thiele helped the girls board the cart. Some of them laughed. Others, in fear, kept quiet. Too used to being put down, none of them knew if their next destination would not be even worse than the one they were leaving.

Max patted his horse and stroked his muzzle. Then he handed over the reins to one of the Turk's assistants. The kaimakam was ecstatic at his new acquisition. Pasha nervously tossed his head a couple of times and kicked out.

Araksi looked at the star-studded sky. She could hardly believe all that had happened but there she was, free from the walls of captivity. She wondered why Max had gone to her aid. How had he found her? After such extreme suffering, her prayers had been heard. She remained silent, her head down. Seconds crawled by like eternities.

One carriage turned about and remained facing the residence doors. Araksi got in, wrapped in a veil. Behind her, Max made sure, his pistol at his waist, that nothing got out of control.

The vehicles started off. They were escorted by Turkish soldiers. Rolf and Friedrich, on horseback, flanked the cart, and Lieutenant Thiele followed behind.

As they climbed the road to Bitlis, Max soothed Araksi. She wept with gratitude.

"Don't cry. Don't show weakness. You're still not out of danger." Dazzled by her beauty, he looked at her from time to time. She was no longer a girl: the Turkish women had brought out all her hidden sensuality. He had thought of her at times, but very often put her out of his mind so as not to imagine her very worst ending. He tried to hide the emotional impact he had experienced on finding her in that harem. As though it had been deliberate, the rescue was no doubt a twist of destiny. Had the kaimakam himself not said so, after all?

She must be written in your destiny.

Finally, they arrived at the big stone house in Bitlis. None of the girls yet dared think what their fate could be. Nevertheless, it could not be all that different from the one they had left, only with a new master. The Turkish guards left and the officers took the freed captives up to the first floor of the house.

Max waited for a suitable moment to lead Araksi to one of the rooms before she got together with her companions. Her emotions welled up and she cried disconsolately.

Max, calling her by her name, spoke to her tenderly. "There's nothing to worry about now, Araksi. Tomorrow I'll speak to all the girls about what the new situation will be."

"I'm ashamed that you should see me like this. I'd given up all hope. Thank you, Sir... My parents were murdered in the caravan... The Turks savagely killed anyone that was unable to carry on... After that, a band of Kurds fell on us... they raped my sister Mavush and my sister-in-law, Vartuhi. The children, my niece and nephews, who knows if they're still alive? Where can those poor innocents be...?" Her voice broke with pain. "My whole family's been destroyed, obliterated."

She broke into uncontrollable sobs. Max embraced her, trying to comfort her. "I'm sorry... I'm truly very sorry. I did what I could... It wasn't enough. Calm down now. You've been able to survive... I really don't know how I found you in that den. Everything seems as incredible to me as to you, Araksi. Someone has decided you're meant to live! You and all the young ladies will travel with us on our expedition to the Russian frontier, or some spot on enemy territory I consider suitable. Maybe when we enter Persia you'll go to your safety, outside Turkey. There you'll be able to find the Armenians on the Russian side, you'll be out of danger."

Araksi looked at him in disbelief.

"But how will we survive, surrounded by Turks and Kurds? They're the ones that murder us, Lieutenant!"

"You'll pass as women for the German officers. Forgive me... And you will be under my own personal protection."

"I thought God had forgotten about me and my people. Why has He allowed this hell of death and hatred towards us? It's so unfair! What I've seen I'll never be able to forget." She was trembling. Events shook her without giving her time to understand.

THE YOUNG WOMEN FELT INTIMIDATED. No one spoke, until fatigue finally took over and all of them, including Araksi, fell asleep amid tears and silent sobs.

The German officers were still sitting around the

fireplace. Rolf and Friedrich could not get to sleep. It was too much excitement for just one night.

"Have you shown the young ladies to their quarters?" Max asked.

"Yes, Max. We've set up some camp beds, and I left someone to watch over them."

Rolf lit a cigarette. Unable to restrain his curiosity any longer, he said, "That girl's cost a fortune, Max, including your magnificent horse."

"A small price for such an exchange. That girl, Araksi, was a volunteer at the hospital. I met her parents, one of the most important families in Erzurum and in the whole of Anatolia. I promised to help them when the persecutions began. I was able to do very little. It seems the Turks murdered them all but her. Fate has put us in this extraordinary circumstance of finding and rescuing her. Have you any doubt we've fulfilled our duty? Any human life that can be saved is beyond all price."

Rolf listened in astonishment. He continued, "Araksi... What an exotic name, just like her beauty. She's an astoundingly lovely girl. Of course! That's why she's been able to survive, or maybe it was a matter of Providence. Who knows? Did you really know her parents, Max? The coincidence is amazing. I find this world impossible to understand. I wonder if we'll get used to the Asiatic mentality, so that what seems impossible now becomes everyday normality. Everything I see seems centuries away from our way of life."

Max sat in a rocking chair. Fatigue was beginning to get to him and he felt that the tiredness and tension of the events were enough for one day. "The Turks tread on and destroy millenary civilizations, but they haven't been able to do it with this flower," he said, as though to himself.

Someone tried to make a joke of the sexual experience the girls must have acquired in the Turk's harem. Max looked at him sternly, putting a stop to any further comment. He had taken his role as protector with true seriousness — and he was especially protective towards Araksi, as the officers whispered among themselves in the days following.

In the distance could be heard the muezzin's call to morning prayer. Max stood up and, addressing all of them, ordered, "Gentlemen — let's get some sleep, though it be just a couple of hours. Tomorrow — or rather today — we'll transfer to the camp with the rest of the army."

THE BAGS FULL OF GOLD POUNDS tipped the small scale. Paying attention, the kaimakam checked that the price agreed on for the slave-girls of his harem was duly paid. Max himself, sitting behind his desk, looked on the procedure in silence. When the proper amounts of pounds had been weighed out, the Turk smiled with satisfaction as he held the bags of coins in his arms. Max stood up and, without much comment, closed the deal.

With this, he had annexed to the expedition a group of women. From there on, all that awaited them was a long journey full of danger on the way to battle, and the difficulties of these women living among them and the Turks, which would require vigilance.

He went out into the garden. The morning was sunny and fresh. The young women were waiting among the wagons. They all had their faces covered and free of make-up. That way they gave the impression of being much younger, almost teenagers, pretty and frightened, the suffering they had experienced more evident in the daylight.

The officers looked at them enthusiastically, smiling, but language differences made conversation impossible. In spite of this, some of the Volga Germans managed to communicate in Russian with some of the Armenians of that origin.

A STRONG DETAIL OF GUARDS had been organized around the wagons, to take them to the army camp. The armed Volga Germans took up their places, keeping an eye on the area. Rolf and his brother kept close watch over the women. Max, accompanied by Memdukh, made ready to speak to them before the departure.

Araksi, next to Noemzar, the girl from Erzurum who had the good fortune of being rescued with the rest, looked on in silence.

"Good morning. I hope you have rested well. Do not be concerned about your lives. I will not allow you to fall back into captivity, at least for as long as I'm in command of this army. You'll always be in our sector of the camp, so no one will touch you." Max looked at the faces of each of the young women, who followed his words with hope. "You will live in tents like the rest of us, and when we arrive at the frontier I will do what I can for you to be able to cross over to freedom. We are in a war zone and we are going forward to battle. This is a very dangerous expedition, but perhaps we'll be able to reach our destination and survive. In the meantime, please bear in mind that the Turkish chiefs will not tolerate the slightest inconvenience you may cause, in which case I would not be able to intervene in your favor."

The wagon got underway towards the outskirts of the town where the army was encamped, waiting to join forces with allied tribes before travelling down the Tigris. Below them the valley extended, and the camp tents which lined the plain could be seen. Some cavalry groups moved in formation, carrying out combat exercises. Tiny in the distance, they raised clouds of dust and the figures resembled moving doodles of uniform color, according to section and regiment, wielding lances and bannerettes at full gallop.

Max sighed. A mixture of troubling sensations went through his mind. He endeavored to conceal from his officers, and himself, the excitement of having found Araksi, which was hugely disturbing.

THE TURKO-GERMAN EXPEDITION PULLED OUT. Max and Omer Nadji Bey rode at the head of the 500 Turkish and Kurdish horsemen, followed by the infantry. Further behind came the artillery and a number of mules loaded with equipment. Bringing up the rear were the rescued girls in four covered ox-drawn wagons, followed by two horses adorned with flags on their backs. Araksi, still frightened and not understanding the changes of destiny that had taken place in her life, observed everything from the wagon.

She could see the kaimakam, mounted on Pasha and saluting the departing troops. A flash of resentment, liberation and fear shot through her, to her core. Her body could not stand any more hatred towards the man that had taken away her virginity.

Max shouldered his sabre as a salute. Out of the corner of his eye he looked at Pasha for the last time. Fanfares sounded while columns of mounted flag-bearers and squadrons of Daghestanis, Chechens and Arabs went by, singing, brandishing scimitars in the air and displaying rifles held by bandoleers across their backs.

After a few hours' ride, Max and Omer Nadji separated from the troops, riding forward on their mounts. They were traversing a rugged mountain pass flanked by woods on both sides.

It was then that Omer Nadji broached the subject for the first time. "I never imagined your zeal in rescuing Armenian women was so great."

Max nodded without saying a word. The powerful politician, laughing, asked, "To the point of giving up your magnificent horse, which we all envied you for. What do you intend doing with them, Swirsden-Righe?"

"I'm going to try and find a way to save them once we get to Russia. Will you be informing the committee in Constantinople about this, Omer Nadji?"

"No, don't worry. Do what you wish with them."

"Thank you, Omer Nadji." Max breathed with relief. At least on his own front the women would be free from danger.

They advanced at a good pace. Seen from a distance, the expedition looked like a caterpillar dragging itself among passes through arid highlands that stretched out to the horizon.

CHAPTER XXXVI

MOONSHINE ON KURDISTAN

THE FULL MOON WAS HUGE as it rose above the tree-tops. The fugitives journeyed on through the forest, barely able to give each other the encouragement to keep on going. They were hungry and dehydrated.

Manuc stopped. The rest, who were walking ahead, noticed him missing. They were panting desperately. They flopped down on the ground and broke off some grasses, which they took to their mouths. Retches preceded the vomiting. By this time, their stomachs rejected almost any plant.

"We've lost our way," observed Manuc, breathing heavily. "How far can the next Kurdish village be? We've been travelling for miles in the wrong direction, let's be honest. We'll die... We'll never make it to the Russian frontier or anywhere else. This makes no sense. How much longer can we carry on?" He broke into tears of anguish.

"We're still alive," replied Diran. "It's a chance thousands of our people haven't had. Let's not give up. We're sure to find something a bit further on. Get up, Manuc. I'd rather die looking for salvation than wait for death under the trees."

"This forest's going to be our end," said Agop.

With effort, Manuc, Diran and the other two trudged on. Climbing over roots the size of mighty boughs, they finally got back on track along a natural pathway, going ever deeper into the very heart of Kurdistan. Every so often they were overcome with coughs, retching and vomiting as a result of the leaves they ate, making their trek intolerable. They would stop for a rest until they got their breath back then, almost dragging themselves along, they would carry on, without any idea of the local geography.

ARAKSI TRIED TO SLEEP. The heat made her turn over time and again on her camp-bed, keeping her awake. The

211

remaining girls slept in the same tent. The night was totally calm.

From her position, an opening in the canvas allowed her to see Max's tent some distance away. He was awake, to judge by the light inside. The gramophone was playing and brought to her ears strains of music familiar to her. She was overcome with infinite sadness and tears came to her eyes. She remembered her father in the study of their family home, unable to sleep, listening to his favorite operas. Memories appeared every night and atrocious nightmares shook her spirit. She was helpless against this nightly remembrance.

During the day she could get away from the ghosts. She would concentrate on each length of the road, on every sound reaching her, but at night her mind turned into the cruellest of torturers, and her thoughts became instruments of horror that defeated all defense.

She looked at Max's shadow bending over his camp desk and thought that, but for this man, she and the others would still be enslaved, perhaps till their dying day, used and defiled night after night, putting up with the kaimakam and his friends' lechery, till they became pregnant and mothers of Mahommedans or, perhaps, being discarded for being barren, falling into pits it was better not to imagine.

She shivered, feeling that nothing was owed to chance: the consul had undertaken to take charge of them if all else failed. No, it could not be chance. God must finally have remembered her and the others. That music wafting over to her was her father's message, communicating with her from Heaven and, together with her mother and dead brothers and sisters, assuring her that they interceded for her in the other world, leading her to freedom. The German was not a coincidence in the tragic turn of events. She told herself it was impossible, otherwise inexplicable. He must be an instrument... but, supposing he were not... having just taken the kaimakam's place? No, no, it was unthinkable, yet... if the lieutenant should fall prisoner or disappear in combat — what then? After all, they were at war, they risked dying, and that could happen at any time. What would her fate, and that of the others, be then? Very near her own tent, hundreds of Turkish soldiers and Kurdish horsemen slept, or kept guard. Woe be to her and the others if that should happen. This was no mere idle fancy of hers.

The light went out in Max's tent. Araksi tried to sleep but realized some of the other girls were getting up from their beds, whispering, and stealing out into the night. Beyond, in the dark, some of the young Volga Germans were waiting for them. She saw the Armenian girls passionately embracing and kissing the soldiers then melting into the shadows. Araksi watched a little longer, until sleep finally took hold of her.

SNOW WAS FALLING GENTLY AND EVENLY on Munich. The military courier stopped outside the Swirsden-Righes'. He took the post out of his big leather satchel, shook the snow off his shoulders, made sure he had the right address, and rang twice. The maid came out to the porch and returned immediately to the study with the mail, to hand it to Countess Hildegard.

The legend on the envelope said 'Constantinople — German Military Mission — General Command'. Hildegard, sitting by the fireplace, broke off the conversation with her distinguished friends to open the letter.

The three ladies wore long skirts, in 1915 fashion. They had just finished lunch and were about to start embroidering, engaged in creating fine designs.

Hildegard anxiously opened the envelope and began to read Max's narrative. She was deeply moved at seeing his handwriting, looking time and again at that sheet of paper that had come from so far. The envelope carried stamps from mysterious places. After reading the first paragraphs, she deemed it acceptable to share some of the passages with her friends. The two of them seemed to be hanging onto each of Hildegard's gestures.

"What d'you think of that... The expedition's advancing into the Caucasus, and all along the way the regiments are acclaimed as conquerors: *'Dear Hildegard, in the villages we are welcomed as liberators. They are ancient, picturesque people...*' Gertrude, Franziska, leave your sewing a moment and listen. Listen to the news from my Max: the expedition under his command is moving into the Caucasus, which no European has trodden in several centuries. No German army has ever passed through it. Do you realize?" said Hildegard in amazement. "They've even rescued several young Armenian slave-women from a harem."

"Slave-women from a harem?" Gertrude was surprised.

Moved, Countess von Swirsden looked at the other two, her sewing box balanced on her knee and about to fall off. Gertrude stretched out and stabilized it, as Hildegard went on reading.

"Poor people. How backward and primitive they are in those far-off places," Franziska opined.

Gertrude seemed amused. She immediately brought forth her knowledge about slavery. "How dreadful, women made sex-slaves — inconceivable in our day and age. Only in parts of the world lost to God's grace could such crude things occur, though it's a well-known fact that Turkish grandees keep mistresses in their palaces in Constantinople, some of whom they even marry. Can you imagine, my dear? What a humanitarian gesture on Max's part. It's truly to be praised."

Hildegard's two friends crossed sly glances. "How proud you must feel of your husband, Hildegard. Who could ever question a legitimate German imperial presence in those lands of infidels? Our officer class impose respect wherever they may go. Why, they even civilize those pagans."

Hildegard read the rest of the letter in silence. Through the windows, the snow could be seen falling ever more intensely. The countess laid the letter aside and concentrated once more on her needle-work. As she swayed back and forth on the rocking-chair by the fireplace, she tried to imagine Max riding a magnificent horse at the head of his troops as they penetrated ever deeper into the Caucasus, cheered by villagers in exotic costumes.

Siirt

THE HOUSES WERE FLAT, built in Arab style. At the sides of the column crowded hundreds of Arab women and children, making a high-pitched ululation as their way of greeting. Max and Omer Nadji saluted the multitude from their horses. Way behind, just in front of the gun section towed by mules, the covered wagon carrying the Armenian girls moved forward. The girls seemed exhausted and rather light-headed after the demanding journey along mountain roads.

Araksi peeked out through the canvas covering, watching how the entire population of Siirt had enthusiastically turned out for the arrival of the expedition. The column turned from the main town towards a broad beach at the riverside, just where the Tigris narrowed between canyons. Araksi thought that perhaps there she would have some space to rest from the compulsory overcrowding among complaining women sweltering under the wagon covers.

A few hours later, an assistant of the local sheikh came to the camp, bringing several Arab horses. The Germans enthusiastically looked at the group of horses appearing across the sand, haughtily shaking their manes.

Max mounted a magnificent animal, intending to try it out at a gallop along the beach. Its mouth being good, responding to the slightest hint by the rider, Max felt at home with the adventure and determined to enjoy it to the full. After riding a stretch away from the contingent, he pulled up, continuing at walking pace.

At a bend in the river, laughter could be heard. Then he heard the women's shouts. He got closer and saw the whole scene. It was the women arguing and squabbling as they washed their clothes in the river. Two of them were pulling each other's hair and on the point of rolling over on the sand. The rest looked on nonchalantly. Legs and arms, bare in the sunshine, moved alluringly even in their shameless row. Certainly feminine beauty in a military world, thought Max. He looked back and saw they were completely out of sight of the camp. There were no soldiers nearby.

Instinctively, he looked for Araksi among the women. He was not long in spotting her, further down the bank. As ever, he felt excited at her presence. She was rubbing the soapy garments then rinsing them in the water. Just then, she looked round and saw Max on the beach, moving closer. She interrupted her task, tidied her hair, which fell to her shoulders, and stood up. The other girls stopped their bickering at once. They looked on attentively, a little awed.

Max dismounted and said, in a friendly tone, "Good morning, Araksi."

"Good morning, Lieutenant."

Her black eyes shone and changed expression on seeing him. Max realized she also felt a little uneasy. An undeniable attraction for the former consul disturbed her. Neither of them managed to speak during the first few minutes.

Araksi broke the silence by stroking the horse. "It's a fine animal, though nothing like Pasha. You've lost him, thanks to me."

They began walking as they talked.

"Pasha helped me fulfil the most important mission I've faced so far. Just forget it — you and the other young ladies are worth a hundred Pashas."

Araksi made a sign of gratitude. She was nervous at noticing her companions gossiping in the distance. She felt targeted by all eyes.

Max laughed. "Don't let it bother you. Tell them I'm a family friend. How is it to all live together? Is it tolerable?"

Araksi nodded. The hem of her long skirt was getting wet as they walked at the water's edge. It was a lovely morning and flocks of birds soared above the waters.

The thoroughbred, nervous and startled by the birds flapping their wings, reared in alarm. Araksi spontaneously reacted, caught the reins, and, walking ahead of Max, calmed the horse in seconds, caressing its muzzle till it was completely pacified.

Max admired her skill and familiarity with the spirited animal. "You've calmed him down like an expert. I wouldn't be at all surprised if you turned out to be a proficient horsewoman."

"My father taught us all to ride when we were children..."

Max stopped and faced her gently, trying to break the barrier that still intimidated her. "We'll never find out if your white-faced chestnut was faster than Pasha. He would have been a formidable rival. They say that, with an expert rider, he could cross the table-land faster than any animal in Erzurum, even the best in the army."

Baffled, she looked at him. "How do you know?"

Max smiled. "We were on maneuvers on the hillsides... It seemed the horse had winged hooves. Horse and rider bathed in the morning light and speeding across the table-land at full tilt. At first I thought it might be a Turk training some bey's horse, but then my field glasses put me straight as to who the horseman was. It was too wonderful a sight to forget. You really are an extraordinary rider, Araksi."

Araksi was dumbstruck. "No one in the world would have been able to catch up with me that time. My life, and those of my parents, brothers and sisters, depended on Akyuz. I went looking for weapons on our estate... But it was all in vain," she lied.

"No, it wasn't. You've survived," answered Max. She lowered her gaze, full of sadness. Max tried to cheer her up, "Let's get to know our surroundings. You may feel a little better if you get away from the camp. Spirits aren't the brightest around here, and I understand it. Would you like to go for a ride with me, Araksi?"

Her face lit up at the invitation. She hesitated briefly then regarded herself, wearing a long skirt and wrapped in rough garments. She felt the eyes of the other girls fixed upon her. She thought of the impropriety of the situation but for the first time since she had left Erzurum, someone was showing concern for her as a person, a human being. Max anxiously waited for her answer, unable to take his eyes off her.

When she accepted, Max experienced a sort of adolescent enthusiasm but the call to mess from the camp reminded him he must return to his duties.

ARAKSI AND MAX GALLOPED AMONG THE HILLS. She had been given baggy trousers and a military jacket. With her hair bunched up in an explorer-type helmet, she resembled an Amazon.

Her new rigout hid her femininity at a distance but, close up, in no way reduced her attractiveness. Two German assistants rode some way behind. Araksi gave the horse full rein and galloped over the meadow. The ride had been the best remedy to interrupt, were it for only a few hours, dark thoughts, and leave behind all humiliation, if such were at all possible. Had those instants not been indelibly etched in her soul for the rest of her existence?

Max spurred his mount and both went up and down the hills, leaving the others behind.

"For a moment, you've managed to remind me of what I was in the past, which in only a few weeks was changed forever." Max looked at her, inviting her to continue. "Everything in my life has become totally uncertain, and there are no longer any plans for the future or anywhere to go back to," she said. "From my parents' protection and the love that surrounded me, everything's become dirty and detestable. And frightening. In less than three months my past has disappeared, covered in blood. It's a wound that can't be overcome. I'm sorry," she apologized tearfully.

"You can't just sweep such a tragedy under the carpet. You don't need to apologize," Max comforted her. "In spite of everything, I can see your courage is untouched, Araksi. I remember your presence of mind among the wounded at the hospital, and then your words, so intense and true when you and your mother came to ask me for help at the consulate. Maybe we have a pre-ordained destiny that brings us together, and mine is to be able to fulfil the promise of getting you safe and sound to freedom."

Araksi avoided looking at him, intimidated by the compliments received. She blushed. It was clear that this man was powerfully attracted to her and was not hiding it. "They're all dead. God has allowed me to live and I don't know why. Perhaps He's sent you as an instrument to save me, that's all I know... Nothing I'd hoped for in life, nor what my parents planned for my future, will be possible now. They're gone. All I have left is the present and it frightens me, I assure you."

"The present is the only thing any of us has, and you'll be able to manage the reins with firmness. Just concentrate on that for now, and the ups and downs of life will finally line up on your side."

Araksi dried her tears.

In the distance, atop the nearest hill, the crumbling wall of a monastery could be seen. Max considered it prudent to avoid any more memories. It was preferable to enjoy the moment. He pointed towards the ruins.

"Ready to accept the challenge, Araksi?" he goaded her. "Let's see who gets to the ruins first. Let's go!"

Accepting the dare, Araksi drove her heels into the horse's side and the animal shot off. It took a great effort for Max to catch up with her.

THEY WERE CLOSE TO THE PERSIAN FRONTIER, but did not know it. The sun was scorching, the region arid as far as the horizon. The four Armenian fugitives dragged themselves across the undulations of the terrain. One vomited bile, suddenly immobile. The others looked at him in resignation. At the end of his strength, the young man died, convulsing from the effects of poison. The grasses had ended up killing Giorgi.

Diran, Manuc and Agop only managed a short distance more and there remained lying on the dunes, faint from the heat of the sun. Light drenched everything. In Diran's mind, the world turned white with blinding brightness. He never knew how long he lay there, until the images began to clear.

Scarcely inches from his head, a horse's hooves reared nervously in the sand. Diran could hear the animal snorting and the smell of its sweat completely brought him round from his sunstroke. On lifting his head up, he saw that several Cossacks were observing them from their horses. Diran heard words in Russian and understood that he and the others were being taken for Kurds, owing to their tattered clothing, typical of herdsmen. Muttering in Russian, he managed to say, "We're Armenians. Water, please, water! Not Kurds... not Kurds... Armenians."

One of the officers dismounted. The Cossacks quickly surrounded the fugitives, keeping their rifles trained on them. Diran half opened his eyes and was able to make out the blurred silhouettes of several Armenian horsemen, bandoleers full of bullets crossing their chests. They wore the typical knotted kerchiefs on their heads. Immediately pulling canteens from their packs, they gave water to the lads, who desperately took long, thirsty gulps. Someone informed them of what they already knew: they were saved.

CHAPTER XXXVII

CAMP ON THE BANKS OF THE BOGHDAN SU

THE CAKE OF SOAP SPRANG from hand to hand. It passed from one girl to another until it fell outside the water. Naked, smiling and frolicking, one jumped out and recovered it, once again to soap herself, lather dripping on the sides of the bathtub. Others waited their turn to bathe, wearing flimsy clothes and fanning themselves in the intense heat of day. Araksi, having just finished bathing, with her wet hair falling blackly on her skin, watched with amusement the jokes they played on each other. It seemed that from time to time, Araksi recovered the joy in life that had always been part of her character.

The fun was interrupted for a few moments and the girls observed the arrival of a Turkish infantry column. In the distance, soldiers passed, marching towards the city of Siirt, the regiments' meeting point. The passage of the troops reminded them all that they were journeying towards the battle front.

KHALIL BEY, COMMANDER of the Turkish troops, had just arrived in Siirt. He carefully moved the tiny flags representing each regiment along on the map. Those of different colour were the majority and stood for the Czar's armies at the frontier. The rest of the Turkish generals and German officers paid close attention to his comments. Khalil walked up and down with a pointer in front of the map as he tapped his tight riding boots with a riding whip.

"My column will continue down the river Boghdan to this sector before the Boghdan flows into the Tigris. Then, my orders are to meet with Marshal von der Goltz's army in Mesopotamia. Gentlemen, let us be certain of victory. The whole advance of the expedition will be a triumphal walkabout, so that the way south remains open to us for the conquest of Kut-el-Amara. Then, from there, no-one will stop us till we seize India away from the English."

Out of the corner of his eye, Max looked at Omer Nadji with a certain complicity. Determined to give his opinion, he raised his hand. Khalil Bey raised his chin with a stern gesture and awaited Swirsden-Righe's intervention.

"Sir, to go up the Boghdan Su will require an enormous effort. It will be a test for all of us. I don't imagine that a march of almost a thousand men fording a large river, then facing the crossing of the high mountains of Persia, could exactly be described as a 'triumphal walkabout'."

"The Turkish army," retorted the general, "knows and dominates every geographical feature in the country. The men are trained to overcome all difficulties. Perhaps you were unaware that the Boghdan Su was the route Xenophon took. We, instead, are going to march in the opposite direction."

Omer Nadji Bey intervened. "The pack animals will transport all the money we have: 5000 Turkish pounds, that is 100,000 gold marks if you prefer, plus 30,000 silver marks. The ammunition will go in chests. If it gets wet or falls into the water, well, gentlemen, say goodbye to the objective. All supplies will be carried on the backs of pack horses, as was done by the grand expeditions of Alexander the Great and the Romans before us. To feel like a conqueror, a price must be paid... The Caucasus is a trial for the men, no matter which army."

Khalil Bey, put off by the objections raised in front of his officers, carried on explaining the maneuvers. Omer Nadji Bey was a civilian, after all, but after the catastrophic defeat suffered by Enver Pasha in the mountains, it was better to keep quiet.

ROLF, WRAPPED IN A RAINCOAT that shielded him from a strong rain shower, endeavoured not to pass over a single detail of what was taking place around him. He was jotting down notes at great speed, to return afterwards to his post on the river bank. Flashes and sheets of lightning fell on the mountains, illuminating soldiers and animals with each downpour. Pressed together in the canyons on the banks of the Boghdan Su, they were waiting their turn to cross over to the opposite bank. Orders were shouted in a range of languages and the terrified neighing and braying of horses and mules mingled in confusion with the deafening roar of the current.

A fierce storm was lashing the expedition. The riders crossed the river via a narrow ford. In another sector, in the dark, the pack animals could be seen carrying huge chests, bearing tables, chairs and all kinds of stores on their backs. Araksi and the other girls had to get down from the wagon and mount horses to cross the river. Gusts of wind soaked their faces and the blackness of night increased the danger of being carried away by the current, unnoticed by anybody. Amid such confusion, Max and the officers took up positions on the opposite bank and controlled the maneuver. A chest fell into the water and was immediately carried off downstream at such speed that it was futile to even try and recover it. Several crates of good wine sailed off, soon to be smashed in the rapids a few miles further on. Swirsden-Righe and his assistants tensely watched the shipment of the cases containing thousands of pounds, swaying on saddles lapped by the turbulent waters; a great fortune entrusted to the fearless mules at every step they managed to gain against the rushing current. The fortunes of the advance upon Russia depended on the fortune of that load.

The noise of the rain was phenomenal. Araksi, holding onto the horse's neck, managed the crossing to the other bank as best she could. Some of the other girls, especially those that had never ridden an animal before, shrieked with dread, scared of being drowned. Finally, by dawn, the whole expedition had made it across the Boghdan Su, without the loss of a single person.

MAX LOOKED AT HIMSELF in the looking glass. Several hours' sleep had brought back his serenity. His facial muscles had relaxed, the tension of the crossing had been left behind. He lathered the soap on his face and sharpened the razor before trimming his thin, dark moustache.

He was thinking about Munich, about Hildegard. He was aware she had received no news from him for several weeks. He would have time to pen her a letter when they got to the big German base at Mosul. Then he thought of Araksi. Lately he thought of little else, and told himself he must put her out of his mind, and that the feeling he had for the young woman was improper. An emotional feeling, or just lust? He didn't want to acknowledge the difference. In any case, it was an uncomfortable, constant sensation, but he was not going to let it interfere in fulfilling his orders, as he had said in front of the Turkish generals before his plea for the Armenian orphans. *'Un consul avec des sentiments'*, they had jokingly called him at the banquet.

That 'sentimentality' — would it not actually be about to betray him, by making him lose control? That girl, Araksi, was absolutely irresistible. In whatever situation and condition she appeared, she was a feast for the eyes. His sexual abstinence had been long and he couldn't help thinking of how she had been the favorite in the harem. She had surely been trained to give even the most demanding man full pleasure. She was no longer the charming, innocent girl from Erzurum: she was a full-fledged female he was not sure he could allow himself to pass up.

Rolf's voice at his side interrupted his musings, asking, with greater insistence, "Would you like me to read again, Max?"

"Why, of course, Rolf. Please do."

Rolf went on with his reading of the chronicle of the expedition. Again, Max lost the thread of the story. Huge responsibilities and decisions to be made from one moment to the next overshadowed any anecdotal commentary. Nevertheless, Rolf advanced to the adventure of the river crossing.

"Almost a whole day has gone by since we forded the Boghdan Su. The new camp has been set up on the bank, and everyone is back at their activity and chores. Men and beasts got several hours' sleep..."

Max interrupted him. "I think I'd better get a good start on Khalil Bey and beat him to Mosul if I want to get hold of supplies and equipment."

WHILE SHAVING, MAX saw Omer Nadji in the mirror, approaching the tent. The Chechen was smiling as he walked. Clean and elegant as usual, he seemed to be in complete control of himself, wearing tails and tall boots.

"*Bonjour messieurs*, Swirsden-Righe, Lieutenant Hüchtinger."

Rolf stood to attention before the commander.

Omer Nadji continued, "Commander Khalil Bey's troops move fast. They're getting ready to move on. This is a challenge to you, Swirsden-Righe. He wants to get to Mosul ahead of you and, to judge by his preparations, he'll probably leave us far behind."

"Indeed? That's what he thinks... I'll leave for Mosul straightaway with some of my men. I must beat him to it to be able to get provisions before he leaves us with the stores bare of everything. I think I know how to gain time."

Omer Nadji, comfortably seated, his legs crossed, lit a cigarette and asked, "Will you travel down the Tigris by kelek?"

Max smiled slightly by way of an answer.

OMER NADJI POINTED at the group of keleks arriving and mooring at the bank. These were the famous rafts built of a framework of pleated reeds resting on inflated sheepskin bags, around 90 per raft.

"Look, Lieutenant, these vessels are the most practical means of travel on these rivers. This has been so since the times of the Assyrians, Babylonians, and Romans. Rivers have been the main communication routes, and keleks the preferred mode of transport in waging war or for commerce. Do you dare negotiate the rapids on a kelek loaded with equipment?"

"If other people have managed it in the past, no doubt we Germans will be able to as well. I'll wait for you and the rest of the troops at our base in Mosul, with all the ammunition and equipment we'll need to face the stretch through the mountains on our way to capture Sautchbulak, my dear Omer Nadji."

The Chechen signified his approval of the boldness expressed by his German ally.

THE YOUNG WOMEN WERE HANGING OUT clothes in the sun. Noemzar was holding a large tub filled with garments while Araksi hung skirts, blouses, and other items belonging to her companions, on the clothesline. Every so often, they would switch. The air was cool and a pleasant wind was blowing, ruffling their hair. They were speaking in Armenian.

"We can go to Tiflis, Araksi. I've heard that Armenians can travel to Saloniki and from there pass through Greece. I haven't lost hope that my brothers and sisters have been saved, so maybe we'll meet there." Noemzar was sad and homesick despite her optimism. Like the rest, she was alone in the world. "You know, there are nights when I can't remember my mother's face. I make an effort and try to see her in the dark, but I can't capture her kind face as she kissed us before we left for school. And yet I can still feel her kisses... and I feel my father's hugs, pressing me to his chest, and my bigger brother pulling my hair when we were tots."

Araksi looked at her while arranging long skirts on the rope. "I've no hope left, Noemzar. I know they're all dead. At times I imagine I can hear their voices. I dream that someone wakes me up and announces the nightmare's over, and then I lie awake, crying... always crying."

Araksi stopped. They were both looking for somewhere to sit down. The clothes, blown by the wind, billowed in the sunshine.

"Diran, my fiancé, you know, he wanted us to go to Russia. He was right — he realized right away that they meant to kill us all." She remained deep in thought for a short while, and then continued. "He was an idealist. At first I thought he was to blame that my father and eldest brother, Tavel, were arrested."

"Why?

"He was a member of the resistance. He kept it to himself until the end." She paused. "How ironic... that we're alive! For the time being, anyway, and on our way to Russia with a Turkish army. If all this hadn't happened, I might already be married to him... and I'd be living near my parents, in the same neighbourhood, just like my sister. We were all very close to each other, my brothers and sister, their children, the little ones... always together."

A silence ensued, and she remained immersed in her memories. Tears of deep sadness trickled down her cheeks.

"We'll survive, Araksi. Maybe some of our people have managed to escape as well. Why don't you look at things that way?"

Weeping with rage, Araksi picked up a stone and threw it with all her might. "Maybe I should've killed myself. You know that too, Noemzar. For the rest of our lives we'll carry that humiliation with us. It'll be so deep, so deep, that it'll never go away. I wish I'd had the strength to kill him. I can't forgive, Noemzar, I'll never be able to."

Noemzar hugged her, trying to cheer her up. "We're alive, Araksi, we're alive. Please, I don't want to carry on remembering. I just want to be grateful to God for another day, and for saving us."

Noemzar stood and walked off with the empty tub. She had noticed Max coming along the riverbank, and did not wish to be in the way.

Swirsden-Righe frequented the women's sector more and more, seeking Araksi's company. She felt especially protected by him, but was confused and still uneasy after the violence she had suffered. She was no longer the same girl and felt she would never be able to give herself entirely to anyone.

Max arrived and went straight to the point. "Good morning, Araksi... Look, there's something I need to decide right away." Araksi looked at him with disquiet. She could not bear any more surprises. "Tomorrow, I'm leaving the camp. I'm travelling down the river by raft with a small group of men. We'll be going ahead of the troops. I want you to come with me."

She did not know how to answer.

"You can choose to stay here and carry on travelling to Mosul with the rest," he continued, "but I'd prefer you to be next to me, for the sake of your safety. At least for a few days you won't have the whole army around you, just a few of us."

So spoke the lieutenant, looking straight at her. He was smiling hopefully, and seemed to be offering her total freedom of choice. She had some doubts as to his true intentions, but knew his behaviour to that point was absolutely gentlemanly and all the girls were witnesses to the kind treatment they received, isolated and protected from Turkish and Kurdish soldiers.

Besides, the German was unquestionably attractive, polite and interesting, and the only person that linked her to her past in Erzurum. Her father had trusted him. What could she lose by travelling with him? In fact, the only guarantee against being abused lay in this officer's figure and authority. No, she did not find him disagreeable in the least. Quite the contrary. She acknowledged feeling attracted to Max and, after all, what else was there to consider but the present, given the miraculous circumstances that had kept her alive? But supposing he wanted something more, taking advantage of his power, what would she do then? But it was surely riskier to stay behind, at the mercy of anyone in the camp until they got to Mosul. The thoughts she was trying to sort out in her mind began to go round in circles. She had to decide fast. Araksi looked directly at him and accepted. Max offered her a broad smile, eager to start out on the adventure without delay. And, making a few recommendations, he left her and walked back to the camp along the riverbank.

Araksi ran after Noemzar. Her mood, all at once, had lifted.

CHAPTER XXXVIII

DOWN THE TIGRIS BY KELEK

AT DAWN, THE GERMAN SOLDIERS loaded gear onto the three rafts. Max, Rolf, the aide Tahir and Memdukh checked the maneuvers on the keleks.

Araksi arrived under the guard of one of the soldiers. She was dressed in military fatigues. On seeing her, Max smiled and offered his hand to assist her in boarding the largest raft moored to the pier. Further back, there was great activity on two keleks about to leave: large vessels that could accommodate the weight of several men and a load of luggage. The rafts were fitted with a canvas shelter as protection from the intense sun on their week- or fortnight-long expeditions.

"The young lady's coming with us," Max announced. The men looked at her without comment. Taking their place on the keleks, the guides began to move away from the bank, pushing themselves off with vigorous thrusts of their long oars. Soon, the pier was left behind and very gradually the rafts drifted into the river until the reeds on the banks and the river bends hid the camp from sight.

Araksi, very taken up with all of this, looked from the corner of her eye at Max, who was sitting on a seat at the stern. She felt excited by the unknown, and the feeling of sailing on a solitary river, caressed by the wind, splashed by the water and swayed by the current. All of it brought memories of a sense of freedom.

There were hardly any Turks travelling with them, save a handful of soldiers on the cargo raft. All the rest were Germans. She felt safe. She had been able to divest herself of her uncomfortable long skirts that covered and stifled her. The baggy Turkish trousers and the shirt and jacket she had been provided gave her an air of exotic femininity and sensual fashion.

The men guided the vessel out onto the Tigris. They were conveying enormous crates of provisions and their own lives on blown-up sheepskins and pleated reeds.

The three large rafts coursed down the river between great rocky sides, crossing a region of wild, rugged beauty. One of the keleks was carrying equipment and 35 boxes of ammunition while the other carried food. They were lightly built and efficient for navigating the Tigris. Keleks had been used by every traveller and invading army since the beginning of time, without ever undergoing any modifications in shape or construction — a design needing no improvement over the centuries, thought Max, imagining his predecessors, Alexander the Great's warriors, looking at the very same walls, the same bends in the river, carrying their spears and swords, their protective shields and armor, anticipating their next battle, penetrating the Persian empire in quest of Darius' throne, under the same sky.

The guides directed the rafts in the current. Handling their oars with great skill, they avoided bumping into the rocks. Max looked up and saw ducks and eagles soaring above the course of the river. Rolf shot two ducks down with his shotgun.

Araksi watched it all with fascination, hanging onto the sides at each roll of the vessel. The keleks were driven along by the current, floating between the jagged outcrops where the water formed dangerous whirlpools, to flow into churning cascades. Araksi lost her balance and half of her body hung overboard. Max caught her by the waist, preventing her from falling. She clutched his arm to steady herself until, the danger past, she let go.

Over the following days, the voyage continued in a peaceful, serene manner. The three rafts moved forward gracefully, and the noise of the water was magnified by the rock walls. Some of the men experienced a sensation of infinite quiet and what for some was drowsiness and leisurely rest was for Max one of the most intense and joyful experiences he had ever known, perhaps akin to one's life-journey.

Araksi, her eyes half closed, sunbathed in the prow of the raft. Her shirt was open, sleeves rolled up, and she was bare-footed. Her straight, jet-black hair fell on her shoulders. Her skin was golden and silky, the result of so many weeks outdoors, in contrast with the Teutons and Russian volunteers, who responded to the sun with burns that reddened their faces and arms.

Max felt a sudden thrill on perceiving her perfect feminine shape beneath her clothing. He looked at her, rapt, as she stretched, lying on her back after a few hours of dozing to the rocking of the waters. She noticed him immediately. Half opening her eyes, she raised her head, turned to look, and met his gaze. They looked at each other with longing. It only lasted an instant, but it was enough. She lay on her hip, tidied her black hair, smiling at him, and went back to contemplating the river.

THE BANK WAS WIDE AND PROTECTED ENOUGH to bring the vessels alongside. They lit a campfire close to the tents. The keleks, moored with ropes and weights that served as anchors, remained beached on the sand. The Turkish guides kept guard.

Everybody gathered around the fire while the ducks Rolf had shot were roasted. The flames illuminated their faces, tanned from the intense sunlight of the last few days. They all looked healthy and happy, far from the anxieties of battle. Max, Rolf, Araksi, Memdukh, and the group of six Volga Germans that made up the crew of the other two rafts laughed and chatted in a relaxed, friendly manner.

Rolf mixed German and French, with a few hilarious Turkish expressions thrown in. As he turned the meat over, he mumbled, chewing a tasty morsel, "What they'd give... back in Straubing, to be enjoying these delicacies by Oriental moonlight instead of the usual tasteless, boring mess rations!"

"Let alone those poor devils in the trenches," observed Max as he uncorked a bottle of excellent Rhine wine. "Duck à la Tigris," he said with satisfaction. "It's delicious, isn't it, my friends? Congratulations to Araksi for preparing it... and to Rolf for his good aim."

"I appreciate your remarks, Max," answered Rolf. "I don't know if it's up to the standard of the gourmet dishes served in your home... I especially remember that evening when we celebrated your receiving the Iron Cross. What wines! And what desserts! What a great lady, Countess Hildegard. We were around twenty back then. I remember the old duke sitting next to Friedrich, having three helpings... and the glasses brimming over with that wine!" Rolf dipped pieces of bread in the sauce.

Araksi did not miss the remark. Suddenly Max, feeling irritated, interrupted Rolf. He went round the group, offering everyone wine. He did not want to hear about his life in Europe, partly out of modesty in front of Araksi and the simple young fellows travelling with them, or perhaps wishing to leave aside homesickness and memories. At that moment nothing seemed more important than to enjoy the present moment without such things interfering. Was there not a certain remorse attached to memories?

"Araksi, how do you say in your language, 'This meal is outstanding; I've never tasted anything like it in my life?'"

Smiling, she spoke in Armenian. They all listened to that ancient language in silence. She smiled, and carried on in French. "Actually it means the same as in any language, 'Thank you, it's more than one deserves. I just made do with what I had available — it's a sweet-sour sauce.' In fact, as a girl it was only occasionally that my elder sister and I went into the kitchen, to ask the cook to make us desserts and sweets and all those things..."

She became pensive as they all paid attention.

Rolf enthusiastically urged her, "Say something more for us in your language, Araksi... In Armenian."

She hesitated, a trifle shy, but finally went ahead, "Heartaches go away like the waters of a river, and the reflection of a new life shimmers in the gentle rays of dawn, comforting the grieving soul." She smiled, a little sadly, and translated it into French.

Max was looking at her, irresistibly attracted. The firelight raised by the wind gave her features an interesting, mysterious contrast. They carried on chatting a while longer.

THE FIRE WAS ALMOST OUT, and they were all sleeping in their tents when the quiet of night was suddenly rent by a woman's scream. Max started from his campbed, holding his loaded pistol. He ran to Araksi's tent. Rolf and the others woke up, and immediately came out into the darkness.

Max found Araksi crying disconsolately. She was still under the effect of her nightmare. Taking her by the shoulders, he tried to calm her. Araksi, sobbing and frightened, embraced him, and Max caressed her tenderly.

"All the dead come back into my head. I see my parents embracing and praying, and the zaptiehs moving in to kill them... I can't bear it... I can't stand it any longer."

She wept, her words rising from inside her, and she shook with sobs. Rolf and the soldiers stopped in front of the tent, their rifles at the ready, keeping guard. They found their commander comforting the girl. Araksi was frightened at seeing the armed men. Max ordered them all to go back to sleep, as the next day they would have a long journey ahead of them.

The lieutenant inspired trust in Araksi and she felt protected; the only protection she really had in the world at that time. She looked at him, and felt she could confess to him her deepest pains, everything that was tearing her soul apart. "He forced me and raped me with all the violence of his body and soul... I didn't have the courage to kill myself, and I haven't had it since, but perhaps that's what I ought to have done." Deep hatred shone in Araksi's eyes. "I should've killed him, all those nights, every time he fell asleep drunk, lying on those sheets. At least that way I would have died with a bit of honor instead of spending the rest of my life remembering my cowardice."

"I don't think so, Araksi... One can't expect that kind of courage in oneself. You can't go against the instinct of survival when what you really want is precisely to live. Your grace was stronger than the horror one finds everywhere. Araksi — nothing is going to happen to you here... All that is behind you. Try to rest. It's over now. I won't allow the demons of night to bother you again."

They remained in silence for a long while. Finally, she went to sleep in Max's arms, as a completely unprotected and abandoned child.

While he held her, Max told himself that no sentimental matter was going to make him deviate from his military duties. He realized that the attraction he felt towards this girl had totally replaced all thought of Hildegard. He could think of nothing but Araksi and he was letting himself in for trouble, there was no doubt about that. She was looked at with desire by all the men. He had done well in getting her away from camp and bringing her along with him.

In fact, it was already a foregone conclusion that, sooner or later, she would end up as his lover. Even Omer Nadji had hinted at it, in his subtle way. What could Rolf and Friedrich and all the other officers that had known him in Germany think of all this? He told himself that any man in his place would understand perfectly. And so he remained there, embracing her for a long time, maybe until daybreak.

THE ENTIRE GROUP boarded the keleks, passing from hand to hand the cargo of equipment onto the rafts. Each time they took down the campsite, they had to pack up and load the bundles, chests, tableware and bedclothes back onto the rafts. They worked non-stop, taking advantage of the morning light.

Araksi came over to the vessels waiting for the moment to leave. There was a hush among the men.

Max seemed to guess what his friend was thinking. "Rolf..."

"Yes, Max."

"Thanks for not giving me your opinion. It's been this way since the very first time I saw her in Erzurum."

Rolf nodded without saying a word, as he carried the last of his backpacks and shouldered his two guns.

WE ARE NOW TRAVELLING THROUGH A SECTOR of fast, calm currents, bordering a more open river bank. Memdukh,

Max's official Turkish translator, is shooting wild duck with his gun. One of the birds falls into the river, close to the kelek. I dive into the river and swim, attempting to reach it, but the current carries me further away all the time. I catch the duck and try to return to the raft. They all have fun watching me from the rafts, although they hide their concern for my safety so I don't lose my calm as they rescue me. The bargemen maneuver so as to get closer to me. Finally, with difficulty, I manage to get back onto the craft.

ROLF, STILL WET FROM HIS DIP, was entering in his diary the day's adventure. Nothing serious had happened. Tired from the effort and the nervous tension, he slept for several hours.

Rocking to the current was usual when they passed into areas with rapids but, by now used to the voyage, none of them got dizzy any longer. Suddenly, the keleks veered round to avoid colliding with the rocks. Instinctively, Araksi caught Max's hand so as not to lose her balance. They held together for several seconds. They could not avoid looking at each other, intensely.

The keleks sailed on uneventfully by day and sometimes at night, until the guides came to a spot they considered convenient and safe to camp.

Through the utterly wild landscape, Max, Araksi and Rolf and, further behind, Memdukh and Tahir, were looking for a pathway among the rocks. They climbed the jagged incline. The keleks had remained securely beached, guarded by the Volga Germans.

An hour later, they came to a great hot spring of sulphurous thermal waters. The place was a wide lagoon amid the rocks; the ideal place, they had been told, to have a reinvigorating, relaxing bathe after so much sailing and the jolts of the Tigris rapids. The sky was perfectly blue. Without having to ask, Araksi moved some distance away from the others to where she might strip away from the men's sight. She undressed calmly and left her clothing on some stones. Stark naked, she waded into the waters. She felt strange, and she smiled. Everything that was happening was a total novelty, nothing like anything she had known before. She had spoken little: that journey was a play of emotions. She imagined the same was true of Max, but his reasons were different.

Perhaps the whole situation was a defense against the horrors pent up in her memory. In that way, each day was a new one and easy to bear, progressing towards the unknown and responding only to the sensations that presented themselves, with the caution she knew she must show, knowing she was in custody, not completely free. The hot spring waters produced an agreeable tingle to her body. They reminded her of Turkish baths.

Araksi tried not to think of anything, but a flurry of situations she had experienced in the harem came to her. She rested her head in the water and looked up at the deep blue, cloudless sky. The laughter and frolics of the nude men going into the water on the other side of the rocks brought her back to the present. One voice she heard was Max's.

They swam and moved slowly, submerged to their necks. Jets of vapor rose from the waters, and a cloud covered the whole surface of the spring. Max and the other men floated and relaxed, loosening their stiffened muscles. Araksi stayed a certain distance away. Max looked at her casually, being very careful not to pester her. In fact, all of them behaved like gentlemen.

When the others came out of the water, only Max and Araksi were left in the spring. They smiled happily. Inevitably, they moved closer and closer to each other. Max, captivated by the situation and unable to hide it, looked at that face with its dark eyebrows shadowing the black eyes, and a sensual mouth that kept him a captive of each movement of her lips.

Araksi, aware of the effect she was having, felt the attraction too. The warm water and the vapour around them increased the excitement for both. They did not speak — they were incapable of uttering a word. The others remained out of sight, drying themselves in the sunshine on some rocks.

Max said, "I think we'll have to go back now."

She assented with a smile. Then she asked him to look

away as she came out of the water. Feigning irritation, Max obeyed. When she emerged, her nakedness was exposed, showing the full beauty of her perfect figure. Max inevitably turned his eyes on her and felt the most uncontrollable physical attraction he had ever known.

Araksi finished dressing behind a rock. Thousands of sensations went through her head. Disturbed, she realized desire was in control of her instincts. All she was waiting for was for Max to make the first move. A few eagles circled the place at low height. Their calls were the only sound interrupting the silence of that place, about to explode.

Araksi took some steps on the stones. Her hair wet her shirt, and her damp skin glistened in the sunshine. Max, a little distance away behind some rocks, was slowly drying his shoulders, his trunk yet bare. Araksi approached to spy on him, prey of an unstoppable desire. It had taken her time to accept the attraction of that foreigner, unknown and unacceptable under the circumstances. But she would not resist it any longer. Here was a man she wanted to be possessed by. Never before had she experienced such an intense desire; not once, in any of the practices she had been subjected to by the kaimakam, had she known such seduction. She had lost her virginity by being raped, and after that traumatic beginning, enslaved night after night to serve the instincts of a disagreeable master she found repellent. Only now did she feel desire united to love.

Once more, Araksi looked at Max's well-built body, sunburnt and trim. Max, with his slow movements, seemed abstracted, enjoying those moments in the sunshine. A little later, he started out among the rocks towards the camp. He found her sitting combing her hair, waiting for him. He gazed at her for a moment. Araksi turned round. Max came to her and gave her his hand, helping her up. They remained face to face, looking at each other in silence and, moving towards each other, unable to resist the powerful attraction they felt any longer, gave themselves up to a passionate kiss.

Araksi slowly drew away and took him by the hand. In

perfect silence, they descended the rocky pathway to catch up with the rest of their group.

THE KELEKS SWAYED IN THE RAPIDS OF THE RIVER. Araksi and Tahir had got off the raft and walked along the stony bank to lighten the weight. The river took a wide bend and the craft soon entered a zone of turbulent waters. The current was flowing very fast and large rocks appeared in their way.

The keleks leapt and dived, producing showers of foam. Several pieces of luggage jumped in the air, while the guides made great efforts to get back on course. Max, Rolf and Memdukh balanced themselves on deck, trying to avoid falling and being swept away by the current. They stretched out their arms, steadying themselves by catching hold of the ammunition boxes.

The guides pushed the rafts with their long poles, moving them away from every rock that appeared. The rhythm of the navigation was devilish. The vessels' wicker decks plunged into the water for a few instants and then, avoiding the obstacle, emerged once again until the next cascade. Some of the sheepskin bags burst on hitting jagged edges.

An hour later, the speed of the current ended up delivering them to a more peaceful stretch, and they were able to leave the last rapids behind. Araksi and Tahir ran along the bank, waving their arms, celebrating coming out of the difficult patch. Araksi felt happy and, the greater the challenges of the Tigris rapids, the more enthusiasm and readiness she showed, feeling part of an adventure with romantic explorers through unknown territories. All of them often felt that way, though they were unavoidably headed for battle.

CHAPTER XXXIX

DJAZIRET IBN OMAR

DAMAGED SHEEPSKIN BAGS NEEDED REPAIRS. The Turkish guides sewed the tears at the riverside jetty. The heat was scorching. A chain of Arab soldiers and Russian volunteers unloaded the ammunition boxes from the keleks to secure them on the backs of mules. The job took a few hours. At the end of the day, the whole crew thought of nothing but resting and recovering from the exhausting effort, but they had to honor the festivities planned for them.

Swirsden-Righe was duty-bound to greet the kaimakam of the tiny town, a village of Byzantine origin and architecture whose chief, on finding out about the arrival of the German commander, came along with his entourage to welcome them. Araksi was ordered by Max to keep her distance from the troops.

The dark group of houses that was Djaziret-ibn-Omar stood out against the desert sunset. Several Arabs were with the sheikh, seated on the ground under the open sky. Max and his companions were placed around the fire. A huge salver of roast lamb and delicious side dishes held center place at the banquet. The men picked the food with their right hands and took it to their mouths, while at the same time laughing and waving long horse-whips, zig-zagging them at the centre of the group. Araksi and Max exchanged glances from time to time, remaining immersed in thought. There was an unspoken understanding between them.

At the end of the banquet, the drumming and music ceased and the Muslims knelt towards Mecca for general prayer. As night fell, Tahir took charge of accommodating the trunks in the quarters provided for them, a white-walled edifice in the desert, having an upper storey with rough windows that prevented the heat from entering. The ground floor had been allocated to their remaining companions.

Max walked in silence. Araksi felt tense but sensual. They mounted the stairs and Max escorted her to her bedroom, next to his. Both opened out onto a common terrace. A large bed had been placed in the middle of the room, and candles lit. Araksi removed the veil covering her head and face. She was dressed as she had become accustomed to, in baggy trousers and an army jacket. She loosened her hair with a shake of her head.

Max went into the room next door, leaving the bags and rucksack with his gear in a corner. He unbuttoned his uniform and went out onto the terrace. The desert extended into the distance. The evening was very hot. At that moment he saw Araksi coming towards him.

"We're a day's cruise away from Mosul," he said, looking at her. This was their first chance to be alone.

"And we'll never have such intimacy again, will we?" she answered. Max shook his head. "I've just spent my time living every instant to the full, trying not to remember the past or wonder where we're going. I think I feel... a sort of happiness. Thank you, Max."

On hearing her naming him for the first time, he came closer until they were touching. Then he tried to kiss her, but Araksi backed away. She was trembling as she looked into his eyes with an expression that required no explaining. Max felt the desire in her, and the need to be loved and protected, a desire that burnt in both of them. She turned round and slowly walked to her bedroom.

In the dim light of the room, illuminated only by candles, Araksi stood without moving.

Max gently took her by the shoulders and she turned around in invitation. They entwined in passionate kisses, caresses and embraces then, unable to hold back any longer, undressed each other, lay down on the mattress and made love the whole night through. At times they said nothing, then gave free rein to exclamations of pleasure, ardent words and loving tenderness. Never before had either felt transported with such special intensity; a kind of explosion that almost frightened them because, as Araksi pointed out, what they were experiencing could well be love.

CHAPTER XL

MOSUL, NOVEMBER 1915

THE CITY STREETS WERE UNMISTAKABLY ARAB, although they showed occasional coiled minaret constructions in typical Persian style. All around, great destruction and abandonment was in evidence. That was Mosul, where the German military had established a consulate, and possessed a great base of operations from which the joint forces would leave on their way to Russian enemy territory.

Max von Swirsden-Righe read the telegram. Rolf listened very attentively. They were alone in the office. In the next room, the telegraphist shut the door on orders from his senior officer.

RADIOGRAM

In the western outskirts of Mosul, where certain Armenian deportees have settled, serious incidents are taking place. In view of this, my orders are that our own troops and any German ones that may be present immediately put themselves at the disposal of the Turkish commander.

Signed
Omer Nadji Bey, Inspector General of the Committee etc., etc.

Max thought this over briefly before going on. Rolf, sitting with his legs crossed, was listening carefully.

"If German troops take part in any confrontations against the Armenians, the Turks won't hesitate in deploying their forces against all Christian citizens — which is already happening in the whole of Turkey. It's unacceptable! No soldier under my command is going to be used for repression," Max said firmly. He resolutely went to the office next door. The German soldier translated as he operated the telegraph.

RADIOGRAM

Orders for Lieutenants Hüchtinger and Thiele. Proceed immediately to Mosul and hand over the command of all Turkish troops and Kurdish cavalry to the Inspector-General of the Committee of Union and Progress Omer Nadji Bey.

Signed
Lieutenant von Swirsden-Righe, Commander.

Araksi and Max were naked in bed, scarcely covered by the sheets. Dim light penetrated the bedroom through the open windows. The lovers took advantage of every moment to be together, caressing each other tenderly after making love. Araksi embraced Max fondly, her black hair falling on her shoulders.

"Listen to me, Max, please listen to me. What if there's some member of my family among the deportees? What if Mavush survived, or someone knows the whereabouts of my nephews and nieces? Maybe the Erzurum group was transferred to the outskirts of Mosul. Please, Max, I can hardly stop thinking about them. Try and understand how this mortifies me."

Max turned over, took Araksi by the shoulders, and placed her with her back to him, and while he lovingly caressed her, said, "No, Araksi, it can't be. You know that. I couldn't even mention it in front of the chiefs. The situation's critical now. The other rescued girls and you yourself must find a way to salvation, but you can't get near any group of Armenians. You must understand this: all of you would be looked at in a very different light, even by Omer Nadji Bey... I'd completely lose control of the situation." Araksi hugged him tightly. "We agreed to live only for the present. We can't afford to think of anything else."

Araksi wept silently. She did not insist.

Max thought of the Turkish soldiers arrayed in the hills, trying to fight Armenian and Assyrian combatants. He imagined the Turks falling before bursts of machine gun fire as they climbed to take the positions of the sharp-shooters nested amid the rocks.

The cabled messages arriving in Mosul that mid-day confirmed that the Turkish officers commanding the troops were ordering a retreat on account of the fierce resistance put up by the guerrillas, carrying away their wounded and dead with their own stretcher-bearers, and retiring from the action. No — there was no way anything could be found out about any Armenian, living or dead. The Turkish military, and no few German chiefs, were more infuriated than ever with all this business that had put the whole territory in jeopardy. If Max wished to carry on having Araksi at his side, he had to make sure the group of women remained under his custody, and maintained as low a profile as possible over the stretches they still had to cover.

WHILE THEY WERE LED by two black slaves down the passages of the governor's palace, Rolf asked Max for the second time, "The Valee, that is, the military governor, is above all the kaimakams in the region, am I right?"

"Yes, but there are vilayets, like Erzurum, that are under the authority of a military governor-general, who's above all the civilian governors in the region. The Valee of Mosul has his own independent military command. You surely understand that by now, Rolf!" Max scolded his friend.

THEY WERE IN AN ENORMOUS, empty room. The Turk sitting behind his desk sported several decorations on his chest. He extracted tobacco from a little silver cigar box and rolled a cigarette with elegance and circumspection. Behind him, the portraits of ministers Enver, Talaat, and Djemal Pashas were a reminder of the omnipresent authority of the Ittihad. The Valee spoke plainly. "We have lost 25 soldiers, apart from several wounded, as a result of the skirmishes caused by Armenians, who are still holding out in the hills."

When Max began to speak, the governor clapped his hands and interrupted him. A door opened and an assistant appeared. The young man, standing beside the desk, began taking notes.

Max began again, "Your Excellency, I'm here to request that troops are not diverted for any other objective from the central purpose of our campaign: the joint offensive against the Russians and the capture of the town of Sautchbulak. I am also requesting that the Armenian girls travelling with our expedition be employed in domestic chores and as nurses. I imagine, Sir, they will very soon be needed in field hospitals."

The Valee smiled knowingly and, drawing on his cigarette, answered, "Young Armenian women for domestic chores... Hmm, stands to reason."

"Indeed, Sir. We have witnessed these nurses' great commitment to Turkish and German wounded at the Erzurum hospital."

The Valee bowed with an air of magnanimity and condescension. The presence of those Armenians among the troops mattered very little to him, in particular what this German might do with them. His government's policy was to keep the German allies as happy as possible, and if they chose to travel with hussies for their pleasure, he was not about to make an issue of it.

"In view of the importance our government places on your presence in the region and the military objective you have set yourselves, I will consider your request... and may even grant it."

Max looked at Rolf. He was satisfied. They stood to attention before the general and made their exit.

And here began the most complicated part of the expedition; the departure from Mosul and the crossing of the high mountains, with the main contingent of Turkish, Kurdish and Arab divisions that would be joining them in Mosul over the next few days.

THE TWO CAMOUFLAGED MERCEDES displaying German army banners at each side went up and down among the dunes in the trackless desert. Enveloped in a cloud of dust, Rolf and Tahir rode behind the cars. A couple of Circassian horsemen followed the convoy as guards. They were escorting Field-Marshall von der Goltz and his officers on their way to Mosul.

The riders gave their magnificent Arabs free rein, galloping flat-out and keeping close to the vehicles. Rolf was lagging behind more and more. He was unused to this sort of terrain and Tahir, on Kismet, and the Circassians were leaving him further and further behind. Rolf urged his mount forward and all at once he found himself flying forward: the horse rolled on the sand and Rolf was flung out of the saddle. Before hitting the ground, Rolf put his arm out to cushion the blow. It was the weight of his own body that caused the fracture.

Tahir looked back and saw Rolf on the ground, while the horse stood up without ill consequences. Tahir pulled up, and galloped back to assist Rolf, who was writhing with pain. The marshall's caravan, not having realized what had happened, carried on across the last few miles of the desert until its arrival in Mosul.

WITH RESPECT AND ADMIRATION, Max guarded Field-Marshall Baron Colmar von der Goltz, hero of Gallipoli, the general who had frustrated the Allied landing attempt in the Dardanelles. He was right in front of them, with his bush-moustached Prussian figure, using a great wall-map to explain the latest modifications to the campaign, as decided in Constantinople by the German high command.

"Gentlemen, some changes have been introduced as regards the initial plan. I'll come straight to the point. As Sixth Army Commander, I have decided to deploy an artillery regiment in Mesopotamia, to invade Persia. Our objective is to annihilate the British. But before facing the enemy on the battlefield, I shall have to relinquish my command to a Turkish general until we get to Azerbaidjan."

With a gesture of resignation and a dry disdain, he added, "The regional Valee will command the troops. This means that as from now there is a single expedition, and that Omer Nadji Bey and Lieutenant Swirsden-Righe report to the Governor of Mosul."

Swirsden-Righe's face showed incredulity and discouragement: he was no longer at the head of the troop, sharing the leadership with Omer Nadji. A Turkish general was to decide the maneuvers.

The marshall proceeded, "We have repelled the Allied attacks in the Dardanelles, but now the British response has been fierce against our forces at the Suez Canal, and they are advancing towards Kut-el-Amara, on the road to Baghdad, which is the Turks' weakest point." He finished talking without greater preamble: the new strategy was underway, and the orders had been given.

Half an hour later, Max and the German officers walked along the columned galleries of the military headquarters surrounding the parade quadrangle on the way to the Officers' Club. They bore long faces. Friedrich, who had been put in command of a horse division, had just reached Mosul by the longest route with the bulk of the army of Turks and Kurds. The trip had demanded great effort, turning out to be much more exhausting than cruising down the Tigris on rafts.

"It looks like we'll no longer be the right flank of the advance on the Caucasus, Max. We've become the left wing of von der Goltz's Mesopotamian Army, which means irrelevant in facing the British. I feel we've been left in a limbo between two campaigns."

They were walking fast. Max said, optimistically, "Our function will be to prevent Prince Nikolai Nikolaevich from joining forces with the British. It will all depend on how many men the Russians deploy on the frontier. Don't imagine it'll just be a pleasure trip, as it's been so far. The possibility exists of going into action via Azerbaidjan and repelling the greatest number of Russian troops possible. It won't be a pleasure ride, gentlemen, in any way. How's Rolf?"

"He fractured his arm and two ribs," answered Friedrich.

"In that state, he can't ride or fire a gun. He'll have to stay behind in Mosul."

The men entered the bar of the Officers' Club. The heat was unbearable. A good number of German officers were having long drinks at tables under huge ceiling fans, which were trying to keep the air in motion. They sat down in the middle of the hubbub. During the whole time he sat with his men, Max did not stop thinking of Araksi. He gulped the last drink down and, as soon as he was able, slipped away to the hospital, which occupied the same precinct as the military headquarters. One had to cross the courtyard to get to the pavilion.

The wounded were attended by Turkish doctors, assisted by Armenian nurses. Max was not long in finding Araksi. She was moving along the aisles between the beds, carrying bandages and medication. She went from one side to another in answer to the beckoning of the sick and wounded. On seeing Max, she left her duties in Noemzar's hands and, slipping past folding screens, sought an exit to the back part of the building, out of everyone's sight.

She hugged and kissed Max hungrily.

"Araksi — all the girls will be in danger on account of the decision I've made, but there's no other possibility. You simply can't stay here in Mosul. That would mean falling back into Turkish captivity as soon as I left. You'll all have to come with me through the mountains. God knows what that'll be like and what'll happen afterwards, but I'll find some way of getting you over to the Russians. Sautchbulak, the village we're heading for, and the whole region around it are infested with Armenian spies. We'll make contact with some of them and contrive a way of getting you over into Russian territory. D'you understand the risk of the situation, Araksi?"

"Yes, Max, I understand... We might be killed... *You* could be killed... I'm not going to be separated from you, my love, knowing I'll no longer..."

"You'll come to the battle-ground as nurses, and there..."

Without letting him finish, she kissed him passionately.

"Araksi..."

"Max, my precious, I don't want to leave you... I know I must, but it's more powerful than any reason... I have no one but you."

Max, overwhelmed with feeling, was hardly able to say, "We agreed we had nothing but the present... Remember?"

He looked at her, wrenched by the whirlpool of

emotions. They embraced and kissed until Noemzar came out to let Araksi know the surgeons required her presence.

IN THE EXPEDITION'S PAVILION, Friedrich and Rolf, the latter with his arm and ribs bandaged, took advantage of a little privacy to go over the following day's maneuvers.

Thiele was presenting a list of requirements and equipment lost on the Bitlis-Mosul trip: saddles, harnesses, deteriorated tents, together with protective clothing for the freezing mountain temperatures. They were coming from the desert and on their way to extreme cold.

While the officers chatted and smoked or drank liqueur, Araksi, in a room next door, was sewing buttons on uniforms and ironing shirts.

"Rolf, you'll stay in Mosul until you're better. You'll be in charge of supplies," Max announced. "The young ladies will travel as nurses, and will then be handed over to the Russians or to some contact of the Armenians on the Persian side. I've been informed that the place is crawling with spies. You should all also bear in mind that we're at risk of being double-crossed by the troops — the Persian officers claim they respond to them... We'll never know for sure until we're face to face with the enemy. They may carry on being loyal, or decide it's in their interest to defect to the Russians. Is that understood?"

"Understood," they all chorused, leaving their tasks and repairing to their bedrooms.

Straightaway, a Wagner opera enveloped the room. Max looked at his watch. It was dark by then. He wondered what time it would be in Munich. He imagined Hildegard at home; far, very far, from all that was taking place around him at that moment.

Araksi came to him and, sitting on his knee, cuddled close in silence. She sensed his distance from her. She remained that way, without asking anything, while he gently caressed her.

CHAPTER XLI

THE CROSSING OF THE HIGH MOUNTAINS

THE CAVALRY ADVANCED UNDER MAX'S COMMAND. Immediately behind came the lower-ranking officers: Germans, Turks and Kurds. Following them were the Daghestani horsemen with their chief, Prince Khoisky, wearing outfits more suited to medieval warriors. The Arab sheikhs, wrapped up in their kaftans, brought up the rear of the column, carrying standards and lances. The infantry followed behind at a pace they had started out at on the way to the mountains, and lastly came the mules drawing the cannons.

They were still crossing the last few miles of desert eastwards. Araksi and the other Armenian girls travelled on a truck, half asleep and calm.

The climate was changing and temperatures gradually fell. The great mountains they had in front of them loomed challengingly and their snow-capped peaks seemed a deadly obstacle. Max looked backwards. He recalled that, a few months previously, those very stone cathedrals had devoured an 80,000-strong Turkish army, without warm clothing or proper equipment for the crossing.

Once the ascent finally began, the soldiers wrapped themselves up in their army greatcoats and other warm clothing. The women left the truck and were transferred to provision carts.

They were advancing along the edge of great precipices where it was only possible to go in single file. The cold was intense, and the snowfall on the high peaks a trial for all the men. The Arabs, merely covered with the robes they used for desert nights, suffered the chilling rigors more than the rest of the contingent.

Omer Nadji ordered a halt to seek protection among the crags. Wind lashed their faces and the animals seemed exhausted by the sleet, making it impossible to advance along the paths. As best they could, and in disorder, they dismounted and huddled together in groups so as to take advantage of each other's body heat. Some pressed against the animals, shielding themselves from the horizontal snowfall. Everything turned white and desolate.

Under cover, inside a large cavern, the soldiers were eating their rations from their mugs. Shivering, they were hardly able to move. Their teeth chattered and they slapped their shoulders and arms to prevent frostbite. Hidden behind large pieces of canvas so as not to be seen by the troops, Araksi and the other girls in the wagons tried to take some food.

Max remained alert. He could not afford to give in to fatigue. He observed his officers with concern and then had a look at the precipices. A gust of freezing wind unsteadied him, making him lose his balance with the same ease as leaves shaking on a tree. The wind thundered in his ears. It seemed as if the blasts of wind from the abysmal depths bounced against the outcrops, producing chords of a bizarre symphony played by brass and cymbals. Tiredness and the cold were beginning to get the better of him.

He returned to the cave. Omer Nadji was studying a map, together with Prince Khoisky and several Turkish officers. The Turkish commander was just finishing his comment, "If we can hold out another two days we'll be on the other side. This is the highest part. The troops will just have to put up with it!"

The men coughed and dozed, huddled together against the rock face. Those that had remained outside the cavern for want of space were practically buried under the snow. "What if it doesn't stop?" Max put in.

"It will be Allah's will," responded Omer Nadji.

THERE WERE THREE DAYS OF UNENDING FURY. The mountain pushed the men to their limits. It seemed that every storm conspired to sweep away those rash daredevils that presumed to travel through the mountains.

When the tempest finally abated and the sky became clear and cloudless, the army came out of its lethargy and the men understood that nature, in some way, had taken pity on them.

The Kurdish guide scrutinized the valley through his field glasses. The landscape was clearly visible for quite some distance. He adjusted the glasses and something drew his attention. The Kurd quickly descended from the boulder and, leaping onto his horse, made his way back to where the commanders were.

A few minutes later, Max was looking out from the outcrop together with the guide. In the distance, surrounded by mountain peaks, was Sautchbulak, an almost imperceptible group of houses.

"Sautchbulak," said the guide, pointing at a dot.

Max felt a certain excitement. He handed over the glasses to Friedrich, who was at his side, contemplating the situation. "It's the Russians' only passage to Teheran and Baghdad."

"Sir, the spies have reported improved roads, to fairly acceptable conditions, that the enemy can use at least for truck transport," Friedrich informed him.

"Ahah... So they've opened up the Caucasus route to Tabriz, all the way from Urfa." Max took the binoculars once more. He pointed into the distance, recognizing the terrain with enthusiasm, knowing he once more had his bearings in those huge mountains after the disorientation produced by the storm. "Look, there on the left. That shining mirror... It must be the great lake Urmia."

Sunshine glanced off the lake. It appeared as a tiny silver spot among small connected valleys as far away as the eye could see. The sighting confirmed their descent from the mountain at the chosen spot.

The Russians were waiting down below, ready to fire from their gun batteries, and the Cossacks would charge against them as soon as they deemed it suitable, Omer Nadji reflected on learning the news.

THE CAVALRY APPROACHED SAUTCHBULAK to a distance of half a mile, headed by Max and Friedrich. Tension grew as the village revealed its features. All the horsemen rode in silence, the horses' snorts increasing the disquiet. Max was reminded he had not seen battle action since the bombardment in Lorraine. Once more, he felt the same resignation to destiny. Danger floated in the air and the silence only increased the nervousness. He observed the faces of the men galloping with him: Turks, Kurds, Persians, some of them veterans, while others would receive their baptism of fire right there. The countryside was desolate, and the Russians had still not shown themselves.

A volley of fire descended on the Kurdish cavalry. Several bodies flew in the air at the site of the explosion. Disemboweled animals writhed on the ground. The riders spread out at a gallop, seeking protection at the sides of the terrain. Only there, feeling under cover, did they rein in their bolting mounts. Then, total silence ensued.

Soon they rallied together and, under Max's leadership, cautiously advanced. Restraining their horses, they entered the narrow, deserted alleys of the town at a trot. Watchful and wary, they kept their rifles at the ready as they rode further in, but there were no enemies to be seen in the recesses and niches among the buildings. Not on rooftops, behind doors, nor anywhere did they encounter resistance. Not even the townspeople of Sautchbulak peered out at the passing cavalry. The horses' hooves echoed on the cobbles, producing a hellish din. Max ordered the column to advance.

At the end of one street they came to a Russian barricade. Machine gun fire immediately swept the cavalry and troops. Bullets whistled and ricocheted off walls. Many hit home, mortally wounding the most exposed of the horsemen.

The officers swiftly gave the order to dismount and take cover behind corners. The Kurds were the first to line up and answer the fire. Several Russian soldiers fell dead at the end of the street. Shouts were heard in different languages and the reigning confusion made the enemy at the barricade retreat.

Far away, on the mountainside, Omer Nadji was commanding the general movements. The Turkish officers saw through their binoculars how the Russian battalions fled from Sautchbulak, dispersing towards the sides of the nearby mountains.

Without wasting time, Omer Nadji ordered the Kurdish cavalry to ride down from their positions and invade the village streets. Hundreds of horsemen, wielding swords and firing their arms like devils, galloped at full tilt into Sautchbulak.

THE VILLAGERS WERE OF CAUCASIAN APPEARANCE and wore long coats and fur caps. The place, which had seemed abandoned by its population, now teemed with inhabitants daring to come out onto the streets after the Cossacks' departure.

At each corner of the town, entrenched posts of Turkish soldiers could be seen, at the ready for any response. Others detained shopkeepers suspected of hoarding weapons, or acting as enemy collaborators.

The government building of Sautchbulak became the army command of the Turko-German forces. The banners of both empires waved outside the large house. Inside, officers and soldiers went up and down the stairs, in and out of offices.

A multitude of civilians crowded at the doors, trying to present their petitions to the new authorities. The telegraph transmitted and received information almost non-stop. Max dictated a telegram to Mosul, thence to be forwarded to Constantinople and, finally, to Munich. Hildegard had to know he was alive, and that they had taken the town without great ado. He was walking to the offices when an officer gave him the news. "Sir, three Armenian men have been arrested as Russian spies."

"Where are they?"

"They were taken to the command office," answered the officer.

"Keep me informed," said Max.

The news reminded him that the time was near to arrange handing the girls over. He felt a pang in his stomach. He thought of Araksi, who was at the hospital tending to the wounded. There were dozens of them, and it was there that she had to stay, serving with the rest.

He felt the minutes, days, weeks, had flashed by like a wisp of breath. It was taken for granted that military duty was above all else. That was his code. But how would their farewell be? How would it be to live without her? He felt the present with such intensity that the danger and mixed emotions penetrated his feelings deeply. Of one thing he was sure: no one would ever be able to replace her. He was crazy about her. He would never again feel passion after Araksi, or physical love with equal intensity. She was the perfect female, the one that fulfilled all his desires, at whose side every hour of every day was one of happiness and a source of intense emotion. Circumstances were sure to prevail and, just as so far everything had been the result of forces beyond them, perhaps whatever they were to experience, perhaps the last moments of life, would be intense and worth living. One thought over-rode all others: he had never told her he loved her.

THEY WERE ALMOST IN THE CENTRAL HALL OF THE PRISON. Several soldiers, Lieutenant Thiele, and some corporals accompanied him. Max and the rest advanced to the passage where they kept the captured Armenians in custody. They had arrived just in time for the execution. Turkish soldiers took the Armenians out of their cell. They were three civilians, still wearing the peasant clothes they had been wearing when they were arrested, dark-haired and with great moustaches, young men between 25 and 30 years of age. They were led in chains to the prison courtyard. Max and his escort slowed down. Walking past them, he felt the eyes of all three on him. Brimming with hate, one of them shouted in their faces, identifying them by their German uniforms, but without knowing exactly who they were.

"You Germans are responsible for our deaths. The head of the woman-trafficker Swirsden-Righe already has a price on it. Long live free Armenia!"

Thiele half shut his eyes, taken aback at the accusation of the prisoner on his way to die. Max felt all the blood in his body rising to his face.

The group of condemned men arrived on the first floor

of the gallery overlooking the courtyard. Below, officers, sergeants and corporals observed the hangman placing the noose round the first man's neck. The Armenian was pushed over the edge and the rope tautened. His head twisted to one side and the young man's lifeless body swung. As the soldiers made ready for the next execution, Max left, unwilling to witness any more deaths.

THE FOLLOWING DAY, THERE WAS NO TIME TO LOSE. The Cossacks would be counter-attacking at any moment. Max and Omer Nadji strode about, organizing the positions of the trenches and the installation of batteries. The soldiers dug without cease and fortified the positions on the mountainsides surrounding Sautchbulak.

Omer Nadji was wearing his tall black fur cap as he played with the sword hanging from the belt across his chest, Chechen style. Max impatiently slapped his boots with his riding crop at each step.

"The Armenians have set a price on your head and, it seems, also on those of your officers. How ironic, Swirsden-Righe: you help them and they don't believe you. Sometimes passions can be deadly, much more dangerous than bullets," Omer Nadji laughed. "Consider this: that Armenian girl you've grown so fond of — now she's placed you between two fires. *Quel consul avec des sentiments!*" he said, patting Max's back. With his incisive wit, Omer Nadji always got to the truth of a situation.

Thick snowflakes began falling on the trenches and the skies darkened. Max thought of Araksi. 'Sentiments' should never be allowed to interfere with one's duty. Once more, he silently reproached himself.

CHAPTER XLII

THE BATTLE

MAX WAS WRITING REPORTS BY THE STOVE. With heaviness of heart, Araksi contemplated the last light of day disappearing behind the mountains. She was standing at the great window, covered only with a colored rug. Snow was falling on Sautchbulak. She turned her sight on her lover and remained that way for a long while. They had just made love. Her shoulders and long legs were bare.

She asked directly, "When will you be handing me over, Max? How much time have we got left?" She went to the desk and hugged him from behind. Her black hair fell on his shoulders as she caressed him as lovingly as she could. Max interrupted his task and joined her in a fond embrace. Araksi felt terribly sad.

"You're not going to die, Max..! Nothing must happen to you, my precious. I just couldn't stand it, you know. I love you, I love you," she repeated, pressing close to him. "But supposing I died? How would you remember me, Max? Would you make it known someday, a long time from now? Would you tell about your love affair with an Armenian girl?" She paused before continuing. "Do you love me, Max?"

Max stood up and, sighing deeply, as though he had long been resisting the confession, embraced her as he looked at her with all the love he was capable of.

"Are you telling me you don't already know?" he asked. "I've loved you since the very first moment, Araksi... even in the face of all I should've been faithful to. I've loved you since that day at the Erzurum hospital. It was unavoidable... or it was written in our destiny. I would have given my right arm to liberate you if it had been necessary. I'll always love you, my treasure..." He released her gently. "We can't ask ourselves such questions, Araksi. We just have to accept the madness of war. We've shared the most vital part of our lives, but weren't able to choose the period or the hour... That isn't for us mortals."

Araksi wept, feeling that what Max had said was true.

There was a knock on the door. Max hurriedly dressed and then opened it. The assistant had a message for him. "Sir, Cossacks and Russian infantry have attacked on the Guldus plain at Miyanduab. The Kurdish clans are on their way to do battle. Prince Khoisky's cavalry battalion has occupied positions on the heights in pursuit of some Cossack patrols. We've taken a few casualties and the wounded Turks and Kurds are arriving."

Max ordered the soldier to wait on the ground floor. Then, turning to Araksi, he indicated, "The hospital is the safest place. You must go there immediately. The soldier will accompany you. Go right away and join the other women!"

Max and Araksi embraced. Her silk neckerchief fell under the chest of drawers without either of them noticing. A few minutes later, in her nurse's uniform, she looked at Max before she shut the door.

THE HUNDRED HORSEMEN UNDER MAX'S COMMAND were making ready in the courtyard. The horses came and went, hooves clattering on the stones. As they were taken from their boxes they were saddled for battle. Other riders were hurriedly lining up. It was almost night and torches shone on the faces of Asiatics determined to face the enemy. The Kurdish officers surrounded Max and gave him the latest report. "Sir, a thousand Cossacks are approaching the town. They're bringing two artillery pieces and several machine guns."

Without answering, Max quickly mounted and placed himself at the head of the first group. Under his direction, almost the whole cavalry division rode out of the barracks. The Turkish and Kurdish group of riders galloped towards the hills surrounding the town. As they neared their positions, the snowfall grew heavier. It was not long before the blaze of Russian cannon-fire was seen. The cavalry climbed as fast as possible in an attempt to get to its own trenches.

Max shouted orders, "Thiele, take charge of the batteries."

Once they had finally occupied their positions, Max urged the officers to charge downhill. The hundred horsemen plunged forward, making their way to right and left in two columns, sword in hand and yelling ferociously to give themselves courage.

They overtook the first Russians. Maddened, they passed like a flock of annihilators, cutting down laggards with their swords. They killed without rest until not a single enemy was left standing. Amid the melee, Max dismounted and, on the ground, fired his pistol repeatedly. The Russians were melting away into the night with their dead and wounded. Then he shouted loudly, "Retreat, retreat, and to the batteries!"

He remounted and, followed by the rest, they climbed the hill at full gallop.

THE SNOWSTORM WAS GETTING STRONGER, enveloping men and horses. In the icy trenches, the swirling eddies of snow made seeing even one's own horses impossible. A white curtain was covering guns and soldiers. Some were already frozen stiff.

From that position, patrols of Kurdish riders left to attack the Russian forces. Max, bent over against the blizzard, ran to Lieutenant Thiele's gun battery.

"Lieutenant, hand over your command to the Turkish officer beside you. Get on your horse and come with me. We'll charge Sautchbulak immediately."

The Turkish batteries expelled fire, each volley like a thunder-peal. When the enemy retreated, Thiele and Max rode down at full speed, followed by a group of horsemen. So it continued the whole night through. They descended once more, but were repelled by the Russian battery still covering the valley. The storm rendered any cavalry charge useless. They went up to the trenches once more to give the horses a rest and try and gather their forces.

The following morning, the mounted battalion rode down from the hills once more into the village. At the head of them, Max observed the movements of the Turkish infantry marching away from Sautchbulak, taking up new positions in the surroundings. Prince Khoisky approached at full gallop at the head of his Daghestani horsemen. On passing Max he shouted, "Lieutenant, two Cossack regiments are advancing on the town from the east. I'm going west to join up with the infantry."

Max did not stop. He carried on galloping towards Sautchbulak. Right away, he thought of Araksi. Perhaps she was still safe at the hospital together with the other girls. There was nothing he could do. It troubled him to imagine the violence the Cossacks might wreak in the streets on retaking the town. They rapidly covered the distance to Sautchbulak, seeking the position of Omer Nadji, supreme commander of the battle.

A group of houses in the suburbs functioned as general headquarters from which the movements of the Turkish troops were controlled. Omer Nadji, surrounded by officers, was studying the general situation on a map.

A young, flustered Turkish lieutenant accosted Max and, gasping, managed to inform him, "Sir, at least two companies of Cossacks are advancing along the river."

Max immediately ordered Friedrich, "Lieutenant, charge with your company and overtake the Cossacks before they get any closer."

The officer obeyed the order and rode forth straight away. Everything was happening at a dizzying speed. The newly won positions had to be held against the Russian offensive on all fronts.

"Swirsden-Righe — change your mounts and return to your forces," ordered the Chechen.

Max did not answer. Each ride uphill to come down again with fresh horses seemed like an uncontrolled cavalcade to hell. It was clear they would soon be overwhelmed. That was all that went through his mind. At that moment, bursts of cannon fire were heard near the town. The Russians were already there, spreading out everywhere. Without doubt, Prince Nikolai Nikolayevich had received reinforcements during the night and was advancing to counter-attack Sautchbulak.

THE WOUNDED AND MAIMED LAY ON BEDS and wherever else there was a space in the hospital. While some died before being operated on, or resisted amputations, the most seriously wounded men underwent continuous operations by the doctors, who tirelessly worked in shifts. The Armenian nurses came and went among the victims, taking them water, cloths, and bandages. Araksi assisted the surgeon. One after another, blood-drenched men were deposited on the operating table. Cannon fire could be heard fairly close by, but the doctors and nurses did not lose their concentration even for a moment. The former captives, now improvised nurses, oppressed at finding themselves amid the gunfire of battles in the besieged town, shuddered on hearing a shell land less than a hundred feet from the building. Noemzar held onto a bedstead, hardly able to hold the surgical instruments she was carrying. Her hands were perspiring in such a way that the metal box full of tweezers slid to the floor. A nervous, uncontrollable tremor produced by the ferociousness of the attack paralyzed her and kept her crouching next to a column.

In the streets, the Russian forces were advancing with artillery pieces and overcoming the Turkish barricades. It was possible to distinguish between the Cossack battalions and the divisions of Armenian combatants advancing elbow to elbow with the Russians. They wore handkerchiefs on their heads and bandoleers crossing their chests.

Czar Nicholas' soldiers ran, crouching, from house to house. An advance platoon was moving ever closer, attempting to take a Turkish army equipment depot. The low building was defended by a barricade. Further on, another Russian unit was setting up its machine guns at the end of the street, taking advantage of the position recently evacuated by the enemy.

In the blocks near the hospital, Lieutenant Thiele was attempting the defense of the storehouses, answering the machine gun fire.

Outnumbered by the enemy, Thiele and his men could barely repel the attackers who climbed over the roofs and then dropped down into the buildings, shooting intensely and constantly.

Russian and Armenian soldiers fought in the courtyards, overrunning the Turks. They killed as many as possible, with bursts of machine gun fire and pistol shots. Finally, they got into the storehouses by knocking down doors and windows. They made a human chain to hasten the pillage of bags full of foodstuffs, and all the equipment they found hoarded in the places. Then they came out onto the streets, protected by their own machine gun units.

Among the Armenians advancing on the hospital a young man stood out, egging the troops on. Pistol in hand, he shot without halting at the barricade that covered the entrance. Like the rest, he was armed to the teeth. Bandoleers crossed his chest and a handkerchief was tied around his head.

A FEW BLOCKS AWAY, trapped in the alleys of Sautchbulak, the Turkish mounted patrol led by Friedrich was barely advancing in the battle, until the enemy immobilized them altogether and they decided to dismount. Protected by the walls of the houses, the lieutenant and his troops managed to reach their own batteries with great difficulty.

The intense fire of the Russian machine guns covered every flank, preventing any Turkish soldier from looking out to respond to the attack or advance a foot in any direction.

Meanwhile, in the hills around the town, fierce combat was taking place. Max galloped across a line of fire. On getting to the hill, he suddenly reined in and the beast reared up.

He looked down at the group of houses. From there he had a full view of the action. The Russian infantry was entering the town on the opposite side, where Omer Nadji's forces were placed. In another sector, Cossacks were fanning out and occupying all the streets. He could hardly hear his own people's shouts in the trenches, so thunderous were the Russian batteries. He immediately ordered the cannons to be fired downhill. The flashes followed one another without stopping.

In the streets, where the fighting had been most violent,

dead and wounded could be seen at each corner. A group of Russian soldiers were setting up a machine gun a hundred feet away from the hospital, to act as backing for the Armenian combatants running in the midst of Turkish fire. On reaching the hospital, the Armenians jumped over the sandbags surrounding the entrance. Some went in through windows and side-doors, smashing every pane of glass as they went.

Shouts of panic could be heard inside. The commander of the group, with the bandoliers crossing his chest, led the attack on the hospital. The young Armenian took the lead, advancing through the wards full of casualties. He gave orders in Armenian, telling the young nurses to evacuate the building without delay.

"All women, outside! We've come to save you. Long live free Armenia! All women out. Out, out! Long live Azad Haiasdan! Get out, quickly! All of you go to the main door. Long live Azad Haiasdan!" shouted the commander time and again.

The group of ten nurses, those captives freed from the harem, abandoned their patients by their beds. They ran yelling to the end of the pavilion. As they arrived at the exits, the Armenian combatants covered their flight. Noemzar quickly joined the group fleeing from the building. She was crying from nerves and relief. She looked back and noticed that Araksi was not leaving her post next to the surgeons. "Araksi! Araksi!" she shouted twice, going back to grip her firmly by the arm while being shoved and jostled towards the exit by a whole throng of soldiers and screaming women.

The Armenian commander stopped short. He looked round in surprise on hearing the young woman's name. He returned, gun ever ready in hand, to the end of the pavilion. Some of the wounded moaned in pain and in fright. He parted the canvases that isolated the operating areas and saw that the Turkish surgeons continued their task on a man covered in blood. No one left their post. Physicians and improvised nurses all stuck steadfastly to their duties.

The combatant then saw the young woman that was

assisting the surgeon. He remained motionless for a moment. He thought perhaps... but no, it was impossible. He was stunned. He walked forward a few paces and approached the operating table itself. The doctors noticed him there, but no one interrupted their urgent tasks. Blood spurted from the wounded man's destroyed leg. Diran stopped in front of Araksi, calling her by her name, almost questioning her.

Araksi did not leave her post but on hearing her name pronounced by that familiar voice and seeing the combatant advancing towards her, she was completely taken aback. "Diran... Diran... Good God, it's not possible, is it you?"

Diran walked a few paces towards her, dumb with emotion and still holding the pistol. Araksi, her facemask still on, looked at him with mixed feelings. Diran took off the mask and embraced her with all his might.

"My God, Diran, it's hardly believable, you're alive!"

"I'm alive, Araksi — we're alive, my love. Our spies informed us about a group of captive women, but I never... I'd given up all hope... Come on, there's no time, keep close to me, we've got to run... My precious, leave everything now... Keep your head down and let's get out of here."

The Turkish surgeon saw with amazement that his assistant was being taken from him, and then carried on with his task, true to his oath.

Diran ran, Araksi's hand in his, almost holding her up, without giving her time to react. They ran alongside the beds and soon they were outside. In the street, Araksi looked back in vain. Some of the combatants were carrying plasma and surgical instruments from the hospital. Diran and Araksi did not stop running. Bullets whizzed above their heads as they made it to the Russian barricade at the end of the block. The girl felt she was again being sucked into the inexorable maelstrom of destiny. Something like a storm was once more tearing her away from her precarious foundations and carrying her back to her past. Everything that was happening defied all imagination. She was still unable to break away from her captivity completely, when the immediate present found her running amidst the combatants with Diran, whom she had in her thoughts given up for dead. She wondered whether she herself had not just died.

FRIEDRICH, FROM HIS COMBAT POSITION, was watching the takeover of the hospital through his binoculars. He saw the Armenians leaving the building with the young women, and suddenly he caught sight of Araksi. He kept looking until he saw them no more as they took shelter behind the barricades. When the last group was safe, the Russians opened a hail of fire on the Turks, and Friedrich ordered his men to retreat at once.

The town remained deserted and in darkness, all the inhabitants staying indoors. It seemed Sautchbulak was empty of soldiers. The Cossacks had retired to recover their strength or perhaps they were just awaiting the arrival of the bulk of the Russian army so as to deliver the Turkish invaders the final blow.

Max rushed into the Command office, where they had lived the first days. He was accompanied by Friedrich and a few soldiers. They busily searched for papers and files. Removing floorboards, they recovered six bags of money. Max went to his bedroom and picked up his books and the gramophone. He had to bend down to gather up some documents, and behind the chest of drawers came upon the silk neck-scarf Araksi had forgotten. With a sense of deep melancholy, he put it away in his jacket.

Almost at once, fearing the counter-offensive that could come at any moment, he left the command post with all his companions and the Kurdish riders. They crossed the plain, yet again towards the trenches, exposing themselves to enemy fire. Max ordered a full gallop till they once again made it to the camp.

All of a sudden, Russian shelling and a burst of shots fell upon the cavalry. Some of the horsemen were killed while crossing the plain. The rest galloped like madmen to find protection in the trenches. Max was forced to throw himself off his horse to avoid the bullets.

A few minutes later, all the officers of the expedition

were gathered around the political chief. Max, Friedrich and Lieutenant Thiele stood face to face with the Chechen.

"I'm going to order a full retreat, gentlemen," said Omer Nadji with sorrow. "The Cossacks are trying to surround us. They've deployed forces on all fronts. Protect the infantry with your troops," he said, looking at Max before asking, "How do you feel about it, Swirsden-Righe?"

"Order an immediate retreat, Omer Nadji... The snow will make camping out impossible. The Russians presume that, by expelling us from Sautchbulak, we'll go back to the frontier. They'll hardly expect us to go deeper into Persian territory... My advice is to go south."

They spread out a map of the region on which could be seen each mountain peak, each river branch, and the possible routes from Persia to Russia. Omer Nadji pointed out the way with his riding-crop, drawing whorls and arrows on the map. "Prince Nikolai Nikolayevich won't try to advance against us via the Mesopotamian plain, putting his back to Baghdad," he mused, almost to himself. "I'll locate the troops in the village of Karawa... and then we'll wait and see what they do."

Max, at his side, walked up and down the trenches. The Turkish soldiers ran, carrying ammunition, and fired the guns that covered the whole of the valley. Everyone had bayonets fixed, ready to repel any attack by Cossacks that might attempt to come up to the position. The wind punished the men's strained faces as they looked out at the village. Omer Nadji and Max stopped every so often to view the valley. The display of Russian troops once more advancing to Sautchbulak could be observed.

Omer Nadji commented, "I've been informed that Armenian guerrillas took away the young nurses, including yours. You should be pleased about this, Swirsden-Righe, since you've been the means of their salvation. Now the girl's among her own. You were Allah's instrument, and Allah always decides for us."

Max said nothing, silenced by a bitter taste in his mouth. Despite Omer Nadji's caustic sense of humor, it could not be denied that his words were true. Whether it was true that there was a being that managed men's fate, or the turn of events in one's life were totally random, or if everything had to be reduced to foreseeable cause and effect, it was not a suitable conversation topic at that moment. All speculation pointed to the accuracy of the Chechen's remarks.

Max looked sadly towards the town. Boxed in among mountains, in the light of sundown, Sautchbulak, now occupied once more by the Russians, was barely visible. For the first time, he had thoughts of failure. No longer was there to be military glory, or fanfares in homage to the conquerors of the Caucasus. Neither would his name be spoken with respect and admiration among the German army officers that might have honored their fatherland by making their flag wave in Russian territory. No — now he would have to face defeat and give explanations to his superiors. Before even that, he had to try and get out of there and save as many men as possible, a dangerous retreat through the narrow passes and abysses of the mountain chain. He pulled up his greatcoat, feeling cold and looking upwards: the grey, clouded-over sky promised new snowstorms.

THE MOUNTAIN PATHWAYS WERE NARROW and decked with snow, and the troops trudged along on their slow retreat. Horses sank up to their bellies and the mules, loaded to capacity, advanced with difficulty. The soldiers, exhausted from so much battling, muffled up, shivering with cold. The less resistant remained behind with their backpacks, freezing to death. Inert bodies and spectral countenances covered with snow lay rigidly in eternal sleep. The Arabs, freezing and dismayed, little used to such frost, muttered prayers to be able to come through those icy precipices alive, and return safe and sound to their camps.

The icy gusts of wind blew into the mouth of the cavern, sounding like a death moan. To have come across those caves in the middle of the night had been providential. No one was oblivious to the fact that they might run the same fate as General Enver Pasha's ill-starred army.

The bulk of the troops rested under the rocks. The men

lit a great bonfire. In silence, they protected themselves, sitting next to each other, rubbing hands and patting their shoulders in the heat from the fire.

Looking lost, Max walked to the entrance of the cavern. Outside, the last soldiers moved wearily, drawing the artillery pieces hitched up to exhausted horses. He hardly blinked. He was experiencing a sort of drowsiness, the result of fatigue and the deep depression he had fallen into. Suddenly he felt a shake that brought him to. Friedrich, at his back, had wakened him.

Max did not answer, just looking at the other with moist eyes. It was dawn.

"Max, we've got to go on. The storm's over. I'm waiting for orders."

One of the Turkish lieutenants that had taken part in the battles at the barricades round the hospital in Sautchbulak came up and offered Max a bottle of vodka. Max took a swig that fired his throat, immediately reviving him.

Memdukh translated the report: "The lieutenant said that the guerrillas that took the Sautchbulak hospital were led by an Armenian from Erzurum, 'Commander Diran'. They took away all the women."

Diran! Max felt a wrench in his stomach. He remembered the young lawyer of that name engaged to Araksi. He told himself it had to be just coincidence. There must be many of the same name, but the certainty that she had vanished forever depressed him completely. He tried to hide it in front of his men.

"He also says that Prince Nikolai Nikolayevich has gathered 300 of his own cavalrymen and a thousand Persian horsemen that are on the Russian side. They are all marching to capture and sack Bukan, the next village," Memdukh continued.

The officers gathered in the cave were paying attention to the advance scout. The stormy sky was clearing, allowing the line of valleys to be seen quite well. Among the neighboring mountain massifs could now be seen a military formation. Looking through field glasses, they immediately saw that the moving dots were riders belonging to the Russian cavalry. Cossacks.

Max asked for the binoculars. "There they come. There must be 50,000 of them... It's a huge army. They've simply lost count. Well, that's it," declared Max. "Order an immediate retreat. Let's go back to Mosul."

CHAPTER XLIII

FAREWELL TO THE EASTERN FRONT

ROLF WAS DRINKING LEMONADE. The heat in Mosul was stifling. His arm was no longer bandaged, his ribs had also healed, and he felt hardly any pain. Leaning on the counter in the Officers' Club, he was looking out through the large windows, awaiting the line-up.

In another sector, a group of young officers were holding a lively conversation at their tables. The raw, arrogant look of them conveyed that they were only recently arrived from Constantinople, replacements for the veterans returning to Europe. They drank to the battles they would be winning, and the promotions and decorations they would enjoy after defeating the Russian enemy.

One of them, holding a glass of whisky, looked with curiosity at the veterans on their way to the parade quadrangle intermixed with Arab and Daghestani chieftains in their exotic costumes.

"Look... Do you know who that officer is... the one walking at the front of that group — yes, the one with the shaven head? It's none other than Swirsden-Righe."

The others pivoted their heads towards the gallery. Amused and curious, they crowded to look through the window.

"That Swirsden-Righe is a fraud, a specialist in squandering energy and resources. After the shameful rout at Sautchbulak, what else can one say about the fellow?"

"A hot-airbag," accused another.

"In Constantinople they were never in agreement with his strategy, but all the same they let him have his way. The results of his ideas are plain to see."

"Big plans, great expectations — that's how he gets others talking about him."

"What's most unforgivable, comrades, is that throughout the entire campaign he never looked into organizing a proper wine-cellar for his officers."

There was general laughter at the comment.

"Mind you, don't make any mistakes. Wine may have been missing, but this one wasn't at all abstemious when it came to women. They say he took a whole harem of Armenian women along on the campaign for his personal provision."

Raucous laughter was heard at the table, accompanied by sly innuendos regarding Max. Rolf was silently choking back his anger. He did not find it easy when his commander was the butt of anyone's jokes. The military band struck up with the first marches.

The Turkish and German troops were lined up on the parade ground. The officers saluted Haidar Bey, commander of Mosul. In Max's eyes the sadness of defeat could be seen. His men deserved the decorations, but they had been overwhelmed by the Cossacks, the objective not accomplished, nor his dreams of glory. Everything Germany desired had been almost within reach of his forces, but had slipped through his fingers at Sautchbulak. Now it would be others that added their names to the glorious list on the altar to Germanic warriors, but not his. Hildegard would not be able to boast that she was the wife of the military hero that had taken part in the conquest of the hinterland, the Caucasus; that part of the world that, for legitimate racial reasons, belonged to Germany. It was the land of origin, from where the Aryans had migrated in ancient times to prevail over all other peoples and become the cream of humankind. No longer would it be he that fulfilled Kaiser Wilhelm II's inspiring mandate, under the orders of which the Teutonic Knights honored the ancestral traditions inscribed in Thule.

The commander of Mosul pinned the decorations on the men's jackets and saluted each officer that had earned the distinction. Max observed Friedrich and then his own translator, Memdukh, stepping forward to receive the honors. They saluted in a martial manner and proudly returned to the formation. Max recalled each of his men's feats of courage and nostalgically listened to the reports of the actions. The tales made him think of Araksi, and he suddenly felt deep anguish. It was hard for him to accept that he would never see her again; would probably never even hear of her.

The sun overhead shone down on the formation. He began perspiring and feeling off-balance. His hands went cold. At his side were Omer Nadji and the Kurdish clan chiefs. Max tried to overcome his giddiness. The sun on the courtyard was dazzling him. Drops of cold sweat began trickling down his closed jacket collar, and the voices of those around went fading out. He thought he heard Araksi, but that was impossible. He realized he would be unable to keep standing much longer.

Rolf, noticing what was happening, caught hold of Max in time and prevented him falling in the middle of the formation. They walked away from the lines. The officers whispered on seeing him go by in a half-swoon, leaning on his friend's arm.

"Now it's our turn, gentlemen. We'll fight with German divisions in command, none of this motley crew of undisciplined tribesmen."

"First, we'll conquer Baghdad," said another. "Then we'll take India away from the English!"

They laughed in celebration of the joke.

MAX WAS SHIVERING AND DELIRIOUS WITH FEVER. Friedrich and Rolf presently developed the same ailment: malaria and dysentery had finally appeared as the final corollary of the campaign. Exposed to tainted waters and travelling through infected zones had weakened the men and their defenses. They lay in bed at the Mosul hospital for several weeks and would remain that way for who could say how long.

Max still held Araksi's neckerchief in his enfeebled hands.

A Turkish soldier delivering the mail entered the pavilion. Without daring to awaken the lieutenant, he left several letters on the little table next to the bed. They were all from his wife, Hildegard von Swirsden.

Max turned his head, his eyes half-closed from the

fever. He hardly noticed the soldier's presence. He pressed the kerchief tightly against his chest, murmuring, "Araksi, Araksi..."

THE ARMY CAR, LOADED WITH LUGGAGE AND TRUNKS ON THE ROOF, went up and down the dunes, projecting long shadows. It travelled far away from any road, trying to pick out the best route. The sun was setting on the horizon and its last rays grazed the sandy crests. They had been underway in the bumpy desert for a week now. Sometimes the improvised itinerary followed smoother ways; others, it required all the driver's skill to avoid getting stuck in the sand.

Max, Rolf and Friedrich were drowsy and convalescent on the journey. They had lost a good few kilos on account of the dysentery. Mosul was far behind, and their mission to the eastern front now belonged to the past. They were on their way to the rail terminal at Ras-el-Ain, the last station built on the Baghdad-Constantinople railway, in the middle of the desert, where they would board a cargo train to travel to Constantinople.

Max wore Araksi's silk scarf knotted round his neck.

From time to time a caravan of camels crossed in the distance: it was a sea of sand that could only be traversed between sunset and dawn, to avoid the heat. When the moon appeared on that wavy landscape, Max, his sight fixed on the bright silvery disk, replayed in his mind the images of all he had experienced. He wondered what to expect in Munich, and the answer produced little enthusiasm in him. He hardly spoke a word to his comrades who were dozing on the back seat. Trying to get hold of himself, he analyzed the campaign. His mind played tricks on him. He tried in vain to correct strategies, telling himself he should have adopted this or that initiative, ordered this or that cavalry charge, but it all belonged to the realm of imagination. Facts were set and no one could modify them now. What was done was done.

His depression would change fronts, and he would delve into his mind in search of the hidden, underlying reason, which mortified him almost more achingly than his military defeat. Ungraspable, inexplicable, without anyone to lay claims against, and even less to seek advice from. It was an obsession that tortured his brain, but it was not in his nature to comment on it.

The memory of Araksi had become a single, uninterrupted thought. He could feel the girl and hear her at his side, loving and embracing each other at the highest pitch. He had no picture of her, though he could still remember her face and fragrance and the sensations her body produced in him. But then he would become aware of her absence. Each mile they travelled returned him closer to the daily humdrum of his life. Knowing it would be without Araksi drove him crazy.

Rolf opened his eyes. The enormous moon was rising and illuminating the desert. From the back seat he looked at his friend, defeated and grief-stricken, his head propped against the doorjamb. On the sandy road, the car's headlights cut a bright swathe in the desert. All at once, a signpost! The driver indicated in a forward direction as, in Turkish, he announced the end of the road. Lights appeared, outlining the profiles of railway carriages stationed alongside platforms in the middle of the desert. The chauffeur drove the car up to the sheds. Several cargo trains waited their turn to be hooked up in the station yard of Ras-el-Ain. Dawn soon arrived.

Still drowsy, they hauled their luggage along with the help of railwaymen. The platform was empty of passengers and the carriages were lined up on the track. They walked the length of the train until they finally chose one. The guards loaded a samovar into the goods wagon, the only comfort for the journey, which would be useful for warming up on cold nights.

"This'll be our carriage up to Aleppo, gentlemen," said Max. "There we'll make a connection with some First Class carriages to Constantinople."

The stationmaster hurriedly came up and spoke in rudimentary French, "Effendi, the railway is interrupted at the Amanus and Taurus passes, effendi. But after going through the mountains in some vehicles you are sure to be able to hire, you will find on the other side a new connection with the branch to Constantinople, effendi."

The locomotive started off. The three sat on some bags on the floor of the carriage. The train gathered speed as it left the station. Soon it was out in the desert. Wind blew in through the open door, ruffling their clothes. The morning light showed the clarity of the horizon. Then the night dew gave way to a hot steaminess that rose from the sands.

The engine kept up its speed along the tracks, moving away from Ras-el-Ain. Rocked by the movement of the train, tiredness grew, getting the better of the young veterans. The open carriage door let fresh air in and allowed a hypnotizing view of the desert. The three dozed on the floor. Max still wore, knotted round his throat, Araksi's kerchief, which flapped in the wind. All at once, a stronger gust loosened the knot. The colored silk slid along the floor and flew up in the air for a few instants, suspended inside the wagon.

Max woke up with a start and, as though from a premonition, his waking reflex made him put his hand to his throat.

The kerchief was by now floating outside the carriage. Max stretched as far as possible in an attempt to recover it. The scarf was still open like a kite, accompanying the swirling eddies produced by the train's movement. It was useless: Araksi's silk scarf suddenly fell and tumbled across the desert, the speed of the train carrying it ever further away.

Rolf and Friedrich, dazzled and sleepy from the midday glare, observed with curiosity as their companion leant half his body out of the train and fumbled in the air, until he was forced to resign himself to the loss. With his back turned, and not having noticed them, Max, leaning against the doorjamb, kept on contemplating the monotony of the desert. He stood there for a long while, showing a silent sadness that his friends would have a hard time forgetting.

PART II

CHAPTER I

MUNICH 1916

THERE WERE INDICATIONS OF WAR throughout the city. Wounded and maimed soldiers could be seen everywhere, sent home from the regiments at the front, or released from hospitals, where they sometimes remained for months, having nowhere else to go — in short, returning to civilian society, incomplete and bereft of possibilities. They wandered around Munich hopelessly, and in the most abject poverty, wearing their frayed uniforms. Others went about like tormented souls, displaying resentment towards civilians that had not been called up for armed service and receiving condemnation for the successive defeats Germany was suffering.

Max von Swirsden-Righe had made a habit of going for a walk in the morning until mid-day. He dressed elegantly, and with a distinguished air contemplated the catastrophic results that the military class and the nobility surrounding the Kaiser had brought upon the country with their war policies, of which Germany's enemies understandably took advantage.

His only business was preparing reports that the Foreign Ministry and the High Command, both in Berlin, had ordered him to deliver regarding his mission at the eastern war front. He crossed the boulevard to the opposite pavement, carefully avoiding the odd carriage or motorcar. He felt irritated. It filled him with impotence to live as a retired war veteran, the same as the poor devils he came across daily. He imagined the mail would have already arrived at his home by then, perhaps with an answer to his repeated requests to the High Command for a transfer to a battlefront.

He entered his residence. The butler respectfully greeted him, taking his top hat and walking stick. Max went straight to his study, eager to open the morning's correspondence. Suddenly he heard his wife's voice.

"Max — are you back? The Senate of the City of Lübeck

has sent you this parcel, darling."

Hildegard appeared almost noiselessly, as though she had been waiting to give him a surprise. With a warm kiss on the cheek, she handed him a box containing a leather case. Hildegard smiled expectantly, waiting for Max to open it.

The countess was still an attractive, highly distinguished woman, with penetrating blue eyes and straight, harmonious features. Her blonde locks escaped from a tall bun kept in place by a hairpin. Just over 40, nine years older than her husband, she had been and still was an alluring and warm-hearted woman. As the legitimate wife of a German officer, as she herself would say, she was accustomed to accepting loneliness and moments of anguish, but when Max returned, their life together carried on quite normally, as if they had only been apart for a short time.

This last mission in Turkey had lasted around a year and a half. Always in love with her husband, Hildegard made a habit of not asking him questions that might make him uncomfortable, showing enough understanding of the vagaries of military life.

She knew that between them there lived on a permanent complicity or rather, a community of ambitions and aspirations that bound them and made them a proper team, very suitable as regards the acquaintances that Hildegard fostered among the high nobility of all of Europe.

Intrigued, Max opened the box and, unwrapping silk papers, took out a cross-shaped decoration. He smiled with emotion and surprise as Hildegard hung it round his neck and lovingly kissed him again, leading him to a small looking glass in the lounge so that he might see himself.

"What's this, Hildegard? The Hanseatic Cross of the Senate of Lübeck. What an unexpected honor! They sent it by messenger. I don't understand."

Hildegard laughed.

"Why are you laughing? It's just that these gentlemen don't seem to hold much store by ceremony. By post, with no prior protocol or warning?"

"Read," said Hildegard, handing him the letter from the

senators in honor of his merits against the Russians at the eastern front.

Max had not finished reading when he almost jumped out of his skin as, from behind the doors of the study, laughing their heads off, Rolf, Friedrich, and several more of his comrades appeared. They all hugged and congratulated him, patting him on the back without giving him time to react.

"In the name of the Senate of Lübeck... For the valuable victories we have taken part in together, and so that all shared experiences during the campaign be the indestructible link of our true friendship," said Friedrich in representation of the senators.

"Thank you ever so much, my friends," said Max, deeply moved.

The butler entered the drawing room, offering aperitifs all around.

Indoor lights were turned on and the celebration carried on till almost 7 p.m. In no time, anecdotes of their Turkish adventure were handed around: it was more comfortable to talk about the past than the uncertain future looming before them all.

Friedrich was the one with most likelihood of being transferred to some unit on the Lorraine front. Rolf had no idea of what the immediate future had in store for him; he was still officially under arms. Max, meanwhile, spent his time writing letters asking for a transfer. But that evening was one of memories. Of course the majority remained forever in reserve. What had transpired in Turkey was private to each of them, as befitted military gentlemen. Many remembrances were sealed forever, and never mentioned in public or in private.

Rolf observed Hildegard, with her bunched up hair and the refined manners proper to a great lady. Then his look fell on Max, always affable towards her, holding her hand as both gaily chatted with their guests.

THE HOUSE LIGHTS were turned off one by one. Sitting in his armchair wearing his smoking jacket, and illuminated by a standing lamp, Max still had his decoration pinned on, like a child with a new toy. An opera was playing on the gramophone.

Hildegard, in a dressing gown, huddled next to him. Without interrupting his writing, Max commented, "These idiots at High Command are asking again about a whole load of irrelevant details. I've sent them a report on these same matters three times already. I have to explain to them what I thought was self-evident."

Hildegard smiled, caressing him enticingly.

"They dwell on unimportant issues, despite the fact that I've reported matters of future importance to the Foreign Ministry. For instance, here I've got a dossier on the Armenians."

Hildegard got closer to her husband. She disregarded the pile of papers and, sitting on his knee, kissed him meaningfully. Max felt a certain discomfort, but contrived to hide it.

"Ah, yes, the Armenians... My love, you're back home now, safe and sound, and we're together again. You ought to forget about all that effort and have a rest. Sometimes I get the feeling that, in your mind, you still haven't come back from Turkey."

"Could be... Forgive me, Hildegard... It'll take time. I find it hard to accept what I'm seeing. Poverty all around, the Empire's soldiers turned into beggars, impotent loafers. Germany's on its knees... and my career's absolutely in the doldrums, in the hands of pen-pushers. I'd love to be fully recovered to go back into service. The weeks and months are becoming interminable, until I'm given a post."

Hildegard was fleetingly glancing at Max's notes.

"What is it you're after, Hildegard? D'you want to hear about the Armenian massacres?"

She brought her lips close, gently kissing his ears and neck. "Yes, Max, I want to hear about the Armenians, above all about the Armenian women. What happened to the girls you rescued from captivity? You never mentioned them again. How were those harem girls? Were they pretty? Were they seductive? Did any of them attract you like me? More than me, eh? Answer me... Were you faithful to me, darling?"

Max sat up straight in his chair. "Some of them were very beautiful." He paused. "A different kind of beauty from the

European... but I never forgot you, Hildegard... if that's what you want to know. The young women were given the best treatment possible, and saved their lives when we took them to the war zone. Their destiny, of which I was an instrument, as the Muslims say, separated us forever."

He checked himself. Memories were betraying him. "What I mean to say is, the sensitive business of passing them over to the enemy happened without our intervention... The Armenian guerrillas, together with the Cossacks, took them away during the counter-attack on the town." Max was trying to hide the discomfort that moment produced. "It was when they occupied the hospital at Sautchbulak. In a way it was natural... We simply never saw them again." An overwhelming nostalgia took hold of him at the memory.

"You surely did the right thing, my love. But for you, those girls would never have been saved from those barbarians," answered Hildegard, looking straight at him. "It's important that the High Command make use of your experience, Max. Without doubt they'll keep it in mind for your next assignment, though they might take longer than you'd wish. Don't you feel that meanwhile it might be wise to spend your time on something useful? Why don't you resume your doctor's thesis at university? Why not, Max? You'd have your mind occupied with other things and I'd take care of you... as when we first met. Remember I fell in love with the brave chemistry student, not the soldier."

Max embraced his wife. It was futile to carry on wallowing in memories. After all, only the present was of any value. To think of Araksi made no sense. Yes, better stick to the present.

"Go back to college? Formulae and lab work, and sink my mind into the library putting my thesis together? The idea isn't a bad one. The student life after so much battling. Why not?"

Hildegard embraced him even more closely and, without further delay, began making love to him.

CHAPTER II

MEETING

MAX WOULD SPEND HOURS IN THE CHEMISTRY LABORATORY, and whole weeks in the university library. His walks around Munich were replaced by obsessive periods devoted to study.

That morning was no different from any other. Light shone in through the library windows. Long desks and stools on each side of the tables took up the whole of the reading room. Full bookcases reached almost to the ceiling, storing the memory of so many experts. Suddenly the venerable silence of the library was broken. Whispers, followed by nervous, repressed laughs, irreverently interrupted study and reading. All those present looked impatiently at the group of youths that had just come in. Max lost the concentration he had kept up for hours.

He looked over at the new arrivals. He took off the round spectacles he wore with increasing frequency and rubbed his tired eyes. The students walked through the room with perfect brazenness. Right away he noticed they were foreigners. Although he did not understand the words, they sounded familiar. They were Armenian, without doubt.

The youths approached other comrades sitting in the room, greeting them with boisterous handshakes and back-patting. One dropped a heap of books on the floor. Muted laughter was heard.

Max left off reading. He observed them with special interest while he stroked the small dark moustache he wore. Thousands of ideas stirred in his mind. When they finally left the hall, Max went over to where they had been sitting. Several papers they had left behind caught his eye. The pamphlets, written in Armenian and German, were an invitation to a meeting of all those living in exile, and sympathizers of a free Armenia, to be held somewhere in the city. The strip of paper with the full address had been torn off. Max carried on reading, curious about it. His heart gave a flip and his pulse began racing. On the list of speakers was Diran's name. Hurriedly, he checked the time on the large wall-clock. The meeting was starting in half an hour. With no time to lose, he ran to the counter and returned the books. Overcome by excitement and a vague hope, he rapidly left the building. He would have to catch up with the youths and tail them if he wanted to find the place.

He walked through the university gardens and soon saw the group of youths. They were walking fairly fast, looking for some means of transport. Max kept a prudent distance behind. Anticipation made his heart beat wildly.

The youths boarded a tram. Max had to make a dash for it to grab hold of the handrails and put his foot on the step. The tram trundled through Munich. The youths laughed and spoke quietly.

Max, hanging onto a handle, could only think of an improbable meeting. The tram left the residential area and arrived at a quarter of parks and squares. The students got off, Max pushed his way through the people, and, disembarking as well, continued, keeping a distance from the youths.

The group walked across the whole park to a pavilion under the trees with a beer garden in the middle. Max felt his anxiety rising. At the tables out on the terrace, people were drinking beer and making casual conversation. Some of them were looking towards the main building, where most of those present congregated, at the invitation of a young man who, from a dais, waved his arms around, emphasizing his speech.

Max was curious and came forward. Several students, almost all foreign, were carefully listening to the young man's words. The speaker was, in fact, Diran, the same as had once appeared at the Erzurum Consulate with the community notables; the one that, as one of the Armenian combatants in Sautchbulak, had taken the hospital by assault, spiriting away the Armenian women and disappearing behind the Russian barricades. He was wearing a dark suit and a small beard, and his features had grown tougher. He was resolutely haranguing in his first language. It seemed to Max that a thousand years of elapsed time, of shattered dreams and loves, of inexplicably interwoven situations and destinies, were present right there in the heart of Munich.

His hunch had been right. He looked everywhere, trying to find Araksi in each female figure. He was sure he would find her. There was no other possibility in his mind. He wandered around, not worrying about how irritating this might be to those listening to the speech.

Further back, among the public, a young woman in European-style dress stifled a scream with her hand on seeing him there. First, it was the surprise, then the stupor: it was real, not a figment of her imagination. The excitement of the meeting made her blush. Araksi resolutely made her way among the people towards her erstwhile lover until she managed to place herself right behind him, only inches away. All she had to do was stretch her arm a little and touch him.

She could hardly believe he was standing right there, but was sure it was her he had come to seek. Once more they had come together. How she had wept for him. How many times had she kept her mouth shut at Diran's pressing queries, forgoing talk about the happy, dramatic times they had experienced on the expedition, so as not to hurt him? How many times had she told herself it was useless to expect the impossible? Araksi stretched her arm and gently touched Max's back. He turned round immediately.

They were face to face. They gazed into each other's eyes for some moments. Headiness prevented either from saying anything. They took each other's hand tightly, as a spontaneous and casual gesture among the people around them, and then let go. Araksi signaled to Max to follow her to the furthest-off place beneath the trees, where they sat down.

The former lovers looked at each other penetratingly, without knowing how to begin. Max took the pamphlet out of his coat pocket and, taking heart, explained, "We're truly tied together by fate, Araksi. A group of lads left this behind near me at the university library."

Araksi looked at him. This was the same Max, without a uniform, among the common folk surrounding them. In civilian clothes he looked less martial, even a trifle defenseless, she thought.

"I'm back on my doctoral thesis. For now I'm just a reserve officer without a post."

"I'm glad you're studying again, Max." Now and then she quickly glanced towards the meeting, which was still going on.

"I can hardly believe I have you here in front of me, Araksi, and know it isn't a dream... an Oriental one... a dream that's never left me." Araksi's eyes brimmed with tears as they held hands again.

"It was never a dream... I'm real, Max. Everything's been real." She paused. "Diran's got to address all these people here, in Munich. He has a lot of commitments, and I usually accompany him. Berlin isn't easy these days, and least for us refugees..."

They remained silent for a few seconds, and Araksi went on, "I often wondered what had become of you, Max, if you were still in Turkey or some other war venue... or perhaps..."

"Or if I'd died," Max rounded off.

Araksi said nothing.

"I'm hoping to be sent to the Front as soon as the War Ministry attends to my requests... Did you ever imagine, even remotely, that we'd meet again, Araksi?"

She was looking at him intensely. She felt a lump in her throat. Finally, she dared, "I've tried to live each day without thinking about the one before. That's a lesson you taught me from the war. I couldn't even know if you were still alive... or not. How could I forget you saved me from every danger, Max?"

He sighed deeply. "After our retreat I heard that Diran commanded the group that took the hospital. And then? What happened after that, Araksi?"

"Afterwards we travelled to Yalta and went by sea to Thessaloniki. Then Greece, then Geneva. Finally, Berlin. The Armenian resistance and others that finance and protect refugees helped us."

They were talking once more as though they had only been apart for a few weeks. He could not take his eyes off her. Her eyes, her mouth, her profile produced the same effect as the first time. He found her even more beautiful. The encounter of his imagination with the real person there, sitting in front of him, had not lessened the enchantment in any way.

"In case you're interested, Max, I'll satisfy your doubts. He doesn't know about us. I just told him about our captivity and how you rescued us." She lowered her voice, a little ashamed of mentioning it, and went on, "The rest would've hurt him more than we've all suffered, and there was no remedying it... or undoing it. That belongs to me — to us."

Applause was heard and they looked towards the pavilion. The audience was applauding Diran.

"Diran's one of the main leaders of the movement," she added.

A waiter left two beers on the table and Max uneasily prompted her, "Are you married?"

She shook her head. "And you? Do you still remember..?" She stopped herself, a little embarrassed.

"I've never stopped remembering you, Araksi. I know I shouldn't, but now everything'll be different. I'm no longer the commander of a conquering expedition, and won't be able to continue... If I can't be with you, knowing you're here, just a few hours away from my life... How beautiful you are."

He caressed her as he glanced towards the pavilion.

"Please, Max... it can't be. I mustn't, Max, I can't. He needs me. Don't ask me, please. It isn't possible for you, either."

"Yes, of course it's possible, Araksi. Did we choose this meeting? Let's not run away from what has to be, what's beyond our own wills."

She was looking at him, seduced by him. A fresh breeze made her shiver. "I'm scared, Max."

The speech came to an end. The people clapped, surrounding Diran and coming forward to greet him. Araksi hurriedly scribbled something on the pamphlet. Then she stood up and, saying goodbye to Max, said, "This evening we're going back to Berlin. You have my address there. Write to me and don't put the sender's name on the envelope."

Looking at him tenderly, she took her leave. Max tried to hold her back.

"I've never stopped thinking about you, but... not now. Please, Max."

Walking rapidly, she reached the winter garden and soon

left the park with Diran and his companions. Max remained for a long while sitting under the trees. He felt strange but happy. A feeling of irremediable loss that he had dragged around since the Caucasus now no longer oppressed him, and a soft caress to his soul was returning him to life, to a joyful illusion.

It must be the closest thing to dying in battle, leaving this world and entering a new existence - free of suffering, he reflected, smiling inwardly.

CHAPTER III

THE LOVERS OF STRAUBING

GREAT JETS OF STEAM DISSOLVED into the darkness of the night when the steam engine came to a squealing stop at the main platform of Straubing station from Berlin. Hundreds of soldiers with their army gear awaited the next train.

Wearing his uniform, a greatcoat, and the tall boots of a cavalry officer, Max was paying close attention to the passengers getting off. Araksi leant out of the window, wearing a little hat. She looked both ways and soon caught sight of him. She stepped off the train and a porter took her luggage.

"Max, my love, here, here," she waved her arm as she ran to meet him. Max pushed through the crowd eagerly, expectantly. The lovers embraced emotionally. They walked along the platform without taking their eyes off each other. Soldiers, about to board the train, passed them by carrying backpacks and equipment. Happy and seemingly unaware of all the bustle, the couple hurried towards the exit.

Max drove to the outskirts of Straubing. Not much was said. They kissed fervently, with looks displaying their deep love then they laughed and embraced once more.

"I counted each hour till we were together again, Araksi. How many letters did I write you? Three? Four? I lost count — until the young lady deigned to reply. Have I retaken the position, then? I'm ready to advance into hand-to-hand combat," he said laughingly, behaving like a teenager in love.

"Don't be so sure of yourself. You're just conceited. You've only had a stroke of luck!"

"Of luck, is that what you said?" he jibed, laughingly egging her on.

Araksi corresponded, snuggling against his chest. "My love, you know it. It's just that Diran put off his trip to Geneva several times. It was impossible earlier... Please, Max, don't ask me for details. Let's not talk about anyone else, just us."

"I have two surprises," he said, accelerating the car.

"Where are you taking me, Max? Will I really have you to myself all this time? I can't believe it — no soldiers, no battalions around us," she said enthusiastically. Max smiled and made signs for her to hand him a rolled-up strip of card on the back seat.

"We'll celebrate."

Araksi unrolled the diploma. "Doctor in Chemistry. Congratulations, my sweet!" Then she added, somewhat dryly, "The peace and serenity of your home have been of great advantage to you."

Max smiled.

"Don't laugh. I really mean it... Mmmm... so then can I come to your graduation party, Dr. Swirsden-Righe?"

They left Straubing by a road leading into the forests. Max drove on a few miles and then left the highway, turning off towards an incline that led to the cabin. Great trees appeared like a dark, impenetrable mass. They were now almost in the heart of the Bavarian woods and the headlights barely illuminated the endless rows of tree trunks at each curve. They were on a deep track that tilted the car to one side. Araksi, leaning on Max's shoulder, felt happiness returning to her life. A landslide of familiar sensations took hold of her uncontrollably.

While they told each other important things and others that were completely trifling, she let her hair down and kissed Max with all the passion saved up from the last time they had loved each other, in Sautchbulak. The world was turning crazily, just like her heart. She could not oppose the whirlpool of her destiny.

THE HOUSE WAS ONE TYPICAL OF THE REGION, cozy and romantic, the quintessence of the Bavarian spirit. They left their clothes strewn over the floor next to the bed and made love all night long. At dawn, a ray of light shone into the bedroom, illuminating the lovers' bodies.

The fire in the hearth was almost out. Max unwillingly got up and threw some logs on, getting them to light with the poker. Naked, Araksi looked at him lovingly. Max stroked her black hair. Then they embraced and as they looked at the fire, Araksi began to speak. The crackling of the logs accompanied the gentle tone she used when speaking her excellent French.

"Time comes to a stop when we're like this. There's no war, no distances, geographies or frontiers, no memories, losses, other people, or anything in the whole world to separate us, my love. When I saw Diran come into the hospital, and afterwards, as we ran to the barricades in the middle of bullets, instead of feeling I was going to my salvation, it was a sort of sensation of death, of the profoundest separation... because you were moving away from me, almost like when I saw my parents die. Different, but the same pain."

Max tried to interrupt, but she carried on, putting her fingers against his mouth. "Then, as time passed — you can't know this, my love — the mind of a survivor becomes accommodating in order to carry on living and not to die of sorrow. That mechanism, or whatever it was, made the unbearable images, the ones that destroyed me just by living them again, gradually disappear, until every recollection was blocked from my memory. What happened between you and me, Max, I also tried to forget. I kept it in the box of impossibilities. But the body also has a memory. It's that of contact with a beloved body, the sensation that remains engraved forever in the deepest part, and is different from any other," she said and stopped briefly.

"From any other, from all others," she went on, "without any possible mistake... It's that inner compulsion that's guided me here."

Araksi knotted the sheets around herself and, thus covered, went to an armchair beside the bed. As she caressed Max's feet, she carried on, "Then Diran came into the story. He was no longer the impetuous, adolescent youth from Erzurum that wanted to marry me and knew as little about life as I did. But his strength was so great that it compelled him to give everything for a cause, to fight for a free Armenia. And there he found me, in the middle of a war. Was it a portent of destiny for him, was it a sign for me, or was it just chance? Diran's the part of my identity that's still alive, that hasn't died in our Armenian world. You can understand that, Max."

"Yes, I do understand it, Araksi — that is, I must accept

it along with you." He stopped briefly, as though searching for the right words. "Though you haven't asked me this, I'll tell you. You may wonder why I don't leave Hildegard and go with you. And as you know the answer, you show me you also have the right to have a companion."

She looked at him in surprise, answering with equal frankness, "I'm not going to ask you, Max. I don't want to spoil this moment. Maybe I don't want to admit it, maybe I can't dream and must just be content with what we have." She took a little pause. "Maybe it would be defying God too much."

Max went over to her. Insistently, with caresses and seduction, he made love to her again.

TOGETHER, IT ALMOST SEEMED as if they were reliving those strange, halcyon days of the campaign. They rode magnificent horses from the regimental stables in Straubing. Sometimes, during the outing, they would look upwards, marveling at the play of light through the highest branches of the forest. Then they would gallop along the paths among the lofty trees. Later, they chose a clearing in the woods, dismounted and, at an elevation at the end of the forest, laid out a cloth to have lunch.

The deep valley, covered in vegetation, extended down between the hills as far as the eye could see. Araksi opened the wicker hamper that held their picnic.

Enraptured by the landscape, Max pensively walked to the edge of the hill. He lay down on the grass. It seemed to him that they were in front of the most exact representation of the best scene in Germanic legends, every sound turning into Wagnerian music. The tree-covered mountains followed each other and the tiny valleys reminded one of an ideal, magical world, peopled by Valkyries and heroic warriors in shining breastplates. Max seemed transported to a different time, far from the prosaic necessities of the twentieth century and even further from the miseries of the war surrounding them.

"Those mountains over there are the Dreisesselberg. Do you see them, Araksi?" he said, taking her by the shoulders and pointing. "And those undulations way in the distance...

That's the Rachel, and the one even further is, let me see...
the Great Arber, I think."

"Do you often come here with Hildegard?" asked Araksi,
untying the bow that held her hair.

"Now and then..." Max answered vaguely. "Look, Araksi,
that's the idyllic Germanic vision. The Germanic soul
corresponds with this landscape. When one's far from one's
homeland, this is the first image that comes to mind, these
forests and mountains, and all the ancestral heroes. Though
my land of birth is in the Baltic, in Riga, this is where our
deepest roots lie. It's like the heights of Erzurum for you."

Sadness appeared on her face. "I don't want to think of
that today, Max. The morning you saw me riding away from
the farm, the morning I was almost killed by our Turkish
foreman, I knew I was leaving there for the last time. When I
remember Erzurum I think of my mother and father and all
the other dead. I'll remember that place with happiness the
day justice is done for my people, for my family. Only then
will I think of my Erzurum."

"I think that day may be close at hand, Araksi, perhaps a
lot closer than we imagine. Look, in Russia the Czar's been
deposed and they've murdered all the admirals of the Baltic
fleet. These events will have enormous repercussions."

"How?"

Max continued, "The idea of an independent Armenian
republic, or even a Caucasian one, isn't unrealistic. On the
contrary, it's quite likely that the Armenians will soon have
their own nation, free of Turks and Russians."

She looked at him skeptically, while they sat on the grass
and he uncorked a bottle of good wine. Max went on, "But I
fear we Baltics will suffer changes greater than other
people's. We'll lose our homeland and won't receive another
in exchange. There'll be no place for our nation."

He was uneasy. He stood again and walked over to a rocky
outcrop. "I'd like to be transferred to Riga as soon as
possible, yet it looks difficult for me, and the Foreign Office
won't attend to my request. That's my deepest ambition,
Araksi." She was paying close attention to him.

"I want a post in my country, to carve a place for myself
in the army elite, and the only place to earn that is at the

front. You don't get to the top by walking along corridors and writing reports in offices while a war's going on."

These were his deepest confessions and her eyes were riveted on him.

"And Hildegard completes that Germanic picture to perfection, right, Max? Although I won't allow myself to think of us two together beyond the present, I can see you have a well-drawn-up plan. How do I fit into your strategy? I'm Armenian. I'll never make a Germanic wife, that's plain to see."

Max bent down and, grabbing her chin, he kissed her. "No one can take your place, my love. What Hildegard shares with me... is a sense of duty." He paused before going on. "So far my marriage hasn't turned out to be perfect... that's obvious. You're here, but... we weren't going to talk about that. I'll always want you near me, and I never want to lose you again."

"It's you that's taking the conversation to those areas, Max."

He embraced her, avoiding any possible argument. Drinking their wine changed the atmosphere, getting ready to lunch amid the imposing landscape around them. After eating, they made love again, and fell asleep in each other's arms. When Araksi woke up, she remained in silence for a long while, without moving. Max was asleep in her arms, and she could not put all they had said to each other out of her mind.

THE TRAIN TO BERLIN was about to pull away. The last passengers on the platform quickly got aboard, and the porters intermingled with the soldiers going to and fro with their luggage. There were sad faces, uncertainty reigned, and sadness in the faces of the soldiers saying goodbye to their families. Then, whistles and jets of steam from the locomotive as it dragged the convoy once more into action.

Max and Araksi embraced and, overcome with emotion, she wept.

"I'll see you in Berlin in a few weeks' time," said Max.

"Yes, Max, yes, my sweetheart. From now I'll be counting the days till we meet again."

Max accompanied her to the steps of the carriage. Once in her seat, she leant out of the window and did not stop crying as they bid each other their final farewell. The guard gave the signal to leave and the train began to move.

Max watched her as she grew distant. He closed his military greatcoat; the night was cold. Even behind the window he could see Araksi's blurred figure waving. He remained that way until the train rounded a curve. The station lights seemed gloomy to him. The noise had died down and the multitude that had crowded the place before immediately gave way to emptiness. He felt a strange sensation on remembering that the following morning he would also be going home, to Munich.

CHAPTER IV

DIRAN

"NO, I'M NOT INTERESTED IN GOING back to Turkey, gentlemen. I can't accept a command without some autonomy — not after having had such responsibilities in the Caucasus campaign."

The government functionaries sitting in front of Max in the plush armchairs of the Foreign Ministry office in Berlin were vainly trying to persuade him.

Max adjusted his round, metal-framed eyeglasses and with an impatient gesture decided to cut the interview short.

"I'd feel useless in what you're proposing. Anyhow, I thank you for your consideration towards me, gentlemen, and pray that in the future you'll keep me in mind for any post I may serve in... but at the battle-front."

He was about to get up when one of the bureaucrats, the eldest of the three, the one with the small red beard, warned him, "Don't rush things, Swirsden-Righe. Your experience in political dealings with the Caucasian chieftains is most valuable. I'm sure you'd be of great use to the Germanic cause in the Baltic. Allow me to explain. Kerensky's revolution will gather in Stockholm several politicians from the peoples dominated by Russia. Who better than yourself to listen to people that wish to get the Russians off their backs?"

Max reflected on this novel proposition. Perhaps it could be seen as a stepping stone, a bridge to getting a post on a war-front. There was no doubt a great danger menaced from the north. *Action goes hand-in-hand with where shells burst,* he thought.

"Russia must be taken out of the war, and the Balts kept under German influence. There's already a great task to be carried out in Lettland and Estonia. The Balts are rabidly revolutionary, Swirsden-Righe. After all, that's the place where you were born."

One of the other functionaries intervened, leaving off chewing his pipe and blowing out a puff of smoke, as he winked, "If you accept, you won't feel an outsider there."

"The place'll be a hotbed of political intrigue. You'll find a bit of everything in Stockholm, including Armenians — although I expect they'll carry on under Turkish influence. They won't be able to break loose easily. As for the Balts, we have to keep an eye on which way they'll go. You'll see how much there is to do in Lettland, Swirsden-Righe, with our German population and the consequences a possible advance by the Russians will bring about."

Finally, the third spoke, "Maybe, after Stockholm, you could be sent to Riga. We might be able to suggest to the army General Command some intelligence mission in the 8th Cavalry Regiment, the 'Rubonia', stationed in Lettland."

"Well, what do you say, Swirsden-Righe? Will you go to Stockholm first as our delegate to the Congress?"

Max's expression changed. "Very well, gentlemen. I'll go to Stockholm."

He left the building with the satisfaction of having put an end to so many months of inactivity. Their proposition meant, at least, that he would be leaving Germany for a time. While others earned promotions, fame, and medals fighting at the front, he spent his time walking around Munich, reading the news. Should he carry on in that exasperating way, reduced to a simple military instructor for recruits at the Straubing Regiment, he would see the end of the war as a laggard in the rearguard.

Turkey, besides being a failure, had spelt a blind alley for his ambitions. Not even Hildegard's contacting some distinguished high-ranking officers had succeeded in landing him a battle appointment. He must get a transfer as soon as possible that would mean commanding troops. The Congress in Stockholm was better than nothing. It would be useful to get up to date with Russian politics, and the possible dramatic incidents about to break out in that troubled land.

He walked a few blocks and decided. Not only did the lack of a military appointment worry him, but he was tempted to succumb to the unstoppable desire to see Araksi. All he had to do was change the address in the taxi he had just hailed. The driver eyed him, waiting for instructions. Max stuck his hand in his overcoat pocket and, fishing out an envelope, checked the address. The driver immediately headed to one of the less affluent Berlin quarters. As they drove along, Max felt an extraordinary nervousness.

His love had vanished. After the time in the cabin and their leave-taking at Straubing station, he had heard from Araksi just a handful of times, and not once in the last few months, in spite of the numerous letters he had sent her every week and then every day.

To turn up this way might be a little imprudent but, should he come face-to-face with Diran, was it not natural to visit his erstwhile protégée, the girl he had saved from the Turks at Bitlis? Max mentally rehearsed phrases, and suddenly wondered, *what if she's stopped loving me?* What if Diran had found out about them and, pressured, she had decided for the Armenian? Given the reduced circumstances in which they lived it was quite possible and even logical. The strange thing was that Araksi should have vanished just like that, giving no explanation.

He got out of the taxi and was left standing opposite a modest tenement. The address was the same one he had sent all his letters to but over the last eight months they had all been returned, unopened, to the sender, with a Post Office stamp stating 'Addressee Unknown'. He decided to cross over, go inside, and ask the caretaker. An elderly woman behind a simple reception desk heard his queries with indifference.

"I'm looking for a young foreign couple — Armenians. I know they've lived here for a few months. They're young, around 22. She has dark hair... Araksi's her name. Surely you'll know on what floor..."

The woman interrupted him. She seemed to know who he was talking about, "Moved out two weeks ago. Don't live in this building no longer."

Max was nonplussed. "They've gone? Where? Didn't they leave an address? Two weeks ago?"

The woman shook her head, a little bloody-mindedly. She seemed to have guessed the reason for such interest.

"That's war fer you, Sir. 'Ere today, gone tomorrer."

Max agreed with her. Discouraged, he came out into the

street. He walked a few blocks at random. A newspaper vendor was handing out the latest news to the patrons of a beer parlor at the corner. The headlines blared out, 'Lenin in St. Petersburg'. Max went into the place.

He sat by the window. A bunch of Berlin Bolsheviks were there, celebrating the revolution in Russia. They raised their tankards to the victory, then downed the contents at a single draught. Froth flowed down gullets as red flags were waved in the bar amid songs and shouts of camaraderie.

Max submerged himself in deep thoughts and right away cut himself off from the general din. He pulled out one of the letters from his pocket and re-read it for the third or fourth time. Her handwriting was clear, calligraphic:

My dearest Max, I know you have always wanted to serve your ideals above any other consideration, so you will be able to understand me. To expect our plans to meet again to succeed is simply impossible. I do not know when you will receive this letter, but when you have it in your hands I would like you to remember me as I remember you, smiling and embracing, oblivious to everything around us, and ignoring time going by, which transforms everything and makes everything distant. That is how I would always like you to remember me. Take care of yourself, dear Max, and God bless you.

Araksi

Max looked up and, with great heaviness of heart, observed the afternoon's patrons. The comrades' songs whirled confusedly around in his head, mixing in with dramatic Baltic and Oriental symphonies. Soon he ordered another mug, and then one more.

LOUD APPLAUSE REWARDED THE LAST SPEAKER, and time after time the same phrase was repeated, "Here in Stockholm..! Gathered at this congress in Stockholm..!" So far, Max had not heard anything of the slightest interest to him, nothing meaty enough that had not been repeated to exhaustion in each and every speech that evening. He felt a little drowsy and tried to will himself awake. He looked to the sides of his box, deviating his gaze down to the stalls.

The theater was chock-full with representatives of various nationalities. On the stage, behind a desk covered with a velvet cloth, the moderators were listening to the Georgian delegate. Max paid attention to the young man's closing words:

"... And lastly, I wish to express the wish of all my countrymen: If the Romanovs have fallen, we are at the turning-point of rising, of rising as citizens of a free Georgia, independent from Russia. This is our opportunity, our historic opportunity. That's all."

Silence fell on the whole theater and, from the stalls, a young man walked up, wearing tails, like the rest of the delegates. He climbed the steps onto the stage, taking his place behind the lectern. Before addressing his opening words, with presence of mind he briefly looked at the audience. Max suddenly came awake: that slim, swarthy young man was Diran. Yes, it was him alright. Max leant forward, leaning on the balustrade, paying full attention.

"We Russian Armenians and survivors from Turkey are struggling for a free Armenia. I participated alongside the Armenian combatants that counter-attacked along the Russo-Persian border, together with the Cossacks. I'm here in Stockholm to make myself heard, for our message to be listened to, which comes from the hopes of those that have been massacred but have not given in, of those that have physically disappeared but are with us in spirit, of those that wish to be considered among the nations of the world as a people that are a part of mankind, with full rights to live in freedom from Russians, Turks, or any other domination. There are those that claim a ruler can do as he pleases with his subjects or citizens, without anyone having the right to call him to account for his acts, for therein lies the sovereignty of countries and those that wield power. But I say it is not so, it cannot be so, that the governor is not like the owner of a farm who, should he feel like it at some moment, eliminates all the chickens on his establishment just because he is entitled to do so."

The audience looked on expectantly, listening carefully to each phrase the young man pronounced. Max, his sight fixed on Diran, felt different sensations. Past and present fused together in the labyrinths of his mind, and Erzurum and Sautchbulak returned to prominence, inspiring all the rivalry he inwardly entertained against that young survivor.

Diran spoke on, "I maintain that a country is not a farm, and I maintain it is about human beings, not poultry in a poultry-run, since there is no international law that establishes it, and this is what it is all about. The crimes these rulers commit against the people in the interior of their countries, as in the case of us Armenians, are contrary to natural law, and therefore cannot remain unpunished. A tribunal of nations should judge these murderers for their abuse of power. What happened with our Armenian people also happened in the Czar's pogroms against Russian Jews. These massacres, never punished by the international community, will increase in scope over the coming years, and new conflicts will break out among the dominant nations against other weaker ones."

The audience seemed spellbound by the young lawyer's remarks. Prolonged applause arose throughout the auditorium when Diran concluded his speech. Gradually, those present went filing out of the theater. The place was a Babel, and the delegates of all the countries walked about the gold-columned foyer seeking some important personality they might approach, taking advantage of the circumstances. Max sought out Diran among the public. The lad was just exiting the auditorium when his eyes met Max's. They spontaneously moved towards each other. Diran was the first to speak.

"How are you, Consul, do you remember me? The last time we met was in your office in Erzurum. War or peace has brought us together again."

Max stopped briefly before putting him right. "I remember you perfectly, but I believe the last time was on the battle-ground. Don't forget Sautchbulak. We also coincided there."

Diran smiled. "I expect you're here as a Balt, wishing to shake yourselves free from the Russians like the rest of us?"

Max accepted a glass of champagne before answering. The waiters moved among the people, balancing trays full of glasses.

"That's correct. There's an opportunity in the Baltic for us Germans... Let me tell you your speech was good, although I feel your 'international community' is wishful thinking. The world powers will never show solidarity above their own interests. In any case, it's possible you Armenians may — perhaps — be able to free yourselves from the Turks. The Russian Revolution is bound to bring about important changes in the regional frontiers."

"Thank you!" said Diran, raising his glass. They walked together to the exit. Before taking his leave, Max stopped. "I discovered you were among the forces that occupied the hospital and took away the nurses, the young women that were rescued, and travelled with my army."

Diran haughtily raised his head. "That's right. I personally was in charge of the reconquest and the women's evacuation." He paused. "This is a good opportunity to thank you for saving Araksi, and of course, for the other girls' lives as well. Had it not been for you and the chivalry you showed in protecting them throughout the whole expedition, I would've lost Araksi forever. Araksi and I will be eternally grateful to you."

Max was unable to avoid asking after her. In fact, he had only wished to find out about her from the start.

"By the way, how is she?"

"We got married two months ago and we're living in Berlin. We're very happy. Araksi tries not to think about the past, although for me this struggle's my prime objective and my job. Now the battle is at desks and offices, in terms of revindications... Araksi and I want a new life, a family, in spite of the war." He added, "I'd like my children to grow up in Armenia. It may be possible one day."

Max politely agreed.

"If it's been possible that we are together after so much suffering and uncertainty, we owe it to you," Diran said gratefully.

They shook hands and Diran departed, mingling among the people leaving the theater. Max, stunned at the news he had just heard, sauntered around among the politicians still in the hall, without paying attention to anything but his own dark thoughts.

CHAPTER V

THE RED ARMY

THE CROWD PARADED, WAVING RED FLAGS. The roar of hundreds of voices singing Bolshevik marches and catches mixed with the cold winter wind coming in from the Baltic. Freezing, protected by their long coats and stepping through iced puddles with their rustic boots, the Bolsheviks took over as they marched down the streets of Riga. Barricades across streets could be seen everywhere. Rolf was observing the demonstrations from a military road he was patrolling at a prudential distance. On his uniform he wore the insignia of the German regiment cantoned in Riga, the Rubonia.

Rolf was alarmed at the constant desertion of German soldiers joining the civilian masses in anticipation of the Red Army's prompt arrival in Latvia.

The army truck drove along the seashore, passing in front of the Russian vessel moored in the port. An equestrian statue of Peter the Great stood unbalanced on its listing deck, never to find its destination in Riga. Beyond, at the mouth of the harbor, a British cruiser constantly trained its guns on the city as a precaution.

The German army patrol arrived at the barracks. The building was an ancient tower that housed the Rubonia. Great tension could be sensed there. A multitude of German soldiers and civilians went in and out, carrying packets of documents. Rolf shook the snow off his greatcoat and entered Captain Max von Swirsden-Righe's office.

The main political functionaries and the chief of the German army in Riga were deliberating on urgent matters. All at once, they were silent and looked towards the telegraph. The tape was running and the tapping of the device was heard. The soldier operator read aloud, "Red flag waving on Brandenburg Gate. City in Bolshevik hands... Berlin's fallen, Sir," he announced, addressing Major Frantz, in charge of the German mission in Riga.

The telegraph immediately went quiet and everyone in the room remained expectant. Max uncrossed his arms. He was standing, as were the others. He still sported an almost shaven head with his metal spectacles singling him out, an inseparable feature of his appearance.

Now he was Captain von Swirsden-Righe, intelligence officer with the task of contriving a possibility of keeping the soldiers loyal to the German nation and army, or what was left of it, in order to prevent them organizing Soviets, ignoring all authority of their natural commands, and joining the imminently arriving Red Army. Chaos reigned in Latvia.

"Governor," Max addressed the highest German civilian authority installed in Riga, "soldiers will begin returning from leave from Berlin and Königsberg as soon as train service is re-established. What are we to do then in the case of insubordination?"

The governor, a quiet man with a large white moustache, did not venture to reply. Disconcerted, he looked at the regimental chief, transferring the question to him.

Max insisted, a little more than concerned, "What should we do — shoot at the troops if they revolt, Sir? I'd also like to know what measures will be taken regarding the civilian population."

Major Frantz walked over to the window. Chiefs, officers and civilians present looked at each other uneasily.

The afternoon was turning ever greyer and gusts of wind and sleet rattled the windowpanes. The small group of ten men responsible for the whole German community in Latvia had to come to a timely decision. German families who had lived for generations in Riga, since the time of Peter the Great, had to be evacuated from the territory before the Red Army invaded. Otherwise, nobody would be able to be responsible for them, their personal safety, or their properties. Major Frantz nervously rubbed his hands. He took a deep breath before answering. His tone of voice alarmed those present even more.

"As head of the General Staff of the 8th Army Division, I take responsibility for the moment we are going through." He paused. "My orders are to open fire immediately on any mutineering elements."

Rolf, standing close to Max, rubbed his hand along his pistol belts in a gesture revealing his concern.

The major continued, "We'll transfer the General Staff command to Mitau." Then he turned to August Winnig, a deputy of the German Parliament in Riga, "Winnig, you're the last German civilian authority here and, as there's no parliament left to recognize, you ought to join your representation with ours and evacuate Riga right away."

Winnig appreciated the difficulty of coming to an immediate decision. "You're right, Major," he replied, "but I must designate some official to represent me, take charge of all the wounded we have in the hospitals, and organize the evacuation of Riga in the shortest possible time. The ferocity of the Bolsheviks when they enter the city will be implacable. That we've recognized the provisional Latvian government will be no guarantee for our German compatriots. We can't leave them at the mercy of the Russian hordes and the local Bolsheviks."

Walking round the desk, Winnig asked Max directly, "Would you, Captain, be willing to temporarily assume my post here in Riga?"

Max responded almost without thinking. "Certainly, Deputy, I accept. But I'd like to keep some officers and corporals with me here," he said, looking around at the officers and civilians present.

Rolf looked on in amazement. Deputy Winnig, highest civilian authority of the unsteady German government in Latvia, waited for Max's list for a few minutes. To stay on in the city till the last moment truly took courage.

Max added, "First of all, I choose Lieutenant Rolf Hüchtinger and Mr. Schickedanz."

"No," answered Winnig. "Lieutenant Hüchtinger won't be able to stay with you here in Riga. He'll be on a mission in Lübeck, his home city, and is to leave for that front immediately. You, Schickedanz, know what you're letting yourself in for by staying to the end."

Surprised, Rolf obeyed the order. As for Arno Schickedanz, he looked with satisfaction at Max. Among the new friends Max had made since his arrival in Riga with Hildegard, Arno represented the cream of Baltic Germanism as a member of societies that paid homage to the great Aryan brotherhood. They were weakened but gathering force among those Germans struggling to recover the pieces of the Empire, dreaming of re-founding a new society based on the old, ancestral traditions. There in Riga, their birthplace, the Swirsden-Righes had rediscovered the patriotic echoes of the call of their race, which seemed to become distorted with each victory of the local Bolsheviks and the imminent arrival in the Baltic of their Russian colleagues.

Winnig said with concern, "I'll be leaving you a large sum of money, which will be useful for the operation of evacuation. You understand, Swirsden-Righe, that by this decision to stay on you're risking your life."

The silence was total.

DEPUTY WINNIG LED MAX TO AN ADJACENT ROOM. He opened the safe and took out a large number of closed bags. "I recommend that you distribute these bags of money among the homes of our most loyal people, so that the Bolsheviks will have a hard time finding them in the case that you should fall into their hands." He clarified, "The rest of the money, the State Treasure of Latvia and Estonia, will leave immediately for Mitau under military guard, before the Communists arrive."

Max, aided by Rolf and Arno Schickedanz, left the room, dragging the bags. The soldiers then helped load the fortune into Max's car.

IN THE LATE AFTERNOON, a convoy of army trucks began leaving the German headquarters. Winnig, the civilian head of the colony, travelled with them. The departure did not go unnoticed. Latvian mobs carrying red flags insulted the convoy as it drove along the streets. The highest authority of the German Parliament was leaving Riga, so putting an end to the short period the Germans had attempted to govern the Baltic provinces after the fall of the Czarist empire.

Riga, founded by Germans in the Middle Ages, enjoyed enormous German influence and tradition. The rapid conquest by the 8th Regiment of the German army, which had responded in aiding the territories of the Hanseatic League, Latvia and Estonia, was coming to an end. Lenin's revolution in Russia had enormous influence among the

Latvian Communists, and the new Baltic republic definitely seemed to be inclined in favor of the Soviets.

NIGHT FELL. A rabble of raging Latvians, carrying weapons and sticks, smashed the windows of large shops. They entered the businesses, assaulting and sacking everything in their path. Torches in hand, they marched along the streets, illuminating the gloom with bonfires that struck fear in the hearts of all that beheld them. Further back, the mob over-ran the streets, waving red flags. One advance group climbed the roofs of the Parliament and hauled down the Imperial ensign. The building, an old three-story mansion, had belonged to the German delegation till three hours earlier.

Political changes in Riga followed one after another at a pace, minute by minute. Gathered in a huge assembly, the fiery Bolsheviks applauded and shouted in the great Parliament Hall, accompanying the nomination of the new president of the Latvian State. From the platform a 40-year-old man was addressing the public with raised arms, and enjoying his comrades' acclaim.

"Studschka! Studschka! Studschka!" chanted the multitude, chorusing his name.

The night was freezing and a deep silence descended on the streets.

MAX WENT TO LOOK OUT OF THE WINDOW once more, and ordered all lights in the house to be extinguished. Hildegard and all his remaining collaborators barred the doors, and sealed off the main entrance and gates with the carriages. They moved about in the gloom. Countess von Swirsden seemed to grow in stature in moments of danger, never showing disquiet; her decision to stand by Max until the last moment of evacuating Riga was not simply a conjugal declaration. She moved throughout the house, carrying weapons and ammunition to each officer and soldier, taking cover behind the windows and waiting with great presence of mind for the Bolshevik onslaught.

Not in vain was she 'the German officer's wife' and the daughter of Count von Swirsden, with several generations of dominion in those regions.

Each German officer carried a gun in a belt at his waist. Once more, Arno Schickedanz looked out at both sides of the street. There was no one in sight. The fall of the first snowflakes increased the silence.

"Strangely calm," said Arno. "They've spent the whole night smashing and sacking dispensaries, and at this moment they'll be designating Studschka in the Parliament. You can't stay in Riga, Max. It's total madness. The Latvian Bolsheviks have had you on their blacklist since 1905. You'll be a certain target of their hatred."

Max calmly answered, "We're staying, Arno. It's my duty. I'm not leaving this town until the last German's been evacuated and the last patient at the hospital is safely on the train. Only then will we leave Riga."

The house was in total darkness. A column of Bolsheviks carrying torches and banners appeared from the end of the street. The glow was moving in their direction. Max felt his wife's hand strongly pressing his.

"I'll be at your side, Max. If you think we must stay in Riga, that's the way it'll be." Hildegard looked him straight in the eyes. "They'll never be able to bend us, will they, Max? We are Germans. If these Bolsheviks have you on their blacklist, bully for you for having defended my father's factory and freed us from them."

The rest of the collaborators, a group of ten people made up of German soldiers and embassy personnel, came to the window. The thick column walked past, shouting death threats. Hundreds of menacing Bolsheviks wielded torches and flags. Max was looking out from behind the curtains and, as though his thoughts had suddenly flown elsewhere, he said, "Soon the shootings will begin... How ironic: in Turkey they were our allies, the Turks that persecuted the Armenians, and now we're the persecuted."

As they passed the German Embassy, the mob increased the violence of the chants that united them to every comrade in the world, threatening death to the opposers of the new regime. However, they did not stop, nor was as much as a stone thrown against the house.

On the first floor, everyone was ready to start firing at the demonstrators at the least attempt to force the doors. For a few minutes everyone held their breath, until the shouts and sound died away.

WHEN DAY BROKE, Max and his officers took themselves to the Parliament. Armed civilian guards of the Bolshevik army kept watch outside the stone palace, warding off a multitude of Latvians with claims and petitions for the new government. They were allowed to pass through the barricade installed on the steps.

The Germans remained silent among the crowd that surrounded them. After demanding identification papers time after time, the guards, with their caps and black coats reaching down to their ankles, continued arguing as to who was responsible to authorize the admittance of the German delegation. Finally, Max and his helpers were brusquely taken to the upper floor. Thus, arriving at the door to Studschka's office, Max said in Russian, "I'm here as the representative of the German government and request that President Studschka receive me as such."

The Bolshevik secretary was wearing a long black leather coat. Of pale complexion, with a beard and eyeglasses that revealed his short-sightedness, he looked the German up and down. He answered with arrogant defiance, "There is no German representative of any other government than the Bolshevik. You have no representation here in Riga. The President of the Soviet Latvian State will not receive you!"

Max took a deep breath. He was wearing a German army uniform and, though unarmed, felt that all responsibility at that moment was invested in his person. Without losing his calm he replied, "I insist on being received. There are still a large number of Germans in this city, and they consider me their representative. Inform the president that I've provisionally assumed the representation of the German mission in place of Deputy Winnig."

Studschka's secretary looked at them all with total contempt. Showing off, with a couple of pistols at his waist, he shrugged, ordering them to remain standing while he disappeared behind the doors. Max and the two lieutenants with him obeyed in silence.

The lights of the chandelier cast a dim glow. Suddenly the doors opened and a functionary they had not seen previously approached Max. Gruffly and speaking in monosyllables, he showed them into the new president of Latvia's office.

Studschka, a middle-aged man, awaited them sitting behind a huge desk. Behind him, red flags hung on the wall. On seeing Swirsden-Righe, he stood and offered his hand, though keeping a hostile attitude.

"I can't consider you a representative of anybody. There is no longer a German mission in Riga. In Berlin we recognize only the Soviet Government, similar to the one I am at the head of here," said Studschka.

"President, I am requesting you grant me a time frame and safe-conducts for the German wounded still in the hospitals, as well as for members of the community that have not yet been evacuated. Then... we will all leave Riga," said Max, not beating about the bush.

Studschka looked down at the heap of papers on his desk as though searching for a solution to a problem that was complicating his life even more than the chaotic situation in progress.

"Alright... I'll provide a train for you all to leave Riga in two weeks' time. But I can't assume responsibility for whatever happens after that, either to you or any other German." Standing up, Studschka indicated the interview was over. "The comrade secretary will hand you the safe-conducts signed by myself," he said, indicating the slovenly individual that had remained at his side throughout.

The Germans went down the inside stairs of the Parliament building, exhibiting the safe-conducts. A veritable swarm of people's army commissars observed them menacingly at the foot of the stairs. The group kept silent until they were outside the building. Max then knew the countdown had begun and that no one, even Studschka, could guarantee the safety of his people. Bolshevik fury was advancing from Russia in sight of all. Not even Berlin would be able to free itself from its Communist comrades.

Germany's polluted, Max kept telling himself.

THE NEXT FEW DAYS CONFIRMED THE WORST PROGNOSIS. Terror took over in Riga. Uncontrolled bands of soldiers from the people's army broke into the houses of those identified as opponents and forced them onto trucks. Whoever resisted was struck with pistols and left lying on the street. Old Riga, of the sumptuous stone buildings, the one that had seen splendor almost comparable to St. Petersburg's, sank into a sea of blood. Latvian regiments who had been faithful to the Czar were transformed into furious Bolsheviks and personal guards of Lenin.

At night, trucks loaded with prisoners drove to the parks on the city outskirts. The morning mist gave a ghostly look to the 'death woods'. Latvians fallen into disgrace, men and women, were forced at gunpoint to enter the woods by Red Army soldiers. Futile tears and supplications were drowned in the vegetation before the dry chatter of pistol shots of the Bolsheviks executing from behind and without delay - the quickest method of getting the victims' bodies into the ditches. For hours and hours, the killings were repeated until men, women and children lay piled up by the dozens and hundreds on top of each other, turning the ancient park used for family outings into a horror of corpses, a graveless cemetery.

CHAPTER VI

THE TRAIN

HILDEGARD WENT TO AND FRO AROUND THE HOUSE. Her movements were incessant. She was packing clothes from the wardrobes and emptying the chests of drawers on the first floor, carrying their contents to the trunks lined up in the embassy reception, ready to be loaded onto cars. On each trip she had to go up and down the stairs. She did this lithely, stopping only to give minimal instructions to the maid who was helping her, wrapping up and packing away everything that could be taken of their belongings. There was only an hour and a half left before the train was due to leave.

Max was heaping up folders and going through files in the office, while papers and books awaited packing. Time was running short and they were already somewhat behind schedule.

Hildegard folded the last dresses and shook the fur coats they would be wearing on the journey. The bedroom window overlooked a better part of the street and all movement along it, although in recent days city traffic had almost completely ceased and the voices of people talking as they passed by could be clearly heard.

The noise of the engines of several trucks was the first thing the countess and her maid heard. Then, the vehicles' sudden braking, and orders in German. Soldiers came down off the trucks at a trot, carrying rifles and taking up positions in front of the house. It was a contingent of German Bolsheviks. Hildegard remained immobile. Still holding clothes, she got close to the window, hiding behind the curtains as she looked down.

She ran downstairs to the office. Max was already alerted and, in the middle of the room, wordlessly made a signal to keep calm. Then he deposited books on the desk. Bangs were heard on the front door as though from several rifle butts. Max ordered the butler to open the door.

"They're coming to detain us, Max. We'll never get to the station. The train's leaving in an hour," Hildegard said with great agitation.

"They're looking for money, Hildegard. Don't say anything and keep calm. The money, the money Winnig left me, where is it? Have you put it in a safe place?"

"I hid it... I won't tell you where so that you don't expose yourself." No sooner had she said this than a bunch of soldiers rushed into the house. Max remained waiting behind his desk, Hildegard standing at his side. The butler looked with fear at the soldiers, who obeyed a yelling corporal. Some ran up to the first floor while the corporal advanced with pointed gun and crossed the reception to the office.

"You're Max Swirsden-Righe?" he bellowed on seeing the couple's presence of mind. "I demand in the name of the Soviet German government that you hand over the people's money. The money Deputy Winnig left in Riga is now the property of the Soviets." Max looked contemptuously at the corporal. Hildegard showed all the composure she was able to with her intense blue eyes.

ON THE STATION PLATFORM, THE LAST RESIDENTS of the German colony of Riga were crowding together, on the point of leaving the city. The dim lighting gave the departure a sordid, sad appearance. Shivering in the cold twilight, Lieutenants Grimmert and Moser, Arno Schickedanz, and several young officers, walked about tensely, clapping their gloves together and trying to reinforce their courage as they eyed the station clock. There was scant room to get close to the carriages and the way was constantly obstructed by porters wheeling trolleys loaded with trunks and bags. Many from the German community of Riga, families that had lived for generations by the Daugava estuary, were ready to board the train that would take them to the frontier, escaping the arrival of the Red Army. The deadline established by Studschka was about to expire. Only Swirsden-Righe and his wife were missing. Arno Schickedanz could not explain why they were taking so long. He did not want to imagine the worst.

THE BOLSHEVIK SOLDIERS SEARCHED EACH DRAWER of the cupboards. They turned over trunks, throwing the couple's clothes about. Even pockets were turned inside out and carefully examined.

The library shelves were looked through and the fallen and piled-up books on the floor were trampled over at each new desperate inspection. Max and his wife were in the office with the patrol chief pointing his rifle at them. As the search began to prove futile, the mood of the intruders deteriorated. Some pulled down wallpaper, while others turned the beds over and smashed furniture in their quest for 'the German people's money'.

Max looked sidelong at the grandfather clock instants before the soldiers smashed it to pieces. He thought that at that very moment the train would be on the point of leaving, and that the officers and Arno Schickedanz would be wondering and worrying about them. From outside, the noise of engines was heard. Once more, from the street the squeal of trucks braking and voices giving orders reached them. Max looked at Hildegard. The situation was getting worse.

The door opened and President Studschka himself appeared in the drawing room. Max felt a sort of relief on seeing him. Studschka immediately began yelling in Russian. Some of the soldiers did not respond to the maximum authority he now represented in Riga, until he was able to impose his will. Enraged and empty-handed, the soldiers left the house. Studschka was irked. He did not want any more problems.

"I warned you, Swirsden-Righe. I can't do anything more for you. Get away from Riga immediately. The train's leaving in a few minutes," Studschka said, consulting his pocket watch. Then, without another word, he about-faced and left the residence.

Max and Hildegard sighed with relief. Max was still intrigued as to the whereabouts of the funds. Throughout the whole time they had been subjected to the search, he wondered where his wife had hidden them. He found it impossible to believe the hiding place had not been discovered.

Hildegard was still cautious. She looked to all sides, making sure there were no Bolsheviks hidden in the house waiting to discover the money. She made signs for him to keep quiet. Taking his hand, she led him to the bedroom toilet. She removed the refuse from the toilet paper bucket next to the WC. Under the dirty cotton wads and soiled toilet paper, to Max's amazement the rolls of bills appeared, untouched. The Soviets had turned the house head-over-heels without ever imagining that hiding place.

Max smiled with relief. He kissed his wife for her brilliant idea. Without delay, they began cramming clothes into trunks once more. The car that was to drive them to the station was still waiting outside.

THE WHISTLE WAS ANNOUNCING THE TRAIN'S DEPARTURE. The last of the sick were heaved up on their stretchers and placed in the corridors. Despite the improvisation of the operation, not even the most crippled of the German patients were left in the city hospitals.

Sad faces looked out from behind the windows. They were gazing, probably for the last time, at the town their ancestors had been born and lived in. All they knew was that an uncertain future awaited them in Königsberg. Meanwhile, on the platform, the German lieutenants and Arno Schickedanz smoked nervously, having not seen their leader arrive. Armed Bolshevik guards walked up and down, with the somber look of ravens, wrapped up in their long leather coats, making the wait even tenser and reminding everyone that the evacuation deadline was getting closer by the minute.

Lieutenant Moser puffed his cigarette hurriedly, nervous and expectant. "Something's happened to the Captain. If he doesn't get here in the next couple of minutes, he's going to miss the train. We can't just go and leave them to their fate."

The others nodded agreement. They shared Moser's concern.

The hands of the clock moved and almost marked the hour. During the next minute, anxiety over the Captain's delay became intolerable. "We can't postpone the departure any longer, gentlemen."

"We can't risk the safety of so many people," concurred Arno Schickedanz. "We have to decide right now. Either we get onto the train straightaway or we go back and find out what's happened to Captain Swirsden-Righe. As for myself, I imagine the worst, gentlemen."

The others nodded agreement as they looked towards the end of the platform time after time.

THE NIGHT WAS COLD. Max and the embassy chauffeur were hauling the last trunks to the car. Hildegard ran in and out of the bedrooms, feeling she might be overlooking something important. She and Max hardly said a word to each other. The concern that they might miss the last train occupied their thoughts entirely, and to have talked would simply have increased their confusion. They brought the last suitcase out. All the luggage was packed into the car. The silence was broken seconds before starting off.

From the end of the totally deserted street, several army trucks advanced towards them. The yellowish headlights were unmistakable. Max's blood froze.

The trucks stopped outside the house. The occupants got down, armed to the teeth and with great speed, blocking any movement of the car. Orders were shouted. The machine guns quickly convinced Max that all was lost. A Bolshevik commissar stood in their way, right in front of the car door.

"Cavalry Captain Max von Swirsden-Righe, by orders of the Red Army I am informing you that you will not be allowed to leave Riga. All residents of the house must accompany us," shouted the Bolshevik. He looked at Hildegard and, lowering his voice, said, "You may stay behind."

Hildegard took her husband's arm and with great presence of mind answered in defiance, "I am not going to be separated from my husband. Wherever you're taking him, I want to go too. Max, I'll go to the prison with you," she embraced her husband.

A young marine in the patrol, admiring her stalwartness, came up to her as his comrades forced Max to advance at bayonet-point. "Your idea is not a very good one, Madam. If you go to the prison you'll be unable to do anything for him, and so there'll be no one to help. Instead, outside you'll be of greater use to him. Take my advice, stay here."

Hildegard, in her helplessness, submitted to the facts.

Max was bundled into the car, squeezed between the guards. All at once, all his expectations had collapsed. He recalled Studschka's warnings. He felt on the verge of fainting. The Soviet patrol, followed by two trucks full of soldiers, went away, merging into the night. Then the house remained silent and Hildegard was at a loss as to what to do.

THE BOLSHEVIK SOLDIERS RAN in formation along the platform. Arno Schickedanz and the rest watched with alarm as the patrol arrived. In seconds, they were surrounded and menaced with pistols and rifles on all sides. Passengers fearfully watched from the windows. A Bolshevik commissar waved his gun for the engine driver to leave.

The steam locomotive moved forward and the cloud of steam enveloped everything on its way. Arno Schickedanz watched in despair as the train slowly pulled out, leaving them stranded in Riga at the mercy of the Communists. When he attempted to find out about Major Swirsden-Righe and his wife, he only received yells in Russian. He and his companions were immediately forced onto the trucks at bayonet-point.

CHAPTER VII

THE NIGHT IN RIGA

THEY LOOKED AT EACH OTHER IN SILENCE. Several hours had gone by, practically the whole night. The Red Army guards watching over them kept the lights of the great hall permanently on. Grimmert and Moser dozed on the sofas, the last pieces of furniture left in the hall save some chairs and a writing table occupied by the guards, who most of the time inspected papers and dossiers of citizens that would later be fetched by the patrols. Armed men incessantly went in and out with papers under their arms, ready to go out hunting opponents. A large red flag hung on the wall. Arno Schickedanz was engrossed in thought, trying to stay awake in case of any change in their situation, but his eyelids kept closing in spite of himself. Very near, though unbeknown to them, the Bolsheviks had transferred Max to another room in the Government House. Watched over by a couple of guards, he was waiting to be subjected to the next interrogation - the third that night.

Max looked at the door opening. Two Bolsheviks came in. They brought in a table and chairs, then a Russian commissar with a dark, straggly beard appeared and sat down in front of him.

"Are you Max Swirsden-Righe, an officer of the former German Imperial Army, posted in Riga to the 8th Rubonia Cavalry Division, in charge of the propaganda office, with the purpose of denouncing German soldiers sympathetic to our movement? Answer my question," the pale-faced commissar curtly ordered, looking out from behind thick spectacles.

Max, weary from sleeplessness, looked haggard under the lightbulb hanging over his head. His uniform was unbuttoned at the neck. He sat up to answer, doing so in Russian, his language of birth.

"I am a reserve cavalry captain of the 8th Cavalry Division of the German Army, with plenipotentiary powers as representative of the German government mission in Riga." Max dug into his pocket and pulled out his credentials. The commissar flung them aside with a stroke of his hand.

"We do not recognize any such power. That government does not exist. We recognize only the German Bolshevik government." With the same disdain, he glanced at the identification papers and demanded, with greater exasperation, "Give me the names and addresses of all employees of your government. I want all of those that worked at that agency. Besides, you are to hand over all the money you received from Winnig for the transport of the Germans! Have you heard me well? I think so!"

"I don't intend to hand over any list. I request that I be given the treatment due to my rank as diplomatic representative of the mission to the government of Lettland," Max answered time and again.

The Bolshevik looked at him, unfazed. The two armed men behind him pulled a face of displeasure at the defiant answer.

MAX CAME TO HIS SENSES once more on hearing footsteps behind the door. He was startled, sitting in utter darkness. He groped the mattress they had dumped him on. He was not in pain. He had not been physically tortured. Maybe he had fainted from tiredness, he thought, discovering a crack of light filtering in under the door. He saw shadows approaching. The door opened and a lamp was lit outside. Once more, guards dragged Max out into the passage. From there, held by his armpits, they advanced to a courtyard along the corridors. Again, he was face-to-face with the same commissar, once again the same questions were unendingly repeated.

"Where is the list of the mission employees? Have you thought it over better?"

"What did you do with the money belonging to the Bolshevik people?"

Max, on his chair, remained silent. The commissar impatiently raised his voice for the first time. With his pistol butt, he nervously tapped on the table.

"You will be transferred to the military prison. The revolutionary tribunal has found you guilty of crimes against the people, for which the maximum penalty will be applied," he said, and then, hardly looking at the prisoner, "The tribunal sentences you to death by firing squad." He signaled for Max to be taken away.

MAX WAS DRAGGED AWAY, held by two soldiers that led him to the back courtyard of the building. His head was spinning. They put him on a truck. He did not take long to learn that everyone on that vehicle was being taken for immediate execution.

No one said a word. Gusts of icy wind could be felt in the back of the truck as it drove through the city. The condemned shivered with cold and fear. The terror of that moment and the wind that cut to the bone quickly dispelled the stuffiness Max had felt.

At the end of the journey they were all taken off and pushed at pistol-point to the inside of the prison. Dozens of Bolsheviks arrived back from their nocturnal roundups, bringing citizens that opposed the new regime. Men and women of Latvia, condemned to be shot in the police yards. Then the trucks left again in search of fresh victims.

Cries of terror could be heard as soon as one entered the building. The place was crammed with prisoners. Max and his captors advanced along the corridors without stopping. They crossed two courtyards.

Max, looking straight ahead, understood that no appeal was possible. His die was cast. He felt it was a drab ending. His death would not be heroic. Maybe a few would remember him for having volunteered to stay behind to defend the evacuees. How far he was from the purpose he had set himself as an ideal of military heroism! To die from a shot in the neck in a grubby courtyard, executed by Bolshevik Jews! Germany, his country, hardly existed now, crumbling at each step, just as he was.

They placed him in the line of those to be shot at dawn. As they approached the parade ground, the gun reports of the firing squad became increasingly clear. Soon he himself would be a bulk, a corpse, a dead object which, heaped onto some cart with the other dead, would be cast into a common grave. He finished his inner dialogue, and the images of hundreds of Armenians appeared in his memory. He smiled wryly at the fate destiny had kept in store for him.

A Russian commissar approached, giving orders to the guards. They shoved Max forward, separating him from the line. They went down a staircase and Max was put in a cell. He was alone. He imagined they were reserving him for a special execution. At least there would be spectators at that last hour.

More than his own death, what tormented him was the thought of separation, the idea of the suffering he would be causing Hildegard.

"Please, please, I wish to write..." he said. "Would it be possible..?"

Right away, the jailer handed him some paper and ink. He felt stunned. He began writing:

My dear Hildegard...

Soon, he immersed himself in a tender farewell and spent a few minutes addressing his last words to the woman who had stood beside him and loyally fulfilled the sacrificial role of the wife of a German soldier during those years of war and separation.

When he was through, several written pages lay upon the little table in the cell.

Max stood up. Suddenly, a rush of pent-up emotions flooded his mind and his heart, and he began to weep. He leant on the table and, covering his face with his arms and hands, he sank into despair. Then he raised his head high, as though emerging from the deepest sorrow, and took up the pen again. He straightened the blank page, hesitated for an instant, and then launched into describing the feelings that oppressed his soul. He felt that in that way he was setting free a true sensation that he had kept hidden and almost forgotten in the depths of his heart. Now, at the final hour of his life, it took over his being, causing the greatest pain that he had ever been able to admit. The idea of never seeing her again, of never being in her company, and the certainty that they would never meet again became unbearable. He was only left the remote hope that these last words would reach her some time:

My beloved Araksi, love of my life, I cannot forget you. In spite of the time that has elapsed, everything brings you back to my memory. During these terrible final moments of my existence I see nothing but you... and in the deep abyss I am falling into, only your warmth... and the sound of your voice as we loved each other...

The creaking of the gate opening made him turn round to face the guards. Resigned to his fate, he stood up from the cot and asked that, as a last favor, they hand the letters to his wife. Only then did it dawn on him that his words would never reach Araksi. Before he could tear the pages up, the guards snatched them out of his hands. Then, obeying orders, he went out of the cell, keeping silent, as the two Bolsheviks kept their guns pointed at him all the way to the central courtyard.

When they arrived at the place of execution, he looked at the sky. It was a misty morning. The firing squad never interrupted its incessant task of killing. He shut his eyes on seeing a man crumple, and imagined himself falling against a wall a few minutes later. He began to sweat and grow restless, but the guard that led the men to the place of execution carried on without stopping. Max became disconcerted but, pushed by the soldiers, carried on walking along the passages to one of the prison offices.

The three commissars presiding over the tribunal looked at him as he went in. He was obliged to stay standing in front of them. Then he understood he had been brought there to hear the definitive sentence.

The Bolsheviks looked at him in silence, adjusting their eyeglasses, and they re-read the letters he had written. On and off, they would smile and exchange little sarcastic comments. One of them began the interrogation.

"You are one of the responsible parties in the repression of our comrades in 1905, responsible for many of the deaths caused by the Cossack regiment you joined to defend the factory belonging to the exploiter von Swirsden. We understand he was your father-in-law..."

Max remained silent, and the Bolshevik went on, "You

headed the Propaganda Office here in Riga until just a few days ago. You watched, and abetted, the denunciation and repression of all those that sympathized with our cause. We want the list of Latvians that were employed there."

The three fixed their penetrating gazes on Max.

"We want the money belonging to the people... You used only a small amount for the safe-conducts. We want to know who Araksi is." The commissar paused. "Araksi? Is that a codename? Or did you have another woman besides your wife?"

He looked at the others with sarcasm.

Max kept absolutely quiet. Then it was the second interrogator's turn. His voice was high-pitched and sounded almost hysterical, although he maintained great self-control. He was wearing a black cap, tight-fitting down to his ears, giving him an even more sinister look. A draught slammed the door shut, which startled Max as he listened to the accusations.

"Did you know that in Berlin they have just assassinated Rosa Luxemburg and Karl Liebknecht? For this reason, our German and Latvian comrades want your head." The Soviet commissar paused before pronouncing his sentence. "All evidence that we find points to your immediate execution by firing squad, Swirsden-Righe. Take him away."

Max shuddered. With contempt and rushing the process, they had just condemned him to death.

The guards led Max away. Several days' growth of beard and the exhaustion produced by the enormous strain he was under made the terror in his expression very evident.

MAX LOOKED UP. THE SUN WAS PEEPING OUT through the clouds. The guards loaded their weapons and waited for the order. He heard nothing more, just a penetrating buzz in his ears. His hands, tied behind his back, were half-numb. He held his breath, waiting for the impact. With foggy vision, he managed to see the squad chief. Then he looked away and saw the rifle barrels aimed at him. He thought he saw the beginning of the order, but suddenly had the impression that all sounds were muted. At that moment, one of the commissars broke out into the yard, running towards the squad. The order to put off the execution paralyzed the scene. The men lowered their rifles and uncocked them. Max, right by the wall, began trembling. His whole body shook and he sweated till he soaked his shirt, despite the cold.

THE MOLDINGS OF THE huge stone building that was Government House were blanketed by snow. From time to time the sun came out. Lieutenants Grimmert and Moser, together with Arno Schickedanz and some corporals, went out into the street by a side door of the building. With concern, they looked at a group of demonstrators shouting outside the building on hearing of their release. The protestors screamed with hate as the Germans went by, waving posters demanding Swirsden-Righe's execution as a reprisal for the deaths of Rosa Luxemburg and Liebknecht; foremost figures of the Spartacist League, a Marxist group put down by the military and the Freikorps — the German nationalists.

However, no one stopped the group of released officers. They walked away with the aim of meeting Countess von Swirsden, who was probably still free and might be able to inform them of Max's circumstances.

CHAPTER VIII

MITAU - KÖNIGSBERG

DEPUTY WINNIG SHUFFLED ABOUT UNEASILY, sitting on the main armchair in his office. On the wall was a large map of the region and in a corner could be seen a German flag hanging from a staff.

The deputy carefully read through the reports on Riga. Facing him, a German government delegate sent by Berlin awaited Winnig's response to the urgent, serious news he had brought.

Winnig, forced out by the Bolsheviks, would have to install his base in the city of Königsberg. He was troubled. After all, it had been his responsibility to leave the evacuation in Swirsden-Righe's hands.

When he finished reading the report, he looked up and said to those around him, "Put me through urgently to the Foreign Ministry in Berlin. They've condemned Swirsden-Righe to death! He's been taken before the firing squad twice, but the Bolshies are still undecided."

A secretary handed him the phone and Winnig immediately became immersed in the communication. When he hung up, his face was somber. "Bad news, gentlemen. According to the Ministry, Swirsden-Righe's under custody of the Red Army. We have it from a good source that he'll be shot within hours. Perhaps he already has been."

He got up and paced round the room, looking at the others as though searching their faces for a way out of the predicament. "The moment could hardly be worse to negotiate with the Russians. While they assassinate our ambassador in Moscow, we expel theirs from Germany for helping the Bolsheviks in Berlin. Swirsden-Righe's really got us in a spot..."

The group of five functionaries that had followed him from Riga nodded.

"I should never have let myself be swayed by his judgment," Winnig said sadly. "Much less fall for his vain audacity. I should have just followed my own instinct."

He reproached himself, as if he could have foreseen these dire happenings.

CHAPTER IX

HILDEGARD

HILDEGARD WAS IN DESPAIR AS SHE LOOKED AT ROLF. Arno was serious and said nothing. Commissars went in and out of Studschka's office. The Countess' fears over-rode the exhaustion of the last few hours. In spite of the fatigue and strain she was experiencing, her distinction, composure and elegance never diminished. She half-closed her eyes and a black shadow appeared before them.

Rolf Hüchtinger had come back to Riga after two weeks, fooling the Lettish border guards, just in time to come to the aid of his friend. Little could he and Arno Schickedanz do against the commissars' power. One word out of place, one wrong gesture, and they could all run the same fate as Max. They barely enjoyed a precarious freedom and the last possibility open to them, at Hildegard's supplication, was to plead alongside her for Max's life at the very doors of President Studschka's office.

The two men sat in silence on the armchairs of a somber reception space, ignored for hours by the circulating, hollow-eyed people. Although they did not mention any details, they imagined Max suffering in some gloomy cell. These hours and minutes that went past were crucial to saving his life, but the information Hildegard and the two friends possessed regarding his sentence could hardly be less promising.

MAX TURNED OVER REPEATEDLY, HUDDLED IN HIS COT. The over-crowding in the dungeons was beginning to affect his body. He closed his eyes, but immediately opened them again in terror on hearing guards passing near his cell.

The place was in deep gloom, and the mechanism of mental evasion was the only possible remedy for the madness and terror that assailed him night after night. If he lost his sanity he would lose all hope, without which, remote as it was, it was useless to consider himself still alive for even one more minute.

He sought his imagination as his last safeguard. When

logical evidence could find no other cranny than to feel defeated, his memories rose up like a series of happy images, transforming the whole place into scenes of light and longing. All at once Araksi, her hair loose, was galloping full-out on the chestnut from the heights around Erzurum on that summer morning, in what felt like another life.

Romantic looks, caresses, passionate kisses, and the fragrance of a perfect body lying next to his own, giving him its warmth and bringing time to a halt. Just that memory, while it lasted, comforted him, and he then understood the profound sense in the words of that woman he was still in love with.

The images arose time after time and in his mind the memories came back shining like the bright sparkles of the rushing waters as they floated down the Tigris. Meanwhile, from the prow of the kelek, Araksi smiled at him with admiration and shyness. Then he wept, curled up on the floor like a child.

A kick in the ribs brought him back to reality. The blow left him gasping and when he looked up, he saw the jailer, shouting at him to get up.

Yet again, Max was seated in front of his interrogators. The doors opened, and in the gloom of the office he could barely make out the figure of the commissar behind a lamp that dazzled him with its bulb.

A guard brought him food. Max hungrily wolfed down the plate of stew. The commissar carried on looking at him as he smoked in silence. Finally, with a sandy tone, he said, "You have admitted being influenced by the theories of Neumann. That arrogant Germanism seems to have poisoned you. You claim you are a Socialist, a National Socialist, but point out you belong to no party... You don't say!" shouted the Russian, as Max, exhausted, tried to keep his head upright on his shoulders.

"You never stopped promoting a propaganda campaign against our government," the commissar went on. "Do you know that your army is crumbling to pieces? Do you realize that you Germans are now very weak, and only defeat is in store for you? We Bolsheviks have initiated a world revolution in Russia, and now we shall take possession of

Germany. That is our next step."

He was silent for a few seconds and then went on, "This tribunal declares you guilty, and sentences you to be shot by firing squad tomorrow at dawn. Take him away!"

THE RED GUARDS CONTINUED executing prisoners. They shot a condemned man. The body slumped and was removed instantly. Max was next. Without delay, he was marched in front of the squad. They tied his hands behind him. The chief ordered rifles to be loaded. Max shut his eyes. He thought of nothing, simply accepting that this was the final moment of his life.

At that precise moment, shouts were heard. A Red Army officer strode across the courtyard and, going up to the chief of the platoon, handed him a paper.

Max opened his eyes; he did not know what was happening. That instant seemed like an eternity. The soldiers were still aiming at him, but no one pulled the trigger.

The chief of the firing squad, clearly irked, read the order. They had just postponed the execution once again. Straightaway, the prisoner was dragged back to his cell. His temples were throbbing and, panic-stricken, he began to shiver and shake with cold.

THE CLOCK ON THE WALL INDICATED 7:30 A.M. Hildegard was slumbering on a couch, as were Rolf and Arno. They had spent the whole night waiting to be attended by the Latvian President.

Soldiers' boots were heard along the passage. Hildegard felt a hand shaking her shoulder. The Bolshevik was concise: Studschka would be arriving any moment and was ready to listen to them. Hildegard started. She controlled herself as quickly as possible, smoothed the fur coat she had on, and fixed her hair with a clip.

Minutes later, they were admitted to the office. Studschka spoke first. He did not have a minute to lose. "Madam, I have been informed that your husband has been reprieved, for this time, from being shot."

Hildegard and the other two held their breath.

"Please... allow me to continue, and listen. Swirsden-

Righe's execution has been postponed only temporarily by the prison governor. As you can see, events are beyond my authority, which is insufficient against the Red Army. The German Foreign Minister is in contact with Comrade Chicherin, the Russian Commissar of Foreign Affairs. They're in negotiations for your husband's life. I myself will now attempt to contact Chicherin. I must ask you to wait outside while I speak to Moscow."

"Mr. Studschka, I implore you to save my husband's life. I pray you, do everything in your power to have him released and enable us all to leave Riga together."

Hildegard and the others went back to the waiting room. They were all primed to hear the decision. The minutes went by unbearably slowly.

Studschka hung up. He indicated to his secretary to have the countess and her two companions come back in. In great suspense, they entered the office again, and stood while they listened to the president.

"Chicherin has ordered your husband to be released. It seems his death would not be considered sufficient reprisal for the murders of Rosa Luxemburg and Karl Liebknecht. Therefore, I am able to hand you this safe-conduct. You and your husband are to leave Riga," he looked from Hildegard to the other two, "together with the whole of the German delegation still in this city, with no loss of time — as soon as possible, Madam and Sirs."

"Thank you," was all Hildegard managed to say as she received the papers from Studschka's hands. Rolf and Arno patted each other in delight as they ran down the passage to the exit, avoiding everyone that got in their way.

WITH ILL-WILL AND ANNOYANCE, the commissars passed the papers Hildegard had just handed them from one to another, inspecting them with great hesitation. One of them, apparently the most senior, shook his head, evidently opposed to Max's release. He waved the papers about, claiming signatures were still missing from the document. The Bolsheviks in charge of the prison were undecided whether to free the prisoner or keep him behind bars. The Russians' looks became increasingly hostile.

ON THE FLOOR, MAX, CURLED UP WITH COLD AND HUNGER and with visible signs of having broken emotionally, was unaware that Hildegard and his friends were pleading for his freedom not far from his cell.

The guards opened the door. He huddled, covering his face as though imploring mercy, such was the panic he felt at having to face the firing squad once more. They did not answer him. In silence, they took him along the corridors once more. This time he was not led to the execution courtyard, nor did they turn off towards the interrogation rooms. And all at once he saw that beyond the glass doors of the hall stood Hildegard and, next to her, Rolf and Arno. He also recognized the lieutenants and corporals of the mission, who had delayed their departure in the train and shared his fate. They all smiled on seeing him appear. He looked haggard, and his beard had grown. He still wore his uniform. Hildegard embraced him with tears in her eyes. No one said anything. Then one of the commissars exclaimed, "We are not going to stop the comrades that are against your liberation. That is not our responsibility."

Outside, a multitude were waving red flags, yelling imprecations against Max. At last, after going through endless controls, Max was able to complete the rubber-stamping of papers and safe-conducts. Then they were pushed out into the street and left to their own devices.

Hildegard walked at the head of the group. They advanced the first few feet amid insults and death threats from a truly intimidating mob. Max looked all around him. He was stunned, but inside him boiled an intimate sensation of humiliation and vengeance.

Several times on the way they were on the point of being mobbed by the multitude. However, no one actually attacked them. Hundreds of hate-filled proletarians accosted and shook their fists at them. They were aware that, at the least provocation, they could end up as victims of a lynch mob without the authorities lifting a finger to save them.

They got to the station. The Red Guards prevented anyone else from gaining access to the platform, so as to avoid any last-minute aggression. Max, his wife, and the rest of their young companions hurriedly boarded the train. Deportee Germans were looking out through the windows, happy to see them turning up alive, and in time — at long last! — to get away from Riga.

SNOW-BLANKETED FORESTS followed each other without interruption. It was night, and a bright moon shone on the desolate landscape on either side of the track. Boundless distances staked out by dark firs appeared like spectral presences beyond the windows. Max kept his sight fixed, hypnotized by the rhythm of the landscape and abstracted in deep thought. Hildegard was dozing, leaning on his shoulder.

The regular rhythm of the carriages was lulling nearly all of them. Given over to sleep and fatigue after the hazardous retreat from Lettland, they slept wrapped up in rugs. Others, wide awake, rested in their seats, focusing their thoughts on the life they were leaving behind and the hardships they would encounter in exile. The carriage was in darkness and was kept pleasantly warm. They travelled on facing seats.

Rolf was not sleeping either. He quickly glanced outside and pulled the curtain to. He smiled in peace, feeling there was no longer cause for concern, they were travelling back to safety as they had done three years earlier from another distant place. Possibly Rolf, better than anyone, could understand his comrade's thoughts. This time they were not returning home triumphant, either. But they were alive.

Hildegard woke and stroked her husband's hand. They spoke almost in whispers.

"These Bolshevik Jews want to see Germany destroyed, Hildegard," Max said, voicing a resentment that was new in him. "The humiliation I've suffered! I'll never be able to forget it. I was scum to them, just like the Armenians condemned and scorned by the Turks. How ironic!"

Rolf looked at him in silence as Max went on, "Bolshevik Jews! They've managed to trample national sentiment underfoot. The commissars have taken over all command posts, and the Russian military have still not clicked to the fact that they're obeying international Judaism in its plans to take over the world."

Hildegard was following her husband's monologue. "We won't let them into Prussia, Max. We'll never allow that. But now just calm down, my love. You're safe... we're all safe, and in a few hours' time we'll be at the frontier."

Rolf could not help reflecting that the captivity his friend had suffered, the psychological and physical torture endured at the hands of the Bolshevik commissars, had left deep scars on Max. His altered mental state was obvious.

"The Russian Revolution has been carried out by Latvian rifles, Jewish brains, and Russian idiots," Max insisted, and then added, "I owe you my life, Hildegard. I don't think I've thanked you adequately for it. I'm enormously proud of you, my love, enormously proud." Hildegard shuddered inwardly on hearing this.

"I never gave up counting on you," Max continued. "I know you've suffered on account of my career, and never as much as this time. I'd never have come out of that Bolshevik hell but for your bravery. You shall always be..." he took a few instants to find the right words, "... my great companion, Hildegard."

Hildegard, deeply moved, snuggled into his arms. "I'd rather have died than leave and allow you to remain there, Max, you know that. Wherever you are, I'll also want to go. I'm a German officer's wife, and that's my duty."

Suddenly, Max stirred, remembering something important. "Hildegard, what happened to all the money Winnig left in our care? Did the Bolsheviks find it? Were you able to hide any of it?"

Their voices woke all their travelling companions. They were all waiting to hear her answer.

Hildegard wordlessly beckoned one of the corporals to help her. They immediately took down some of the trunks and suitcases from the rack. The men opened jars of preserves, bread, butter and honey containers, and food for the journey. Presently, wrapped in their food supplies, the wads of money were revealed, to everyone's amazement. The whole sum Winnig had entrusted to them appeared before their eyes.

"It's all here, Max, well hidden, safe and sound," she said with a smile.

The lights were extinguished once more, and sleep finally overcame everyone but Max. He opened the drapes and, while he contemplated the snow-covered scenery, thought that some Oriental music was impinging on his ears, bringing to him memories and images that appeared like a continuous caravan of memories. He remained that way for a long time. Then he shut his eyes and leant on Hildegard's shoulder. When the clicks of rifles being cocked by the firing squad finally faded from his ears, he was able to sleep soundly.

CHAPTER X

BERLIN 1920

DIRAN CAME DOWN SOME STEPS and went in through the red wooden door of the tobacconist shop. Outside the building, a sign in golden letters read, 'Manuc, the Tobacconist – Cigars and Tobaccos imported from Turkey'. He had to stoop a little and then went down a small ladder. He went through the routine by heart. No sooner did one go into the shop than he smelt the pleasant, unmistakable aroma of tobacco. On the shelves, imported cigars of every quality were lined up in wooden cases. A woman behind the counter was wrapping parcels as she attended to a couple of Berlin customers. On seeing Diran, she greeted him in Armenian as she usually did, while concentrating on getting her customers' orders ready.

"Hello, Crisdine... How's business? It seems people are smoking more and more in this country, eh?" answered Diran, in a very good mood, removing the bowler hat that matched his dark suit.

"Thank God... Manuc's downstairs, waiting for you with the others. Ah, Diran, I've got something for Araksi, which she ordered weeks ago."

"Thanks, Crisdine. Remind me when I leave." He passed behind the counter and went to the back of the shop. Going down some steps, he came to a small patio. He saw a light on in the back room and went there along the corridor.

The place was stacked high with boxes of cigars, tins of tobacco, and Oriental spices, hard to come by for any European in those post-war times. Dimly lit, the storeroom served as a meeting place for the leading members of the exiled Armenian community. Six middle-aged men were talking in an undertone, emphasizing their words. Manuc and Agop had maintained their ties with Diran. Not in vain had they saved their lives together, fleeing from the death caravan through Kurdistan to the frontier. This was a new stage in their lives.

It was their lot to live as refugees in Berlin, with the

responsibility of keeping open any political opportunity that might allow negotiations for the much-cherished liberation of their land.

Diran greeted them in Armenian. They seemed pressed for time.

"Sit down, Diran. We'll get straight to the point," said Agop. "There's an extremely important bit of news for the movement and all our compatriots — rumors, but reliable ones: Talaat Pasha is here in Berlin."

Diran jumped on hearing this, "Talaat, here in Berlin?"

Manuc continued gravely, biting a cigar in his mouth. "Yep, just as you've heard. That murdering son of a bitch is living in anonymity, supported by the generals. He's living somewhere in Berlin."

"How are we going to find him?"

A third individual, somewhat older than them, nodded at each comment. Looking at his companions, he considered the moment right to intervene. "We haven't the resources... for the moment. Talaat's protected by the German government, and they'll keep all related information in this regard very much to themselves."

The man had a bushy moustache. He spoke Armenian with a thick German accent, which showed that he had left Anatolia as a very small child. Moving away from the stool he had been leaning on and sticking his thumbs in the suspenders that scarcely held his trousers up, he said in a friendly tone, approaching Diran, "Diran, listen. Nostalgic German monarchists are preparing a coup — a military coup to overthrow the government. Everyone knows that by now. Berlin's a hotbed of paramilitaries and nationalists."

He paced among the boxes and then carried on, "Someone... an individual you know from the bad days in Erzurum, has been recently recalled to Berlin." Diran looked at his companions, intrigued, "Sorry... I don't understand."

Manuc took a long puff of his cigar. Then he took one of his best cigars from a case and handed it to Diran, taking over the conversation. "The individual in question is nowadays an active member of the Freikorps, the nationalists that support Kapp as head of the future government. Kapp enjoys the support of the military

335

commander of Berlin and the Baltic paramilitary forces... among which is our man: Swirsden-Righe. Do you remember him? He's the chap we're interested in. Without doubt he'll be in a position of power after the coup."

Diran was following Manuc's discourse without fully understanding. "The fellow's become an active propagandist, and is a high-ranking Intelligence officer in the Freikorps. To locate Talaat we need to get hold of that vital information. D'you understand, Diran? We're convinced Swirsden-Righe knows Talaat's whereabouts."

Diran took the magazine Manuc was offering. It was called *Klarheit*, meaning 'clarity'.

"Have a look at it." The rest remained silent. Manuc continued, "As you can see, it's seething with National Socialism. You'll notice the affection he feels for Jews after miraculously saving himself from being shot in Riga. The guy has become ultra-anti-Semitic."

"Maybe Swirsden-Righe does know about Talaat, but where do I come into the picture?" asked Diran. "Besides, I still don't understand why Swirsden-Righe might be willing to reveal the information to us. No German Intelligence officer in his right mind would be ready to."

All of them looked at Agop, as though waiting for his intervention. "It won't be you that asks him, Diran. You know that our commitment to our people is forever, and will endure for as long as we live. We're not asking you to do it, Diran. Swirsden-Righe would never tell you. However, we believe there's someone he'd reveal any information to, someone able to make him confess every important detail."

Diran looked at his companions with ever-increasing confusion.

Agop completed his statement, saying, "That person is Araksi."

"Araksi... Araksi? But why are you involving my wife in this business? What are you insinuating?" Diran's face was red with fury.

"Diran, it isn't my intention to offend you, but we know she and Swirsden-Righe were involved in a relationship at a certain moment. You must understand we've got to take advantage of that circumstance..."

"Be clear, Agop. Be careful with making any comment about my wife because I swear I'll break your face! I won't have it from you or anybody else." Diran swooped on Agop, delivering him a punch full in the face without giving him time to react. Agop noisily fell on the boxes, rubbing his jaw.

"Diran, calm down, calm down." Manuc restrained him from behind, locking his arms and trying to calm him. "We thought you knew. We haven't wanted to offend you. Diran — it's our mission. There's no room for pride here. This is the price we all have to pay," Manuc insisted.

With the help of the others, Agop got up with difficulty, rubbing his jaw, which was already showing bruising at the level of his chin. "I never imagined you didn't know what went on between them... but you've got to know. It's better that way. Araksi was his lover throughout the mission to Persia. The German was crazy about her."

Diran was disconcerted. He broke loose roughly, not believing what he had heard for the first time.

"D'you remember the rest of the girls you saved in Sautchbulak?" Agop pressed on. "They talked about Araksi's affair with Swirsden-Righe. You can't change what's already happened, Diran. What we're asking you for is difficult, but it's little if you think of our responsibility to our people."

Heavy-hearted, Diran tried to take hold of himself and quieten his mind, though not his heart. He felt hurt and furious. In spite of the shame of not knowing, it was unfair to take it out on his friends. He managed to catch Manuc's words, "If Talaat gets away, justice will never be done."

Diran remained silent for a while, and then continued, "If Swirsden-Righe gives Araksi that information, what'll happen afterwards, Agop..? I don't want either her or me to be accomplices in any action. Don't count on me for that. Who's going to do it? Which of you will cover his hands with blood the same as they did?"

Agop came forward. "Look at it this way. Talaat, though he's outside Turkey, has been sentenced to death *in absentia* by a court in Constantinople, the same as Enver and Djemal. None of us will do the deed. Someone else has been designated for that mission. Neither you nor Araksi will find out the details, I promise you... but justice will be done."

"Every last atom of my being cries for justice for the crime against our nation, you know that better than anybody, but I can't accept exacting vengeance ourselves. We can't lower ourselves to their level. We're Christians and don't believe in applying an eye for an eye, or taking justice into our own hands. To kill here isn't the same as in a war."

When he finished speaking, he picked up his hat and, turning, left the meeting. The others looked at him without saying a word. He crossed the courtyard and went up the steps. Under his arm he had some copies of *Klarheit*. He passed by Crisdine, absentmindedly ignoring her, but the woman held him back for a few moments. She pulled down some small jars wrapped in delicate papers.

"Wait... take these relishes. They arrived today from Constantinople. I promised them to Araksi weeks ago. They'll make you feel closer to Erzurum."

"Thanks, Crisdine... Closer, as before..."

"There's hardly anything left in the grocery shops. What's going to happen when people can no longer afford a bit of tobacco or food? I'm scared this is going to happen, Diran. This country's going to explode. There's nothing but hatred all around. We should go to America. That's what I keep telling Manuc."

Diran put on his hat, stuck the parcel under his arm, and made a sign of agreement. He hurriedly walked out into the street, avoiding further talk.

BERLIN WAS A DANGEROUS PLACE AT NIGHT. Only beggars and prostitutes walked the city at those hours. Diran strode along the middle of the street to avoid being surprised by some assailant. His steps clicking on the cobblestones were the only sound to be heard.

Everything was in turmoil in his head. He had been the last to find out about Araksi's and Swirsden-Righe's love affair. The community of survivors would surely whisper about it behind his back. The proof of this had been shoved right under his nose by his closest friends. As he walked along, the Talaat business became secondary to him and, try and avoid it as he might, a single thought ran through his mind.

"Shit, shit, what a damn fool I've been," he kept telling himself. Then he reminded himself it had all happened during a period of the most absolute uncertainty and suffering, in the worst conditions for survival. Maybe Araksi had been forced by Swirsden-Righe and the son of a bitch had taken advantage of his wife just like the Turks in the harem. Diran had heard the story of the captivity from Araksi's own lips, but he never dared ask her for details. Actually the two of them, in an unspoken agreement, had resolved not to remember those hellish times.

Turning a corner, the yells of a man in an alley startled him. Further on, a group of prostitutes around a fire waited in vain for some pedestrian to happen by, with whom to ply their trade. Diran felt cold. He pulled up his overcoat lapels. He was just a few blocks away from the apartment and he quickened his pace.

He thought for a moment outside the door then let himself in.

The apartment was medium-sized, cheerful, and sparsely furnished. A gramophone was visible on a table in the main room. Araksi, on hearing her husband arrive, embraced and kissed him lovingly, helping him to take his overcoat off. He seemed a little distant.

"Why were you so long, love? I was worried. You know how it worries me when you come home alone at night, in the dark. What kept you so long?"

"I had a meeting with Manuc and the others. Crisdine gave me this for you," Diran answered, flinging his hat on the rack.

"Wasn't the meeting at the tobacco shop for tomorrow, Thursday? How pale you look, Diran. Are you feeling alright?" She was keeping an eye on the saucepan, which was emitting a fragrant smell of stew.

Diran unwrapped the packet Crisdine had given him and put it on the kitchen table.

"Pepper and cumin! It's months since they disappeared from the markets. Good Crisdine never forgets my requests... I'll make some of the sauce we used to have at home. D'you remember how Papa loved it? It's a luxury we'll allow ourselves this evening, my love. Open the bottle of wine, please. It's the one under the cupboard. I think it's the last we have."

"That's right... The meeting was going to be tomorrow, but Agop and Manuc wanted to hold it earlier on account of something important," Diran said, with evident irritation.

Araksi was chopping vegetables on the kitchen table. "Ah, yes? What did they have to say? Pass me the knife."

"They suppose Talaat Pasha's taking refuge here in Berlin."

Araksi stopped cutting and looked at her husband in amazement.

"Talaat! In Berlin? So how did they find out?"

"There are confirmed rumors. Actually, no one knows where the bastard's hiding out."

"And if we bumped into him round the corner, Diran, in our own neighborhood, what would we do? What would our reaction be if we came across that beast? Would I become paralyzed just to find him facing me? I think I'd cover my face and run. What would you do? How can such an abominable person live an ordinary life, walking around like anyone else, without the weight of his crimes driving him mad?"

"Conscience isn't the same to everyone, Araksi. Some can live hiding their crimes and meanness without the slightest qualms. There are individuals that, by hiding heinous actions in their deepest recesses, end up anaesthetizing their memories." Diran was looking at her with a penetrating expression.

"So what will the people of the resistance do if they find him?"

"Execute him."

Araksi briefly interrupted what she was doing, "So what will our people do if they find him? Take justice into your own hands? You'll become murderers just the same as them. Is that what you want, Diran?"

"Do you remember what they did to us, Araksi, what they did to our families? Do you remember we had parents... brothers and sisters, and homes... and there were children, innocent of any evil, and even a great fortune... Do you remember that? Can you remember millions of our people being murdered in the cruelest way imaginable?"

"Enough... enough, Diran, please."

"Would you rather bury the memories and pretend nothing ever happened, Araksi?"

"Don't talk nonsense, Diran, as if those things had never happened to me. Especially me! I can't stand that sarcastic and foolish tone you use sometimes."

The stew was done. Araksi caught hold of a dishtowel and lifted the saucepan off the fire, placing it on the table. She indicated to her husband where the dishes were in the cupboard. The conversation continued while they sat down at the table. Diran was making an effort to keep in control in front of her.

"There's someone else involved in the business, Araksi." He fixed his sight on her as he paused. "Agop and the others believe that person could know Talaat's whereabouts, someone you know very well, Araksi. Intimately..." he said, wiping his mouth with the serviette and getting up to fetch the magazines. Araksi watched him in surprise, without understanding. Diran returned to the table with the copies of *Klarheit*.

"Max von Swirsden-Righe's in the city."

Araksi stifled all reaction at the mention of Max by her husband.

"They presume there'll soon be a military coup against the Berlin government, led by a certain Kapp, with the support of the Baltic paramilitaries, and the Freikorps, among whom is Swirsden-Righe. Do you remember him?"

Araksi became uneasy. "Why the question, Diran? Of course I remember Max Swirsden-Righe... I have an unforgettable memory of him. If it hadn't been for his bravery and humanity, I wouldn't be here with you. Why this suspicion, Diran?"

A blush immediately rose to her face. Diran, determined to hear the whole story from her, pressed forward, "Swirsden-Righe's become a staunch supporter of the struggle against the Bolsheviks. It seems the man's suffered a radical transformation." He leafed through the magazine, showing her the articles signed by Max. "He repudiates the Jews and blames them for Germany's ills. It'll end up turning into hate of all foreigners, until the hate turns against anyone different from themselves. Have a look... your humanitarian consul is obsessed with the purity of the German race."

Araksi turned over the pages in silence, until Diran faced her with no further delay. "Araksi... the organization has given me... has given *us* a mission. They want you to contact Swirsden-Righe, appealing to the protection he provided you and the others in Turkey. They believe you'll be able to find out Talaat's whereabouts in Berlin. Swirsden-Righe's always been an army intelligence officer, and any information on that butcher Talaat will be vitally important for us."

Araksi stood up, trying to contain the violent anger overcoming her. "They want me, your wife, to look for Swirsden-Righe and seduce him? And what did you say to that, what was your reaction? Have you allowed that affront against me, Diran? Against us?" Diran looked at her in silence. "You can't ask me for that, Diran. If my father lived, he'd surely have answered such an offence with a punch. What sort of man are you?"

"Araksi, I've respected you and accepted everything without asking questions since we've been together, listening to you for hours and being understanding for all these years... But this matter requires looking deep inside ourselves, beyond our own pride. I love you, always have loved you. It was a miracle to meet up again when each believed the other to be dead. The nature of this mission obliges me to humiliate myself before the organization and, it seems, also before you. I have no alternative, Araksi... I have to be told everything, what really happened during the expedition, between you and Swirsden-Righe."

Diran looked expectantly at her. He had made use of all his common sense and bent his self-esteem, but a deep sadness was coursing right through him.

Araksi saw the time had come to make a clean breast of the memories she carried deep within herself. She walked over to the window, looked down into the deserted, dimly-lit street, and turned round to face him. Before she began talking, a gleam of emotion dampened her eyes. "We were lovers during the expedition. Max... never exerted pressure on me, the contrary of what happened to all of us in the kaimakam's harem. He was always a gentleman, and my protector. In spite of being a captive and travelling with Turks and Kurds all around us, he gave me the rank and place due to me. Not a single man ever dared look at me all the time I was under his protection."

Diran let himself sink heavily into the armchair.

"I fell in love with Max, and he with me. We just lived for the present. I couldn't afford the luxury of it being otherwise. Everyone... including you, had vanished in a nightmare that had been atrociously real and irreparable. I imagined you to be dead, Diran, as all of my past. He bought me from the kaimakam, he pulled me out of hell."

Diran looked surprised.

"Yes, just as you heard. Max bought us all to save us. He bought the kaimakam's slave-girls. He paid a special ransom for me... a fortune in gold... for me... the Turk's favorite. Does this scandalize you? The rest of the details aren't worth your knowing. I just didn't want to hurt you, I promise you. D'you think one can forget something like that in one's life?"

Diran was quiet for a long time, not daring to say anything. Everything he had not wanted to think about in the years after the rescue was being revealed to him now, in a foreign land. Destiny, once again inscrutable, was embroiling him with the only man that had ever really been Araksi's before him. For some odd reason, right from the first he had felt an aversion towards that fellow. His nature had put him on guard against the German since their first encounter at the consulate, but now everything was indicating that his intuition had been right.

"I know you met him again in Munich," he said with wounded pride.

Araksi passed it off, "That was pure chance. It happened during one of your speeches. I was with you and didn't think I should comment on it. After that, I never heard from him," she lied. "Is that all Agop and the others told you about me?" she asked, feeling uneasy.

"Araksi — do you love me?"

Araksi herself wondered what feeling it was that united her to that young lawyer she had married after living an impossible passion. There was no room for any further deceit. "There are loves that brand our lives and are inevitable, and there are others that help us to live. I respect you and I've chosen you, Diran... but you have no right to ask me to forget episodes of my life as though they'd never happened, or hadn't marked me forever."

She was thoughtful for a while. Diran waited in silence.

"I'll go and see Max Swirsden-Righe... but I want to warn you that you're forcing me to risk awakening feelings that I'd decided to keep away from."

Then Araksi and Diran remained in silence and did not speak again for the rest of the evening. She felt she had freed herself of a great weight in her heart. Deep melancholy took hold of both of them. The past and an uncertain future once again strangely mixed, as if the web of their destinies were inseparable and deliberately placed them in a constant challenge. They had invoked the past, and all the dramatic images and memories had filled the little apartment. The ghosts, so often warded off, were there again.

ON THE FOLLOWING EVENING, Araksi made her way to the seedy old Berlin hotel, following the instructions Agop and the others had indicated as the right place to meet Max von Swirsden-Righe. The hotel was the meeting place where Kapp's followers mingled with nostalgic monarchists, rabid nationalists, and old die-hards from the German army who barely found a niche in the contorted politics of a defeated country, strangled and isolated by the conditions of the Treaty of Versailles.

Araksi briefly hesitated before going through the doors of the elegant building. She stopped in the entrance hall, dominated by golden moldings and reddish, opaque velvet curtains dividing the salons.

As she advanced into the reception area, men's glances were directed towards her. The lines of the dress she was wearing had been taken in, emphasizing her waist and bust. Her dark, gathered hair and a small hat gave the natural sparkle of her eyes a kind of shade. Her exotic beauty in no way went unnoticed among those flush-faced Germans.

The men were arguing at the hotel bar. Cigar smoke

pervaded the whole room. Women of easy virtue giggled and shared the uniformed men's tables. The place resembled a big brothel in which uncertainty was intertwined with the ambition of the political slogans and chants. Everywhere the harangues of those beer-hall orators were to be heard, with a tendency to join whichever movement might recuperate their disputed nationality.

With caution, Araksi asked a concierge where to find Max von Swirsden-Righe. The employee pointed at the tables. Araksi advanced to a kind of dining room full of people, an improvised location for conferences and ceremonies. She passed a mirrored door and walked through a sector of rather small private rooms. Along the narrow passage, she felt intimidated and doubted whether she should continue.

"Excuse me, do you know where I can find Max von Swirsden-Righe?"

The young Balt looked at her with fascination and, smiling as he looked over his shoulder, winked at his companion to make way along the narrow passage.

"Max von Swirsden-Righe? Are you sure you wouldn't prefer me?" Araksi attempted to get through between the two without paying attention, but the soldier insisted. "Don't get cross. Have a look there, in that room on the right. If you don't find him there you can come back. What's your name, darling?"

Araksi moved on a few feet. The door was ajar and allowed one to see the meeting that was being held. A cloud of cigar smoke enveloped the whole room. Her heart beat fast and she felt intimidated. She scanned the group of 20 men sitting there, and suddenly her look fell on Max. He looked a little older. At least that was her first impression. As ever, his head was shaven, a small moustache gave him an air of severe intellect, and a few furrows had appeared on his face. Araksi stood without moving. She remembered it had been almost three years since she had last seen Max, in Straubing at the cabin in the woods, and then the farewell at the station, but she was unable to let the memory progress: Max had just spotted her. First, he made a gesture of absolute amazement at seeing her. Then he rose from his seat and, excusing himself, made his way to the passage.

They were face to face.

"Araksi, what are you doing here?" he said, disbelievingly. "What are you doing here?" he asked again in a tone denoting joy and confusion.

Araksi smiled as they looked into each other's eyes. "How've you been, Max? Please excuse this surprise appearance, this intrusion, let's call it, after... some time. I needed to see you. I'd heard you were here. Perhaps I should have..."

Feeling uncomfortable at the attention she aroused among those around, she lowered her voice. "Perhaps we could find some quiet place to talk. Or perhaps my visit's just been untimely..."

"Untimely? Totally unexpected... How beautiful you're looking, Araksi. As ever."

Araksi felt flattered and Max, taking her by the arm, made signs to her to wait a few seconds while he looked into the meeting room.

"Gentlemen, please excuse me. This is a matter of absolute priority. We'll carry on later," Max said to his companions, who laughed and felt he was right.

"Let's go somewhere we can talk. How did you know where to find me, Araksi?"

"Does it matter, Max? The whole of Berlin knows what's going on."

They climbed the great stairway that led to the bedrooms. Everywhere, they came across Freikorps paramilitaries going in and out of bedrooms in the company of women. Max smiled on seeing Araksi's expression.

"Comrades of arms... of ideals. These men are going to save Germany, Araksi. We're struggling to become a nation again, and great changes are in the offing. You're about to be a witness to history being made."

When they arrived at the door to the room, Max unlocked it and invited Araksi in. The place was spacious, with a small reception leading to the bedroom. Max turned all the lights on. It was almost night. Next to a window with drawn curtains stood a table with flasks of liqueur. They looked into each other's eyes without speaking. Max filled the glasses. Araksi moved to a large couch and sat down, taking her coat off. Then she removed her hat with a sensual action, letting down her dark hair. Max looked at her and as ever felt an irresistible desire. The attraction that woman produced in him remained intact, despite the years of separation, despite all that had happened between them, despite everything; like the first time in Erzurum, thought Max.

"I met Diran in Stockholm, at that congress... That was the last news I had of you."

"Diran and I are married... It seems an eternity in perspective, and at the same time a headlong dash. Max, everything I've experienced inevitably repeats itself."

Max took a sip of his drink and imagined he perceived a certain seductive tone in her speech. "You're as lovely as ever, Araksi." He paused. "You haven't forgotten me, then?"

"D'you think it's possible to forget?"

Max stood and, going over to her, took her in his arms and kissed her with passion. She resisted for an instant, then yielded. She felt troubled.

"Max, please... It's true I needed to see you. It's our destiny, as you've always said. I let my wish to see you guide me. It was easy to find you. All Berlin knows about Kapp and the fragility of the government. But tell me about yourself in all this time. Tell me, Max," she insisted, and he sat next to her, gently caressing her. His vision focused on a point in the past, as if with the telling vivid images paraded before him.

"I was a hair's breadth away from being shot by a firing squad of the Bolsheviks in Riga, Araksi. During those nights of prison, I turned and turned on my bed with terror. Those weren't nightmares. They were the most certain reality. They would drag me out for interrogation by the commissars, and once more, at dawn, I found myself facing my executioners, who loaded their rifles and aimed at me; but at the last moment they would postpone the execution for one reason or another and take me back to my cell. They shot hundreds, thousands in the prisons and woods, and threw their bodies, piled on top of each other, into common graves in the forest. At those moments I would cling to the best memories of my life... and it was always you that appeared. I held on to your memory with desperation."

Max filled his liqueur glass and, emptying it in one go, seemed to give himself the strength to carry on the story. As she listened, Araksi began to realize that this man was no longer the unbendable knight of olden days. A deep wound had been opened in his person, and she was able to recognize it. It was the kind of imprint borne by those that had been ill-treated or humiliated, and only a great inner strength, and nothing else, would enable them to carry on standing upright for the rest of their lives, carrying their horrors around in body and soul. She knew well what it was all about.

Mellowed by Max's words, she put her arms round him like a child and began caressing and kissing him tenderly. Max, resting on her lap, lifted himself up. They kissed, dragged along by the passion that still seemed to exist between them.

"Now you seem a lot more like me. Now that you've had a taste of hell, your soul must understand the agony I went through," murmured Araksi.

DIRAN DINED ALONE AT THE DINING ROOM TABLE. As the minutes and hours dragged by, depression overcame him.

He went to the kitchen and threw the leftovers away. A porcelain dish slipped out of his hands as he was rinsing it and smashed on the floor. Impatiently, he picked up the shards until, overwhelmed by his feelings, he threw them against the kitchen slab. A metallic clatter resounded in the kitchen while he yelled and insulted destiny and himself in equal parts. Back in the living room, he looked at the clock on the wall, which marked 10 p.m. That made five hours since his wife had left in search of Swirsden-Righe.

Diran sat on the sofa and with resignation poured himself a glass of liqueur. He lit a cigarette and remained in the semi-darkness. A dim light came in through the window from the street. He examined his thoughts once and again, fearing that this meeting between Araksi and Max might spell the end of his marriage, wondering if he had not made the biggest mistake a man could make: to push the woman he loves into the arms of his rival.

MAX AND ARAKSI KISSED and caressed each other with tenderness. Then Max got up and paced round the room.

"I'll never be able to forgive that humiliation. At those moments, I understood who the real enemies were, Araksi. The enemy is and always has been the Bolshevik Jew, advancing on our nation with intent to dominate it, to Judaicize it. First it was Russia, and now it's Germany's turn. We're not going to let that happen. That's why we've come to Berlin."

Araksi was watching each of Max's movements. The heat of the passion that had previously taken hold of her suddenly went cold.

"We'll soon stage a military coup to get Ebert out of the government, you know, that fellow that's pretending to be Chancellor. At the same moment, our companions will rise up in Munich, and when they triumph I'll be part of the government. The time's arrived when we Germans must stand up for ourselves. The German people's conscience is asleep. Everything's rotten with Bolshevik and Jewish ideas, Araksi! The German nation needs a thorough cleansing... That's inevitable. In order to be able to revive our ideals of greatness, the scum will have to be separated from the good part. Do you know, Araksi, we're not even allowed to train our army on our own national territory. We're obliged to send it to Russia for maneuvers. Do you know who's in charge of our troops? The Turk, Enver Pasha — yes, the murderer of your people, and that's because our enemies have tied us hand and foot. They've got the German people on their knees, so that we'll bleed to death and disappear as a nation. But the humiliated, defeated German nation will once more rise from the ashes, not without first eliminating the rot that's poisoning our race."

He talked non-stop. He went to Araksi to offer her more liqueur. Araksi was startled, then remembered her mission. She had to get away from any personal feeling and concentrate on what she had been sent to do.

"Max — is Enver Pasha collaborating with Germany, then? Hasn't he been condemned *in absentia* by a tribunal, together with Talaat and Djemal? Hasn't he been sentenced to death by the very Turks of Constantinople?"

"Everything's been a great farce, Araksi. Talaat Pasha, the Minister of the Interior, walks along the streets of this city — Berlin — protected by his anonymity and abetted by all those stiff-collared generals that sank us into failure."

Araksi redoubled her attention. Max was naturally getting close to the information she had been instructed to obtain. At the same time, she felt there was nothing honest in her attitude. Nevertheless, she quickly assumed her responsibility.

"You terrify me. Talaat in Berlin? If I inadvertently came across him some morning, maybe in my neighborhood, who knows, I'd feel paralyzed with terror, or maybe I would not respond for myself, in the name of my parents, my brothers and sister, and for all the Armenian dead... We've moved to the Augsburger Street," said Araksi in a hushed tone, as though she wished to give her former lover information he did not know. She stopped there.

"Augsburger Street? In that case I hope to be able to visit you very often... But don't worry — the Turk's nowhere near your neighborhood. They've lodged him near the zoo... But why should you want to know that? Forget it. We've already left that war behind... All I know is that I can't take my eyes off you. That's all that matters now."

"You're right, Max. Talaat and the others must now deal with their conscience. In spite of everything, I've forgiven, otherwise I wouldn't be able to carry on living. You must also forgive, Max... Otherwise hatred will eat you up from the inside."

"I don't think you've understood my ideas, Araksi. I haven't changed my way of thinking in the least. For you, I have only love, as it's been since the first time I saw you in Erzurum, and perhaps now I need you more than ever. Hildegard did everything to save my life in Latvia. She's my greatest ally, but I can't forget you. And I know it's the same for both of us. We'll never be able to fully separate, Araksi... This is the proof that you haven't been able to resist the distance between us, and you've finally come back."

Max embraced and kissed her.

"No, Max, please... Of course I'm fond of you and always will be, and I'll be forever grateful for your having saved my life. Please, Max! I can't." Araksi struggled, trying to free herself from Max's embrace. He unbuttoned her dress, leaving her cleavage exposed, which only intensified his lust, until she managed to break loose.

With reddened face and ruffled hair, almost without intending to, she shot at him from her innermost being, "Please Max! What have you turned into? Who are you..? I've never heard you talk with so much hatred about people's condition or race. Your fanaticism is very much like the Turks'. Baltic Blood-brotherhood... the people destined to rule over everyone! What nonsense is this? Why do the Jews deserve your hatred? Are we Armenians also on your list..? Won't we also be eliminated from your new world that only accepts Germans? I loved you for your humanity, and that's no longer there. It's gone. All those people around you, Max — I think they've forgotten every Christian principle. Turkish, German, Armenian, Russian blood is the same in the face of suffering, at the time of death. I only saw men in the same condition, horrified at the fragility of their lives, which they lost in an instant. There is no superior race, Max. We all have a right to exist. In any case, my people are over 3000 years old. We became Christians before any other kingdom or country on earth."

Weeping, she went from one side of the room to the other. She fetched her coat and purse and, without stopping, walked to the door. "Never as much as now, Max, have I understood my father's words so well. I'm proud to belong to a civilization that, for centuries, has struggled to keep its traditions alive. Have you forgotten Turkey, then? Have you all turned pagan? No nation has the right to believe it can subdue all the rest!"

Max vainly tried to stop her from going out into the corridor.

"Don't give me history lessons, Araksi. Either you stay here tonight with me, or else never again intrude in my life, and even less in the sacred principles that govern my acts."

Araksi opened the door. Max was inflamed, and seemed on the point of losing his self-control. His hands were shaking. Araksi looked at him straight in his eyes.

"I was scared of being face-to-face with you again, Max.

Many times, I felt regret at having fled from you out of cowardice. After all, is it a sin to doubt one's feelings and want to be sure about what we really need? You know, I have the dream of one day leading a completely normal life... as I was brought up for. Let's not humiliate each other any further, and say goodbye with respect for what we had before. Don't lose your soul, Max. The glory you're looking for is no reward at such a high price. Your new world's no longer mine... Goodbye, Max, may God protect you."

Araksi went into the passageway and, after walking faster, broke into a run. Max followed her insistently, trying to keep her there. She went down the main stairs as fast as she could to the central hall. Max then stopped. He followed her with his eyes, leaning over the balustrade on the first floor, without daring to go down.

"Araksi, don't go. Araksi, wait... Come here at once! It's an order! I'm ordering you to!" he shouted several times, beside himself.

Some uniformed men turned round on hearing the shouts. The spectacle was nothing unusual in that hotel, frequented by women that visited the paramilitaries every evening. Soon they lost interest and gathered in one of the rooms. They crowded together and, oblivious to anything else in the world, sang military marches, drowning out any din that might be coming from outside that room.

THE CLOCK SHOWED IT WAS 2:30 A.M. Diran was smoking in the gloom. The sound of a key in the lock made him look at the door. Araksi came in noiselessly. Without turning the lights on, she left her purse at the entrance. Right away, she saw her husband's profile, sitting in the dark. The ember of his cigarette gave him away. Still wearing her coat, she went over to him.

She knelt by the couch and began stroking him tenderly. Diran remained silent, without blinking. They looked straight into each other's eyes. Araksi kissed him and moved between his arms. Then she nodded. Diran embraced her, and then she felt safe. She immediately recalled that night in her father's study in Erzurum, when in Zareh's arms she was able to feel that everything was alright, that nothing wrong would happen, and nothing could harm her, even in the middle of madness that seemed to have no remedy. And without wanting to know anything more, she gave in to tiredness, like a tiny girl, and soon they both fell asleep.

CHAPTER XI

A FAILED PUTSCH

THE BERLIN STREETS WERE COMPLETELY DESERTED. For three days people stayed at home in sympathy with the workers' general strike. The real surprise for the monarchists staging the coup was that every civil servant of the Republic also seemed to have vanished from government buildings. Kapp's followers found themselves with no one to rebel against.

A truck loaded with Freikorps soldiers pulled up suddenly in front of Government House. Paramilitaries got off, rifles at the ready. One of them was the flag-bearer. Max von Swirsden-Righe crouched down, protecting himself against bullets, and ran in combat position, pistol in hand. But no bullet downed him. Silence was total. He ran up the outside stairway. No one resisted the advance, no missile responded to the takeover of the seat of government. Max entered the building. The Erhardt brigades set up their machine guns, determined to evict the socialists and kill any worker or politician that got in their way.

Max ran through the empty halls. He went into a room on the second floor and saw some books piled on the floor. They were all that had been left behind in the whole office. From the end of the passage came the voice of a brigade captain ordering an immediate retreat from the place. There could be no government coup without anyone to detain. Still, Max took a few more minutes. He went over to the pile of books and, on leafing through them, his brow furrowed with concern. He took several folders and ran back along the passages. The paramilitaries aimed in all directions without finding anybody. In that ghostly absence the brigades had just been defeated by an invisible enemy. They soon came back out onto the street and Max and the Baltic soldiers boarded the trucks and left.

The Berlin population, in the midst of a general strike, had turned its back on the Kapp putsch and its attempt to take over the reins of government. One thing was certain, thought Max: they must flee to Munich as soon as possible if they did not wish to end up facing firing squads once the workers' strike was over. He looked up at the dome of the building. The red flag of the Bolsheviks still fluttered on the flagpole, and this final attempt by the monarchists to take power was already history. Mentally, he began looking ahead at a novel strategy. Perhaps the time had come to find new companions that would set out a different route to power.

The nation was falling to pieces before everyone's eyes. The Treaty of Versailles kept the country in a stranglehold and Kaiser Wilhelm was an exile in Holland without a throne. Only a negligible collection of Nationalist die-hards with no political identity raised their voices against the humiliation imposed by the defeat. The individual that led them referred to himself as 'the drummer of conscience'. Captain von Swirsden-Righe put his hopes in him, and took himself to Munich. After all, there lay his home, his wife, and all the contacts for survival and progress once the nation emerged from chaos and Germans discovered a leader that would carry them to a destiny of greatness.

CHAPTER XII

BALTIC ACQUAINTANCES

"COUP ATTEMPT FAILS," read Arno Schickedanz aloud from the newspaper he was trying to keep steady in the lurching taxi. Sitting next to him, Max was looking out to prevent the driver from taking a wrong turn and making them arrive late for lunch. Arno had arranged the meeting weeks before. Max remembered very well his friend's comment, his companion in Riga, about the men they were about to meet. The phrase had been convincing enough to make him think that new, suitable acquaintances might guide him to positions of power in those dark, anarchical, labyrinthine times. "People essential to acquaint oneself with for anyone considering himself a proper German," Arno had said, and he considered himself German from head to toe.

"Read on," said Max, which Arno did.

"Mr. Kapp's coup was the armed response to the Social-Democrat government seeking to dissolve the Freikorps; but it only lasted four days. The conspirators fled from Berlin. Shall I go on?" he asked.

Max smiled and, adjusting his tie, said to his friend in a somewhat embittered tone, "It was the general strike that defeated us. Tell me, Arno, how the hell can you take a government over when there isn't a soul around to depose?"

"At least you found the guest book during the four days we took power. That was valuable, Max. The Bolsheviks would have come across our names in the interviews with Kapp. No doubt by now they'd be out searching for us to knock us off."

Max had a look at his pocket watch. It was almost 1 p.m. "Tell me a little more about this Rosenberg. Why do you say he's essential for our political future? Incidentally, unless the driver gets a move on we'll be late for lunch with him," he said impatiently.

Arno looked out of the window. They still had a good stretch to go to the best hotel in Munich. The tram up ahead turned off at a curve, squealing against the rails, freeing the boulevard. The chauffeur accelerated and Arno answered. "Alfred Rosenberg is an old comrade from the Baltic. He's really influential. He manages a number of publications, as I told you."

Max interrupted, "I've read his translation from Russian of the *Protocols of the Elders of Zion.*"

"That's good. He'll be happy to know it. He has close links to the Thule Society, and is highly regarded by one of the figures it's convenient to know here in Munich. I mean Adolf Hitler, as well as his associates. Rosenberg and Hitler are on intimate terms and it's said Hitler's the man that best promotes our ideas nowadays. Everybody in Munich is talking about him."

"Adolf Hitler..." mused Max. The car stopped outside an elegant hotel.

"It's here. We've arrived." Max and Arno quickly got out and soon made their way to the dining room. The *maître d'* escorted them among the tables to where Alfred Rosenberg was sitting. On seeing them arrive he stood up. He greeted Arno affably and then shook hands with Max.

Rosenberg was 35 years old. His deportment was elegant, unmistakably Germanic. Right from the start he showed sympathy towards Max von Swirsden-Righe. Of Baltic origin as they were, he had earned a certain fame as an anti-Jewish theorist with his well-known translation of the *Protocols*, something like the bible of fanatical racists and zealous nationalists, who found in that decalogue attributed to Zionists all the evils of the world, holding them responsible for Germany's war disaster and the fall of Czarist Russia.

Rosenberg dealt with his roast beef and vegetables as he underlined his theories with ancient ideas based on the mythology of the Aryan race and their modern-day representatives, with the conviction that it was the German people's mission to rule European civilization. Max felt he had found the exact measure of the deep resentment he nurtured after his exploits in Riga. As the editor of the periodical *Völkischer Beobachter*, Rosenberg was building a political career and was on good terms with Adolf Hitler.

They soon came to the point and after dessert, amid drinks and anecdotes, Rosenberg invited Max to the next meeting at which Hitler was the speaker. "You'll see for yourself an electrifying personality in action," he said with assurance, and Max looked at Arno, satisfied with the new acquaintance he had introduced him to. He had the feeling that at that moment a new destiny was opening up before him, the doors of a great ideal putting him back on the path of his political ambitions. The failures in Turkey and the humiliation at the hands of the Bolsheviks in Riga would find their revindication, and he would devote himself whole-heartedly to the cause of that renowned Austrian propagandist who promised to make the enemies of Germany tremble.

THE THEATER, THOUGH CRAMMED WITH PEOPLE, was in absolute silence. No one dared break the suspense created by the speaker seconds before he began his lecture, leading them, by the spell of his vibrant words, to levels of intense excitement as his propaganda grew more extreme.

Adolf Hitler was not tall, nor did he have the typical Germanic build. His hair was dark and straight, swept over to one side. A lock fell over his deep blue eyes, and he constantly had to restore in place. He roared behind his dark moustache and, as he progressively identified with the character he had created, he kept everyone on the edge of their seats. The audience enthusiastically applauded at the end of each of his explosive, disquieting promises.

From a preferential place in the theater, next to Alfred Rosenberg and Arno Schickedanz, Max Swirsden-Righe and Countess Hildegard listened attentively, almost in ecstasy.

Rosenberg looked at them sideways, watching their reactions. When the lengthy speech finally ended, he exclaimed over the tumult, "Well, Countess, what did you think of this presentation? This exceptional state of communion with the audience happens at every meeting Herr Hitler addresses," he said euphorically.

"Well, Alfred, I think we may have found the man that can bring Germans together to save the country from the enemy within and all the rubbish invading us. We'd like to meet Hitler, wouldn't we, Max?"

"That's what we're here for, Alfred. I'd like to shake hands with and congratulate such a speaker."

They nudged their way through to the stage and then Rosenberg took them backstage. Hitler, surrounded by bodyguards, broke away from the group on seeing his friend Rosenberg appear with two important visitors. "Herr Hitler, what a stunning performance. Allow me to introduce these distinguished friends, who have come to one of our reunions for the first time: Dr. Max von Swirsden-Righe and his wife, Countess Hildegard von Swirsden."

Hitler offered his hand with affability and flamboyant courtesy, making everyone feel comfortable. "How d'you do? Very pleased to meet you, Dr. Swirsden-Righe... Countess... What did you think of the speech?" he asked, casually appraising them.

"Your words... energize, Herr Hitler. It's what we've really been wanting to hear for years. They contain the essence of the German response to our enemies," Hildegard said with enthusiasm. She immediately felt the magnetism of that unique man, while dozens of euphoric people attempted to approach him. The place was getting stuffy. "When one listens to you, a vibration arises in the soul that comes straight from the deepest atavic German conscience. We'd be delighted to attend another of your speeches. I swear that, listening to you, I've the conviction as never before that there is a live and fighting German spirit."

"Thank you, Madam, I'm honored by your words. It's what I intend: to wake our slumbering minds, like a drummer alerting our people's conscience. It will be a privilege to have you in the audience again, Countess von Swirsden. No doubt Rosenberg finds valuable and distinguished members for our cause."

Hildegard looked at him, spellbound. Hitler then put his arm on Max's shoulder, inviting them to a celebration at some other, quieter, place, together with Rosenberg and Arno.

CHAPTER XIII

THE SOGHOMON AFFAIR

THE GUESTS EDGED ROUND A TABLE full of Armenian delicacies, including traditional desserts and assorted sweets. Champagne flowed generously, glasses were refilled all the time. Others helped themselves at the buffet, seeking a seat in Manuc's and Crisdine's spacious apartment. Every friend and leading character in the Berlin community of Armenian exiles was there.

Araksi and Diran chatted on a sofa. Araksi was dressed fashionably but not ostentatiously, in keeping with their modest estate. Her hair was shorter and as usual she shone like a beacon among the 60 or 70 people present. As they made short work of the delicacies, they exchanged lively conversation with friendly couples. Drinks and cigars relaxed the men and some couples danced enthusiastically to the rhythm of Oriental tunes, without a care in the world.

Manuc observed his guests with satisfaction. Holding a king-sized cigar and circulating among them, he took charge of keeping the gramophone going without stop.

Suddenly a deep voice boomed out above the jollity, "Attention, friends. Listen up, everyone. I propose a toast to our hosts, Manuc and Crisdine. May they long continue celebrating happy anniversaries such as tonight's," said Avedis, a little tipsy. All stood up, raising their glasses and wishing their hosts the best, and Avedis, his eyes shiny, once more spoke up. "Countrymen! I am proposing a toast because justice has been done. I invite you to drink to Soghomon Tehlirian, who has avenged 1.5 million dead compatriots by assassinating Talaat Pasha in a street of this city.

This time, glasses were raised in silence. Araksi looked inconspicuously towards Diran. A woman anxiously said, "Avedis — you were called as a witness at Soghomon's trial. Tell us what happened in court. I can't believe such an odd, shy person could've dared to kill the pasha. Is it the same Soghomon that once or twice came to our dancing classes?

That man was incapable of killing a fly."

A pretty young woman next to her immediately recalled him, and, as the festive spirit had faded from one moment to the next, commented, "Yes, that's right. Do you remember that reserved young man, awfully shy, that kept looking at me in silence, trembling the whole class through, without daring to invite me to dance? I think his hands were sweating from nerves." She spoke with an element of contempt.

Another of the young women intervened, "What happened at the tribunal, Avedis? Tell us about it, the part that didn't appear in the papers."

Avedis took a sip before launching into the story and becoming the center of attention. "Well, you've all read that young Soghomon was from the town of Erzindjan, just like you, Manuc... and that all his people died in the massacres in June 1915, and he saw them die in the deportee caravan. I'm sorry, my friends, we know how painful it is for all of us to remember those days, but you asked me."

A pall of melancholy fell on everyone present. The story affected them all like a dark cloud that shrouded their enjoyment, forcing them to remember. Avedis went on, "And later he himself — I mean Soghomon — was able to come out of the deportation alive by hiding among the bodies and then, in the dusk of evening, escaping to the forests, and hiding among Kurdish mountain villages, together with other fugitives until they made it to Persia."

Someone interrupted Avedis. "It sounds identical to your story, Agop and Diran. Doesn't it sound like your own story, Manuc?"

Agop, Diran and Manuc looked at each other. Soghomon's story had been constructed on the basis of their own survival tactics. Diran did not want to know the details. The matter had never again been mentioned in front of them, but it became evident who was responsible for putting together a credible back story for Soghomon.

Diran lowered his eyes. He was bothered by any act of violence, having lived through too much of that in the past. Avedis carried on, all the guests hanging onto his words. "Then he crossed the Russian frontier, etc., etc. Years later, he arrived in Berlin and, once living here, a totally chance event was to change his life. One day he saw Talaat in the street, and hardly crediting his discovery, followed him. He purposely moved to the Hartenberg Street, in front of the minister's building, close to the zoo. You already know the end of the story."

Diran took hold of Araksi's hand. As the story unfolded, she grew increasingly upset. Mentally, she went over that night when Max von Swirsden-Righe had given her the information about the Turk. The consequences were obvious. Agop, standing amid the guests, observed without showing any emotion. Avedis' tale illustrated the scene prior to the murder.

"Birds flit around on the tiny balcony of Soghomon's apartment here in Berlin. The slender young man of 25, Armenian of course, appears on the balcony and waters the plants, anxiously looking at the building opposite. He looks across time after time. The windows of the apartment he's watching open up. Talaat comes out onto his balcony and sits in the sunshine. Soghomon panics and hides behind the balustrade, spying on him. He begins trembling and tries to control himself. The Turk goes in and shuts the windows. Soghomon comes out again and sees Talaat gone. He looks down and sees him emerging from the building. Soghomon opens a suitcase and, from among the clothes, pulls out a 9mm Luger pistol. He puts on a coat and hat, sticks the gun in a pocket, and hurriedly leaves his building."

All of a sudden, someone carrying a tray tripped, and a glass landed on the floor, smashing into pieces. Everyone was startled but Avedis went on.

"Talaat Pasha calmly walks along the pavement. The street has a boulevard in the middle, dividing the two-way traffic. Soghomon looks both ways, and sees Talaat some 100 feet away, walking with his back to him. He hurriedly closes the distance. His face shows concern at what he's about to do. He hides his right hand in his pocket. Further ahead, Talaat walks on, totally unaware, and enjoying the morning sunlight. On overtaking the Turk, Soghomon goes a short distance in front of him, looking into his eyes for just an instant. Talaat has no time to react. Soghomon dashes back behind him, takes out the pistol, points at Talaat's neck, and shoots. Some people have seen the whole episode."

Everyone was carefully listening to Avedis' narrative, as he had heard it at the tribunal in front of the judges.

"Soghomon races away as fast as he can, with the body lying where it fell. The people in the street pursue him. 'Murderer! Murderer!' they shout. In his flight, Soghomon drops the pistol on the pavement. A group of men push him down to keep him from escaping. Furiously, they begin kicking and punching him. A mechanic hits him with a pair of pliers. Soghomon shouts, 'He was a foreigner. I also a foreigner. I foreigner... he Turk, me Armenian. No harm to Germany in this matter!'"

When Avedis finished, he looked around. The group of friends still retained the images of the murder in their minds, ruminating on what they had just heard. Right away, some of the women made signs of rejecting the violent crime. Others, the more fervent, nodded approval, feeling themselves avenged by the young man's deed.

Avedis added, in conclusion to his tale, "So, justice was done."

"I can't believe such a psychologically fragile man, so un-self-possessed, can have committed such an act of retribution. I've been told Soghomon wasn't all there, upstairs," said a woman, as a starting shot. Immediately everyone's comments were heard.

"Precisely, my dear... The jury should have deliberated whether Soghomon Tehlirian was in full possession of his mental faculties; that is, whether he was in his right mind when he did it, or if his act was carefully planned and premeditated, maybe in association with others, as the prosecutor insinuated," speculated an older gentleman conversant with criminal justice.

Diran casually looked over at Agop and Manuc. Neither had opened his mouth. Araksi felt a sudden heat. Her hands began perspiring. Avedis' booming voice was heard again.

"As for myself, I told the judge I knew Soghomon from before. I made clear that the little I knew about him was from having seen him at some of our meetings. The fellow — Soghomon — kept repeating before the judge that he'd killed Talaat Pasha with premeditation. He said it quite clearly and without doubt. He was fully convinced as to what he'd done."

A short woman with close-set, light-colored eyes and an intelligent look asked, "Then, what was the defense based on? How was he found not guilty? If he declared himself guilty and is in his right mind, I don't understand. You're a doctor — tell us," she said to the young man in a blue suit and red tie next to her.

"Well, yes... I know the results of the medical inquest in the Tehlirian case. His dead mother's face used to appear to him, inciting him to take vengeance and commit the crime. Therefore, in view of these confessions by the defendant, the court doctors concluded they were in the presence of a person with a serious mental illness, who suffered a permanent state of nervous depression."

The guests all began talking at once. The doctor attempted to round off his opinion. "Listen! Listen! Let me finish... They said he often experienced a repulsive smell of dead bodies, and would then faint. In short, despite his diagnosis, the doctor considered Soghomon was conscious enough to appreciate the criminality of his act."

Araksi was perturbed and her face was going pale. Diran got her a glass of water. She listened in a daze to the voices around her. The smoke and stuffy atmosphere lowered her blood pressure and a deep anguish led her down the passages of her mind she tried to avoid.

The commentaries made at the tribunal continued. "The medical expert from the chair of psychiatry declared, 'A man can resist incredible horrors without becoming sick. Only some pathologically predisposed persons suffer mental changes when coming face-to-face with supreme ideals.' Finally, the professor added something very interesting... something I'll never forget. He said literally, 'Every fanatic, every man that obeys the impulse of a great ideal, has a certain amount of mental illness and, should he be exposed to the motivations of those great ideals because he is under the influence of an acquaintance that triggers them, then the mental imbalance of the fanatical state comes to the fore once again.' Interesting, isn't it?"

Araksi held her perspiring forehead and, feeling sick, leant against the sofa.

"It is, but in spite of everything, the jury declared him innocent. Remember Talaat had previously been tried *in absentia* by a Turkish court in Constantinople, which found him guilty, together with the other murderers, Enver and Djemal."

"Yes, my friends, that's what the jury members here must have thought... acknowledging that the beast was at large and unpunished," Agop reminded his friends, who were already on the verge of tears as they remembered the million dead and, especially, their own families that had remained in Turkey forever.

Manuc, also wanting to contribute to the debate, essayed, "Talaat Pasha, my friends... bumped into a psychological victim of the war... Soghomon, quite deranged in fact, smelt cadavers everywhere and saw his dead mother indicating his duty to do justice. In this way he became the avenger of a whole people. With that kind of mental imbalance, Soghomon Tehlirian escaped a death sentence because that's the way a local jury decided. It's evident Germans have wanted to downplay their responsibility in the killings by not calling on officers that were present in Turkey to declare. I'm referring to an old acquaintance of some of you, Major Swirsden-Righe." His eyes fell on Araksi, drawing attention to her from all the others. Then Manuc raised his champagne glass.

"Let's drink to Soghomon and to the memory of all our dead."

Araksi, despite her queasiness and being made the object of an accusation, made use of the presence of mind that had always been hers and was her greatest strength. She was not about to be fazed by the ungentlemanliness of those that were rudely singling her out in front of everyone.

Standing up, she looked Manuc in the eye. She had wanted to put him in his place for a long time, and now she would do it. The delicate relations among the group of exiles had distorted the social standing each had once upon a time in far-off Anatolia. Araksi was aware of her family background in contrast with those that were pointing her out that evening. After all, they had all been united by chance, in some cases their only tie being their condition as refugees in Berlin.

"Can it be that you're all unable, every time we meet, to lay aside the violence we all experienced?"

A woman sitting next to Manuc, whose sufferings still stood out in deep bags under her eyes, replied, "I find it good to remember so that these things never happen again, my dear."

The other guests began feeling uncomfortable, but Araksi was determined to answer any snide reference against herself. "Most of us have lost our parents, brothers, and relatives. Some of us are the single survivors of whole families, as are Diran and myself. We've witnessed the deaths of those we loved, and will never be able to forget it. We're carrying around our horrific suffering, impossible to accept. Is it even necessary I should mention it? Yet, each of us chooses to remember and live in the past or remember and live in the present, so that we and our children may lead, finally, an existence as happy as possible... and in peace. Otherwise, the hatred will never end, and will pass from this generation to the next, and to the one after, poisoning us forever."

Everyone was staring at her, not daring to interrupt. Diran firmly stood beside her. He seemed to be backing her up in each of her words. He looked straight ahead with dignity.

Araksi continued, "Can't you understand that the seed of hatred is growing each day and with greater strength right here, in this country where we've come to take refuge? Before, we were the persecuted. Now it'll be the Jews and, after that, perhaps anyone that doesn't think the way they do. Here we might even become the target of hatred for being different or foreigners. Then will come all those that aren't accepted by nationalists and fanatics. Maybe all the sick, and weak, and unnecessary will be eliminated... Don't feed that hatred anymore! We've already had enough of it!"

Moved, she took Diran's hand to steady herself, feeling unwell. "Diran, please take me home. I'm sorry — I didn't mean to spoil your anniversary."

Araksi and Diran made their way among the guests. Diran was feeling quite upset, but did not say a word.

One of the women whispered, "She's also remained affected. It's impossible she can have forgotten her past, because it's a terrible burden: she was a harem slave, imagine."

"She was Swirsden-Righe, the German consul's, lover," added another.

THE LIGHTNING STORM PROJECTED flashes against the bedroom wall, anticipating the crash of thunder. A heavy curtain of water was falling on the city. Araksi stirred between the sheets in a deep but unquiet sleep. All at once she screamed out. Diran, startled, shook her by the shoulders to try and wake her. She seemed to be talking in her sleep, then opened her eyes and with great anguish embraced him, crying. Diran caressed her soothingly.

"What's the matter, my love? What's wrong? Easy, I'm here with you."

Araksi muttered, and with half-words tried to explain, "The same images as ever, they come to torment me... I saw them die again... Then... we were all... I don't know where... You were also there... Suddenly, a crowd gathered, there were shots, someone else died, and I ran to save myself, mixed in with the crowd. I was looking for you, Diran, and then everything blotted out... There was no one else there. I was back on the Kemakh mountain pass, the place they murdered my parents. Papa no longer looked at me. His eyes were closing. He couldn't see me anymore. Mamma was lying on the rock... The zaptiehs came with their whips and yataghans. Then everything gleamed with a very strong light... Everything was desolation and death, and a wrenching pain here, right here," she said, touching her breast. "The demons won't leave me in peace," she cried, tears wetting her face.

"Take it easy, my love, calm down. Nothing's going to happen while you're with me. No one will harm you, ever again."

Araksi adjusted the strap of her nightgown and sat up. She drank some water and looked at the window with despair. The rain banged heavily, bouncing off the windowpanes.

"Let's go away, Diran. Let's get away from Germany and go somewhere very far away from here, where there are no memories, where everything's new and we can live in peace. We'll never be able to go back to Armenia. No one will. You have to accept this... The two of us together, wherever we go, never mind where, or how far from Erzurum. We'll be the roots and memory for our children. I've no one but you, Diran, my love."

Diran remained quiet for a few moments, then said, "And I you, Araksi. But first I have a mission to fulfill. I'm pledged to it for life. There's a whole people waiting for us to wage a war, but an office war, to gain independence. We're the only hope for those that have remained in Armenia, for all those that carry on fighting in the mountains... Here and now, the future of Europe can be decided and perhaps that of the nation our parents always wanted, Araksi."

The bedroom was in half-shadows. Araksi watched the rainstorm falling on the roofs and streets. Water ran, flooding pavements and overflowing drains.

"It's just a matter of a few more months, Araksi. If the German Nationalists triumph, they may help us against the Turks to gain independence. D'you realize? Sometimes... when everything seems useless, I even think I ought to fight again, Araksi... once again wield a rifle in the mountains."

Araksi sobbed in silence. "Don't worry, my love. We'll stay until it's the right time to leave Germany."

She dried her face. Instead of calming her, Diran's words increased her confusion. It was clear that their life was adrift once more. "All I know is that the danger we're in is constantly growing, and that I won't be able to stand any more misfortunes. I wouldn't have the strength for it, Diran... I just couldn't."

He hugged her tenderly and she nestled between his arms. With a tiny voice she said, by way of a confession, "And thanks for putting up with the gossip and sarcasm at the party. Thanks for putting up with my past, my love."

They were silent for a long while then began making love, while lightning illuminated every corner of the room.

CHAPTER XIV

THE FUND-RAISER

ADOLF HITLER WAS USED TO making the rounds of Munich nightclubs. He was already acclaimed and praised by many people, and enjoyed a growing popularity among certain social circles. Everywhere he went, he was accompanied by Eckart, Beckstein and Rosenberg.

The car stopped on account of the traffic and Hitler, inside the car, saw a newspaper vendor shouting out the latest news. At a sign from him, Rosenberg quickly got out, bringing back to his boss a copy of the paper. On the front page it carried headlines relating to the murder of Talaat Pasha: *ARMENIAN KILLER OF TURKISH MINISTER FREED.*

Hitler quickly read the extract, and commented to his friends, "An Armenian that goes mad and kills an exiled minister... If you ask me, he can't have been that mad... nor has he acted on his own. There must be an organization behind this."

The others passed the paper round. Beckstein was the first to speak, "Swirsden-Righe'll be able to give us details of what happened in Turkey. Remember he was consul at Erzurum."

Hitler looked fixedly at Beckstein. An idea had just flashed into his mind. It was no more than a fleeting, unformed thought, but one that somehow made the whole drama clear. It would need a lot of ripening and time. He remained silent for the remainder of the journey, brooding on terrible schemes. The night light of the street awnings illuminated his pallid face, his pupils alight with a dangerous glow. He held back the impulses pushing their way up from his innermost abysses and reaching his mind, inscrutable to those around him. All of them, comrades from the first hour, competed with one another in offering ideas at every opportunity, hoping to earn the privilege of his confidence in exchange for an absolute and unquestioning allegiance.

"Hmm, yes... the Armenian question," Hitler mused aloud. "The Young Turks harbored no doubts as to what to do about a minority that was getting in their way. You're right, Beckstein, and we do have a lot to learn about the matter. Incidentally, I found this Swirsden-Righe a determined individual, one of our own kind. He already was before he met us. Let him give you a hand with the newspaper. He could prove a good propagandist. Alright, Beckstein?"

Beckstein nodded, adjusting his felt hat. Next to him, Eckart did not want to be left out in offering Hitler a few useful details. "Hildegard von Swirsden could be an extraordinary source of funding for the party, Adolf. Her acquaintances among royalty are very close, especially with Princess Victoria of Saxony Coburg-Gotha and her Romanov husband."

"Ahah," broke in Hitler, "Grand-Duke Kyril, the self-proclaimed principal heir to the throne of Russia and his wife, Princess Victoria Melita... Interesting... Surrounded by a whole bevy of nobles — decadent, useless, but very rich!"

Soon he seemed to give no more importance to monarchical references, though he had certainly taken note of the usefulness of the Swirsden-Righes. "You deal with that matter, Eckart."

The car stopped outside the cabaret. Several people crowded around the doorway. On seeing Hitler get out of the car, they came up to greet him effusively. He was treated as a celebrity and his charismatic presence gathered people around him wherever he might be. Hitler, Eckart and Beckstein pushed through and went into the place. The orchestral music filtered through to the hall from the stage. The light-hearted strains and irreverent laughs promised an evening of fun and frivolity with gay dancing-girls and champagne on the house, for this popular person and his friends.

THEIR IMPERIAL HIGHNESSES,
GRAND-DUKE KYRIL AND PRINCESS VICTORIA MELITA
ARE PLEASED TO INVITE YOU TO A GRAND BALL
TO BE HELD FOR THE PURPOSE OF..............

GRAND-DUKE KYRIL AND THE PRINCESS stood with imperial majesty, greeting each guest entering the castle foyer.

According to protocol, after being announced with their titles and functions, they were presented to the couple of pretenders to the throne of Russia, snatched by the Bolsheviks in the 1917 revolution. Subsequently the long line of Russian and German nobles and a pleiad of important figures arriving at the ball mingled at this great event of the highest of European society, gathered to contribute towards the imperial cause — funds that were to be destined to build an army that would overthrow communism and restore the crown to the Romanovs, in exile since the murder of Czar Nicholas II, his wife Alexandra, and all their family.

The huge, blazing chandeliers with their dozens of glittering crystals played on the women's diadems and the men's decorations. The two-headed imperial eagle of the Romanov dynasty stood out on the standards hanging from the moldings several feet up and the whole length of the palace's grandiose Hall of Mirrors.

Max von Swirsden-Righe and the Countess mingled and chatted in high spirits, circulating in an environment they were completely at home with. Every so often, they would excuse themselves to receive and exchange pleasantries with elegant dukes and generals of the old regime, enveloped in flashy uniforms and covered with medals. Max was wearing tails and Hildegard set off her beauty, together with the distinction of her character and place in society, with a long sky-blue gown and a valuable necklace of emerald pendants to go with it; an heirloom from her maternal grandmother. Her hair was gathered up, crowned by a tiara of precious gems.

The other ladies wore the best jewelry in Europe, for some of them the most important items they had managed to come away with, in their escape from Russia.

"As you see, Your Highness, times are changing rapidly and the new political forces are adapting according to what is convenient. Indeed, we're the best evidence of this, gentlemen. We've been opposed in the past, but today's politics are turning us into natural allies against a common enemy," commented Max, bringing into the conversation the other gentlemen around him, all drinking champagne.

The Russian nobleman facing him, wearing a white

uniform with large golden epaulettes, gave his opinion, "Actually, that's quite true, Swirsden-Righe. It's funny to see the turn of historical events. Not so long ago, I myself was charging against Sautchbulak under Nikolai Nikolayevich's orders and you attacked us from the Turkish side. How ironic! Here we now are, gathered for a common purpose, and on the same side. This is a lopsided world, gentlemen."

A venerable old gentleman standing among them immediately touched on a topic that had been worrying him since the start of the conversation. "If you will allow me, gentlemen, regarding the here and now. Swirsden-Righe, kindly tell me, are we to understand, as I've heard you say, that our purpose of reinstating the Romanov dynasty is compatible with the ideals of the German National Socialists? How can that be, my dear sir, because for a good while I have not been able to make the connection in my head."

Another elderly gentleman, whose family descended from Aleksander Nevsky himself, was even more direct. "It's said that you and Countess Hildegard have become fervent collaborators of that Adolf... Hitler, and that you commonly foster backing for that gentleman. Forgive me, but personally, just the same as the prince, I cannot understand what there can be in common between us and this... army corporal turned orator..." said the old Russian Count, looking at everyone with an edge of skepticism, and seeking complicity. "How can that man, unknown, with no rank or background, be creating so much excitement, etcetera? Kindly explain to me what the benefit could be in my contribution for the installation of Duke Kyril to the throne also going to the party coffers of this *Mister Hitler* or whatever his name is."

Max remained utterly calm. In order to answer the count's question, he went straight to the point. "Very well, Sir, consider this: ousting the Bolsheviks from both countries will be possible only with contributions from the great fortunes of Europe. And Adolf Hitler is the right man to head the necessary cleansing of those elements that have made our nation sick. If I may, I ought to say to both our nations, 'Gentlemen, we National Socialists are the only possible response to your objectives. Without Bolsheviks in Germany, those in Russia will soon weaken. Don't forget, gentlemen, that the Jews are always behind their plan of world domination, never mind the form of government, riding astride the Communists, or exploiting peoples and concentrating wealth in their own hands under monarchical regimes or even republics. That is the cause of our misfortunes, gentlemen, and Herr Hitler is the chosen man... the only one that will put things in their proper place. Of that I assure you... And now if you will excuse me, my wife's making signs at me."

The Russian nobles thought over the unequivocal answer. Max went to Hildegard. The opening strains of the orchestra were heard. Grand-Duke Kyril pushed forward with Princess Victoria and started off the waltz.

Soon the guests were gracefully revolving to the music in the Hall of Mirrors. A few pieces later, with perfect steps, the Romanov prince himself was leading the glamorous Countess von Swirsden in his imperial arms.

Max felt satisfied. He thought to himself that he was witnessing an evening of triumph. Nearly all the white-collar aristocrats had promised their contribution to the party. Hitler would be pleased, and he and Hildegard would be ever more highly regarded in Hitler's inner circle. The political campaign was moving forward smoothly.

CHAPTER XV

ROLF SAYS GOODBYE

MAX AND ROLF GALLOPED THROUGH THE WOODS at a break-neck pace, hooves sinking into the damp ground that was covered with leaves. Shafts of sunlight filtered through the branches of the huge trees. Rather than an enjoyable canter, it seemed the old comrades-in-arms were out to re-live the rhythm of the cavalry charges shared on the campaign in the Caucasus and even earlier, at the regiment in Straubing, when they were reserve recruits. They had forged a friendship that now, almost eight years after dangers and adventures, they still kept up. They reined in and dismounted in a forest clearing. They were both in uniform, as in old times.

Looking up, Rolf saw sun rays breaking through the tangled roof of the forest, projecting spots of light amid the shadows of the path. "For a moment I felt I was back in Kurdistan, among the mountains and rivers of Persia," he said nostalgically.

"Your brother's missing, though," said Max. "I can hardly stop remembering Friedrich at Sautchbulak. I can almost remember his voice shouting out orders between the reports of cannon-shot, running along the trenches and ready to mount at the head of his platoon.... He was truly brave, your brother — a good soldier, our dear Friedrich...."

Rolf made a gesture of sorrow at hearing memories of his brother. "That's right, Max. Best remember him on horseback and full of life than imagine his death in Lorraine."

"No, Rolf. You're mistaken. What a fine death for a soldier! Friedrich died in combat, the death every German soldier must aspire to."

"Maybe... but my parents are still awfully cut up about it.... And I want to get away from so much pain for a spell, Max. This is getting more uncertain by the minute." Rolf tied his horse to a branch then they looked for a log to sit on and stretch their legs. He said, "I'm thinking of spending a good long while in the States, far away from everything."

Max looked at him in surprise. "The States? What are you going to do there? I'll find it odd not having you nearby, Rolf."

Max, just like his friend, had been won over by a feeling of nostalgia. Increasingly, there were fewer opportunities to spend a relaxed time together. Times were changing giddily and in those years following the war, his life had been taken up by political matters. Suddenly, he asked his friend, "Tell me, Rolf, d'you still write your diary?"

"Of course. It's still in the making."

"Rolf, there's something I've been wanting to ask you for a good while — have you jotted everything down there — I mean, strictly day by day — everything you and I know happened on the campaign?"

Rolf looked at his friend, understanding, "No, Max, not everything. Of course not. Just military and political aspects. If you're referring to matters belonging to your private life, they're none of my business, and belong to you... I never intended recording them, nor would I have any right to."

Max was quiet for a good while. Birdsong festooned the forest, and deep calm seemed to pervade the setting. His tone of voice was melancholy. "I find it impossible to remember Erzurum without Araksi... But that's all gone. I'm at peace with my conscience. I was able to rescue her, and that should be enough for me."

In all those years and especially after the escape from Riga, Rolf had had few opportunities to see his friend. Never before had he heard him mention Araksi's name.

"What became of her? Have you heard anything about her life? Forgive me if I offend you."

"I was told by the Armenian that rescued her in Sautchbulak that they had got married and managed to come to Europe — Geneva, I believe. I came across him at the Stockholm conference. He thanked me for Araksi's rescue... and that's all. I never heard any more of either." He remained thoughtful, idly doodling with a twig. "You know, Rolf, Hitler's asked me to head the Bavarian Combat Union. There are very resolute guys among them." He stood and began impatiently pacing up and down. Rolf observed. "It's a pity you're leaving us, Rolf. The country needs people like you. We're alone, and either we come out of it on our own strength, or we go under. We've got to get rid of the illusion that anybody external is going to free us, and now, Rolf. We've got a new prophet, I assure you, and his name's Adolf Hitler." Max's doodles on the ground were beginning to take shape.

"Hitler has been able to wake Germans from the yoke of Marxist thought. You should hear his speeches. I swear, my friend, that they make your insides vibrate. You know, Rolf, this is where the future of Europe, and maybe even the world, is being decided. It's going to be an unrelenting struggle against our enemies."

Rolf kept watching his friend.

"When the German spirit becomes compact, united, and popular, then we'll be ready to face other nations. It'll be the Bolshevik star against the Swastika, and the Swastika will come out on top."

Max was becoming impassioned, his words issuing in torrents. It was as if a deep-felt wound, almost a resentment, surmised Rolf, was guiding all his choices and actions.

"Germany must stop being the plaything of other nations, as if it were at the mercy of a changeable, ungrateful woman that comes and goes in one's life as the whim takes her, motivated only by her own vanity. And you, unable to stand her absence, humble yourself before her, so that she won't leave you again, sentencing you to the uncertainty and solitude of her absence."

Rolf felt the comment strange and understood that there was a lot more to the Araksi business than he would ever be told. He asked no questions.

"No, Rolf, that will come to an end, wait and see. We won't allow it again. We don't need anyone else. Germany will need no one else from now on."

They remained in silence for a long while, then untied their horses. They knew they were about to follow diverging roads, and might never meet again. Before mounting, Rolf looked down at the damp ground. There was the doodle Max had drawn with the twig. Rolf moved his horse closer to see it better and the sketch now made sense. It was a fylfot-shaped cross — the Nazi Swastika.

CHAPTER XVI

MEMORIES OF HELL

THE SCENE WAS TREMENDOUSLY VIVID, the barbarians coming from the Eastern forests destroying the last bastions of civilization with their spears and swords. The terrified citizens, cornered among the last columns of the buildings and temples in flames, offered futile resistance against the invading hordes. Bloodstained stairways, piled high with mutilated bodies and faces distorted by horror. Women raped, others on the verge of being abducted, tied onto saddles and snatched away from their own people on the horses of fierce Germanic barbarians.

The enormous painting by a prominent Flemish master hung on a wall at the Munich Academy of Fine Arts. The long-haired, bare-chested warrior-heroes wearing spectacular helmets were collecting their conquerors' booty.

In front of the masterpiece were visitors of every age. Awed by the picture, they could scan the whole scene by raising their eyes and looking at each angle and corner of the huge canvas.

Hitler, hands held behind his back, beheld the scene with ecstasy, together with Max Swirsden-Righe. Next to them, Emil Maurice, a heavy-looking character with an unfriendly aspect, who for some time had not moved away from Hitler for even a second, brandished a riding-crop against his tall boots. Behind them, an unremarkable looking man, at some distance from the group, kept a lookout for any suspicious movement in the place.

"This corporeal beauty, this magnificent composition the painter has created, is the very representation of the Germanic people. Those mythological semi-gods of the Aryan people have their descendants, my friend Swirsden-Righe, the best individuals in our nation, the chosen among the best people of the human race, don't you agree? It only needs to awake from its lethargy to fulfil the ancestral mission God has assigned it: to rule civilization and be the custodian of values from the whole of human history, of the best that humanity possesses. The day will come when we are strong, and no one will stand against us. For that we must begin by cleansing the nation of any element extraneous to our Germanic model. Look at the image of those beautiful Aryan warriors. Imagine them wearing the uniforms of our present youth."

Max nodded as they walked on through the great salon. Hitler took his arm, a distinction he seldom conferred on any of his collaborators. "Tell me, Max, there's something... regarding some news I've read in the papers and would like to understand better. You, as consul in Turkey, were a privileged witness of events at the Eastern front. How did the Mohammedans manage to kill so many Christians, and in so short a time? Not much is known about that episode. Was it a purely Turkish affair, or did our high command intervene? Tell us about the Armenian Question, Max. Probably no one else knows as much as you about it."

Thoughtfully, Max seemed to be knitting the idea together in his mind. "That is so, Herr Hitler. I'll make it short and sweet: the German mission's position was a privileged one. The ambassador, Baron von Wangenheim, and the army chiefs of staff were informed daily about what was going on in Turkey. Enver Pasha, the War Minister, was constantly accompanied by high-ranking German officers."

Hitler seemed very taken with all this, and encouraged him to continue.

"The Intelligence Department, the Istikhbarat, was led by a German officer. This was the center where all political and military secrets of the empire converged. The chief? A Turkish colonel. Above him was a lieutenant-colonel of our army, in charge of the central control at Ottoman General HQ. Its main function, you may wonder? The deployment and direction of executive units of the Special Organization of the East and the transfer of operations to the annihilation camps."

"Annihilation camps?" mused Hitler with interest. "You mentioned a Special Organization, Max. That means there was a method, a systematic action, which would therefore have been in correspondence with the civil laws. Did the German High Command also plan those actions?"

Max lowered his voice. Some visitors were taking their time viewing the magnificent works. He waited until the last of them was vacating the area and then resumed his explanation. The impulse to confide everything to his leader seized him at the same time that a thirst for vengeance nestling deep inside him swelled his mood. As he spoke he had the conviction that those figments in Hitler's mind were giving form to a dangerous darkness. For an instant he felt his words were swaying Hitler's stormy, inscrutable mind.

"Well, not exactly, Herr Hitler. Although the Treaty signed between the Kaiser and the Ittihad allowed Germany to manage the Turkish military organization in time of war, there was no meddling on our part in Turkey's internal affairs. Priority was limited to war actions." He paused to adjust his glasses. Hitler and his assistant Maurice remained expectant at the exposé. "We always knew what was going on in the interior of the country. I was there and saw it all with my own eyes. We were ordered by our own General Command not to get involved under any circumstances."

"Tell me, how did the Turks go about killing one and a half million Armenians in two years?" Hitler impatiently asked, point-blank. Only a small bench was available to sit on in the next salon. The two men sat down without interrupting their chat, while Maurice remained standing.

"The Turks wanted a country exclusively for Turks, do you understand? They considered the Armenians the Jews of the East, who soon became a nuisance. First, they annihilated the politicians, clergymen, the influential figures in Constantinople. They liquidated them from one day to the next in the street, in their offices, in their own homes." Hitler was listening to each and every detail. "Then they disarmed all Armenian youths. They grouped all military officers and soldiers in forced labor battalions, turning them virtually into pack animals of the Turkish army, and using them in the construction of roads and bridges. They all died — no one survived the snow and mountain roads."

"Tell me about the Organization of the East, Swirsden-Righe, who its members were, all the details..."

Max stood and got into his stride. As if he were speaking

before his Commanders, he adopted in front of Hitler the erstwhile martial tone he had used before his superiors on so many operations. "Herr Hitler — the Special Organization of the East was presided over by a military governor, under whose command were six provinces, each with its own governor, all of them subservient to Mehmed Kamil Pasha, supreme military and civil chief. This Organization had absolute authority over the total elimination of all the Armenians in the Empire, a secret policy efficiently implemented in every corner of Turkey, in each vilayet, from which very few were able to escape. Then... shortly after, the time came for the deportation of the Armenian population from cities and villages. The central idea of the method was to send them to the Syrian and Mesopotamian deserts from one day to the next, without a fixed destination. Mile-long columns of women, old people, and children died in the mountain passes, victims to the sun and thirst, and attacks by the Turkish and Kurdish populations of the villages they went by."

Max saw Hitler's gaze wandering, dark, unfathomable, over his shoulder, beyond the present, into a time as yet not come, but already tangible in the leader's mind.

Emil Maurice broke the silence, "We should take better advantage of those able to work before they die. German science will surely come upon a less primitive, more effective method, *mein Führer*." Without any concrete allusion to anybody being made, the three understood the content and purpose in their minds.

Max added the odd detail to complete his veiled resentment. "As regards the prettier young women and girls... they all ended up in Turks' harems, sold to them, or simply sequestered from the caravans... After all, who today remembers the Armenians?"

Hitler found the Turks' attitude reasonable and nodded his agreement. Then he stood up, took Max's arm, and, as they headed to the central hall of the Academy, asked, "And tell me, Swirsden-Righe, what did they do with valuables... I'm referring to properties, money, Armenians' accounts in European banks? Under what system were the goods that those people went leaving behind re-allocated?"

At his back an immense painting, in front of which they had been sitting all along, *Christ on the Cross*, hung solitary and doleful in the silence of the great hall, mute witness to the confessions just set at large.

CHAPTER XVII

CRISIS – BERLIN 1923

AN INCREDIBLY LONG QUEUE OF BERLINERS was braving the sleet. Lined up along the market stalls, they hoped to be able to buy some of the scant foodstuffs still exhibited. Every so often, sales would be interrupted, the stall-keepers taking down price tags and replacing them with higher ones. A sense of tension and panic pervaded the atmosphere, many rising up in protest while others begged for help at not being able to afford the outrageous prices caused by inflation.

Stiff with the November cold, most people were downcast and quiet but from time to time scuffles would break out with somebody snatching the last vegetables or cakes of soap from others. With mild resignation, people carried bags full of paper money to buy the bare necessities of subsistence. Araksi and Diran, clapping their gloved hands and hugging each other for warmth, were waiting their turn to obtain something of the little remaining on the stalls. No one was exempt from the general hardship, and the economic rigors obliged them to spend several hours a week in queues or walking about, simply to change money and then see it turned into an immense pile of depreciated paper. Just like their neighbors, they were also borne along by the economic whirlpool that was undoing the country, but still kept their little apartment, and Diran's income in dollars had not yet been stopped.

Araksi, her cheeks reddened with cold, looked at the queue opposite. Clerks and workers were waiting outside a bank, while others emerged from the building, pushing wheelbarrows loaded with bills.

A dull noise arose in the area but not among the people queuing up. The chanted strains were heard as a far-off echo. Everyone looked at the end of the street. Soon the chants and shouts became recognizable. A group of ultra-right-wing demonstrators were approaching, carrying sticks and placards, smashing shop windows. Exclamations of panic were heard, and the outcry and sound of breaking glass blended with the barked orders of the paramilitaries. Blows fell on the backs and heads of Jewish shopkeepers. The cruelty increased, brought on by fanatical youths who, after striking their victims, would oblige them to get down on their knees and paint the Star of David on the outside of their shops. Araksi then saw that the huge queue was breaking up and the disbanded crowd was advancing on them. Now the danger was from the opposite corner. Another mob, carrying red flags, was approaching.

Araksi shouted and caught Diran. "Look, over there - Bolsheviks! My God!" she uttered in panic, and then continued observing, covering her mouth.

"Come, Araksi, run for it, let's get away from here, quick. Hold my hand and don't be frightened."

All at once, a free-for-all broke out in the neighborhood. Everyone ran towards street corners, trying not to be caught up in either of the two demonstrations. Both were striking anyone in their way and smashing windows. Bleeding heads were seen on all sides, and of every age. Diran and Araksi ran hand in hand, seeking some crevice to escape by. They looked at the house fronts in the hope of finding some passageway to take shelter in.

All at once, the doors of a little church appeared as a last possible refuge. "This way, Araksi.... In here.... Quick, run, the doors are closing!" The parish priest was pushing the main door shut with the help of his sexton. On seeing them approach, he held up for a few seconds, urging them to hurry before the mob over-ran the temple. Immediately he bolted the massive doors, securing them with locks in use since the Middle Ages. Outside, the demonstrators engaged in hand-to-hand combat.

In the gloom of the church, the sounds of the fray seemed distant. The place was cold, and a few candles were alight on the side-altars. Araksi and Diran ran almost halfway up the central nave. It was an old Catholic church, built in stone, not far from their apartment. Strangely, they had never noticed it. They sat at the end of a pew. They were flustered and sweaty despite the cold, and Araksi felt her heart beating fast.

Both looked at the Custodia on the main altar. Araksi

knelt. Diran inspected the lateral naves. Images of saints stood in the prayer altarpieces, in the darkness of the church. Suddenly, a movement caught his eye.

The shadows stopped moving, hiding in a corner. Then a tiny child's voice was heard, followed by a whisper to keep quiet.

Diran stood up, looking for a better angle. Beyond the column interrupting his vision, he saw a man with a dark beard and wide-brimmed black hat and his wife, wearing a long skirt, also dark-colored. In silence, sitting on the steps of a small side-altar below the image of the Sacred Heart, they were holding their two little children. They were Jews. The girl huddled in terror in her father's arms. Diran pacified them with a friendly gesture, then returned to the pew.

From outside, the shouts and sounds of shattering glass were getting louder. The great doors of the church were shaken several times under the pressure of the throng. Araksi said with a tiny voice, "It gives me the shivers. I feel as if I were in Erzurum once more."

She paused. Diran's eyes were moist as both contemplated the main altar. "He... has been kind to us, but won't He get tired of giving us opportunities? We've got to get away from Berlin, we've got to leave Germany. Please, Diran!"

Her husband looked again at the family, immobile in their hiding place. Diran's eyes filled with tears. A sob he had contained during a whole lifetime shook him. He had never allowed himself such weakness. He had been able to overcome a lot of pain without ever showing it but, at that moment, the uncontrolled images in his memory came to the fore, overwhelming his character hardened by events, bringing out the deepest emotion. He wept like a child. Araksi looked at him in surprise, tenderly.

"All at once, everything comes back to me in a rush... In my mind I can see my parents as if they were right in front of me... Do you see those over there?"

Araksi nodded.

"Papa and Mamma... were taking refuge in a church when they were murdered, together with my brother."

She knew the story perfectly.

"They'd separated us by force. The maid had to escape

with me. There was no time for all of us to be together. You've heard my story innumerable times, Araksi, but I never told you how they were discovered. My little brother, Armen, loved his marbles. He was never without them. Anywhere he went, his pockets were full of them. I still remember their colors and odd shapes inside the transparent glass. Hiding in the church, the same as those poor terrified devils behind the altar, were my parents that morning. Armen tightly pressed the marbles in his hands. They fell on the floor at the worst moment, bouncing and spreading out everywhere on the tiles of the church. The noise immediately alerted the Turks that had gone in and were about to leave without having found anyone. And they took no pity on them!"

Diran wept disconsolately. He could not stop himself, despite Araksi's efforts, holding his hand and never ceasing to caress him. Once he recovered, he went on. "It's always been a blurry story in my memory, an explanation given by adults, the monks who protected a child that had been left alone in the world. Now I've been able to live through it in the flesh. Look at them over there, behind the altarpiece, as if the picture of what happened to my parents were alive. Why... such divine injustice? And all at once everything has been cleared up, Araksi... I've just understood it all in an instant. My whole life without an answer to so much pain, asking myself the same question for years, and now I've been able to understand it. The reason we've been spared, Araksi, is to tell about the horror we went through."

Araksi comforted him lovingly, stroking his back. Diran sobbed, until he finally recovered.

"I know you can't stand these months and years invested in useless proclamations and all this sterile struggle any longer, Araksi, but there's something you've got to know, something that makes our possibility of breaking free more difficult, and which I can't turn my back on. The Allies have just signed a treaty with Turkey in Lausanne. Listen..."

Araksi bowed her head.

"Listen, please listen," he said almost pleadingly. "They've excluded all mention of Armenia, and we Armenians will carry on not being worth a shit to anyone in this world. The Turkish Nationalists have obtained international recognition, and we've only one card left to play. The Armenian movement needs the support of this country and its National Socialists."

Araksi looked at him disbelievingly.

"The patriots still fighting the Bolsheviks in the mountains are desperately asking us to look for political accords in Europe. Come with me to Munich, Araksi. That's where they are, getting ready to take over, and they'll look favorably on the Bolsheviks' not seizing power in a free Armenia. We won't stay another day in Berlin, I promise you. This is the last I'm asking of you: let's go to Munich!"

Araksi remained silent a few seconds. The banging on the church doors had ceased, and the yells had subsided. She sighed and then, fully convinced, answered, "If I can't lead my own life with you, Diran, I'll leave forever. I will not stay in Germany to die once more."

Just then the sexton approached them and, almost in a whisper, told them, "They've gone away. You can go out. Hurry, my children."

Araksi and Diran walked down the sacristy aisle, led by the parish priest, to a side door giving onto a safe, clear alley. Together with them, the Jewish couple and their children left one at a time. As they gratefully took their leave from the priest, they crossed deeply understanding looks with their companions in refuge as a parting gesture.

CHAPTER XVIII

THE COUP

HILDEGARD TURNED OFF THE DINING ROOM LIGHTS. The butler had just served coffee in the little side room and quietly awaited her instructions.

Hildegard seemed especially worried that evening. She had felt that way all through dinner, until the last of the guests left. She hastened the servants' evening routine by doing some of the work herself. She dismissed them to their quarters and nervously went to the study.

Max, in shirt sleeves, divested of his dinner jacket, was wearing suspenders and still had on the tie he had not loosened. The room was warm despite the November cold, and the fire crackled in the hearth. He dropped cigar ash in an ashtray and, holding a glass of brandy, had a third or fourth look at the map of Munich spread out on the study table. Hildegard served coffee and sat down on a little armchair — the same corner where, during the war, filled with uncertainty, she had read the letters arriving from the Caucasus, which in the afternoon she would read to her friends as they embroidered.

She glanced at the city plan marked out with arrows and directions indicating troop movements and tried to ferret Max out of the hermitlike state he had adopted throughout the meal.

"Max... Max... Can you hear me?"

"Ye-es, my dear, I'm listening." He immediately perceived her disquiet, so unusual in her.

"I'm worried, Max. Tell me the truth: are we really ready to take over the Bavarian government?"

Max did not look up.

"You know well I believe in the party and consider Hitler a providential man, but to lead a military putsch against 3000 men, the most influential and powerful in the country, taking them hostage and with the highly probable risk of producing a blood-bath right in the Bürgerbräukeller, if things don't turn out as planned... It would just need someone to put up some resistance to produce a disaster, Max..."

He interrupted, "That isn't going to happen, Hildegard. There'll be no failure. You heard what Hitler said at the meeting at the Krone circus, and repeated here tonight: 'The dictators Stresemann and Seeckt governing in Berlin say we will stage a coup... And I tell them we don't need it. That's the strategy we'll use, Hildegard — acting unexpectedly. Surprise them all together where they're least expecting it."

"But Max, do you really believe the Bavarian regiments will side with Hitler instead of following direct orders from Berlin? Do you imagine von Seeckt and von Lossow are going to sit idly back and not intervene, only for fear of the National Socialists and a popular reaction in Bavaria?"

Max paced up and down. His wife's worries were making him impatient, but they were not altogether unrealistic: the coup they were planning at the Bürgerbräukeller could well end up a resounding failure, costing all of them their lives. Shot by a firing squad or life-long imprisonment would be the options.

"If I keep wondering about it, I won't be able to sleep tonight, or any other until after 9th November," added Hildegard. "Won't this be just an enormous plunge into the dark? Won't the confidence we've placed in Hitler have perhaps blinded us?"

Max sat in the armchair in front of the fire. The glow of burning logs gave the conversation a disquieting character. He seemed tired and, with a gesture typical of him, removed his glasses and rubbed his eyelids. With a cautious voice he tried to hide his own doubts, "I'm responsible for the plan, together with Rosenberg. There's a great risk, I won't deny it. Hitler won't be on his own because we'll be there with him. Besides, I trust Rohm and Goering's courage and, most of all, I trust myself."

Hildegard was worried. That evening, after dessert, when the men had got up from the table to smoke and deliberate, she had hardly been able to hear Hitler and his inner circle deciding the final points of their plan of assault at the Bürgerbräukeller.

The idea was rash: to trap the highest Munich society in

the beer-hall and, consequently, take power in Bavaria at machine gun point, bringing about the collapse of the government with all its members present there. Hildegard was unable to rid her mind of all the fears accumulated over the last few years. For the third time she listened to Max's explanation as to how they would give the Bavarian government its *coup de grace* and then call for a general rebellion in the whole of Germany.

"The SAs will surround the place, and the Combat League will carry out its parallel actions. The surprise factor will be fundamental, Hildegard. Look at it this way, my dear. Adolf Hitler has distinguished me with his friendship, has announced his plan — *my* plan — to nothing less than take over the whole of the nation. Do you realize? Can you see where such a situation places us? Can you imagine the reward? I'm his favorite collaborator. He's told me so. Can you understand, Hildegard, that this is the highest political position we've ever been able to imagine — the summit of power, at Hitler's right hand?"

Max vehemently stood once more, again pacing round the room. He helped himself to another glass from the brandy flagon. "When I came back from the mountains after the retreat from Sautchbulak, at the Mosul base a group of young officers whispered behind my back about me, 'This big-headed Swirsden-Righe, so full of himself... look at the way the generals in Constantinople dress up his defeat by decorating his officers.' In my embarrassment I made out I hadn't heard them, but I felt they were right. Those officers arriving to replace us said what I was thinking of myself and my command: Failure."

Hildegard was deeply moved. Max continued, visibly embittered, "When Winnig received me in Prussia after our disastrous retreat from Riga — you know, you were there — he said to me, 'Swirsden-Righe, I should never have left you in charge of the mission.' What he really meant was, 'You undertook a task you were unable to fulfill, and that's the way it turned out.' My dear, this is the greatest opportunity life has giving me as a soldier. I'd never hesitate to run this risk because the prize is glory. Hitler will triumph."

Max was standing in front of the fireplace, his look

disappearing among the vision of the flames. He seemed to be lulled to sleep as he watched the logs disintegrating, falling onto each other.

"There'll no longer be anyone in the German army considering me just a 'bold and boastful reserve lieutenant, conceited and looking for notoriety.' We," he said, approaching his wife, "together... will be able to rebuild a great Germany, freeing it from that rotten rabble of Marxists and foreigners invading us, Hildegard."

She enveloped him with her arms, and for long seconds remained that way, without saying a word. The fireplace glowed even more intensely than before, giving the room a reddish tinge.

TWO NIGHTS LATER, ARMED to the teeth, he was travelling by car along the streets of Munich towards the objective. Max thought of his wife's embrace. He was tense, sitting next to Hitler. No one spoke. Hitler was wearing tails. From round his neck hung the Iron Cross, received for acting as messenger at the Front as part of the 4th Battalion, when he was a corporal. Now, eight years later, the National Socialists led by him were advancing in trucks crammed full of paramilitaries, determined to seize power.

The surprise plan of attack was no doubt rash: to topple the governor of Bavaria, Gustav von Kahr, and replace the government, setting up elderly General Ludendorff, the hero of past glories — perhaps the greatest war hero — as the new President of Germany. The measure would leave the conservatives happy and calm everyone down. Besides, old General von Lossow would be easily manageable for Hitler. As for Governor von Kahr, they would catch him with his pants down before he even started his speech. Max looked at his companions' faces and mentally went over Hitler's orders: they would barge into the hall, weapons in hand, while in a box on the first floor Goering installed a machine gun pointed at the gathered assembly.

Then Hitler would force the ministers on the stage to resign and proclaim himself the new authority. Meanwhile, Max would go and fetch old Ludendorff from his home, informing him on the way to the Bürgerbräukeller of the success of the putsch, where Rosenberg and Rohm, with the assault forces, would keep all the captives in the building under control. These lads would cover any hesitation or error by Hitler, Max thought. They were almost there, and all doubts would be cleared up in the next few minutes. For good or ill the die had been cast once more. As in the past, this was a pre-emptive strike in which everything was put in play. Without doubt this was to be the riskiest bet ever.

COMMUNIQUÉ TO ALL RADIO STATIONS IN GERMANY
ARMY GENERAL HEADQUARTERS – BERLIN

The soldier operator raised the volume of the transmitter and repeated the order issued by the Berlin Headquarters for the second time that night. The clock on the wall indicated 4 a.m. and the army garrison soldiers, armed for combat, ran to the trucks parked in the barracks.

To all German radio stations. Bavarian Minister-president von Kahr, General von Lossow, and Colonel von Seisser in Munich condemn Hitler's putsch. The takeover by force of arms at the Bürgerbräukeller lacks all legitimacy. Repeat: lacks all legitimacy.

Hitler and his collaborators are considered usurpers by the Reich Government. I repeat: Hitler and his collaborators are considered insurgents...

ARAKSI WAS FEELING COLD. Although she was travelling well muffled up, she covered herself with the thin rug and not even by wrapping herself in it did she stop shivering. Through the weather strips of the sleeper-carriage windows, an icy draught came in. The movement of the train in her half-slumber, and the cold going right through her, immediately transported her back to the uncomfortable ox-wagon Max had provided for the women on that journey through the high mountains on the way to Sautchbulak. Memories crowded her mind. She could never will herself to remember the past. Rather, images and sensations came back to her unexpectedly; but when they took over, they did so with such intensity that she relived even the slightest details, not only in her memory but body and soul. Sometimes she found them intolerable and seemed to be hearing the Turks very close by once more. Other times, she would wake up from dreams believing herself in the camp tent, embracing Max. Why was she still remembering him? Actually, it was all part of a great nightmare and it was futile to separate the horror from happy memories. A state of despair overcame her straightaway. The half-sleep came to an end and Araksi opened her eyes, uneasily. Without full awareness of where she was, it took her a few moments to realize the train was travelling across the country in the middle of the night. Diran was asleep in the upper bunk.

She sat up and reached out for the water bottle and a glass. She had a few sips and then raised the blinds a few notches. Outside it was totally dark and her face was reflected in the window. She was still young and beautiful. Men turned round to look at her wherever she was. It had always been so. What strange luck, hers. It seemed that now her destiny was a permanent journey, moving from one place to another, rootlessly, unable to fulfil her innermost dreams. She got closer to the reflection and fleetingly saw a resemblance to her mother. Silent tears ran down her cheeks until another train's lurching passage in the opposite direction brought her back to the present.

She looked up. Diran was a heavy sleeper. As she looked at him she thought that there he was, still by her side, in the middle of nothingness, as from the very earliest moment. She found this frightening: maybe she was afraid of losing him, and straight away her musings would go back to Max and the wild love story they had lived through. Those days in the past kept her from flying, from fulfilling her dreams. Every thought always led back into the same labyrinth. Or was the answer simply war, the awful tragedy that had come between her happiness and her youth?

Something had to happen.

Diran was sleeping uncovered, the blanket hanging from his berth. She covered him and lay down again. There were still a few hours left before Munich. She found it hard to sleep again. Her eyes remained fixed on the window until darkness turned into daybreak.

CHAPTER XIX

THE MUNICH PUTSCH

THE LOCOMOTIVE CAME TO A STOP. Under the station clock a large sign announced they were in Munich Central Station.

Signalmen and the train-guard approached the train and the passengers started getting off. Bustling porters wheeled luggage around, then rapidly trundled the trolleys to waiting cars and the taxi rank. A long line of soldiers cordoned off the length of the platform. Inside the sleeper, Araksi had just finished loading hats and coats into boxes. She looked out of the window and, on seeing so many soldiers, worriedly exclaimed, "What's going on here? Diran, come, have a look. All these troops! This is even worse than Berlin."

"They're Bavarian army regulars, Araksi. They must be guarding against an imminent attack by the National Socialists. Come on, hurry. Grab your bags. And don't say anything, just let me do the talking. Have you got your documents?"

Araksi nodded. The guard was going up and down the corridor, knocking on each door and repeating, "Munich Central Station, Bavaria. Passengers kindly get off the train. Quickly, please, be so kind. Munich Central Station..."

When Diran and Araksi got off, a stony-faced officer approached them and asked for identity papers. He looked at them steadily, holding a large Alsatian dog while a couple of soldiers stood in front of them. Diran pulled out the papers from his overcoat.

"Armenian refugees," observed the officer, comparing photographs. He briefly said nothing. Then, in a tone that was almost friendly, he remarked, "My brother fought at the Eastern Front." Diran and Araksi forced a smile. "What's made you come to Munich at a time like this? Haven't you heard what's going on here?"

"When we left Berlin, everything was quiet, Officer," answered Diran. "What's the matter, why don't you tell me? Why are there so many troops around?"

"Mr. Hitler has taken over the government, and the Reich

army aren't ready to allow it. That's why we're here."

Araksi looked around uneasily.

"But are the streets safe? D'you think we'll be able to get to the Marienplatz?" inquired Diran.

"We're staying with relatives, very near there," Araksi added.

"Streets safe? At the Marienplatz? A column of 2000 Sturmabteilung and Combat League men is now lining up to go there, with Hitler at the head. The police have set up strict control in the area. They won't let you through. Nice day you've chosen to come to Munich." The soldiers smiled.

With no further delay, Araksi and Diran picked up their luggage and, following the porter, left the platform. As he watched them walk away among the crowd, the officer shook his head, unable to understand, and said to a lieutenant standing next to him, "They were saved from the Turks and now they've come here."

They walked with difficulty, dragging their belongings. A thin drizzle was falling on Munich and at each turn they came across Bavarian troops. The soldiers, posted at corners, sitting on trucks and holding rifles, looked on with indifference. Others passed with fixed bayonets, occupying the whole length of the streets. Hardly a civilian was to be seen.

"This is certainly crazy, Diran," Araksi commented, out of breath. "We left Berlin to come precisely into the cave of all Germany's problems. What are we going to do afterwards, watch how they kill each other? Do you realize what a bad idea this is?"

"Araksi — we're about to be witnesses to an historical event... unique," he answered as they approached a coach for hire in front of the boulevard. "Get a move on. That coach'll take us there."

"What I want is to get away from unique, unrepeatable historical events of the 20th century," she flung at him while pushing a large suitcase with bags and hatboxes hanging from her shoulder. "I already have stories enough for our grandchildren... if we ever get round to having any and, besides, I can't go a step further lugging these bags around. Are you listening to me, Diran?"

"I'm listening, woman." Diran walked faster. They were carting along all their worldly possessions. "Araksi, my love, we're only a few blocks away from the Marienplatz. Nobody was expecting this. What a show! Everyone in Munich, maybe even in the whole of Germany, could join the nationalists. I must find some way of interviewing the leaders."

Diran ran across the street and went up to the coaches. A run-down horse was patiently slumbering under the weight of harnesses and garlands. The driver, sitting at the front, was an old Bavarian with a bushy white moustache. A canvas roof covered the passenger seat. Nothing seemed to bother the driver, not even the cold drizzle he protected himself from, wrapped in an ample cape, or the troops going by in ever increasing numbers towards the Odeonplatz, posting soldiers round about.

"Good morning. Can you take us to the Marienplatz?"

The old coachman smiled doubtfully.

"Or as near to it as we can get?"

"Marienplatz? I don't think so," said the man, shaking his head. "The police are erecting a barrier to stop Mr. Hitler getting through. But I can get you fairly close. But listen... Are you foreigners that haven't understood what's going on in Munich? You wouldn't be Jews, would you?"

"No, we're Armenians, Christians just like you Germans," Araksi retorted, resolutely and proudly standing straight; completely characteristic of her, this resoluteness only added to her appeal. The coachman understood immediately and, by way of reparation, changed his tone, "Ah Madam, don't worry, then. I said it because the S.A. people are unforgiving. Once they take power, a whole lot of innocent people are going to suffer. A lot of blood's going to flow. God protect the Jews from these people. Get on and let's go."

The coach started off at a fast trot, avoiding army trucks and closed-off streets. Araksi and Diran looked attentively around them. As they got nearer to the square, the multitude of demonstrators and onlookers grew. Some argued at street corners, alarmed at such a concentration.

Further on, the coach made its way through groups of people, clerks and workers that spontaneously moved forward, waving flags and parading along pavements and boulevards. All hoped to join Hitler at the Marienplatz.

Once in the center of Munich, the coachman slowed down and the horse went on at walking pace until further progress became impossible.

"This is as far as we can go. You can carry on walking. The square's just up ahead," the coachman indicated. A barricade interrupted the way and the police forced them to keep behind the throng of curious onlookers. From one of the corners giving onto the Marienplatz, they hoped to see Hitler and all his forces march by. Suddenly the dull noise of the demonstrators marching in step on the cobblestones made all eyes turn towards the side streets.

Diran and Araksi ran the last few blocks, dragging their baggage along as if at that moment all their packs had become lighter.

The Sturmabteilung; 2000 resolute, grim-looking men wearing brown shirts, marched behind their leader, singing and holding banners high. They were carrying carbines and steel helmets. A hundred bodyguards covered Hitler's back. Further behind, three units in columns of four abreast were still crossing the Ludwigsbrücke. Then came the cadets of the Army Infantry School, dressed up in their golden uniforms. Araksi and Diran could see no further than the first row. The number of resolute National Socialists wearing the swastika as armbands and ready to face a police force with fixed bayonets at the end of the street was impressive.

MAX — DR. VON SWIRSDEN-RIGHE according to the title which party members used when addressing him — was marching on Hitler's right in the front row, alongside other party personalities.

The Führer wore a raincoat reaching down almost to his ankles, and a beret.

General Ludendorff, the elderly military hero and darling of veteran soldiers, was parading in his Field-Marshall's uniform, one arm linked to Hitler's on his right.

A car bristling with machine guns followed immediately behind them. Rosenberg, who had introduced Max to Hitler, was in the second row, somewhat offended at the snub.

Together with him were other important Baltic Nationalists. To the left, always covering the Führer, the Bund Oberland, the Munich paramilitaries. On the opposite wing and in the center were the assault forces. Himmler carried the Imperial war flag at the head of 2000 combatants shouldering rifles with fixed bayonets. They kept in step, singing a stirring military march.

Closing the demonstration were war veterans in ragged uniforms, workers in working clothes, and businessmen — all wearing the Swastika and sharing the same anti-Bolshevik frenzy.

Max felt invincible. That triumphal parade was the closest thing to anticipated glory: the recognition he had pursued throughout his military career had finally arrived. To march elbow to elbow, his arm linked with Hitler's on the way to take power, was more than had ever been his ambition. They did not talk amongst themselves. They still had to cross the stretch separating them from the Odeonplatz. Then they would arrive at the Defense Ministry, where they would meet up with Rohm's men. At that moment, Max imagined he heard Hitler saying, looking ahead and pressing his arm, "Max — today's the 124th anniversary of the Brumaire. Nothing happens by chance."

Max recalled Napoleon's genial coup that made him the master of France.

He half closed his eyes. The force they had unleashed was advancing like a powerful engine launched to overcome however many might oppose them on the way to the highest ideals of the fatherland. 2000 men backed Max's thoughts, and perhaps another 50,000 in the whole of Bavaria might be waiting in the wings to join them as soon as they proclaimed themselves the government at the Defense Ministry. The whole nation would be at the feet of whoever finally united all Germans under the Third Reich: that leader was marching elbow to elbow with him.

Such thoughts sent a shiver of excitement right through him. Max's legs carried him mechanically, involuntarily: rather than marching to the Marienplatz, he felt himself floating.

The crowd's cheers became the most profound sounds in

his memory. All at once, it seemed as though a strange silence were cutting him off from all the giddy events round about, the same silence he had experienced on the field of battle in Lorraine with howitzer shells falling on his regiment and he, in a fit of courage, finding the strength to carry away wounded men over and over, pulling them out of the mud without waiting for a second volley of the French guns to pulverize whoever tried to take shelter in the bog-like corridor of the trenches.

Images followed upon each other at break-neck speed in his memory. He saw himself leading the cavalry charge at Sautchbulak in the dusk of twilight, as the Cossacks fired their artillery at the hillsides of the valley, hurling riders and horses, which moments earlier he had been galloping alongside, in the air.

He was unable to explain why his soul was suddenly overcome with infinite nostalgia but an intense feeling of love embodied itself in him at that instant.

It could hardly be possible — his sight had to be deceiving him — that woman running among the throng right there, as they advanced, could only be Araksi! A fashionable little grey hat covered her silken black hair, but even so, the figure of his beloved was unmistakable. Max doubted his own mental balance. He tried to follow that couple with his sight, moving among the teeming multitude, that tried to keep watching the demonstration going by. He recognized Diran by the same hook-nosed profile that came to him in dreams every so often, renewing the pain of imagining her with him.

"Araksi!" he said in perplexity on making sure it was no delusion.

Hitler glanced sidelong at his companion, not understanding. They were close to the Feldherrnhalle, the monument honoring the generals of the nation's wars.

DIRAN AND ARAKSI FINALLY SECURED a privileged position from which to look on, exactly at an abutment formed by the crowd of curious Munich people enveloped in cheers of patriotic fervor. The spectacle of the National Socialist forces marching was impressive. They seemed an unstoppable wave, determined to fracture any barrier put in their way.

The young couple's gaze immediately fell on Hitler, that leader every newspaper was talking about. Then Araksi's sight turned to the man on his right. She felt overwhelmed. It was Max, of course. It could be none other — a little older and wearing his unmistakable round metal-rimmed eyeglasses. A shiver ran down her spine. Max had recognized her and his sight was fixed on her eyes. He seemed to be smiling and, in the disbelief of the encounter, as astonished as she was herself, gazed at her with deep tenderness.

Diran, giving voice to so much amazement, shouted out, "Look..! There in the front row, Araksi, next to Hitler. It's Swirsden-Righe!"

Araksi remained immobile, without being able to say a word: she mumbled as she tried to pronounce her former lover's name. In a gesture that over-rode her will, she took off her hat and shook her hair loose.

The shouting was deafening, although for Araksi and Max the multitude ceased to exist for an instant. In the exchange of looks, it seemed that scenes of unending giddiness transported them through time, and that sanity and all reference to space were changing beyond control. It was not words or concepts that found an answer in Araksi's heart and mind: it was the inexplicable union of emotions and her destiny joined to that man's that arose before her at every turn of events, in unimaginable situations, without her ever being able to understand the reason.

General Ludendorff stepped forward a few paces. The column was almost at the Odeonplatz. There was a shout and the report of a gunshot. Dozens of police began shooting at the men. Ludendorff carried on walking, his head held high. One of the combatants fell, wounded. Goering received a shot in his thigh.

Araksi could hardly believe her eyes. She felt Diran's push and saw the crowd running madly in search of shelter. Her eyes remained fixed on the scene but she was unable to move. Their luggage was spread out all around, trampled on by the crowd stampeding from the square.

Max continued advancing, still looking at Araksi, his arm linked with Hitler's. A fresh shot from the police hit home in the first row. Max fell. It was a well-aimed shot that killed him instantly. Hitler toppled to the ground, dragged down by Swirsden-Righe's body.

Araksi gave a muted little cry of horror at the sight of his death. Diran, crouching next to her, did not move for a few moments then he decided to pull her out of the emotional trance that was paralyzing her. They both crossed the square. With one arm, he led his wife, in the other he carried the only suitcase still in their possession.

Hitler, wounded and lying on the ground, struggled to get free of Swirsden-Righe's body, lying beside him in a pool of blood. He dragged himself as well as he could under a nearby car. He was bleeding, and a piercing pain of broken bone bored into his sides. Around him the entire column of 2000 armed men ran helter-skelter, escaping along the side streets of the square.

Araksi and Diran reached an entrance-passage. Prey to an attack of nerves, Araksi held on tightly to her husband. They said nothing. At that moment she understood that life, destiny, or the Heavenly Father, had determined the exact time and place in which the roads between her and Max were to separate forever and that, in a secret way Diran was never to appreciate, she would begin to be really free — free to follow the direction she wished without any presence ever being able to chain her again.

The sound of shooting died away little by little and calm returned to the Odeonplatz. Thus ended the failed putsch attempt on that morning of 9th November, 1923. In this way began the rise to power of Adolf Hitler: with serious blunder and several deaths on the way but free from any repression, and suffering no greater harm than a fractured arm as the police closed in to arrest him.

Max von Swirsden-Righe lay dead, in front of the Feldherrnhalle.

CHAPTER XX

THE END

COUNTESS HILDEGARD POURED HERSELF ANOTHER CUP OF TEA. She was impatiently embroidering by the window. She had not wanted to go to the square, assuming Max would call her from the Ministry of Defense, with the news that the country was in the party's hands, the takeover in Bavaria a fact. But what Hildegard could not stand was the suspense: there had been too many emotions over the last few years, what with changing conditions and so much uncertainty brought about by the war. Waiting was almost worse than the danger of action itself. She remained stoical at her home, only hoping Max was safe. Although she hid it, showing herself to others and to her own self as cold and in command of herself, that morning Hildegard was trembling inwardly at a feeling of dire foreboding.

The doorbell rang several times. Hildegard jumped at the sound, finding it odd that they should insist for so long and, raising her voice, ordered the servants to attend. She remembered the telephone had been mute all morning, and felt disquieted.

Two men in civilian attire, wearing long overcoats and crumpled hats, handed the butler a message and left. When he opened it, he went pale. Half shutting his eyes and stretching his gloves, he waited for a moment in the darkness of the entrance hall. Then, picking up courage, he walked to the study.

Hildegard kept her eyes fixed on the window, lost as though delaying what she was anticipating.

The butler opened the doors, his eyes tear-filled. "Madam, a message has been delivered for you: Dr. Swirsden-Righe has just died."

Her head slowly shook from side to side on hearing the message. Then she rose from her armchair and changed the water in the flower vase beside the window. She had to lean against the back of the armchair so as not to topple over.

The butler made as though to hold her arm, but she

stopped him. "This is... terrible," she stammered. "But I'm the wife of an officer.... A heroic death is the best death for a German officer."

CHAPTER XXI

BUENOS AIRES

THE STEAMER SAILED THROUGH THE ENTRANCE to the river plate, where the currents of the great estuary and the Atlantic Ocean meet. Two hours later, Buenos Aires appeared on the horizon.

On deck, Araksi and Diran breathed the humid morning air that ran across the murky waters of that immense river, almost a sea, which is poetically named the *'Plata'*, the 'silver' river. It was for them, thought Araksi, better than any other precious metal. Freedom was as valuable as any fortune that had remained buried in Erzurum. Sometimes those episodes seemed so distant, almost a remote past belonging to another Araksi. Ten years had gone by since then. She found Diran's choice wonderful.

"Argentina. The Argentine Republic..." She had never before heard of the existence of that far-off land of pampas with swaying wheat fields and livestock numbering millions grazing on plains teeming with opportunities, the place Europeans chose to travel to in search of the Promised Land, as emigration brochures had it. And she reminded herself that it was all she knew about it. Anticipation made her a little anxious. All the passengers on deck looked at their new destination with amazement and uncertainty. Families with children, men from every part of Europe, packed together and curious, with homesick and hopeful looks, and speaking diverse languages, leant on the railings, lessening the distance that separated them from the landing-pier.

Yet nothing could be better than a new and peaceful life, the promise of an unwritten destiny in that city, whose name sounded strange but happy: Buenos Aires — 'Good Airs', Araksi repeated aloud, in an incipient Spanish, huddling next to Diran. With wonder, they looked at the profile of factory chimneystacks along a quiet branch of the river, dividing the banks, crossed by a great, dark iron bridge and plied by small vessels of every color, like the fishing boats of Naples. Already visible were the port cranes and the masts of hundreds of cargo ships lined up and loading grain in the Dock Sud (South Dock) basin.

Tugs maneuvered the ship to the pier, sounding their sirens and expelling water towards the banks.

The April sun peered through the clouds and a deep blue sky shone above the harbor. Araksi hugged Diran again and, looking at each other, deeply moved, they kissed. They were young and, by some conjunction of inexplicable vibrations, felt that neither violence nor grief had been able to cross so much ocean, and that at last they were safe.

Diran handed over their papers and, after checking that everything was in order, they walked down the gangway and were led to the pavilions to collect their baggage.

Hundreds of people queued up on the pier, waiting to enter the Hotel de Inmigrantes, an enormous Italian-style building where the majority, without means or recommendations, would be put up by the authorities until they found work.

It was early in the morning. The river breeze played along the docks. Araksi walked a few feet along the esplanade away from the customs sheds while Diran was dealing with porters and transport. Beyond the port railings she could see European-style buildings. Araksi sat on a bench under a willow tree. The air brought the sound of an accordion-like instrument and guitar playing. She thought she recognized the tune. Getting up, she walked over to the railings separating the harbor from neighboring areas.

The singer, a rugged, handsome 'nightbird', wearing a felt hat that fell over his forehead, was practicing a tango accompanied by a negro guitarist and another fellow playing the bandoneon. There they were, under the eaves of a railway shed, heating water on a small stove. Araksi moved closer, curious and fascinated. The men looked at her meaningfully, winking.

Araksi returned the compliment, smiling at them through the railing, and the singer raised his hat, dedicating the next tango to her. The tune was played to the end and Araksi allowed herself to be led along the fast by-ways of memory. A tear rolled down her cheek. From behind, she felt Diran's loving embrace. The music carried them away and their throats tightened with emotion. The rustic, genuine tango, sounding its welcome, was the same one as was played in her parental home, amid stolen kisses and children running about; the same that they had danced to on that happy Sunday in Erzurum. A good omen for a new beginning.

EPILOGUE TO THE UNFINISHED TRAGEDY

August 1939

STORM CLOUDS WERE ROLLING ACROSS THE STEELY BLADE OF THE MOUNTAINS, escaping towards the horizon. When the winds had cleared away the bad weather, the sky appeared, blue and cold, over Berchtesgaden. Mountain peaks rose nearby, majestically surrounding the Eagle's Nest, the place where the fate of Europe was about to be decided, close to the Austrian border. The dogs' barks on the terrace resounded fearsomely. One by one the generals arrived, climbing the road in their cars, in immediate response to the Führer's call. That meeting was not an ordinary one at the center of power during the summer holidays. The highest military chiefs could sense their leader's purpose.

Hitler was playing, laughing and excited as a teenager, with his Alsatians as he raised his arm to the military that stood to attention before him. When they were all gathered, a deep silence prevailed. Hitler walked a few paces along the great terrace, overlooking a cliff that dominated an impressive view of forests and lakes.

He kept up the suspense during a few minutes, as was his custom. He was wearing his uniform with the swastika on his arm and unexpectedly, raising his voice, said, "Gentlemen, I have ordered your divisions to attack Poland tomorrow, and exterminate men and women without pity or consideration."

Not one of those present batted an eyelid, remaining immobile, martial, unresponsive, hanging on to each of the Führer's words. They all knew that it was the order leading to war. Hitler half turned and looked towards the mountains. He seemed to be reminiscing about someone absent, as though responding to a conversation stored in his memory with someone that had inspired him in the past. Then he remarked, as though the force of the words had overflowed his innermost thoughts, "After all, when all is said and done... who today remembers the extermination of the Armenians?"

BIBLIOGRAPHY

The following books were consulted by the author in performing research for *Araksi and the German Consul*:

Posten auf EWIGE WACHE by Paul Leverkuehn, published in English by the Gomidas Institute, as *A German Officer during the Armenian Genocide"*

German Responsibility during the Armenian Genocide by Vahakn Dadrian, Blue Crane Books

Las Memorias de Henry Morgenthau in Spanish

Operation Némesis by Eric Bogosian, Little Brown and Company, New York

Hitler by de Marlis Steinert Vergara, Grupo Zeta

The Third Reich: A New History by Michael Burleigh, Hill and Wang